The Book of Secrets

'Part generational history, part detective story, part social
chronicle, the novel is a "living tapestry to join past to
the present", a continuing commentary on the act of
storytelling, which is being dramatized as we read'
ALICE MUNROE, MORDECAI RICHLER, DAVID STAINES
– Citation from the Giller Prize Jury

'M. G. Vassanji masterfully weaves an extraordinarily colourful
and richly complicated carpet . . . *The Book of Secrets* is a big
book in every sense. It contains both love and forgiveness.
And at its heart is an enormous generosity'
Toronto Star

'As I read this book about exiled people squeezed by
circumstance, I thought of other novels that seem its cousins:
Timothy Findley's *Famous Last Words*, Michael Ondaatje's *The
English Patient* and Graham Greene's *The Heart of the Matter*'
Globe and Mail

M. G. VASSANJI was born in Kenya and raised in Tanzania. Before moving to Canada in 1978, he attended university in the United States, at M.I.T. in Massachusetts and the University of Pennsylvania, before moving to Canada in 1978. In 1989 he was writer-in-residence at the University of Iowa in its prestigious International Writing Programme. His previous novels are *No New Land* (1991) and *The Gunny Sack* (1989), which won a Regional Commonwealth Prize. His most recent book of fiction was a collection of stories set in Dar es Salaam, *Uhuru Street* (1992). *The Book of Secrets* was the winner of both the Harbourfront Prize and the prestigious Giller Prize in 1995. He lives in Toronto.

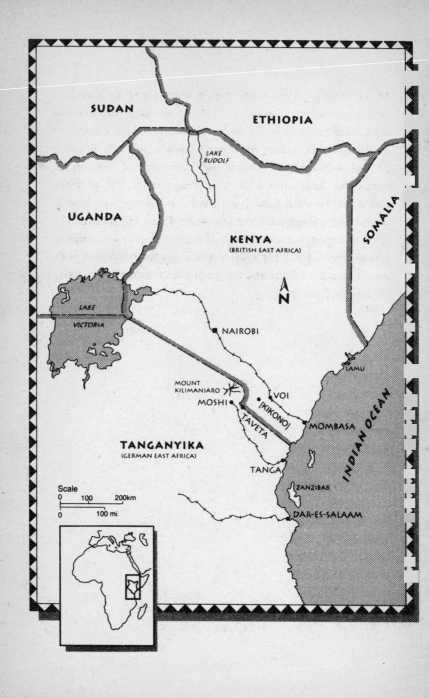

M.G. VASSANJI

The Book of Secrets

PICADOR

First published 1994 by McClelland & Stewart Inc., Toronto

First published in Great Britain 1995 by Macmillan

This edition published 1996 by Picador
an imprint of Macmillan Publishers Ltd
25 Eccleston Place, London SW1W 9NF
and Basingstoke

Associated companies throughout the world

ISBN 0 330 34401 3

The Publishers are grateful for permission to produce four lines from
The Ruba'iyat of Omar Khayyam translated by Peter Avery and John Heath-Stubbs
(Allen Lane 1979) © Peter Avery and John Heath-Stubbs, 1994;
and to Faber and Faber Ltd for permission to use seven lines from 'You'
from *Collected Poems* by W. H. Auden, edited by Edward Mendelson.

A CIP catalogue record for this book is available from
the British Library.

Printed and bound in Great Britain by
Mackays of Chatham plc, Chatham, Kent

for Kabir
who wouldn't wait

I passed by a potter the day before last,
    He was ceaselessly plying his skill with the clay,
And, what the blind do not see, I could –
    My father's clay in every potter's hand.

— *The Ruba'iyat of Omar Khayyam*

The Book of Secrets

Prologue

7 July, 1988

They called it the book of our secrets, kitabu cha siri zetu. Of its writer they said: He steals our souls and locks them away; it is a magic bottle, this book, full of captured spirits; see how he keeps his eyes skinned, this mzungu, observing everything we do; look how meticulously this magician with the hat writes in it, attending to it more regularly than he does to nature, with more passion than he expends on a woman. He takes it with him into forest and on mountain, in war and in peace, hunting a lion or sitting in judgement, and when he sleeps he places one eye upon it, shuts the other. Yes, we should steal this book, if we could, take back our souls, our secrets from him. But the punishment for stealing such a book is harsh – ai! – we have seen it.

They were only partly right, after all, those wazees – the ancients – who voiced wonder-filled suspicion and mistrust at the book and its writer, the all-powerful European whiteman administrator who had appeared in their midst to govern. They could not know that this mzungu first and foremost captured himself in his bottle-book; and long after it left his side – taking part of him with it – it continued to capture other souls and their secrets, and to dictate its will upon them. Even now it makes protagonists of those who would decide its fate.

Because it has no end, this book, it ingests us and carries us with it, and so it grows.

But it began simply, the story of this book, an unusual discovery put into the hands of an out-of-work schoolteacher, who at last found his calling and began to work with an industry and enthusiasm he had not mustered since his apprentice days.

I am that former schoolteacher. In my time I taught a generation or more of schoolboys. I have watched this place grow from a small colonial town into the bustling city that it is now. Many of my students have left, gone abroad to different corners of the world. Professors, businessmen, and engineers now, who left during the trying times that gripped us in the last decade, or even earlier. They've gone beyond me, so many of them, but I carry no regrets. They are proof of my success. Wistfully sometimes I wish I had been born later than my time, so as to be able to make the leap from this periphery into that centre, where all the important and exciting things seem to happen. But as I am, I have never desired to leave.

When I complain – and who doesn't? we've lived through trying times as I said – Feroz laughs at me. When I mention how I miss my old Morris to transport me around, he says with his shopkeeper's logic, "Sir, if you had left, with your talent and experience you would own ten cars!"

They still call me Sir, or Mr. Fernandes.

Three years ago, officialdom caught up with me and discovered that I had passed retirement age. I was given no option. Spending idle days since then was not easy, in this city where I had no family or close friends and was after all an immigrant. A few months ago in the beginning of March, I had found myself treading along the footpaths of Dar es Salaam's back alleys when by accident I met Feroz. It was not the first time that a former student had come to my aid. He is not what I would count as one of my successes, and he knows it (I mention too frequently and indiscreetly my prize achievements). His once muscular body now distends, and the loose mouth gives him a friendly look that I suspect hides bad teeth and a nervousness about what he says. Financially he has not done so badly. Mixed with that Eastern respect for the guru, there is in him, I know, also some of the shopkeeper's contempt for the low-paid teacher and self-styled thinker who ultimately does not seem to amount to much. But he came to my aid. I must confess, so straitened was my circumstance that I had been reduced to searching for a pair of shoes at the open-air mnada in Congo Street. It was as I emerged from the madness of the mnada, pushing my way through the solid throng of shoppers, raucous vendors, and jostling thieves, clutching my parcel and hastening away surreptitiously into Uhuru Street, that I bumped into him. He had, it appeared, stopped his car to give me a lift, and then got out and watched my sorry little sojourn into discount shopping.

When he heard my story, Feroz's sense of propriety was offended. He was outraged. The very next day he took me on a round to see some people of means and influence in the city. He even telephoned a few people upcountry, he lent me money. And, failing finally to find me the kind of job he believed I deserved, he offered me a flat to live in, here at the corner of Uhuru and Viongozi streets.

What is it like to step back into a tomb? The name on this building where I've been put up is Amin Mansion 1951. Downstairs, outside the corner shop, the partly obliterated sign "Pipa Store," at the intersection nicknamed Pipa Corner, brings to mind the one possible image when I think of the name Pipa: a plump wheezing man in singlet and loincloth inside a produce shop, perched atop a tire-seat in the middle of all his wares, his fingers constantly at work folding and refolding squares of paper into packets of spices, dropping them in one fluid motion into a basket at his side, measuring time as it were with grains of turmeric, coriander, chillies. . . . A man with a reputation for stinginess, dirtiness of his store and person, the shadiness of some of his dealings. The store now belongs to Feroz, who uses it as a secondary business place, selling shoes, radios, and watches, his primary sphere of action being the bustle of Msimbazi, just beyond Congo Street where he found me.

It is good to have as guardian a former student, if one allows to slip by the occasional glimmers of contempt that show themselves in the gracelessness of a joke, the rudeness of unexpected familiarity, and gives due recognition to the genuine kindness and respect that are also there. The ambiguity of this breed of shopkeeper was brought home to me in the most startling fashion by Feroz one day, over tea in the shop.

"What is history, sir?" he asked.

Carefully, I pressed cup to saucer to stabilize them, and looked up and stared at him. The expression on the face of this former D-student: a smile composed equally of embarrassment and pure mischief.

"You taught history, sir. Can you write it?"

"You mean . . ." I began, groping in vain for some loose change in thought with which I could extricate myself as he pinned me with that look, apologetic, embarrassed, cunning.

"Let me show you something, sir. Come, sir."

I followed him, into that famous backroom of Pipa's day, thought then to harbour in its darkness all kinds of mysteries and evidence of shady dealings which the police could never lay their hands on. Now it was a bright fluorescent-lighted room, shelves of shoeboxes covering the walls, the sharp smell of vinyl and rubber and fresh packing filling the air. There was a table in the

4

middle, covered with a freshly wiped, gleaming plastic sheet of a white-and-red checkered design. On it was an object, distinctly foreign to the scene, and the purpose, I sensed by the expectant stillness of my companion beside me, of our entry into this former hideaway. It was an old brown leather case, the kind used to protect passports in former days.

"Take a look at it, sir." He took a step forward, leaned over and flipped it open, and stepped aside for me. I went to look at the book that was now exposed.

A faint odour exuded from it with the turning of the pages. It had seen some very dirty places – and what place more fittingly dirty than Pipa's dark backroom.

"I found it in the store, sir," said Feroz behind me.

What value could the old miser Pipa have attached to this book, I wondered. Did it come with the junk he gathered patiently over the years and sold in his crowded shop? Had this single item simply, by accident, been left over, missed the fate of the numerous pieces of paper that wrapped spices or started wood fires? Or had it been deliberately saved?

I turned to look at Feroz.

"Is it important, sir?" he said anxiously, goading the historian in me.

"It could be," I answered.

In the last decade and a half, many relics saw the rubbish piles of this city, as people in a frantic rush to seek a new life abroad thought little of throwing reminders of the old one away. Passports, driver's licences, books of every kind, magazines, letters, handwritten manuscripts – all rotted among unpicked garbage or met the flames or were auctioned off as scrap. Later there were fervent but mostly futile attempts to salvage these pieces of jettisoned lives.

"Tell me, where – how – did you find it?" I said to Feroz.

But at this point a servant came to call him. A consignment of shoes had arrived in the store, the Zanzibari blackmarketeer was waiting to be paid. Feroz turned to go, saying to me, "Later." I hurried out with him, taking the book. Seeing it clutched under my arm, he stopped. "I have to look at it carefully," I explained. I promised to guard it with my life. There was no time to argue. The anxiety on Feroz's face as he extracted the solemn oath from me was a thing to ponder.

It was a diary. A 1913 edition, published by Letts, and of the "Explorer" variety, which could be used for the following year, presumably by those confined to those regions of the globe with limited access to amenities. Five by eight inches, it allowed for three days a page. The cover was soft board, beige with black type, except for "Explorer" flourished diagonally in large red italics. The endpapers were covered with advertisements of the day – Indo-European Telegraph Company Ltd.; Royal Insurance Company; Eno's Fruit Salt – "A Pleasant Way to Health Before Breakfast, The Natural Way." There followed two pages with the sunrise and sunset times for 1913 in Capetown, Bloemfontein, Bulawayo, Pretoria; postal rates to South Africa; cable rates; and 1913 customs tariffs to South Africa.

After this information came a clear page, inscribed with the owner's name and address in the centre:

Alfred Corbin
Kikono, British East Africa

and the first part of a Latin inscription: "at nos hinc . . ." the rest was stained and illegible.

Inside were brittle, yellowed pages, encrusted with open, dry capsules of cockroach eggs; insect remains, thin like fossils, releasing the pungent dust of their own decay. Several pages were torn off, many were stained; there were sections which had been neatly burrowed through by silverfish.

The ink was faded, the writing often unreadable. Much of it

consisted of typical diary entries against dates – scrawled, cryptic, the obligatory reminders or notes (for example, the entry for 27 February, 1913: "Crossed the equator. Parades, dinner, ball; weather wonderful so far . . ."). And then, intermittently, there were neater long journal entries written in sloping hand. I gathered that Corbin must have been quite a letter-writer, and probably shared his observations with correspondents.

Sir Alfred Corbin was, of course, Governor of Uganda in the late 1940s, after which he retired from the Colonial Service, though he was called upon later to advise the British government on the independence of that and other African colonies. He had served a long time in the British administration in the area, and even worked on the policy that went under the name of Indirect Rule. The diary in my hands was a record of an early posting, one forgotten fragment of an addendum to a well-documented history. And as such, of what interest to me, these personal outpourings, the scribblings of a young colonial officer, drafts of letters to mother or father, or perhaps notes for his eventual memoir?

This is how I have come to picture him: seventy-five years ago, in 1913, the only white man in an African village, sits at a rough, crooked wooden table in his rough wooden house. Above him, from a beam, hangs a pressure lamp. Outside, pitch darkness interspersed by the light of a few lamps and candles. The man at the table puts down the glass he's sipped from, picks up his fountain pen, and writes in his diary. By this writing he begins to weave the thread that will connect to me.

Even before I began to pore over Corbin's entries which would subsequently so grip me, I could not help but feel that in some mysterious manner the book touched our lives; was *our* book. There was, I felt, much more there than the contents of its pages; there was the story of the book itself. Written here amongst us, later perhaps hidden, and now found among us, it must have left a long and secretive trail, a trail that if followed would reveal much about the lives and times it witnessed, and tell us why the diary finally surfaced where it did.

I remember my moment of decision exactly – this book, this burden before me. It had, as I sat contemplating it, the aspect of a portal. Should I enter, give to it my retired days? . . . I wrote a letter, to a very dear former student from whom I had received a postcard a few months before, and proceeded to meet a librarian and coax him to open a certain locked cupboard at the Dar es Salaam Library. I entered headlong into an engagement with the book.

I would – I told myself – recreate the world of that book. I would breathe life into the many spirits captured in its pages so long ago and tell their stories; and I would revive the spirit of the book itself, tell *its* own story. And so I would construct a history, a living tapestry to join the past to the present, to defy the blistering shimmering dusty bustle of city life outside which makes transients of us all.

In the weeks that followed I discovered the dark, passionate secret of a simple man whose life became painfully and inextricably linked with that of an English colonial officer. I saw that the ephemeral tie between them – the tragic young woman Mariamu – would become the most tenacious bond of all. I saw an old uncertain world give birth to a new, no less fragile one, and I followed the trail of this book, from the pen of a lonely man to the obsession of another, from ancient lives caught up in imperial enterprise and a world war to these, our times: and finally to myself, and the hidden longings of my past. At the end of it all, I too lie exposed to my own inquiry, also captive to the book.

PART ONE

1

The Administrator

We carry within us the wonders we seek without us;
There is all Africa and her prodigies in us.
- Sir Thomas Browne

And now, sir, I come to Africa . . .
- William Pitt
(in the House of Commons), 1791

1

"We seem to have sighted Mombasa at last," wrote Alfred Corbin in his diary on 1 March, 1913, aboard the German vessel *Prinzregent*. He concluded his brief entry with a reminder to himself to order more pipe tobacco the next time he wrote home. After that he strolled out on deck. Passengers had crowded on the starboard side to gather in the new vista which presented itself to eyes long weary of the sea and the ghostly distant shapes of land.

How fitting, he thought then of this sight of Africa, that it should greet you so gently; how melodramatic and unaffecting if it were to show you straight away its power and wildness, its strong colours, the pulling force. It was in order to be impressed, to confirm his schoolboy expectations fed on tales of famous adventurers and explorers, that he had strained his eyes seaward ever since they'd left Marseilles with a fresh load of passengers from the British Isles. He himself had boarded the *Prinzregent* at Hamburg. It was the sixteenth day at sea, the ship had turned southwestwards to round the island town and bring into view the town's full glory in the sun. A sight that even then he knew he would never forget. The coast of Africa, the harbour of Mombasa. Its modesty, the composed exoticism of its orientalness, stayed with you like the strong lines of a deceptively simple masterwork. White houses shimmered on a hill rendered lush green with vegetation. A fringe of palm trees decorated the shoreline, a white road came up to the beach where a restless waving crowd awaited. The waters were dark blue but choppy, the sky spotless that day. Even before they entered the southern harbour, dhows and bagalas hailed them, smaller craft hustled cheerfully alongside with expectations of business.

On the ship, his fellow passengers would have noticed a man of medium build and average height; he had fair hair and a thick moustache, droopy eyes. He would have been observed as being somewhat shy.

Alfred Corbin had spent his childhood days with governesses and in schools in Stockholm and Prague and Hamburg, speaking more of the languages of these foreign lands – at least in his youth – than he did his mother tongue. His father, Charles, after a stint at cattle farming in Argentina, had settled on a career in the Consular Service. The family had a house in Devon, and the only claim to distinction it could make was through relation to Sir George Corbin-Brown of the Punjab, and through a vague connection on his mother's Scottish side to William Pitt's war minister, Dundas. Of his two brothers, Robert was an officer in the Indian army and Kenneth was an Area Commissioner in Nyasaland. To start off his youngest son in a different direction, Charles Corbin found for Alfred a post at the Hamburg agents of the Union Mail Shipping Lines. This job was not without interest for Alfred – it was in Hamburg harbour that he first laid eyes upon natives of Africa, ship hands conscripted from the west coast of the continent – but Alfred was soon eyeing other opportunities. A chance came when he was returning from London to Hamburg via Paris.

Years later, in his published memoirs, he would describe how he was conscripted into the Colonial Service. In Paris he'd been told the undersecretary for the colonies, Mr. Winston Churchill, was resting in a local hotel, having returned from a trip to East Africa. On an impulse he went and presented his card at the hotel, noting his relation to Sir George. "If he is related to Kenneth Corbin, send him up," came the reply. Mr. Churchill, it seemed, had met his brother in British East Africa (as Kenya was then called). In a room strewn with paper and filled with cigarette smoke, the undersecretary, in the midst of a late breakfast, accepted Alfred Corbin's application for a job, which would require from him, as he put it, "his whole life and soul."

Even though it would be a few years later that he took up the offer (having become involved with a woman in the meantime), Alfred Corbin would always consider it propitious to have been initiated into the Colonial Service with these credentials, whose value would grow with the years. And he never left the Service until he retired.

2 March, 1913

We were taken into dugout boats, called "ngalawas," and were rowed to the shore by boisterous boatmen who sang in clear voices to each other. As soon as we stepped on solid ground we were completely taken over by a surge of porters wearing that white Swahili cotton smock so popular here and called "kanzu." Cranstone the surveyor, who had been chattering so tiresomely since Port Said about Mombasa, the eye in a socket, the leafy hiding place where Sinbad must surely have wandered through and perhaps seen the roc's egg, began muttering now about the den of forty thieves, saying "apana-apana, enda-enda" and more. Two Indian policemen in enormous beards and red turbans watched the scene calmly; a group of scantily dressed Indian men searched nervously among their arriving compatriots whom we had picked up in Aden. Many of the Europeans on the boat were met or knew their way about. It was unbearably hot and noisy, the clamour contagious and unsettling. As I looked around me uncertainly, the focus of a cacophony of solicitations, an Indian man pushed through the throng and introduced himself with a restrained smile.

"Sir, please allow me," he said in a soft voice.

Gratefully I relinquished my holdall to this short dark man who was wrapped in a black tunic with a shawl around his neck. He said his name was Thomas and would I follow him. He had a rather musical voice and the curious habit of moving his head from side to side as he spoke. He turned around and I followed, keeping my eye fixed on the back of his glistening black head. It took me the rest of the day to realize that the man was perhaps attempting to muffle his cold with the silly-looking woolly shawl, for there was a faint whiff of camphor in the air . . .

Thomas led him to a corrugated-iron shed, a blazing furnace of a place. This was the Customs House, where a long line of Europeans and a few American hunters awaited inspection. An Indian clerk sat at a table, filling out forms in quadruplicate, periodically releasing an angry or fuming passenger with a hoarse "Next!" and a stamp on a passport. He saw and acknowledged Thomas. Beads of sweat fell visibly from his brow onto the papers he wrote on. From time to time he would move an index finger across his forehead and sweep a rain of sweat onto the earthen floor.

"You have a gun, sir?" asked Thomas.

"A rifle . . ."

"Not to worry."

Thomas looked away with the air of someone ready to wait indefinitely, and Corbin looked outside through the barred window at the sunny courtyard, ready to do the same but with less composure.

"Please point out your baggage, sir," said Thomas suddenly.

Corbin did so. Then by some unseen magic all his belongings appeared at the head of the queue and he was summoned with a deference the other Europeans could not challenge. His gun and ammunition registered, he was whisked with style out of Customs and his baggage loaded by a porter onto a cart bound for the Mombasa Club up the road.

Only then did it occur to Corbin to enquire about the man into whose hands he had put himself, now walking solidly beside him. "Don't worry, sir," said the man, but the special treatment at Customs had cost five rupees.

They walked through the exclusive English settlement called The Point, strewn without regard for economy or geometry with picturesque villas in lush gardens connected to each other by roads barely better than tracks. The sun-hat was heavy on his head; without it, he understood, he would collapse. The temperature was ninety, he felt clammy, and the slight breeze from the ocean lacked the spirit to revive. Not too soon, it seemed, the large white building of the Club appeared in sight. With a relief that overwhelmed him, Corbin almost ran into its spacious shade.

The manager, Hanning, greeted him with a lemonade. He was a big red-faced man with thin yellow hair and a handlebar moustache, and wearing a rather sparkling white shirt and tie for the time of day. He'd had a swim and a bath, it appeared. Thomas left, promising to return. Corbin took a small table inside the bar, next to the doorway, through which he could look out at the verandah and the garden. There were two other entrances to the bar, one leading from the dining room where lunch was being served by black waiters in kanzus and red fezzes. There were African hunting and war trophies on the walls; a niche held an Arab copper-work jar under a pair of daggers. Behind the bar, at which stood a barman looking busy, were three group photographs of men with hunting or fishing spoils. A corridor past the snooker room led to a small number of guest rooms, to one of which Corbin was presently shown. The window faced the back, and he could see part of the road leading down to the old town.

3 March

The room is large and airy. It has two beds, two chairs, a chest of drawers and a mirror, otherwise it is absolutely bare. There is no carpet. Several passengers on board ship called this club the best in Africa! . . .

4 March

"Venice has its gondola, London its cab, and Mombasa has its gharry, as I always say," says Hanning. He is a drifter, who answered the Club's notice, which was placed in the Cape Town *Times*, and came over to see the place, he says. The gharry is a tram running on rails and pulled by one or two natives. It is the only way to travel on the island, I am told. The PC is away and I might as well enjoy the metropolis while I can, before I get posted somewhere where I'll be lucky to have a roof over my head. He has given me a list of the sites to visit. The Club has a small guide book, which he has lent me to browse through. The old Portuguese fort is a must. The old name of Mombasa was Mvita, for war. . . . Then the ancient mosque, the northern harbour where the dhows anchor, the water gate. And, no visitor to Mombasa misses the boat ride around the island . . .

The Club verandah looked upon a dense garden of brilliant colours running all the way to the cliff edge, which was demarcated by a wire fence and white stones. Beyond lay the ocean, its shimmering, misty horizon a fitting sight for an expatriate or tourist or colonial servant to contemplate over a cocktail.

He began his sightseeing the same day. A tram had been called, and it emerged now from under the shade of a bougainvillaea bush. It was rolled noisily to the rail and lifted upon it, after which he sat on the wooden seat under its canopy and was pushed and free-wheeled all the way down the tree-lined shady Kilindini Road.

If The Point presented meditative vistas – dreamy groves, brightly coloured gardens, vast ocean, coral cliffs – Mombasa town assailed all the senses at once. The smells of overripe pineapples and mangoes, the open drains, animal droppings; costumes of a dozen cultures and the babble of as many languages.

He played tennis every evening at the Sports Club while he waited for the Provincial Commissioner, the PC. At the new and already potholed cricket pitch he watched a friendly game on the first Sunday he was there: Indians versus the English, one tribe on either side of the pitch. It was a clear rout of the ragged Indians, most of whom had never held a bat before and had merely been assembled for the Englishmen's pleasure. Dinner parties at the Club degenerated into drunken orgies, after which members had to be assisted into their trams. On the second Sunday of his stay, he participated first in an oyster picnic on the shore, followed by a "cocktail parade," in which the object was to mix enough drinks to knock oneself out.

There was one lion trophy on the wall beside the bar. A fierce, huge head, its mouth stretched wide open, the contemplation of which could make your stomach turn, your hair rise. As you turned away uneasily from this meeting you might be told by the barman that this lion had carried off twenty-seven victims in Tsavo: a coolie from an open railway carriage; an unknowing porter from a campfire away over a four-foot fence before his companions discovered him missing, the following day finding his bloodied clothes, some bones, and a severed head; a sleeping labourer dragged out from between two oblivious companions inside a tent . . . and so the bloody toll went. If it was late in the afternoon, your attention would invariably drift, from that vanquished terror on the wall to the oversized human head below it, belonging to its hunter, Frank Maynard, who was sitting at a small table holding a whisky. There were stories about him, too, but they were told in his absence.

He was a big man in army khaki, who came every day for his sundowner. From where he sat he quietly watched all the goings-on in the room – the bluster and chit-chat, the deals and complaints, the dart and card games, of the merchants, the officials, and the engineers. His presence, once he arrived, like the man-eater's above him, became part of the character of the room. The hair on his large head was brown and sparse, he wore a small moustache, and the cold green eyes revoked any trace of warmth betrayed by the faint toothy smile at his lips. Nevertheless, he was liked and much respected for what he was, the more so for the predicament in which he had (unfairly, it was said) been put.

Frank Maynard was a captain in the King's African Rifles who would pursue a recalcitrant animal or tribesman with like ferocity and ruthlessness. Currently he was on suspension pending an inquiry regarding his conduct on a punitive expedition against a tribe and was biding his time on the coast.

On several occasions Corbin's eyes had met and acknowledged that searching look from the trophy wall. Then one day, after he had been deposited at the Club door by a tram after a sightseeing tour, as he sat in the bar wiping sweat from his brow and contemplating his second bath, despairing over yet another change of clothes, Alfred Corbin's eyes fell briefly on the soldier. That momentary look seemed to spark a resolve, for Maynard got up, and with slow deliberate steps came straight towards his table.

"Frank Maynard," he said, shaking hands and sitting down.

"Corbin, Alfred Corbin."

"So I've heard, old chap."

Corbin tried not to feel like a mouse under that overbearing smile, that brilliant predatory gaze, not to become too conscious of the heads turned to stare at them from the bar. He was waiting for his first posting in Africa, and this was a man who had trampled the land from corner to corner, slept in the forests and killed its wildlife and natives.

"I knew your brother in India. Robert. Good man."

"In the Punjab?"

Maynard nodded. The same amused look.

"And I met Kenneth in Voi. Didn't get to know him well, though, he was on his way out — home leave, it was, and Nyasaland after that, I believe."

They had a drink together. The lion on the wall, Maynard told him, catching his gaze, had measured nine-foot-eleven, tip to tip, nose to tail; it took eight men to carry it.

The following evening Corbin was invited for supper.

Maynard kept rooms on the second storey of an Arab house on the Kilindini Road, not far from the Club. He greeted Corbin at the door in a yellow kanzu and a tasselled red fez. The reception room was furnished simply in the Arab style and they sat on pillows. Maynard produced a hookah and Corbin a cheroot. By this time the younger man was more composed, the other relaxed and less intimidating. A woman suddenly entered the room with a sharp rustle of clothing which made Corbin start. She was strikingly beautiful, a half-caste of partly Arab or Indian blood, partly African. The short length of buibui, worn around her shoulders over a colourful dress, was what had rustled; she hovered around them for a while before finally taking a stool some distance away.

"Stop gaping, man!"

Corbin raised an eyebrow. Maynard chuckled.

"A few years ago practically every man in Nairobi kept a native girl — or two or three. Now they are more civilized and busy with each other's wives."

The night was cool, a light breeze blew in through the open

window; there was a mosque not far off, from which the muezzin's "Allahu Akber" presently came through clearly. Below, from the courtyard of the building came the sounds of boys playing, men chatting on stone benches by the little garden, probably over their coffee. Over whiskies Corbin and Maynard talked of their schools, their families. Maynard's was a banking family; his refusal to join his father caused him much guilt and brooding. He was now estranged from his family.

The woman got up and left the room again with the distinct rustle of her buibui. She returned with a pitcher of water for washing hands. Then she brought their food: meat curry, and rice and bread. They drank more whisky and had plum pudding from home for dessert.

"I don't always eat this much, but in company I tend to indulge. Africa teaches you how little food you really need, and how much we in civilized England tend to overeat."

They sat up late into the evening. Maynard did most of the talking, mostly about Africa. He loved it and he hated it, above all he feared it for what it could do to him. "This is a savage country, and it could turn you into a savage. It is so easy to be overcome by its savagery, to lose one's veneer of Western civilization. This is what I have learned, what I dread most. So in a way I look forward to leaving it. But I have nowhere to go. India, perhaps. Egypt . . ."

He respected the African, yet would call him nigger. He loved animals. He had killed scores of both. He believed in Empire, but had no patience with settling the country with whites. "I," said the soldier, "respect the African – as a redoubtable enemy or as a friend. I would kill him with as little compunction as he would me. But the settler, and the low class of official we have in East Africa – excuse me, Corbin, but there are not enough of you here – despises the black and would use me to kill him."

They sat in silence for a long time. The courtyard below was quiet now. The moon had risen and passed the window and was somewhere above the house. From outside came the sound of frogs and night insects, with the richness of a symphony, it seemed, when he paid attention to it, and from the kitchen came the occasional clatter of utensils. One more time Corbin glanced around the room, preparing mentally to leave. There was one question he had about this man, based on what he had heard at the parties and picnics. But it was not his place to ask.

As if sensing this unease, Maynard began explanations.

"Imagine," he said, "the centre of the village where they hold the baraza. Cleared hard ground. A white man – an Englishman – pegged to the ground. Lying on his back, mouth wedged open. Savage men and women come and urinate in his mouth. Men standing and laughing, women crouching, all drunk on pombé. The man drowns in nigger urine. He is disembowelled, used as a latrine. . . . Imagine the insects feeding on him . . . the stench . . . the scavengers . . . hyenas who would not leave a scrap of meat on a bone, vultures, crows. It had to be avenged, Corbin. For the white man, for authority, for order – they are the same thing here.

"We went in at dawn. Spies had given us the layout. No man or woman to be spared, I ordered. We set fire to the huts, waited outside for the niggers to emerge. I myself bayoneted them, men and women they came running out. . . . No mercy, I said . . .

"You'd be surprised at the ease with which a bayonet enters a human chest. . . . How cheap human life is really . . .

"You disapprove – obviously. Tell me, what would you do? I myself am not sure I did the right thing – I am haunted at times – but I believed then I was doing the right thing. To show strength, fury. This is a savage country, it makes a savage out of you. What would you do?"

"I'm not sure I can say . . . not being a military man. I do think the Colonial Office holds vastly different views of the natives."

"Yes. I wonder which will prevail. Yours, obviously, when I've cleaned up and subdued the land for you to administer."

But they departed on cordial terms. "I disapprove of his actions, not of the man," Corbin went back and wrote. In fact he was strangely drawn to the soldier, and joined him several times for drinks, until his posting came.

17 March, 1913

"Send the poor devil in," I heard the Provincial Commissioner say, and the secretary looked rather apologetically at me. "Poor devil" because I had been posted to a place called Kikono near the border with German East. It is a substation that has been sporadically manned depending on the availability of junior staff. There are a few mission stations in the area that lies to the east and next to the foothills of Kilimanjaro. The town is populated by a community of Indians and some Swahilis from the Coast. Henley, the PC, is something of a student of African tribes, hence his sympathy for me. He had just returned from a field safari in Giriyama. I must say I was not a little disappointed. In Africa one does not expect to be saddled with overseeing Indians. These, I am told, already have a conflict under way with local missionaries. Nevertheless I was eager to get away. And so, after yet another dinner party and dancing at the Grand Hotel (grand in name only, as everyone here hastily explains – but the Club is no good for such events, as it is out of bounds to women after 7 P.M.) and a picnic lunch the following morning with a charming couple called the Unsworths, I set off on the Uganda Railway for Voi.

I had resolved to catch up on duty, to write letters to Mother and Robert, but as soon as I sat down with paper and pen I realized how futile it was to attempt that mundane chore, to conjure up England out of a night in Africa. The darkest, blackest night that simply shut out the world of European Mombasa. From where I sat contemplating my epistolary failure, the window of the Uganda Railway coach sent back an eerie reflection of myself. I pressed my face to the pane and watched the darkness fly past . . .

shadows in the moonlight swiftly rushing by, shadows that could be trees or some species of wildlife. . . . It was impossible to surrender to sleep with the knowledge that finally I was entering the interior of Africa . . . the huge and dark continent that had defied the rest of the world for millennia, now opening up to European civilization, to a great Empire of which I was a minor but privileged functionary. "Life and soul," Mr. Churchill had said. My body had blistered in the heat and swelled to the bites of insects, and as I lay on the most uncomfortable bunk the Uganda Railway possessed, my soul was stirring.

19 March

Thirty porters were engaged for me at Voi, from where I set off this morning after spending two nights at the Dak bungalow. There has been much singing and merriment. The porters are of the Wataita tribe and speak a little Swahili. They wear a strip of cloth around their waist. Their front teeth are sharpened to a point, and some carry objects such as tin boxes or small animal horns in the slits in their ears. With me is Thomas, who was the first person to welcome me in Africa and has doggedly stayed with me, willing to serve me for anything I can pay him. He has told me an interesting story of how a woman from his people was once Queen of Mombasa for a very short period during Portuguese times. Thus the vanquished clutch at straws of glory. . . . He has a rather irritating habit of equating his status with mine, and never tires of pointing out the shortcomings of the poor Wataita. He doesn't realize that they all have fun at his expense.

Part of our way is thick, thorny bramble, which we have to cut through. I am utterly in the hands of the porters and guides. What do they think of me? I feel strange and nervous, helpless with the smattering of Swahili I picked up in Mombasa. Sometimes I am the subject of their song, but whether they ply me with compliment or abuse I cannot say. Baboons chatter in the trees above us, rhino spoor has been pointed out to me, I have seen a snake cross my path. At one time we were followed by lion grunts, and even now in the dark night perhaps I hear them growl. I am reminded of the lion head at the Mombasa Club and the red-fezzed Captain Maynard sitting under it. I cannot help thinking that if the blacks in my caravan decide to butcher me and my Indian, it would be Maynard or someone like him who would be sent to avenge us.

2

Kikono, "The Little Hand," lay some thirty miles from the border with German East Africa, a convenient stop on the east-west trail from Voi to Moshi that connected the two colonies. The mighty snow-capped Kilimanjaro attended by fluffs of cloud loomed in the near distance: a presence at once enigmatic, benign, and mystical; a symbol of the eternal. But the heart of this town in the thorny desert country was the little mbuyu – baobab – tree, a short thick deformity struggling out from the side of a hill, from which twisted, mangled branches grappled uselessly against the sky. In somewhat light-hearted fashion, and in keeping with legends surrounding mbuyu trees, this one was sometimes called "the little hand of the devil"; but at night, and especially at sudden encounter, it would appear quite ghostly, not to say satanic, and was avoided. During the day it was a shady meeting place. Facing it in two rows perpendicular to each other were the shops and houses and two mosques of the small town.

Early one afternoon the townsfolk began to prepare to welcome the new Assistant District Commissioner. The rest time had passed unnoticed. At last, amidst much anticipation and after a few false alarms, a boy was seen to go up to the little mbuyu tree, from under whose branches he began to beat on his drum, at which signal the shopkeepers stepped out from their shops to join the gathered crowd. The men in the police band, twelve-strong, set themselves up under the tree, and the drummer boy sat with them. The Indians stood in a row, somewhat solemn-looking in white drill suits and red or black fezzes, or in dhoties and turbans. Next to them formed a shorter line of Swahilis, in kanzus and embroidered caps, some in waistcoats. There was a third, large group of vendors, servants, and occasional labourers, and, with them, tribesmen and women from the neighbouring area. Thus they stood waiting, occasionally looking up, turning or craning their necks towards the road that entered town and would bring the new representative of the King.

What manner of town was Kikono, an Indian haven improbably placed miles away from the railway at the western edge of Taita country? It was said, with some truth, that open one Indian duka, or shop, in the middle of nowhere and soon you'd have a row of dukas, in the same way as a potato or yam proliferates. The first duka appears when a wind-riding seed falls on the ground and decides to make its home there. So the first duka appeared, so the town grew.

A young English naturalist and sportsman had one day taken off from the ancient port of Lamu on the Indian Ocean, where he had been a guest of the British Consul. He had borrowed a large sum of money from his unofficial banker, an Indian shopkeeper of the Shamsi sect called Jamal Dewji. The shopkeeper sent one of his sons along with the explorer-naturalist, ostensibly to assist him and even cook for him, but actually to keep an eye on him. "In his country he may be king," he bragged in mosque, "but here I trust nobody." "Stick to the hat-wearer's heels and don't come back without him or the money," he told his son. Indeed, it was known that the Englishman, who had done much prying around town, had slipped into his bag an antique China bowl from an old tomb, and the news of his departure was received with some relief. He first went off to Zanzibar, from whence he sailed to Bagamoyo and marched with a caravan to Moshi and Taveta and finally to the station of the Mission of Christ in Africa, in the Taita country. At the mission he stayed two weeks, spending his time hunting and exploring. During this time Jamal Dewji's boy, Abdul, fell in love with one of the converts, a Swahili girl called Hannah, and convinced the explorer to release to him some of his father's money so he could set himself up in the area. The eminence was only too happy to rid himself of the watchdog at a discount. The boy and girl married, the girl reconverted to Islam and reverted to her original name, Khanoum.

Abdul Jamal Dewji, known thenceforth as Jamali, started his shop some miles down from the Mission at the little mbuyu tree which was long known as a resting place for caravans. The Shamsi community to which he belonged was well-organized, and news of this single-family settlement spread to Mombasa and beyond. There is a railway to the north and a railway to the south – how can a town fail to grow between them? the young man's father boasted in Lamu. All that is needed is a line to join the two and pass through the village for it to become a town, a city. A few months later two men arrived from India, and later their families. Grocers, dispensers, sellers of cloth, jewellery, and hardware: a line of dukas sprang up. Where there are two Shamsis, as the adage says, let one be the headman, father and priest – the mukhi – and let the other form the congregation. That is, let them without further ado start a mosque.

The mukhi of the Shamsis here was currently Jamali himself. Like mukhis everywhere, he was paid not financially but with honour and respect, and promises of rewards in the hereafter. He was a shopkeeper, tall and lanky for his kind, with a face a little short of humble and the doggedness of a hyena when he had to

27

help a community member. His Swahili wife spoke Cutchi to add to her mission English and had borne him three children.

Thus setting themselves up, loyal British subjects – and vociferously so – with visions of growth and prosperity for the town, they had applied to the government for official township status. While it made up its mind, the government responded by sending an Assistant District Commissioner of the Mombasa Province when it could spare one. The current ADC was Fred Axworthy, now on a march out of town to welcome and initiate his successor, Alfred Corbin. Word had reached town earlier in the day that ten of his thirty porters had deserted the new ADC the night before. Four of the ten were apprehended on the road outside Kikono, and now languished in the lockup.

Apparently heralding the arrival, a bevy of little boys in kanzus, loin cloths, or nothing at all, came running down the road, followed by a man rolling on his heels. They all joined the more irregular sections of the waiting crowd. The Indians formed a straighter line, the Swahilis stirred. All eyes were on the road now. There was a sudden silence, then everybody clapped hands as the two Europeans in white suits and sun-hats came striding into town at the head of a trail of porters. The police band broke into "For He's a Jolly Good Fellow," and the Englishmen stopped to hear it out.

And this was what appeared to the new ADC as he approached the town: fleeting glimpses caught between bush and tree and anthill – a figure draped in white, dashing from left to right, cutting across his path in the distance. It could have been a man in kanzu but for the black hair flying, the lithe movement, the nimble step . . . then a red head-cover over the hair to complete the female figure. So amazed was he by the sight that he had stopped to watch. She disappeared behind an incline, where he was told lay the settlement . . .

. . . a mound really, of red earth, covered sparsely with the predominant vegetation of the area, namely thorn. Soon after that apparition disappeared, into one side of it, as it were, there emerged from the other side and directly in front of us a party lead by a white man in sun helmet.

"Dr. Livingstone, I presume, what? I dare say you must be the new ADC, the replacement I've been begging for on my knees, for months. Axworthy's the name."

Red-faced and stocky, perspiring freely, he was jovial, if anything. I introduced myself.

"We've caught some of your porters who absconded, so we've been expecting you rather. I dare say you'll have to prescribe some strokes of the kiboko as deterrent. I don't believe in the whip myself, too damn humiliating, but it's what works best."

I don't remember what else he said, but it was a lot. I glanced briefly behind to see poor Thomas trudging along, bringing up the rear.

The entire town came into view almost instantly. To our left ran a row of shops and houses, meeting another row at a right angle at its far end. We were at the head of the only street and the town square, its centrepiece a baobab, or mbuyu, tree that led to the administrative centre and the ADC's house.

This was Kikono, its inhabitants gathered under the mbuyu tree waiting patiently to greet me. As we approached, the police band struck up a tune. I was introduced to the local dignitaries, Indian and Swahili, the chiefs and dignitaries of nearby villages, and the local police force. After a supper of chicken stew and fried plantain, served by a young African girl who was rather scantily dressed, followed by pudding, brandy, and tobacco which I contributed, we retired.

The following day a rather unpleasant task awaited me. Those porters who had deserted on the way from Voi and had been caught were lined up to receive their dues. One fellow was brought in that morning with fervent protestations of having lost his way, so his case had to be heard. It was decided against him. Each received 10 strokes of the whip. "6 is too little, 20 too much," said Axworthy.

It seems to me there has to be a better way of making the native willing to carry burden for a wage, some attractive inducement at journey's end perhaps . . .

It's been 5 days since I arrived, and Axworthy left this morning. The girl who cooked and waited at table for him has also disappeared, having joined the departing entourage, so Thomas swears. I am now lord under this mbuyu tree.

26 March

. . . My powers are modest. . . . In criminal cases I can inflict only one month's imprisonment and a fine of Rs 50, whilst in civil cases my jurisdiction amounts to fines of up to Rs 250. . . . Bothered by boils, saw dispenser.
Ask for –
½ doz whisky
6 tablespoons
biscuits, any kind
. . . already Mombasa seems far away – and Europe?

He administered with a quiet, forceful diligence, a monastic rigour, in the unquestioned belief that what he did in his small way was part of a bigger enterprise in which he had some stake. His method – for he was a methodical man and thought carefully about what he did – was to understand the motives behind his people's reluctance, recalcitrance, or hostility, and to make them understand his own position. He was there to administer in the name of his king and nation, to bring the land into the twentieth century in as painless a way as possible, in the belief that the British Empire with its experience of ruling other lands and with its humane system was the best nurturing ground for an emerging nation, for backward Africans and Orientals to enter the society of civilized peoples.

Governor's Memoranda for PCs and DCs (1910)
(Native Policy, pages 5-6)

... The Fundamental principle and the only humane policy to be followed in dealing with peoples who have not reached a high stage of civilisation is to develop them on their own lines and in accordance with their own ideas and customs, purified in so far as is necessary. Whilst retaining all the good in their government, which makes for manliness, self-respect, and honest dealing, only that which is repugnant to higher ideals of morality and justice should be rejected; and the introduction of so-called civilisation, when it has a denationalising and demoralising tendency should be avoided. It is not from the present generation that we may look for much; the succeeding generations are in the hands of the Provincial Commissioners with their district staffs. . . . It must certainly be their endeavour to lift the natives to a higher plane of civilisation; but this can only be achieved by gradual methods and by observing existing conditions.

He was police chief, magistrate, doctor, tax collector and, when his superiors demanded, surveyor. It was a job that required infinite patience, a certain amount but not an excess of good humour, an ability to turn cold, a knack for improvisation, an ability to forget the day's concerns. Only by the most abstract idealism could you try to convince tribes to send their sons to work with the Indians, or of the benefits of paying taxes. How to convince them to abandon their own laws, their universes, for a

31

European view of being? How to explain that an ugly girl was not an evil omen, when if the people really believed in the portent they could will bad luck and prove their prophecy right?

Much of his work involved arbitration and administering British justice. The former took cajoling, reasoning, using threats or the lockup, always with native custom as guide. But imposing British justice was like constructing a marble edifice, irrelevant and alien to people governed by their own laws and ways of doing things. Even so, his waiting room was full when he began hearing shauris – the petitions from the people – in the morning. He believed he was often used as a curiosity, as a test, or for an opinion, while the real, the binding decisions on the cases were taken elsewhere by tribal councils.

17 April, 1913

The powers of an ADC are greater than I at first suspected. I can give imprisonments up to 6 months, but beyond 1 month the sentence has to be approved by High Court. My Court entirely independent of the DC's . . .

Governor's Memoranda for PCs and DCs (1910)
(Native Policy, cont'd, page 7)

By upholding the authority of the Chiefs and Elders, I do not wish to imply that officers are to sit down and enforce blindly – possibly at the point of the bayonet – all orders issued by these men who, after all, are only savages. The main object of administering the people through their Chiefs is to prevent disintegration amongst the tribe . . .

There was a Government Station in Voi and a temporary one in Taveta, between which his small dominion lay, and every quarter an ADC arrived from Voi to assist for a few days and to collect reports. The first one of these was a big, bluff man called Woodward. Corbin was lucky, Woodward told him over brandy, his area was so sparsely populated: "Mostly coastal people and foreigners." But even so: "Won't be long before a real test case comes along, old chap."

"Such as?"

"When a real hard one comes along, you don't know what to do – that is, you know what you have to do, but it doesn't feel right. It's a case you never forget. Welcome to the Colonial Service."

He wouldn't say what his own such case had been. But he had a word of advice: "Whenever you find things getting a bit too much for you, *go on safari*." He emphasized the words. "And women . . . it's easier on safari. But don't bring them back. Concubinage is not tolerated any longer."

There were regular football matches in town, in which all the races participated. The post office was active; mail was collected and taken to Voi once a week. The *East African Herald* arrived regularly from Nairobi, and it was in one of its issues that Corbin learned of Captain Maynard's transfer out to Palestine. The settler community in Nairobi had picketed the Governor's residence in protest, and the paper carried a strongly worded editorial. On King's Birthday they had a march-past, the mukhi Jamali donated sodas, and that night the Indians held a function to which Corbin was invited.

As he surveyed the district he ruled over like a king – some of the tribesmen even confused him with his own monarch, King George – Frank Maynard would come to mind. A man who returned savagery for savagery, no longer needed in East Africa. Throughout the country, towns like Kikono were springing up, full of life, the whole land buzzing with a vitality it had not known for millennia, all due to European intervention. The likes of Maynard would be needed only if the imposed order broke down, a prospect that seemed remote.

11 May, 1913

Imagine waking up in the middle of the night to the sound of trees rustling, a hyena barking . . . and, of all things, a dissonant, whining hum. What could it be – some animal, a sick donkey braying, a lost calf – perhaps the stray dog Bwana Tim was wounded? Then gradually I realized what it was. What is it in human intonation that makes it identifiable? For that's what I could swear it was. People singing! I could not believe my ears. A faint sound of human singing, a chorus not in full control. Was I in some ridiculous dream? I sat up, pinched myself. The singing ceased after a while, but voices persisted intermittently. Something was going on. I walked to the window but desisted from opening it, if only because it would create its own racket. By this time the sounds had ceased altogether. It was eerie. I have never believed in ghosts, although in Mombasa I was told not to be too sceptical. Fortunately it was almost dawn, and soon the town was stirring. Upon inquiring later in the morning, I was told that the Indian Shamsis wake up at 4 A.M. to pray!

The administrative centre of Kikono consists of the government buildings, situated on the top of a low hill. My own "jumba" is a crooked wooden house with iron roof and no ceiling. The furniture has to be moved during rains, and the creaky verandah gives ample warning of any arrival. There are two bedrooms on one wing, facing back and front. In the rear of the house are the kitchen and a servant's hut. The office is an even more dilapidated affair. Beside it is the police station and post office. Out in front, in the compound, are a mbuyu tree and a large thorny bush, which overlook a sharp drop, itself covered by scrub. And beyond that is the rest of this little town, the brown mud-and-wattle huts that make up the business and residence section where the Indians and Swahilis live and run their dukas. The dispensary is in the rather lethal hands of the Indian Chagpar. A footpath runs down the hill on the west side, from my house, arrives in the town, and goes beyond to join the road to Voi.

Roughly half the Indians belong to the Shamsi sect of Islam and have a separate mosque. They are in touch with Voi, Mombasa, Nairobi, even Bombay and German East. Once or twice a year it seems they hold large feasts, and when they do not go to Voi for that purpose they collect in Kikono community members from the neighbouring towns and give themselves a regular jamboree. There are also Hindu, Punjabi, and Memon families, but quite often the distinction blurs.

Nowadays I mostly sleep through the pre-dawn Shamsi hum, but in the morning am awakened by the flapping wings of a flock of birds on the move and then the *cockorickoo* of a cock crowing somewhere.

The simple quiet of a town early in the morning – the gentle slap of the cool air, the sun just beginning to warm itself over the hilltops and trees. There is the very occasional clink of utensils – reticent, as if the woman frying vitumbua or tambi in some dark interior of a house is wary of shattering the peace – the yelp of the dog Bwana Tim, reputed to have been abandoned or lost by a European traveller, the angry protest or whine of a loose iron roof. Corbin would walk into his office next door and occupy himself for a while with the odd piece of correspondence or report, or even an unread newspaper. Then, with the sun a little higher up, he would go on a stroll through the town as it prepared to go about its business. "Jambo!" he would call out to someone.

"Jambo, bwana!" would come the reply. Sometimes he stopped at the little canteen for a cup of sweet black tea with ginger, which he liked but would not admit to Thomas, who looked after his cooking. The stall was owned by a man called Baruti, meaning "gunpowder," and the strong-flavoured tea was famed among travellers, who would gather there for refreshment and news.

He relished these early moments of the waking hours, without the bustle of activity, the irritating little petitions from the people that so often stumped government regulations and which would soon clutter up his day and take everything out of him.

3 July, 1913

. . . Indians came to petition for permanent status for the town. I told them the town plan would have to be approved by the Land Office, who were likely to recommend changes to the present plan. They were agreed in principle. Prepared memo. Man from Voi arriving 7th.

. . . Trying hard to get rupee balance right. . . . Thomas has dysentery. He has the annoying habit of singing "Once in Royal David's City" unceasingly.

There were no European settlers in the area, but the occasional travelling party, if it cared to stop, was welcomed, and indeed escorted into the village by the children and met with an askari. Once a family of Boers with two servants passed through on horseback and ox wagon, retuning from German East, disappointed at their reception there by people they had taken for their kin (they left some German newspapers, which the ADC read with much interest); and weeks later a similar Boer family stopped for refreshments on their way into the German colony. At another time two Irishmen came away from a foray across the border with two ox wagons full of sisal bulbils in sacks, stolen from the thriving German plantations.

Kikono was situated close to where the seasonal Kito stream dipped southwards before meandering back north and away. To the east, in an area heavily wooded with shrubs and thorns, was the station of the MCA on a ridge that marked the beginning of the Taita hills. Somewhere else, Corbin was aware, was a French mission. The town of Taveta, which had grown because the CMS (Church Missionary Society) had set up there after being told to leave Moshi by the Germans, lay to the west, and in the distance along the road could be seen Kilimanjaro, Queen Victoria's present to the German Kaiser. In the south was shrubbery and the Taru desert, and the Pare Mountains were dimly visible directly in the southwest. It was a beautiful country. There were forests, lakes, and craters, and hills overhung with blue mist. And there were plenty of animals.

Some ten miles away from Kikono, beyond a gauntlet of thorn and bush that had to be hacked through, on a crag a thousand feet high, stood the MCA station overlooking a vast territory. Its buildings of wood and iron stood out strikingly in the distance as one approached from the town. At its lonely, high perch it seemed to have the appearance of having fought off the bush forest and kept it at bay. The only way in, as you approached from Kikono, was to round the hill and come from behind.

On Sundays a handbell announced service in the mission; its peal ringing merrily through the countryside greeted Corbin as he climbed up the low rise on the beaten path. He was in the company of a curious, wonderstruck crowd of people, the more ragged of whom he had picked up on the way, the better dressed having descended the hill to escort him in. Behind him, as always, followed Thomas. This was their first visit to the MCA station.

SEND US, O ENGLAND, YOUR MEN said a wooden plaque

37

hanging from the gate and decorated with a painted floral border. England had sent two women instead.

Miss Elliott and Mrs. Bailey, who had been waiting for him, welcomed Corbin anxiously and served him a drink of water. The place was truly an oasis, he observed. The compound was swept and tidy, and large trees provided shade. There were several modest buildings to one side, but the main building, where the two ladies had rooms, stood prominently apart. Immediately after he had drunk the water he was taken to where the service was to be held, under one of the trees.

A hundred or so converts, many in European-style attire, sat attentively on the ground. An equal number, perhaps more, of curious onlookers stood some distance away in the sun. Deacon Kizito conducted, leading with a sermon in English: "So he bringeth them into their desired heaven." He then spoke in Swahili with a peppering of Taita words. A boy in shorts and tucked-in shirt gave a five-minute discourse in Taita. A group of children sang, first in English and later in the local dialect. Finally Miss Elliott got up and announced the day's schedule of activities.

After the service Corbin was shown around the station – the hospital, the school and workshop, the staff hostel, the chapel. There were fruit and vegetable gardens. The Sunday school had thirty students, whom he left in the hands of Miss Elliott, as she recited Longfellow, to take a tour of the surrounding area with the deacon.

Corbin returned for lunch and tea with the missionary women. Thomas had been found useful in the kitchen and had even helped in the teaching that day. The deacon disappeared for some work.

Over tea they sat in the Mission house, on the verandah. Immediately below them was a drop of rock, bush, and trees. The countryside presented to their view was dull, languorous, and hazy in the afternoon heat. There were large stretches of thorny bush; mountains covered the horizon towards the west; a forest in the east looked black and impenetrable. Somewhere in the distance there was a play of lightning, a few quick strikes, and then came the muffled roll of thunder. For some moments they were preoccupied by the sight of a dusty trail – Masai youths herding cattle.

At length Miss Elliott stirred. "If there ever was an Eden . . ." she said.

"What do you mean?" demanded her older companion severely.

"Surely Adam must have walked here in these very plains and hills, in this region of the earth . . ."

"Before he was expelled to Europe?"

They had a curious relationship – the plain Miss Elliott, frail in mind and body, it seemed, though obviously not in faith, and the stern, protective Mrs. Bailey, who might have bounced bar brawlers in another life. She had served with her husband in West Africa, then, after his death there, she joined the floundering Mission of Christ in India, where she met Miss Elliott. The two decided Christianity could be served better in Africa.

They discussed the fact that the Mission had no following in Kikono. The women felt bitter about it, this town impregnable to their attentions, which nevertheless their Mission had had an unwitting hand in founding.

"The Indians are half-savages," Mrs. Bailey observed, beginning an explanation she had obviously thought out conclusively and in detail.

"And therefore worse," said her companion. "You can do nothing with them."

"Gone too far the other way, she means. At least the African you can mould. But the Indian and the Mussulman are incorrigible in their worst habits and superstitions. They will always remain so."

39

"As Bishop Taylor said, 'The African yearns for our top hat and elastic-side boots, but the Indian will never let go his dhoti and will forever remain half-naked.'"

At this juncture his own Indian cook with the very Christian name Thomas arrived, in his parson's black, and Corbin got up to go.

14 August, 1913

Fortnum & Mason hamper arrived, all intact. (Thank you, Mother.) . . . socks and darning needles – where *do* mine disappear? – cards from: Ken, Robbie . . .

Ken: Do I want a post in Nyasaland? No – but, Oh for a day by the sea with a g&t! (Mombasa Club.)

I suppose it's all right for Thomas to take Sundays off for services at MCA.

∽⌒

Governor's Memoranda for PCs and DCs (1910)
(Promotion of Officers, page 20)

Junior Officers are required to pass an examination in Swahili and law, and only those that have passed will be eligible for promotion. But whilst proficiency in native languages, a sound knowledge of law and of the local ordinances and regulations, and skill in topography, will form important qualifications for promotion, the main tests will be the success of officers in their dealings with the general public.

3

"It has been a festival," wrote Alfred Corbin when it was over, "at the end of which a young man with the preposterous name of Pipa (meaning barrel) is in the lockup for creating a disturbance – and could very well be charged with spying, if I had a mind to do it. The Indians are sulking at this outcome – and my cook, for entirely different reasons, seems determined to poison me."

It had begun innocently enough.

"The King's representative is invited to our festival," the mukhi Jamali said. He had come with the invitation the week before, wearing a new blue-and-white embroidered cap, the kofia, perhaps in anticipation of the event. "Everywhere, they are invited and come," the mukhi added.

"Why, mukhi, I would be offended if you did not invite me," Corbin told him. "I would be delighted to attend."

And so he had gone.

Eight men dancing round a tent pole, each with an eighteen-inch stick in his right hand, the left holding onto a long red or green ribbon which descended from the top of the pole. To the steady, seductive beat from the tabla and dhol, the intermittent screechy wail of the harmonium, and a rich Kathiawadi voice from the old country revelling in the happy occasion, the eight men weaved in and out past each other around the pole, over and over, in a movement as regular and intricate as the mechanism of a timepiece. And as they went swinging past each other they brought the middle of their sticks together in a sprightly click. The men wore loose white pyjamas and long shirts, coloured sashes round their waists, bands round their heads. Their shirttails went flying as they danced.

As the men danced past each other in ever smaller circles, their red and green ribbons wove a checkered sheath around the pole, until finally the eight limbs of the dance, the loose ends of the ribbons, were so shortened the men stood shoulder to shoulder, beating time with the sticks. Then the process reversed as the men spiralled outwards and the ribbons unwound.

At the back of the festival tent, called the mandap, Alfred Corbin stood beside the mukhi, in casual shirt and trousers and somewhat dazzled by the celebrations. The air was laden, a heady mix of strong perfumes and sweat, incense and condensed milk, and dust stamped through the mats after a long day. Boys raced about, babies wailed, old folk sat quietly in their corners, sherbet servers beseeched people to drink. And in all this chaos, the uninterrupted drumbeat in the background, the sharp, regular clicking of the dancers' sticks, which made him flinch, the dancers' dizzying motion, the weaving and unweaving of the checkered sheaths.

As he stood watching, a garba dance got under way with much excitement: a whirling circle of joyous, brightly clad women, nose studs glinting, bangles jingling. The garba enacted the first conversions of the community from Hinduism, several centuries ago in Gujarat, he was told. Corbin saw in it a flower opening and closing. The women, bending forward, clapping hands, approached the centre, then with a snap of fingers stepped back into the spinning circle. Corbin wondered if it was appropriate to stare and turned away his gaze.

A chair was produced for him and wearily he sat down and accepted a drink of sherbet. The men's dance had wound down, and the din had reduced somewhat, though there were shouts of approval as the garba grew faster, the women now performing with brass pots which they would release and catch again with their hands, clanking their rings upon them to the beat. Momentarily Corbin let his eyes close, held the cold sherbet glass to his forehead, felt the pleasant restful sensation.

When he opened his eyes again it was as if he had been transported, was in the midst of a vision. A striking young woman in white frock with a red pachedi around her shoulders was approaching, then receding, doing a rapid brass-pot dance with lithe movements of waist and hip and unconscious of the eyes upon her – envious, wondrous, angry – her own eyes large, black, and deep, on her lips an indifferent even arrogant smile. Her features were markedly distinct from the other women's, so that she seemed an outsider of some sort: tall and thin, fair, with long face, pronounced nose, full lips. The circle of women had broken, a few of the younger ones were dancing solo, and in between them danced this siren. The tabalchi-drummer beat faster and the agile dancers kept time, feet thumping, hips gyrating without inhibition, breath drawn sharply, faces glistening with sweat.

Embarrassed at what looked like exhibitionism for the sake of the white man, the mukhi turned towards Corbin, and the Englishman took his cue. Thanking the leaders, wishing them a good evening, he walked out of the tent and started up the path to his house, in the company of an askari, just as a group of boys came running into the tent breathing out kerosene-smelling flames from their mouths.

43

This was the first of three long nights of celebrations, which lasted till dawn, followed by a few hours of slumbrous stillness before the next day's festivities began anew. Many visitors were in town. There were processions with banners and ceremonial costumes. The police did a daily march-past, and there was neverending food for all and sundry. It was an occasion for kofias and kanzus, turbans, frocks, and pachedis. The ADC felt good that all this happened in his domain; under, so to speak, his benefaction.

21 October, 1913

... This I suppose is administration at its most rewarding, a vote of confidence and honour for the Government's representative.

❧

Each afternoon of the festival there arrived for this lord an offering of the day's food in a covered brass tray. The first offering produced an open altercation with his cook and personal servant.

"Heathen food, your eminence," said Thomas, shaking his head dismissively.

"Let's uncover it and see, shall we?" said Corbin indulgently.

The aromas were strong, and his askaris hovered nearby in case the mzungu rejected the offering. But the mzungu was not going to let it go without a try.

"All the same, sir, I will bring English food. Christian. I give this witchcraft to the police."

"Uncover it, man!"

And so, for three nights Corbin went to bed satiated on unfamiliar cooking he quite took to in the circumstances, relieved of the dreadful "English" cuisine usually provided by his cook. Long into the night came the beat of the dhol and drums, the screeching of a harmonium, bringing visions of whirling circles, the girl in white.

How would he replace Thomas? The man had become insufferable; from the deferential and unassuming small man Corbin had met in Mombasa, he had turned into an overprotective and domineering mother hen. His disapprovals were many and openly stated, especially concerning Corbin's relations with the "heathen" townsfolk.

Every Sunday, stuffed into a black suit and wearing a black hat on top of his glistening hair, Thomas made his way with much ceremony to attend service at the Mission station, where he had been welcomed, his Indianness notwithstanding. Corbin himself only paid short formal visits, but on several occasions Thomas brought for his ungrateful master scones that he had evidently pocketed.

23 October

I feel sorry for poor Thomas . . . but to forgo saffroned lamb "biryani" for a curried shepherd's pie and a kedgeree he calls trifle. . . . He has sulked mightily, exaggerating his attentions to increase my guilt all the more. Once he read in my presence a letter from home, whose details he refused to divulge, becoming resentful and aggressive at my questions, and I wondered if the missive was genuine at all. I recall how he insinuated himself into my patronage the first time we met. I did not question who he was, not very deeply that is, assuming Mombasa, like all large ports, to have all sorts of characters washing upon its shores whose backgrounds are not worth the trouble of inquiry. He has even punished me, I fear, with curried concoctions that have done my stomach no good at all.

27 October

We have made up, and I have dutifully swallowed Thomas's shepherd's pie, nothing less. And I have learned something about his life. He was born Hari, and was brought up, he told me, in a mission centre outside Bombay, and recalled two ladies not unlike the

45

two stalwarts of the MCA, one of whom he spoke of rather fondly. He has left a wife and child there. He joined me in Mombasa, he says, at an impulse, when he thought he had been recognized by a priest who had known him in India. How much of the story is true I dare not conjecture. East is East . . .

Yesterday, an astounding event from which only now I sit down to recover.

The "happiness" had been over for two days, the last of the visitors were leaving. The local Indians dutifully went about their business. It was approaching noon, and I began drafting a reply to a query regarding our police contingent. (It seems Government House wants assurance of the preparedness of administrative centres for emergencies such as sudden attacks by the natives.) Suddenly there came shouts, sounds of scuffling and violent quarrelling outside. At first I only momentarily looked up. The askaris know their job (as I was in the process of saying in my memo). But something, the significance of which I was about to discover, made me get up and step out onto the verandah. What I saw was a brawl in progress outside the post office, involving none other than my servant, Thomas, an utterance from whom must have drawn me out. The sounds of the scuffle, with promise of general excitement and diversion, had travelled sufficiently far by now – the first spectators were already racing up the hill. I might have been amused, telling the askaris to get on with it, but this time I was irritated and walked down to the scene, barely beating the crowd to it.

Of the five men involved in the brawl, two were askaris barely holding on to a burly young Indian man, who stopped struggling at the sight of me. As if on cue, Thomas turned and saw me approach, which having done, he quite unnecessarily took hold of one of the Indian's ears and said rather ridiculously, "German spy, eminence."

"Enough," I said, and curtly asked the postmaster, who made

up the fifth, why he wasn't at his job, and what this childish matata was about.

"Wasn't I on duty when this pig teased me?" he said.

"Mfalme!" roared the Indian at this provocation. "My lord, it was they who insulted me." He would have charged at someone had he not been under restraint by the askaris.

There followed an exchange, the foulness of which did not endear this Indian to my heart at all. He is called Pipa, I learned, and is a most surly sort. He has short-cropped hair on a large round head that gives him the appearance somewhat of a dolt. His clothes – shirt, trousers, and shoes – are quite respectable, so he appears to be a man of some means.

Pipa, it seemed, had come from German East for the celebrations. The morning after they ended he took to the post office a sack of mail, which he had brought with him from across the border. The postmaster showed annoyance, naturally, at this unusual quantity of mail. Thomas, hovering nearby, started scolding and abusing Pipa, who gave him a box on the ears.

I gave orders for Pipa to be put away in the lockup for the day, asked Thomas to go about his duties, and accompanied by two askaris proceeded to examine the mail in the office.

Letters by Indians of German East to kinsfolk in Bombay and Porbandar and assorted villages in India – "Desh," as they call the home country – were understandable; as were letters to relations in Voi and Mombasa and Nairobi. They are, after all, subjects of the King, and their reliance on the British government for this most important service was touching. But most irregular were 3 letters from the Oberleutnant of Moshi Fort to Germans on our side. I opened all the letters. Most of them were in Gujarati or Swahili; a handful were in English and there was one in Greek. I allowed them to go with the regular mail. They were, of course, correctly stamped. I will send the German letters, appended with my translations, to Voi, though they seem harmless. One was for hand delivery to a Herr Lenz in Mbuyuni, through which Pipa would pass on his way to Voi. He has to be watched, but I cannot hold him.

28 October, 7 A.M.

About the Pipa affair –
Last night the Shamsis had mosque (as usual). Considerably less singing, much discussion, the purport of which I had no doubt. I was resolved to be firm – the young man had to be taught a lesson. He had after all assaulted my servant – for whom . . . I have no great love but who after all is of my household. Later I heard a commotion outside, approaching up the hill, then coming to a halt not far off. The booted steps of the watchman outside on the verandah were reassuring. Suddenly the door was flung open. A young woman, head covered, walked in and fell at my feet. Behind her stood the helpless askari.

(Later)

"Mheshimiwa," she said, "Great Sir," and looked at me with pleading eyes. (I was on my feet in surprise.)

She was the girl I had seen dancing at the celebrations. Even in everyday, simple attire she was striking in her looks. Her head-cover had fallen back and there was a wild look about her. She was speaking in Swahili and I could not wholly understand her, but I surmised that she was the betrothed of the lout Pipa whom I had locked up. She was at my feet yet had had the nerve to burst in past my askari, for which she had not even apologized. I was not seeking her apology, though, and reassured her about her young man. She smiled a little, in thanks, and left. As I watched her from a window I observed a man come out from the shadows and follow her.

I stood reflecting on the inscrutability of the alien – how there must be matters of which one will never have an inkling – when there was a gentle knock on the door. Now the whole community picks up courage, I thought. I called out, and the mukhi walked in, fez in hand. I took a chair, and offered him one. "Bwana Corbin," he said.

He is a man of the world, his position involves travel. In spite of his humble and respectful approaches, he no doubt knows the place of an Assistant District Commissioner in the government's hierarchy. Powerless though the individual Indian is beside a European, as a community they have a voice that is heard. In Nairobi, as the *Herald* regularly reports, they are making a lot of noise; more than three-quarters of the country's business passes through their hands, in towns just as small as this one. And no less a personage than Mr. Churchill has supported their cause publicly. I reassured him, as I had the girl. The sergeant had been instructed to release the prisoner at ten o'clock. He thanked me. I offered him tea. My guardian angel Thomas showed displeasure, but hastened to the kitchen. The mukhi, having gone outside to pacify his community members, returned. Over tea I asked him in a friendly way if his community held themselves above government punishment even if they violated the law.

"Ah, Mr. Corbin. . . . But this was a small thing . . ."

"But your man could be charged with spying," I said.

At this he was genuinely agitated. "Mr. Corbin! He was given those letters. What could he have done? We are a subject people . . ."

I laughed, and he joined me. I asked him what his people sought in this country, in the wilderness, so far from their own country and culture. "Peace and prosperity," he said. I repeated his words. "Yes, sir," he asserted, "with your protection. We seek but little. Already we have contributed to the Uganda Railway."

He did not remind me that he had an African wife, and children from her, of his commitment to Africa, or of the troubles in

India from which his community was running. His discretion and reserve impressed me. In him his people have a good leader, I told him. The British government was pleased with his community, I said.

I asked him about the girl. Her name was Mariamu, he said. She lived with her mother and stepfather. She was his niece, moreover; her mother was his own sister Kulsa.

"Who is the stepfather?" I asked.

"Simba," he answered.

The word means "lion" and was obviously a nickname. I asked him who this "lion" was and he laughed. "Rashid the transporter," he said.

Apparently this man Rashid was a former railway coolie (therefore strictly speaking not one of the Shamsis) who like many others deserted his job when the man-eating lions at Tsavo seemed invincible, picking off the labourers at will. To the terrified Indians, their tormentors were not real lions at all but the spirits of those who had perished in the desert. How to explain, the mukhi said, when one minute a man is sitting next to you by a fire, inside a four-foot-high protective stockade, and the next minute you see his place empty and hear his screams in the distance? Or when a companion is snatched from the top of a tree where he's taken his bed, and lions are not supposed to climb?

"According to the coolies," the mukhi said, "the spirits of the desert were offended by the railway of the mzungu, and came to attack them as lions."

"Then this Rashid must be called Simba in jest," I offered.

The mukhi smiled assent. "Now he handles mules. That's what he knows. But he's a good provider . . . and a very protective father. He's fond of the girl – perhaps too fond."

"Would he take to following the girl about?" I asked.

To which he responded, "Bwana Corbin is a keen observer."

"The girl is wild," the mukhi said. "She's inclined to go away by herself and the family is worried."

I wondered if it was she whom I had seen running in the distance the day I came here to take up my post. She had been coming from the direction of the river.

"And she is this young man Pipa's betrothed?" I asked.

"Yes, sir. He came to set the wedding date. He, too, has problems, but inshallah, God willing, they can give happiness to each other."

"And when is the wedding to take place?"

"In a few months, Bwana Corbin."

Pipa, meanwhile, will return to Moshi, where he has his shop and his mother.

The Indians were grateful for the lenient treatment of the young man, and they showed their gratitude in abundance. Crates of tinned milk, a bottle of whisky, socks, underwear, soap, landed in Corbin's home. One result of the whole incident was his discovery of Thomas's practice of extorting favours from the businessmen using threats of influencing the ADC against them. After receiving a severe dressing down, Thomas fled.

It was some days later that Corbin found out that his servant had gone and joined the Mission station. Word got around that Bwana Corbin was looking for a new cook, and one day a plate of fresh chapatti arrived at his doorstep, which he ate with much relish. The askari told him it had been left by the girl Mariamu. The offering was repeated every Thursday, the eve of Juma, an auspicious day when orphans and beggars were fed.

4

The nights were cold and dry, the blackness so absolute, so palpa-
bly dense he felt that if he reached out a hand from where he
slept he could pull it aside and let in the lighted world of London,
Paris, and Hamburg. The mbuyu tree rustled outside, in the
distance was the cackle of hyenas, the grunt of a leopard or hog,
the constant *crick-crick* of insects. Sometimes there would be the
maddening, eerie pelting of rain on the roof, a sound which
should have been welcome in this semi-desert. He had heard of
spirits resident in mbuyu trees and naturally had ridiculed the
idea, but in this menace-filled darkness, in this loneliness, all one's
scientific objectivism seemed vulnerable. He knew it to be four
o'clock when the rich and rising cry of the brave muezzin rallied
against the thick darkness. Such a desolate cry of the human soul
in the vast universe. Was there an answer, a response? And then
the Shamsis preparing for their mosque. They were a hardy lot,
who could match the early Christians in their zealousness. First
the mosque caretaker got up and went around the village knocking on doors. Gradually those who felt inclined would make their

way to the mosque. Then for a space of half an hour there would be silence – while they meditated, so he was told.

He had read accounts of the explorers, the great travellers, read reports of their lectures, including one at the Geographical Society of Hamburg given by Krapf. As a boy in England he might have heard Stanley. Didn't they ever spend sleepless nights, these men, or waver from their purpose? Maynard, the seemingly indomitable Maynard, who had stalked the length and breadth of the country subduing intransigent natives, had confessed to him to bouts of sleeplessness, depression, doubt, taking to his diary to kill time and tire the brain, taking a local woman to kill loneliness. And also he had admitted to that snapping of nerves, an outbreak of savagery.

That irregular journal for the junior official, *The View from Down Here*, had recently carried an article on the dreaded "disease" that often struck the lonely administrator in Africa, and dubbed the *Furore africanus*. "The thing to watch out for," said the writer, "is a welling up of uncontrollable anger. Before the storm breaks out in a bayonet charge against a tax-evader or witch-doctor, it is a good idea to go out on safari." An official in German East Africa, he read further, had hanged eight mothers in a row for infanticide. This was in the Pare region, not even a hundred miles away.

Outside there would momentarily be the murmer of human voices as the Shamsis came out of the mosque and went home. Looking towards the shuttered window he could see the first rays of the morning light streaking in through the cracks. There would follow a few minutes of absolute stillness, and then the familiar flapping sound of birds on the move signalled that the day was at hand, and he would get up.

After such nights of desolation he longed for European society; a round of bridge, which normally he did not play or like very much, a game of chess. Several attempts at chess with his now-absent Thomas had proved disastrous. They could not agree on rules, had quarrelled like schoolboys. They had played draughts sometimes, and even card games for two hands. Once, the Indian community had invited him to play carom, and six-handed whist, amidst tea and snacking and much giggling and staring on the part of the children and women. He realized they had made much accommodation for him, and the experiment was stopped – both to his relief and disappointment.

He pored avidly over the Nairobi papers when they came, the *Herald* and the gossipy *Globetrotter.* The arrivals, the departures, the controversies were many. The outbreak of bubonic plague in the Indian quarter and the resulting outpouring of vituperation against the "unhygienic brown man," the shooting or lashing of an African, the arrival of royalty or a flamboyant Chicago hunting expedition with balloons, a new chief at the Norfolk, the new Governor, the newspapers were a wonderfully exuberant source of news.

25 December, 1913 (Christmas Day)
. . . pantry bare, but there were spare tins of biscuits and corned beef under the bed. I had rather expected an invitation from the Mission, though I suppose with Thomas there it would have made for an awkward situation . . .

The town was quite noisy for a holiday, and when I stepped outside to look I saw that preparations were afoot for what turned out to be a garden party. This "happiness" was for my benefit and quite pleasant, but the speeches were long.

Perhaps Mrs. Bailey and Miss Elliott had thought he would be spending Christmas Day in Taveta.

He had familiarized himself with the towns in the area,

including Mbuyuni, where he finally met the German resident Lenz, who had been sent the letter (intercepted and read by Corbin) from the German commandant of Moshi Fort. A few times Corbin had been required in Taveta, the pleasant oasis town at the German East African border, with a resident ADC and the large Church Missionary Society station whose incumbents – Miss Campbell and Miss Knight – were more amiable than those of the local Mission.

He hunted on occasion, having first begun when a leopard attacked a woman behind her hut in a nearby village. The animal was not found, having perhaps met its fate elsewhere. But on his tours upcountry he shot for meat. Only once, when he sighted a beautiful stray zebra, did he shoot, wantonly, for trophy. The animal seemed to have sensed its fate, standing perfectly still and hopeless, only its ears twitching slightly. His companions on such trips were the village dog Bwana Tim, some askaris, and a gold-bearded albino with the rather strange nickname of Fumfratti, who appeared always in the same black trousers and waistcoat, red shirt, yellow bandanna, and a wide-brimmed hat, as if to mimic an American hunter.

Taveta: 13 February, 1914

A trying journey, from which I recover at this CMS Mission in Taveta in the hands of two solicitous missionaries . . .

On our way down from Kikono, with much relief we arrived at a stream. It was overhung with great trees where we stopped, and the ground was cool. The water level was low, and the flow down to a trickle, coming from the general direction of Kilimanjaro. That eminence had by now both peaks behind cloud covers. Behind us was the local village, whose children had come out to watch us and receive their presents (sweets from the mukhi's store). But we were not to have peace in this arbour, it was already

occupied by baboons. At first they remained content with shriek-
ing and shaking of branches farther upstream. Soon, however,
they became bolder. One peeped out from the foliage fairly close
to us, then another crossed the stream in three or four rapid
bounds. At this point Fumfratti, caressing a smooth grey stone in
the palm of his hand, told me very casually that we should put a
collar on Bwana Tim. Surely the dog wouldn't stray so far, I said.
Whereupon he stood and began walking up the stream, stepping
lightly on stones to do so, and then for a moment disappeared
from sight. There came then, from where he presumably was, a
mighty commotion from the monkeys, after which the albino
reappeared, holding something white in his hand. He came and
placed it in my hands. Imagine my shock when I saw what it was –
a skull! I almost dropped it from my hands.

"The nyanyi play with it. It is a nyanyi, a baboon, skull."

The flat, declarative remark is often the prelude to a story. I
waited for it.

14 February

A few years ago, Fumfratti said, a mzungu and his party – which
included himself, he paused to add – had walked by this spot with
a dog. A small dog, kadogo (he gestured, making a dog shape
with his arm and the flat of his palm), brown, with a lot of fur on
his back, ears like fans (another gesture). This mzungu was also
on his way to Taveta. While he was preoccupied with arrange-
ments, his little dog strayed. (Here Fumfratti paused to look at me
as if to prepare me.)

A pack of yelling baboons jumped upon the dog from the trees
and quickly tore him limb from limb. When the mzungu's party,
having heard the commotion, reached the site of the slaughter
they saw what must surely have been a most grisly sight – baboons
at play with pieces of the body. One monkey bounded away with
a limb, another had his mouth covered with entrails. I told him to
stop. The mzungu went mad with fury, continued Fumfratti. He

was foaming. The man responsible for the dog's care was lashed to within an inch of his life. The party decided to abandon the site, but they left some meat lying around where they had rested. After they had gone some distance, the mzungu turned and crept back up the path they had walked. He entered the bush, walked on farther, approaching the baboons from behind. Cunningly, and with caution, like a lion. The baboons were at the leftover meat, fighting over the pieces, rowdy as only monkeys can be. The mzungu went and waited behind a large bush, observing. "Kwa taratibu yule mzungu akalenga," said my man, conscious of his audience. Carefully the white man took aim, and with his rifle shot as many of the stupid baboons as he could. About ten in all.

"Truly, that was a mzungu," said Fumfratti.

I wondered what to make of this veiled judgement of me. "Describe him to me," I said.

"Menandi," he said. "That was his name. Big, head like a rock, two teeth like this . . ." he gestured with two fingers.

And yes, the CMS ladies tell me Maynard was here, on his way to Moshi (ever the soldier) to see what the Germans in their colony were up to.

But this was not all. The stream had more for us than a reminder of that grisly episode. As we prepared to leave, some villagers approached: a young man in the company of older men. They had so far kept their distance, fearing, I suppose, that I was after taxes. After humming and hawing, in broken Swahili and a mixture of local languages, they made their plea. They wanted the bwana – me – to kill a python who had moved into the vicinity. But surely they could kill snakes, I put it to them. But the mzungu had a bunduki (a gun). And all the wild animals fear the mzungu.

So off we went in search of the snake. It was a strange, bewildering procession through the bush. My companions chanted all the while: "Dudu . . . dudu . . . dudu-dudu . . ." Why, I asked

Fumfratti, why dudu – insect? "They want to fool the snake, make him think the mzungu is after a dudu."

Why the snake should understand Swahili, and why a white man should go after an insect armed with his rifle I did not bother to inquire. Finally we stopped. We were at a boundary of sorts. The growth became dense ahead of us, and small trees littered the area. "What?" I said. A villager pointed at the ground beneath a tree, and I saw the snake slithering away into the bush rather unhurriedly. It was a pretty large one – about nine inches in diameter. The villagers, by creating a racket, forced it to turn back, whereupon Fumfratti said, "Shoot," and I shot it twice.

Any resistance it had left was bludgeoned out of it with clubs and sticks, and it was finally dragged out in front of us, belly swollen with its latest prey. Very skilfully it was cut open, lengthwise, so it could be skinned later, and out of the slimy inside that still twitched, they brought out something so revolting I shudder even now. It was a human baby.

We stopped at two other villages, at the second of which there was a long case involving a father and his sons . . .

Fumfratti has proved invaluable on this journey. He has travelled widely as a scout, and is a mine of information. My askaris and porters defer to his age and experience, and his wit. Several of them can carry a tune, lead the company in song through forest and grass, but Fumfratti is the storyteller. In the evenings, by the fire, his long stories continue from the previous night and (I believe) change plots and characters. During marches he keeps the men's minds off their loads, their pangs of hunger, and the intense heat with a marvellous supply of riddles. Not surprisingly he was greeted like an old friend when we arrived in Taveta. We had been on the road three nights and a little over two days.

In Taveta Corbin was shown the graveyard, which lay in arcadian peace and shade behind a mango grove. There he saw two European graves built up as shrines. He was taken to the site where the explorer Thomson had struck camp thirty years before. Kilimanjaro loomed even closer here, and he learned that an underground stream from the mountain practically surrounded the town. From the top of the hill where the Mission offices were, he could see the green belt of dense vegetation that followed the water line. The water surfaced first at a crater lake, called Chala, in the hills to the west. It then came up in a spring, and later at Lake Jipe, before flowing towards the Pare mountain range back in German territory. He was told the area had been explored by Maynard two years before.

In Taveta the government station was now vacant, though a new ADC was on his way. Corbin stayed four days, to hear petitions and dispense salaries, and he ordered a clean-up of the town on the last day.

On their way back they made a detour to see the hallowed site of local legend, the peaceful Lake Chala, which lay secluded among the hills and mountains. They were taken to it by two Masai youths they met in the vicinity, who without a word but understanding their purpose led them through coarse bush up a steep path on a hill. They arrived at the summit abruptly, and found themselves looking down upon a breathtaking sight: a blue lake, crystal-clear below them, wavelets stirring across it, and presiding in the distance the mighty snow-topped mountain that fed it. The Masai each carried a long staff. They grinned proudly at Corbin, then proceeded to climb down, leaping from clump to clump of shrub and sliding towards the water. Their young voices cut sharply through the pristine air. Corbin, a little nervous, felt compelled, followed, then hesitated halfway. The youths stopped to wait for him, then one of them threw the mzungu his staff, and doggedly Corbin descended after them.

For a long moment he crouched on his haunches at the lake's side, under a clear sky, watching the clean, irregular edge of the water with the land rising steeply all around it, breathing the cool air, feeling it play on his skin, oblivious to anything else. It was a place so unique in its beauty, so much at peace with itself, so unviolated, he felt he had come to the site of Creation itself.

5

There couldn't have been a greater contrast between that nature's secret, the Edenic Chala, and the pioneering hustle and bustle of man-made Nairobi, where Corbin found himself unexpectedly but not unwillingly a few weeks later. In his isolation he had often longed for even a brief foray into the European life of Nairobi. His application to sit for the language examination in the capital, and to show his face at the Secretariat, was considered an indulgence, but was approved, by his DC, Hobson of Voi.

It was the morning of the day before Nairobi's Race Week when he arrived.

"You realize, of course," Mrs. Unsworth said to Corbin with a glint in her eye, "that the Norfolk, Torr's, the Embassy, all the clubs – everything in Nairobi – is absolutely booked. You can put up in our guest house, if you don't mind."

"Oh, but he must!" said her niece Anne.

"That's very kind of you," he said.

The girl was radiant with life.

Edwina Unsworth and her niece had come to collect him at the railway station. There was something charmingly childlike about the way Anne was dressed, and yet decidedly odd – the safari skirt with pockets and leather belt with gun holster, the collar and tie, the wide-brimmed hat.

"I told you he'd recognize it," said Mrs. Unsworth pointedly to her niece.

As he did, of course, from the outfit of Princess Amelia in the recent newspaper photographs of a royal hunting expedition. Like the princess, Anne was small in build, and she had golden curls under her hat.

"It suits you better," he said graciously, and everybody was pleased.

Mrs. Unsworth was a bigger, middle-aged, woman. She wore a simple dress and on her head a double terai lined with the customary red as protection from the sun. "Jack couldn't come away," she explained as they got into the buggy. "He'll meet us later." A larger party near them was having their luggage loaded into a wagon drawn by two mules in the charge of a huge man in riding boots swinging a long whip. "That's Omar Khan," said Anne. "He's from South Africa and absolutely indispensable in this town."

Corbin had corresponded with the Unsworths unevenly since meeting them in Mombasa when he first arrived, and while planning this visit he had asked if they could arrange to have him met, this being his only imposition on them. For the two ladies to come to meet him, instead of sending a junior official or a store clerk, was a kindness greater than he expected.

This was the capital of the land, where the rulers lived, he told himself. From here the Governor and the Secretariat sent directives to the Provincial Commissioner in Mombasa, who directed Corbin's own master, the DC in Voi. This was the "up there," or "God's-eye view," in contrast to the "down here" or "worm's-eye view" of the lowly ADCs. There were hand-drawn hamali carts on the road, bullock carts with turbaned drivers coaxing their charges in Indian vernacular, rickshaws with tinkling bells, their African drivers calling out for passengers or right of way. There were a few motorcars.

Edwina's husband, Jack Unsworth, was a civil engineer who had stayed on, after completion of the railway, and was now part-owner of Unsworth and Mason, importers of machinery parts. Anne was the youngest daughter of one Edwina's sisters. She had come on holiday and decided to stay.

The Unsworths lived in a bungalow on a two-acre plot. Like so many of the newer buildings, it had the cold grey look of the stone now being quarried in the area. Solid and squat, respectable yet dreary-looking, especially on the cold misty mornings of Nairobi. There were stone steps descending to the driveway under the shade of a large tree, where the Ford was parked; an askari in khaki uniform and a red fez but no shoes kept watch from the top of the steps.

After a game of tennis, a sundowner, a rubber or two of bridge, the servants pampering you with morning tea, the smell of frying eggs and bacon, the clink of china and crystal, a late round of brandy or port, the soft bed immaculately prepared by the trained servants . . . after all this the African night seemed as tame as it could be made. And you could eliminate it with the flick of a switch. Yet, he thought, there seemed a fraudulence in this little England in Africa – fraudulence in the sense of a conjuring trick – and fragility. He was told, however, that with persistence it could all be made real, like America. If only there could be self-government. Ten years ago this was all bush, dry grass. The Masai and Kikuyu walked around half-naked then. Now they would take loose hand-me-down tweeds if they could.

Nairobi, even white Nairobi, was not a homogeneous society. Some wit, commenting on the scandals for which it became known, called it a "square" society. At one corner stood Mrs. Hollis, brothel-keeper and fortune-teller, who could also be hired to preside over seances. Her Syrian girls had been put on the train, and Nairobi was bracing itself for the Japanese girls due to arrive before Race Week. At another corner were her customers, the low-level railway officials, salesmen, drifters, out-of-work hunters and scouts. On the third point of the social square were the few aristocrats and their fawning toadies, playing public-school pranks at the Norfolk. Then there were the high officials like Ainsworth and Whitehouse, responsible for much of the development of Nairobi, and respectable businessmen like Unsworth.

With Anne, who wrote the occasional witty column on colonial life called "Our Way" for the *Herald*, Corbin visited some court hearings.

4 April, 1914

... A lord of the realm who shot a servant for serving bad cream with dumplings. A Jesuit priest who confiscated the possessions of his converts in the name of the church and was contesting them in earnest. A farmer who had a servant flogged fifty times, until senseless, for eating the kitchen rice and denying it afterwards; another who shackled his workers by their pierced earlobes, causing infection and death in one. . . . Two brothers, Londoners, who desperately sought for the graves of their parents while the land went unused. And so on. The case of Captain Maynard is still remembered with some bitterness here . . .

. . . Went with Anne to the new bioscope – a place called Garvie's. The film caught fire, and amidst catcalls and bottle-throwing we departed in haste . . .

A number of young men in town had their eyes on Anne. He met them at dinner or dances at the new Nairobi Club, all apparently willing to wait on her hand and foot. It was a wonder, as Edwina remarked pointedly to Corbin, that she was not yet engaged. No girl coming in from England survived Mombasa, they all arrived at the capital well after their honeymoons. Only Anne was holding out, but, she gave her guest a smile, not for much longer.

"Would she mind," he asked Mrs. Unsworth, "a life far away from the city, almost in the middle of nowhere?"

"Anne," she told him, taking the cue with a grateful look, "is an unusual girl. She is an adventuress. That's why she is here. If you ask me, she's bored with society."

He found Anne intelligent and attractive – perhaps even a little glamorous. Her spontaneous nature complemented nicely his reserve, and it was obvious she preferred his company. But a matrimonial step would have to be thought out carefully. For one thing, his own DC's approval would be necessary.

During Race Week, Nairobi was covered in a perpetual cloud of dust kicked up by horses, buggies, and motorcars. Many visitors simply set up tents on open ground. At the Turf Club, which was decorated with flags and bunting, people of all tribes gathered to watch the horse races and polo matches. Elsewhere in town there was tennis and cricket, fishing and cockfighting, gambling and boxing. And throughout the week, everywhere it seemed, bands of the police and the King's African Rifle added a touch of smartness, not to say music, to the whole affair.

He had earlier on called at Government House and signed his name in the official book. He sat for the Swahili and Hindustani language exams, and his interview with the Acting Governor, in the middle of Race Week, went well. Before his departure he and Anne agreed to write to each other.

He took a crowded, festive train back, getting off at Voi, where he spent the rest of the night at the Dak bungalow, sharing rooms with a Swiss farmer and a young South African. The next day, with some askaris given to him by the DC, he marched to Kikono.

When he arrived he was greeted warmly, welcomed back, and it struck him this time, having just come from European society, how much this was home to the Indians and Swahilis, who had resigned themselves to it, a place that was for him only a temporary stop. He could not imagine the future they dreamed of for themselves and their children.

On his first day back he had his midday meal at the mukhi's, in the shed in the backyard, amidst much peeping from the women and children. But the children of the family he now knew by name, and when he called them they came to him.

The ADCs at Voi had promised to keep an eye open for a good servant. Meanwhile, there was still the plate of chapatti delivered at his doorstep every Thursday, the auspicious eve of Juma.

In a few days Nairobi seemed far away once more, belonging to a world as distant as London or Prague, the world of news reports and memories, from which, however, he soon received the first letters from both Anne and Edwina. How far his domain was from the city he had recently left became apparent in the most shocking manner by the events that followed.

6

8 May, 1914

This instant darkness descends from the heavens. The mbuyu stirs outside, Bwana Tim barks . . . in this dusk which the Shamsis call maghrab and imbue with mystic significance and dreadful possibilities. A time for prayer, or close to it: twilight, the sandhya. The lamp hanging from the beam above me stirs in the slight breeze I presume is there, disturbing shadows. It is eerie, but for the stern tones and vigorous sounds of the missionaries Miss Elliott and Mrs. Bailey in the kitchen.

Today I had a most distressing confrontation with the maalim – the teacher and exorcist – and because of it, I fear, with much of this town.

This is what happened.

It was close upon 10 o'clock in the morning when I went out for a stroll, as I do by custom, leaving roughly half the day's petitioners waiting. I would have a chat with the dispenser, Chagpar, against whose prescriptions a complaint had been lodged by

67

an angry father. Having warned the man against carelessness (he responded by saying the father did not know his derrière from his head), I proceeded back, intending to walk around the village. As I passed the Swahili mosque I heard a terrible scream from behind the adjoining house. I stopped in my tracks and, sure enough, there came a sharp, threatening voice, then again a child's scream (as I thought then) – this time muted – and then another voice, hoarse with protestations . . . all of which I put down here as best as I can:

"Unaenda?" (Are you going?)

A grunt, a swishing sound as from a whip, a scream, a hoarse cry thinning into a pitiful heart-rending wail.

"Je? Ume nyamaza . . . unaenda?" (You are silent . . . are you going?)

"Ndioooo!" (Yes!)

A swish, a wail.

"Mbona yupo!" (Why are you still here?)

A swish.

"Naenda! Naenda baba! Naenda!" (I'm going, I'm going!) the cry trailing off into a whimper.

I don't know how, but I had left the street and was in the backyard of a house. And it was amazing to see that the cries, the screams, the energetic and clear replies to the shouted questions were all coming from one source: the girl Mariamu. She was seated on a stool, clutching at her hair with both hands, looking at the ground in sheer exhaustion. Her feet were bare, the clothes on her back shredded. She was being beaten. The old maalim, the exorcist, in kanzu and cap, stood over her glowering, a whipping branch in one hand, a tin box in the other. It was his voice that I had heard from outside, putting the questions to the girl. A fog of incense smoke rose from a brazier on the ground in front of the girl and had filled the area. Looking on, stood Rashid, the girl's stepfather, the mukhi, her uncle, and the girl's mother (holding an open book, it seemed, for the maalim), all of whom had moved aside when I appeared.

What does our law prescribe for such a situation? Instinctively I cried "Wait!" and the maalim stopped the proceedings and prepared to leave. Firmly, but not without reservation, I took the switch and the tin from the old man. The tin contained red pepper, its contents flew towards my face – I swear not unassisted – and I choked and sneezed. "Don't play with what you don't understand," I heard the old man say.

In a rage, I had the girl removed to my spare room, once used by Thomas. Then I despatched an urgent message to the Mission, and both women later arrived and went straight to my charge. And there the matter stands.

What I witnessed was a crime under the law, and I could not let it pass. And yet I had come upon what was evidently an accepted ceremony, involving respectable members of this town. The maalim's disrespect and defiant attitude could be the beginning of a rebellion. My authority has suffered. And my reputation, certainly, at the Mission. I have to decide upon a suitable course of action.

A short while ago the girl became hysterical and I heard one of the ladies deliver what sounded like two sharp slaps, at which moment the girl gave a startled yelp, almost of surprise, and then became quiet.

To add to Corbin's sleeplessness that night, a drum started beating in the dark somewhere: a long, monotonous beating that left him nauseated and sweating, tossing and turning restlessly, waiting for sleep to come. Were they trying to frighten him, calling up spirits to harm him, playing on his jangled nerves? The two mission ladies slept in the spare room with the girl. He had no idea of when he fell asleep, it was after a strong whisky, but he woke up to find himself on the floor beside the bed and Miss Elliott in the room with breakfast. Outside, the sun shone brilliantly, everyday sounds came reassuringly from down the hill, and it seemed that the worst was over.

That morning, the ladies took the girl with them to the Mission, Miss Elliott leading her triumphantly by the hand.

A Shamsi girl in the hands of Christian missionaries was sure to bring the mukhi over, and Jamali came that evening to see Corbin.

"Bwana Corbin," began the mukhi.

"Yes, mukhi."

"Sir . . . our daughter . . . taken away by the missionary lady . . . most inappropriate." He was referring, of course, to the "daughter of the community," his niece.

"I did not see your daughter treated at all well, mukhi."

"Bwana Corbin. You don't understand . . . excuse, please. It was not she but a shetani, a spirit. The shetani had to be driven away . . ."

"Do you believe in all that stuff . . . spirits?"

"But of course, bwana. Everyone does." And he murmured something.

"I beg your pardon, mukhi?"

And the mukhi quoted from the Moslem book in Arabic, then gave a translation: "We created man from clay, and the djinn We created from fire."

The girl's condition had been desperate, the mukhi said. She had always had strange ways. Going to the river to wash at dusk, which was the hour when the shetani came out. As a child, climbing the twisted mbuyu – the hand of Satan. The shetani resided in mbuyu trees. Did Mr. Corbin know how many slaves had died under the little mbuyu many years ago during the famine? It was where the caravans had rested. And the captives who were too weak were left to die – meat for the lions and hyenas. That twisted mbuyu tree projected their agony. And it housed their spirits. Some good, some bad. The girl had come under their influence.

When a shetani entered her head, she became a tigress, this quiet girl. She would attack her mother using all sorts of language. Ate like a demoness. Only Rashid the transporter, her stepfather, could speak to her then and calm her down. This had gone on for many months.

"But this time, when Bwana Corbin was in Nairobi . . ." the mukhi said.

"Yes?" Bwana Corbin waited.

One evening, just after the long prayer had begun, the one with the recitation of the avatars, the incarnations of God, the lamps inside the mosque flickered out. There was deathly silence. The sounds of people, animals, fires crackling outside – all ceased. Then suddenly came a peal of shrill laughter. It stopped. And the prayer continued with the roll-call of the avatars: fish, tortoise, man-lion, Rama. . . . After prayers they found that every light in the town had either dimmed or gone out. They were frightened but went about their business.

The next evening, again, this time when the roll-call reached man-lion – a scream. They all got up and ran out. Others had already run towards the sound. Lights had dimmed. They came upon the girl in her house. She sat wide-eyed on the floor, indecently, laughing hysterically. Her stepfather went to help her, but she rudely spurned him. It took several people to restrain her. It was then that the maalim was told to take over and proceed with his ministrations.

He had tried all kinds of remedies. Prayers, potions. What Bwana Corbin witnessed had been the last resort, for which the maalim had asked permission, warning against faint-heartedness.

And the old man had driven out the invader. "Pray God, he will stay out. The girl is to get married."

"Such treatment . . . is illegal," the ADC told the mukhi hollowly.

They stood in silence.

The missionaries had the girl, he thought. They could try to make a fuss out of the incident.

"Let's wait. Give the girl some time to recover at the Mission. Then we'll see — we'll get her released."

The mukhi was not quite satisfied but agreed to wait.

"And the drumming in the night," Corbin said cautiously. "Was there a festival in one of the villages?"

"Yes, sir. Another spirit. You see, sir, the villagers were driving out the devil of fever. Another girl, suffering horribly."

"And is she doing well now?"

"No doubt."

Corbin stared long and hard beyond the doorway through which the mukhi had walked out. What had gone on in that village? He would probably never find out. Was it something British law would approve of? Most likely not. He felt frustrated and helpless, uncertain. A dark thought fluttered into his mind, which he could not entertain, articulate — something he felt was too big for him. He let out a sigh and made an ordinary observation: administration's all right, but how the devil do you deal with another culture's ghosts?

In the following two weeks, the mukhi came several times to see Corbin, demanding the girl's release.

"What if she doesn't want to return?" Corbin asked once.

"You joke, bwana," said Jamali. "She is our daughter."

Finally the ADC asked Jamali to take a delegation to the Mission, including the girl's mother, to see for themselves how Mariamu was doing. And if she would come with them, they were to take her. They should show appreciation, Corbin told him, that the girl was happy, and they should give the two missionaries their assurances that the incident would not be repeated. He himself sent a note to the Mission with his own guarantees for her well-being, adding that she was already engaged to be married.

And so Mariamu was released.

7

The rains, it seemed, were over, and a dry spell was upon them. Outside the ADC's office the Union Jack on the flagpole would give brief intermittent flutters, ever sensitive to the slightest motion in the surrounding air. Down below, the town of Kikono lay still, deadened by the heat of this afternoon hour.

The tensions following the episode involving Mariamu subsided, and on some pretext Corbin had the police band do a march-past. The children loved it and the people were reminded of the dominant yet generous force in their midst. At a football match the government team had gracefully accepted defeat from the locals, Mr. Corbin's half-time chat with his sergeant not going unnoticed. There were afternoons of music from the ADC's new gramophone, which he had brought from Nairobi. An askari would sit under the twisted mbuyu with the machine, alternately playing two records for the listening pleasure of an audience that sat quietly on the ground in front of him. And finally the old exorcist had come to visit him, not exactly to apologize so much as to pay respects, which was really the same thing. The maalim explained to Bwana Corbin the "ways of our ancestors," when, long before the Europeans came, the people lived peacefully, families were without strife, and elders were given respect. The incident of the exorcism was not mentioned. The coffee-seller approached, clicking his china cups – Corbin assumed that someone had directed him this way – and the ADC graciously accepted the maalim's hospitality. Finally the old man gathered his kanzu and got up, and, promising Corbin some lessons in Arabic script at a future date, presented him with a beginning reader. The ADC walked him to the door. "And one day I will cure you, too," the maalim told him with a nod and a sharp look, and strode off, his kanzu waving behind him. Corbin smiled indulgently at his back. He was happy. All was well, a crisis had been averted. This was what administration was all about. He despatched a letter to Anne to that effect.

West of Kikono, beyond the bushes that formed a natural boundary of the town, was a small wood, which he had observed from the hilltop Mission, a dark green stretch running northwards, following a seasonal stream. There were native villages there, in the oasis, but he had never visited them – the villagers came regularly to town, for celebrations and to buy provisions, and brought their hut taxes with them. On more than one occasion he had been tempted to change direction and go towards that silent green presence, so distinctive in this landscape of red dust and thorny scrub. But each time something else, farther, had tempted him away. This day, though, he gave in to his instincts and found himself walking towards the wood. The mysterious drums in the night had beckoned from there, had finally proved irresistible.

He crossed the thorny scrub behind the line of buildings that included the Swahili mosque, and a little later realized that he was walking along a footpath. The grass was taller and greener, the ground was soft and falling gradually, but overhead the sun was merciless on one so foolhardy as to forsake shade at midday. Suddenly the path stopped, and a few yards farther he was inside the forest. He was struck by several sensations at once. The cool shade, the tall, still tree trunks around him, interminable ranks of them stretching in front of him, the silence so deep he could hear his heart beat, his breath draw. Only when he looked directly above him did this darkness seem to have any limit – birds flying, leaves fluttering, sunlight trickling in, filtered by the foliage.

He walked a few steps, leaves and twigs crackling beneath his feet – wondering if he should turn back, sighting a chameleon, wondering further if he should have brought along a rifle or companions at least – and then he stopped, pricking up his ears to the sound of running water. He walked towards the gurgling, now more distinct and reassuring, almost animate, and arrived at a swift stream, brown water rushing between steep banks. At this juncture, where the trees held back to let the stream through, the sunlight fell vertically and broke into shimmering fragments upon the water surface. There were several ways of crossing. Stones had been placed at shallow points, but to reach these he would have to climb down the bank. A little farther upstream the banks rose and came close together. Here a log had been thrown across, which he covered in three steps. He walked some more through the forest until he came to a clearing where stood a village. It was from here, he guessed, that the drumbeats of a few weeks ago had come down to oppress him.

He was welcomed with shouts of "Jambo!" and "Shikamoo!" and given a stool to sit on and milk to drink. In the common area some women in khanga cloth were at work; two toddlers played on the ground. A herd of goats passed in front of him, in the charge of two almost naked boys with spears and shields. He was brought mangoes and bananas to eat, but declined. He was seated in shade, where a host of mosquitoes descended upon him, so he moved his stool out in the sun. An older man arrived and bowed to him, then sat on the ground close to his feet, asking if he had a cigarette. Some young men arrived, with friendly smiles, and asked what he had come for. Just to see how they were, Corbin replied. He talked with the men in Swahili and was told that there was fever in the village. He asked if there was a mganga, a healer, there who cured sickness. They smiled. He said they should come to his office for medicine. He told himself he should talk to the Mission ladies about quinine and write to Mombasa about supplies. He did not know what he had expected to find here; it seemed so ordinary, like dozens of villages he had seen. And yet the drumbeat in the night. . . . There were layers of life here clearly inaccessible to him, deliberately hidden from him. Finally he got up to go, realizing he had been away too long. As he turned he saw two of his askaris come to meet him. He was a little annoyed, and not a little relieved.

As they emerged from the bushes and reached the edge of the town, in some haste now, a figure appeared from behind the line of houses there and stood near the mosque. It was Mariamu. He had not seen her since her release from the Mission. As he passed she did not look at him, but turned her covered head away as modesty and custom demanded.

He was now walking parallel to the row of houses. She was behind him. In a sudden mischievous move, he turned, catching her unawares, and met her eyes. She stood tall, her red pachedi having fallen on her shoulders, revealing her long thick black hair, her eyes dark and deep – a vagrant with the bearing of a queen, as she refused to turn away a second time.

Who should be waiting for him when he got back but the indefatigable mukhi, with a suggestion.

"Two birds with one stone, bwana, as the proverb goes." Jamali nodded his head in affirmation of his brilliant idea. "Mariamu will be your housekeeper and cook for you — better even than your Thomas. She has training — both in Swahili and Indian . . . Punjabi, Gujarati. She will sleep in the kitchen outside. Until the young man Pipa comes and takes her away. God willing."

Corbin couldn't have agreed more. The girl was now his responsibility too. As Jamali put it, what better arrangement than that the girl be housekeeper to Bwana Corbin, who could keep an eye on her? The girl's wedding had been postponed too long, said the mukhi, due to her problems with the spirit. It would now take place in five weeks, during which time it was better if she lived where she was not reminded of her unhappy experiences. Corbin was pleased at this outcome, this show of the towns-people's renewed trust in him. And Jamali went away happy, rubbing his hands, very much the successful troubleshooter. "Perhaps you'll invite us to dine next," he grinned from the door-way, pointing to an oversight that brought red to the English-man's cheeks.

The mukhi was right about Mariamu's cooking, though the ADC's one-person residence made little demand of her gifts. And she slept not in the kitchen but in the spare room.

7 June, 1914

2 cushions. 6 tins cake (raisin). 4 oxtongues.
Oatmeal biscuits. ½ doz. whisky. Tins of marmalade and jam.
— disabuse Mariamu — extent of ADC's resources and kitchen.
— Sunday breakfast for the local bigwigs — maandazi and baazi, which the coast is so famous for. Fish. Fruit.

11 June

Poor wretch, she has a temporary home now before that brute of hers comes to take her away. . . . I do not know what to make of her — the impetuous girl who walked in past my askari and

78

spoke directly to me, then the silent girl who left chapattis for me on Thursdays, the girl humiliated by the maalim's switch, the proud girl holding her uncovered head high and staring directly at me, and now the quiet and shy housekeeper. Which is the real one?

∽◠

There was a rustle of clothing, and he looked up from his diary, giving a start at the sight of her sitting on the floor in the doorway that led to the back. She was staring intently at him, her chin resting on a fist supported on her drawn-up knees, her pachedi fallen from her head. She lifted it over her head and turned her face away, but she did not get up.

He did not know what to say at first, but then grinned sheepishly and came out with "What do you see?"

"You write many letters."

"Some," he said. "But mostly to myself."

"To yourself?"

"Why, yes. In this book." He gave it a thump.

She smiled, and then got up.

"May I have some water?" he said.

She fetched him a glass and looked away as he drank.

This became a regular rendezvous, a ritual, and he started looking forward to it. After supper and a stroll outside, he smoked his pipe, then sat down to write, and like a genie (were there female djinns, according to the mukhi's Book?) she would appear.

"What did you write today?"

"That you are a good girl."

"But you wrote for a long time."

Naturally afraid and shy of him because of his status, and because he was a man, she became forthright only when he opened up to her. Perhaps this was also because he was a foreigner. He was surprised, startled at this rapport, and he rather enjoyed it.

79

He had never talked to anyone of her race like this before. He asked her about herself, and she inquired about him. Bit by bit, a little reluctantly at first, they let out pieces of their past, those that would be understandable to the other.

Her mother, she said, was the mukhi's sister. Her father had died in Mombasa and her uncle had arranged a remarriage with a local Kikono man that had turned out to be a disaster. The step-father was a railway coolie who had run away and never stopped dreaming of returning to his native Punjab.

"Don't you think of your home?" she asked.

They talked in Swahili – his, broken – and in gestures, and some misunderstandings were comical.

23-24? June

. . . I found myself explaining the political map of Europe to her – the countries, the languages – drawing crude comparisons. How to explain my reason for being here, leaving that fairyland to come to this darkness, where the kerosene lamp casts our long shadows on the walls and outside the hyena barks and the night owl shrieks – where I have no one of my kind. To help you, your people, I offered. She looked nonplussed. On orders from my Sultan, then. That, she understood.

Her stepfather . . . she said.

"He's called Simba, isn't he, Rashid the transporter?"

She laughed, apparently at his use of the nickname.

Her stepfather knew about spirits, she said. He had seen them come as simba, lions, when he worked on the railway. And because his journeys took him places, he knew the local languages and so could talk to the shetani who haunted her.

The shetani hated her mother the most, after which he hated her uncle Jamali, the mukhi. She didn't know why. He made her say cruel things to her mother, and do *evil* things. Her mother would sit all night beside her when the shetani came, she would call her brother the mukhi to come and say prayers. She wrote letters to a holy woman in Mombasa and received many prayers from her. She bought tawiths, with Quran inscriptions inside them, and made bracelets for her. But the shetani was too strong. Finally, with her brother's permission, Mariamu's mother went to the maalim, who was not of the community.

"What evil things did you do?" he asked gently.

She lowered her eyes. "What the spirit told Rashid . . ."

To tell her about Nairobi, the big city, he once showed her some photographs: the bead market on Government Road; himself at the wheel of a car; Dr. Ribeiro's zebra-drawn buggy; Anne and Edwina in front of their house on the verandah, servant in kanzu beside them.

"Your two mothers," she called the two women. He wondered if she was mocking, and eyed her sharply.

One night as they talked he heard an unusual sound outside – an uncertain step, an exclamation, not the reassuring thump of the askari – and he went out to look. Flinging the door open, he saw the stepfather, Rashid, sneaking away, and shouted angrily at him, threatening to shut him in the lockup. Then somewhat amused and embarrassed he came back inside. The girl had fled to her room.

Then, some days later, he saw the mukhi's wife hovering at the back of the house. "It is new moon's night," she said. "The girl doesn't have clothes for mosque, so I brought some." Later when Mariamu came out, she looked, he thought, rather lovely. Through some quirk of fate, he mused, the ruffian Pipa had been most lucky in his choice of bride. Corbin had a drink, went out for a walk in the dusk, and passed the mosque, where ceremonies were in progress. He would, he thought, offer his patronage to the girl: if she was in trouble, wherever her fate took her, she could call on him for help. It would never be hard to find him. He went back and waited for her. When at ten o'clock she hadn't appeared he went to bed.

He woke that night shivering horribly, realizing in that feverish state that what he had feared had struck. He got up, stumbled to the table to look for water, found some, mixed it with brandy, and drank it. He stumbled back to bed, fell into it. Later he became conscious of a cool sensation, hot aching eyeballs, the smell, the weight on the bed of another body. Mariamu was putting compresses on his forehead.

He was up in two days, weak but otherwise recovered, with an appetite that promised a quick return to his normal condition. But seven days later, fever struck again. Watching the mzungu turning into a yellow ghost of himself in her care, Mariamu called her uncle, who arrived with the dispenser. The two men, recognizing the symptoms of blackwater fever, at once raised the alarm. Voi was notified, the MCA station appealed to for help, and Mrs. Bailey arrived, taking over the household.

2 July, 1914

. . . all sorts of powers I am told were invoked to cure me . . . including brandy blessed by verses of the Koran . . .

At night the mukhi came, a little apologetically, with the maalim. The ancient exuded such an authority – Mrs. Bailey was practically pushed aside, though she managed to come back with force into the picture. He had said one day he would cure me, and here he was, book in hand. I did not believe in his powers, of course . . . it was disconcerting. He sat by the bed and started taking my pulse and so on – I don't know what for except to disarm Mrs. Bailey, who stood by sternly, observing very closely. His face – the skin dull and wrinkled as old leather under the white kofia – was without expression, except for the eyes black and burning. He did not refer to our previous meetings. Presently he motioned to the mukhi, who produced several incense sticks, which he proceeded to set up all over the room. Mrs. Bailey was enraged.

"I will not have this!" But the maalim had put a very firm hand on my forehead and she was forced to take notice in case he did me harm. His other hand, palm downwards, was on the open book in his lap. The hand on my forehead felt heavy . . .

The maalim began to utter prayers in Arabic. As he finished he turned around to stare towards the mukhi. He looked distracted, distant. He began now to mutter in a dialect that even the mukhi did not understand. He spoke in harsh tones, stone-faced, his hand remaining pressed on Corbin's forehead. Finally he came to himself, for the mukhi heard a familiar word, "maji," water, and saw the maalim's face relax, his hand lift from the mzungu's forehead. Mrs. Bailey went to fetch water. As soon as she was gone the old man carefully laid the book aside, on the table next to the sick man's head. He took the bottle of brandy which was on the table and, holding it in both hands, he muttered some verses and blew over it, then put the bottle back. Mrs. Bailey returned with the water, the maalim took it and prayed over it, then offered the water to Corbin. "Give it to me," said Mrs. Bailey sharply. The maalim obliged without protest, and she took the glass and firmly put it away. "He doesn't need it now," she said.

As the mukhi and the maalim left, with one final glance at the patient, Mrs. Bailey proceeded to remove the incense sticks. Then she took the water and threw it out at the back of the house in the dark.

"Brandy!" groaned the ADC, stretching out a hand, when she returned.

And he drank the brandy, with its promise of alcohol and the maalim's prayers for recovery.

8

Corbin's illness had served to narrow the gulf between him and the two missionaries. Since he had refused to be carried on a stretcher to the Mission, first Mrs. Bailey then Miss Elliott had stayed to look after him. Mariamu had assisted them, staying a week longer in his service before going to stay with her uncle, the mukhi, to prepare for her wedding.

The Shamsis gave Mariamu a full wedding. She wore a dark green frock and green pachedi that was full of wonderful affects: needlework, sparkles, and sequins. Her hands and feet were covered with henna in detailed bridal patterns. She shimmered and jangled as she gracefully moved. The frock-pachedi was a gift from her people, the earrings, the bangles, the finely wrought necklace were all lent by them, in a collective gesture that Corbin found deeply touching. Only the sparkling little nose stud was actually hers, and it looked humbled by all the finery upon her. The pale, rouged face framed by the black hair – is this what an Eastern queen looks like – the full moon in the embraces of the night, he remembered reading somewhere, perhaps in

FitzGerald. There was an element of exaggeration, of unreality about the whole thing, but the mukhi said there had not yet been a wedding in the town, and so this was something special.

It was an evening ceremony at the Shamsi mosque. All sat on the floor facing the mukhi, except the ADC, who stood in the doorway. He knew he was not allowed in, yet he watched with an obstinacy they did not know how to handle. The Swahili sheikh read the nikaa in Arabic, and the bride and groom then signed the register, Mariamu writing her name as Miss Elliott of the Mission had taught her during her short stay there. When the marriage was announced by the mukhi, all stood up to congratulate the couple, wishing them a happy new life, and Corbin, seeing her husband looming large in turban and suit beside his fragile bride, yet looking humbled by the experience, thought perhaps there was something good in him; after all, the mukhi had praised his enterprise.

Later the couple sat on chairs outside, near but not quite under the little mbuyu tree, which had been decorated with coloured paper and from which hung a few lamps. On both sides of them were single rows of chairs for the elders and family. On the hard ground in front of them were geometric designs drawn earlier by the women using coloured flour, and beyond these auspicious markings the remaining guests sat facing the couple. The bride was presented gifts by a delegation of two men from Moshi, representing the groom's family and community, and the groom received gifts from her family. It was an event that drew many from the neighbourhood, even the Englishwomen missionaries. Afterwards a meal was served and sherbet flowed freely. Music was provided first by Mr. Corbin's gramophone, then a harmonium and tabla and dhol appeared, and an impromptu concert began.

Later that evening the Mission ladies sat with Corbin on his verandah and indulged in small talk and a little brandy. The couple had been escorted in a procession to the small house that had been arranged for them, and the guests had dispersed. But the festive air appeared to have lingered down below in the town. There were lamps still lighted in the shops, where the men were perhaps playing cards, and occasionally there came a snatch of chatter, a burst or two of laughter. A song began and broke off.

Miss Elliott lamented the passing of the girl from her influence. "She was such perfect material for conversion," she said. Over his pipe Corbin offered the opinion that perhaps she was best off with her own people. "Surely," said Miss Elliott, "no one is better off for not accepting Our Lord." Her companion agreed forcefully.

Corbin had nothing to say to that, and they lapsed into silence. After a while he asked how Thomas was doing.

At first the women did not respond. One looked towards the other, who was staring into the darkness.

"I hope nothing's the matter," he said.

Mrs. Bailey finally abandoned her contemplation of the night and turned to her companion. "Jane, we should tell him," she said.

"You tell him," Miss Elliott replied.

It turned out that Thomas had set covetous eyes upon Miss Elliott. The ladies became wary, but hoped the man would change. Then one morning, while Miss Elliott was arranging flowers inside the church, she was accosted by the Indian, who proposed to her in the most odious manner. And that was not all. He had been put in his place, of course, but later that limb of Satan had seduced a girl convert, with the argument that only those women who had had intercourse with a real Christian man would be saved.

"Something about holy water," murmured Mrs. Bailey.

Miss Elliott choked on her drink, turning very red.

"I'm sorry I ever let him attach himself to me," said Corbin, coming to the rescue. "He did have a way of ingratiating himself with one —"

"He's been sent away, of course," said Mrs. Bailey. "We are keeping eyes and ears open in case he's done more damage." She shuddered.

"Do you think there's going to be a war in Europe?" said Miss Elliott, demonstrating her recovery.

There had been rumours in Mombasa and Nairobi, which had leaked out in Voi, about the worsening political climate in Europe.

"As likely now as any time before, if you ask me," said Mrs. Bailey. "Nothing unusual is going on."

"Oh, but it is," said her companion. "Fighting in Serbia. Mobilization . . ."

"What mobilization?"

"There are rumours."

"In any case," offered the ADC, "we hardly have the armies to fight in Africa. I can assure you, there are no preparations afoot for war with our neighbours."

They went back inside and prepared to retire.

The ADC had learned to gauge the depth of the night's quiet by the clarity of its non-human sounds: the hoot of an owl, the bark of a hyena, the whisper of leaves. As he lay in his bed it seemed to him that the town which was his charge had now finally retired, had accepted once more the embrace of quietude.

Through this night there rang a shrill cry, all too human, then angry shouts half muffled as though coming through open doors, and sounds of thumping and shuffling feet, and at least one person as always during commotion approaching up the hill to make a report.

Corbin walked out on the verandah, taking the spare lamp with him. An askari approached in the darkness. "The girl, bwana!" The ADC's heart sank. He hurried down the path, following people already running to the scene, which presumably was the house near the Swahili mosque designated for the couple.

He walked through the small crowd that had gathered, until only a few men stood in front of him. He caught glimpses of the mukhi standing at the doorway, expostulating with someone inside, whom Corbin saw was Pipa. The bridegroom of a few hours ago was shaking his head from side to side in vehement denial. When he saw Corbin he took a threatening step towards him which the mukhi blocked. The young man, in loincloth and singlet, was sobbing; the mukhi gently pushed him back inside, and then said to Corbin, "Please, sir, go. Not now." The door closed behind him. Slowly Corbin walked away, back up the hill to his house.

The mukhi came early the following morning. He stood with his fez in his hand, a pained, hesitant look on his face, his head tilted sideways questioningly.

The ADC was sitting at his table with a cup of tea. The Mission ladies were not around.

"Now tell me, mukhi. What was that matata about? Did the boy have a change of heart?" Corbin said.

"Bwana. Most unfortunate matter. Tragic."

"What happened?"

"What to say, sir? Boy says girl not pure. She was touched."

"How do you know . . ." Corbin began foolishly, then stopped and stared at the man.

"What to do?" said the mukhi.

The Englishman continued to stare.

"What to do? Now the stepfather, sir, he spreads poison, the boy is in grief . . . and your good name, sir . . ."

"What about my good name, mukhi?"

"Forgive me, bwana. But Rashid says the girl was in your bed one night."

I have denied the stepfather's accusation in the strongest possible terms. The man has to be watched for mischief. I told the mukhi as much. When the mukhi left, I saw Miss Elliott walking about on the verandah, having just returned from her walk. She came in as soon as we exchanged looks – I wonder how long she had been there. Mrs. Bailey soon came in from the spare room, and the two women discussed their needs at the station in a rather formal way.

No more was said about the accusation. The ADC kept a low profile and applied for leave. The girl and her husband would soon be on their way to Moshi in German East.

But the war came first.

Miscellany (i)

From the personal notebook of Pius Fernandes
April 1988, Dar es Salaam

And so ends the diary, with more than four months of empty pages. As far as is known there is no record of any other diary of Alfred Corbin; no indication that the Englishman ever again committed his thoughts, his observations to paper (until, more than five decades later, he published his memoir entitled *Heart and Soul*, a terse – not to say soulless – account covering his several decades and posts in half a dozen colonies).

But the story doesn't end here, of course. Questions remain. Like a snoop I must follow the threads, expose them in all their connections and possibilities, weave them together. What else is a historian but a snoop? But, no, the urge is stronger. Like a bloodhound I will follow the trail the diary leaves. Much of it is bloody; it's blood that endures.

The questions. What are we to make of Bwana Corbin's denial of involvement with the girl Mariamu? What became of her in the years that followed? What evil acts did her stepfather, Rashid, purportedly able to communicate with lion spirits, make her commit? How did the diary leave the Englishman's hands? How many times did this diary change hands before landing in mine now? What of all those people whose lives it touched?

The diary is not a voice in the wilderness. There are witnesses. Think of a name, a place, a time, and immediately there are witnesses who come to mind – those who know the place, the person, the time, who passed through and wrote about them, who received letters, who spoke about them, who heard the stories.

There are many paths to choose from. And no one path is quite like any other, none of them will return to quite where it began. The path one takes is surely in large measure pure accident; but in equal measure, it must be determined by predisposition. And so I know, am forewarned. Ultimately the story is the teller's, it's mine.

Correspondence

Toronto, March 25, 1988

Dear Mr. Fernandes:

I am *thrilled* by your request and what it purports. I have always railed – given the opportunity – against the lack of a sense of history in us. (Recently I gave a talk to that effect entitled "What Is Not Observed Does Not Exist" – an idea stolen and adapted from physics.) My own researches – which have brought me to Toronto – have taken me in the direction of showing that the bhajans (hymns, gyans), which have been considered exclusive property of a religious community, with specific attribution of authorship, did in fact belong to a milieu, a collective – think of what that does to people for whom every word has been considered sacred. . . . Already battle lines have been drawn between the traditionalists (dare one call them fundamentalists yet?) and the academics. A world conference on this sticky problem, which no one dreamt of when they told us to educate ourselves, is to be held in London in a week.

More from London when I've had a look at what the libraries have to offer regarding the colonial bwana of your interest . . .

Regards,

Sona

London, April 9, 1988

Dear Mr. Fernandes:

In 1963 the Oxford Colonial Records Project was founded, in which former colonial officials or their families were asked to deposit at Rhodes House Library the personal records of their years in service. Most of the material was donated. The library is interested in the *content* of the material – even Xeroxes would do, and so they would pay little or nothing for the diary in your possession. Now if it belonged to a famous poet, things would be different. But a mere colonial bwana, when Empire is an embarrassing reminder. . . . I'm sorry, you'll have to disappoint your benefactor.

Also, regarding the material relating to Sir Alfred Corbin. I'm afraid these bwanas did not write much – or else did not donate the juiciest stuff. The Corbin family has not donated any personal effects. Of course there are records of official correspondence (Governor to Colonial Secretary, price of groundnut oil, etc.), but hardly anything personal and nothing from the period of your interest.

That fox Maynard wrote a journal, but access to it is restricted. He did publish a version of it, probably edited. A typical entry runs: "Saw 20 zebra, 10 oryx . . ." Corbin is mentioned as a "sound but stodgy chap." Maynard stopped at a town called Mbuyuni, near Taveta, and there had an encounter with a German or Swiss resident called Lenz. An incident in which a dog gets killed by baboons gets mention, as does a passionate defence of his punitive attack on a village – the event that attracted publicity and got him transferred out. The published diaries end before the War; the restricted version goes up to 1917.

I am sending Xeroxes of interest under separate cover.

Keep me posted!

Sona.

Appendices

(1) Sir Henry Johnson, Cambridge naturalist of independent means, writes in the introduction to his published diaries about a hunting and exploring safari planned in 1895 with his older friend and hero the author H. Rider Haggard. But the older man, wary of the entailing physical hardship, "cried off" at the last moment, and the young Johnson went on his own. He stayed several months in Lamu as a guest of the British Consul. In his diary Johnson mentions his "banker," one Jamal Dewji, whose son, "a rascal," accompanied him on his voyage round Zanzibar and inland, until he seduced a young convert at the MCA station in Taita country and stayed on at a village there. Johnson sent many details of local colour to the author, who subsequently based one of his characters on him.

(2) One of the three German letters confiscated by Corbin was addressed to an H. Lenz of Mbuyuni, a town some ten miles away. It reads as follows:

Moshi, 19 October 1913

My dear friend:

Herr Braunschweig is of the opinion that the map of the Taveta region published by the Voi District Office is in error. Could you ascertain if new information is available. Our own maps can only remain incomplete without it. I am afraid the British are rather lackadaisical in matters of accuracy.

We hear a new ADC has arrived in the area and seems like a nice fellow. Perhaps he is of a more scientific disposition.

With kind wishes from all of us here,

(Signed) W. Greiner
Oberleutnant

From the personal notebook of Pius Fernandes
April 1988, Dar es Salaam

My patron Feroz comes once in a while like the fairytale dwarf to judge the progress of my industry, in these rooms he has provided for me. "So, sir, what do you make of the diary?" He already knows it has no financial value. His interest now is in what I make of it, as he puts it. Patience, I tell him. Meanwhile I have some questions.

"What do you know of shetani?"

"You mean shaytaan . . . well, sir . . . you know, people believe in them."

"And exorcisms – do they still go on?"

"You don't hear much about these things these days. Zanzibar – that's the place for them – full of shetani. There was a case recently in Dar, but. . . . There's a Memon who does it, removes the shaytaan. I'll find out for you."

Sometimes he takes me to his home for the afternoon meal. At heart he is a lonely man, I think. He lives with his wife and daughter above the other store, the main one. The second child, a son, is studying in England. Running two stores, the husband and wife keep out of each other's way. She is quite his opposite in temperament.

There is a hubbub in the main store when we arrive. In the noon-hour rush, a thick-set Arab in a kanzu has been accused

95

of attempted shoplifting, and unconvincingly but not without humour he attempts to clear himself: hasn't he just been to Juma prayer? But to no avail. Shouts and verbal abuse from Zaynab follow him out. Feroz and I have one meal, after which we depart to the store on Pipa Corner. I am only too aware that in her eyes I stand very low and under suspicion: an unemployed teacher with ideas. But she is polite, has to do the necessary to reflect the harmony of her home, and so she gives us a thermos of tea to take with us.

"Any news of the visas?" I ask Feroz. There is some action, I know, to remove part of the family to Canada.

He looks up. "No."

I interpret this to mean failure.

"I'm happy here. Perhaps I'll send the kids for education, and the wife can join them there."

We have tea. From time to time something gets sold, something is in short supply, and he phones the other store to request stock. He has a code, every item has a nickname: "brown plastic," "Hong Kong maridadi," "Taiwan with buckle." . . . He knows his inventory by heart, knows on precisely which shelf he can find how much of anything, what the cost price is. It occurs to me that this is what one means when one says that business runs in the blood; the monetary worth of anything is at the fingertips.

"I have news for you. Do you know Rita . . . Gulnar?" asks Feroz.

"Gulnar Rajani?" I try to sound calm, but it's impossible; that name means too much, and he knows he's hooked me.

"Former student of yours, wasn't she, sir?"

"Yes . . . quite some years ago – what about her?"

"She's coming to Dar."

"What, here? What on earth for? Isn't she fabulously rich in England now –"

He's had the effect, and he looks away, busy with a customer, enjoying his fun. At length the customer leaves and Feroz returns to me.

"Well, as you know, Rita is Pipa's daughter-in-law. I wrote to her about the diary – and that you were looking at it. So she telephoned. She said she had been planning a holiday here – she also owns property in Dar through her father – and she was very curious about what we had to say about the diary. She's very keen to see you again."

Keen to see me, or the diary? What, if anything, does she know about it? I wonder at this intrusion of the personal into my research.

"It belongs to her, then," I say.

"That remains to be seen," he says, impassively.

In the locked cupboard of the Dar es Salaam Library, there is an old exercise book in which the title of every book in the cupboard is neatly noted down. There are even the names of absent books and where they were last known to be. A copy of Henry Johnson's *Diaries* is in this cupboard. Against the entry for Alfred Corbin's *Heart and Soul*, the writer has penned, "Sent to Moshi Library, upon request," followed by the date of the entry: 16 February, 1967.

Last month I placed an ad in the Dar es Salaam *Daily Herald* for two days running, requesting information from anyone whose family had anything to do with the First World War in Kilimanjaro region, especially in Moshi, Taveta, and Kikono. There was no response, which means nothing; everyone is too busy existing, scraping a living. A question like mine sounds ludicrous, and if I have the time to pursue such questions, I must have time to pursue witnesses. Which is what I decide to do. And so I take a bus to Moshi.

The Moshi librarian wants to know who told me about *his* locked cupboard. The cupboard in Dar, I tell him. You have to get permission, he says. From whom? He is not quite sure. Come back in the afternoon, he replies. I decide to look around the town (there's nothing like the sight of an old building for confirmation that, yes, there was a past) and, inquiring in the streets among the elders sitting at corners and outside mosques ("Eti, mzee, are there old buildings here – or cemeteries . . ."), I am directed finally to the Utamaduni (Culture) office. The Party cadre at the reception booth asks much, says much, commending my interest in history, even introducing me around as someone doing valuable service. But before divulging anything specific, he directs me to the Cultural Officer, a tall man of about thirty-five in blue jeans and jacket, a drooping moustache, looking like a Swahili with much Arab blood.

He takes me to his office – a large room with a large wooden desk littered with paper, some filing cabinets, and a table and chairs for meetings – and agrees with me, yes, much research needs to be done on local history. Archives need to be preserved, buildings need to be maintained, but there is no money. The Germans are interested, are busy looking up sites, marking them, preserving them. He works part-time with them. But most of their efforts are in the Tanga region – their favourite town then and now. It was here that the British suffered their biggest and most humiliating defeat in East Africa. He smiles faintly.

"When they were defeated by a swarm of bees," I say.

"Yes," he smiles.

His name, he tells me, is Jamali. He was brought up in Moshi.

"Your babu-bibi? Grandparents?"

"I saw my grandmother."

"In Moshi?"

He nodded.

"And where was your grandfather from?"

"Lamu," he says.

This man sitting across from me is, of course, the grandson of Jamali, the mukhi of Kikono.

He has much to tell me, does Young Jamali, as I will call him.

II

The Great Riddle

The two quarrel by day and make up at night.
    – Swahili riddle
(Answer: the panels of a door)

9

The wedding procession that with music and ceremony had escorted Pipa and his bride to their room had dispersed, the last of its members leaving reluctantly with suggestive, even lewd, remarks to relieve the couple of their bashfulness, remind them of the night ahead. The room was off an empty store, separated from it by a curtain of gunnies; there was an entrance at the front and a doorway to the backyard. The bed had been strewn with jasmine flowers, sprinkled with perfumes. The air was filled with the sweet clinging vapours of halud to rouse the senses. There was a tray of fruit by the bedside, slippers had been placed nearby.

Outside, the evening's mood lingered a bit in the occasional shout or burst of laughter; inside was very quiet and still. The bride and groom sat on the bed next to each other, exactly where their happy escorts had left them. He in grey suit and red turban; she in green frock and pachedi. She was staring at her red henna-dyed hands clasped in her lap, waiting. Throughout the evening he had caught only glimpses of her – this girl he was taking away, this gift he had been given but could not look at yet. He had been aware of the shimmer of sparkles and sequins beside him, the soft movement of the pachedi – the occasional thin clink of the bangles on her arms the only sound emanating from her. Looking at her now beside him, finally his to relish, he realized that the jewellery was not hers. People had lent it to her, putting trust in her groom; they had dressed and anointed her and had sung wedding songs for her, a daughter of the community.

He took his turban off and placed it beside him. Then very slowly, delicately, he put his hand to that richly decorated pachedi at her forehead and pulled it back over the hair and the garland of flowers behind it and let it drop to her shoulders. She turned to look at him, and took his breath away.

"Eh, Mariamu, you are truly beautiful," he said almost reflectively.

How could it be? Pipa thought. He, a former street urchin, without even the dignity of a father's name to attach to his, and beside him in this little room this houri – a celestial being such as was promised only in heaven. She was so perfectly beautiful, there was such a nobility in her. He could not deserve her. The long oval face, the chin and cheekbones, the long nose – not the round features of the shopkeepers' wives – and the thick wavy hair he caressed, and the long smooth neck under it that felt so hot to his touch.

"Come my little dear," he said, fingering the necklace. "We must put away the jewellery carefully. We must change."

He got up, and from a trunk took out a checkered loincloth, and turning low both lamps that hung in the room, he went into a shadow to change. Then taking one lamp with him, he visited the backyard. When he returned, Mariamu was sitting on the bed, changed into a simpler frock, her other clothes folded neatly beside the bed.

Does she know what to do? he thought. How much have the women told her? Tonight I'll be the teacher, he thought, recalling an analogy given him earlier that evening. I'll be the teacher, and teach by inflicting a little pain. This is how it has to be, how it always is. He felt magnanimous in his manly gentleness and consideration.

Putting the lamp back in its place on a wall, he came to bed. He got into it, behind her, and gently, taking her forearms, pulled her down beside him, saying, "Come."

"I am your wife," she told him as she went to him, in a mixture of yielding tenderness and anxiety.

No longer was she a celestial being but a woman in his arms. The smell of halud and the taste of flesh. Under her frock she was obligingly ready, she had been told well. The first time he was all rage and she patience, and when his fury was spent he lay back satiated, waiting for renewed desire, which had to come. It did, and he entered her again, lasting longer, watching her face in the dim light and meeting her eyes so that this time it was a shared act. Then he lay back.

And as he stared at the dark ceiling above him, slow waves of doubt lapped at his unwary brain. The deed was done, twice. Come morning he would show the soiled sheet, banner of his triumph — it had been easy . . . had it been too easy? And suddenly a crashing realization destroyed his composure — banner of his triumph or *shame*? Quickly he sat up. There was blood, but only a trickle.

"What —?" she began, but in a moment he was out of bed. He looked at her, at the sheet, in revulsion. "So this was the trick!" he said loudly. And then he shouted "Jamali!" towards the door, his anger worked up. "So you thought you would cheat Pipa, you! Take your whore back, Jamali!"

"Please —" the girl pleaded, and he pushed her away violently. She screamed as she fell on the floor.

There came shouts from outside, urgent knocking. The door was flung open, Mariamu's uncle, the mukhi, almost ran in.

"What happened? Aré, what happened? But tell me, you, what happened?"

Pipa, staggering like a drunk, swung at the mukhi.

"You cheated me – you bastard – you gave me a –"

Jamali pushed him into a chair, telling him for practical purposes not to be a fool and publicize his shame.

Jamali had closed the door, but now there was pandemonium outside and suddenly it was flung open once more. Jamali went to close it but faced a crowd of people. Pipa came to stand behind him.

Then Pipa saw the ADC push his way forward through the crowd and heard a voice in the darkness outside say: "It was the mzungu who deflowered the girl." Pipa looked at the mukhi, then at the approaching Englishman, and heard the chuckles and murmurs in the background, and knew he had been cheated, robbed.

Following that first night she had slept on the cold floor of pressed earth, until one night he told her to get up and helped her into bed. He had not touched her. He found it difficult, his heart heavy at the mere thought of it, his loins completely dead to it.

He could reject her. It was in his bounds and the community would support him. She would fend for herself, become somebody's woman, a prostitute . . . but even as he cast a glance at her beside him he saw a wife.

They were two lonely people, he thought, as he watched her scrape the pans, helping herself after him. Two people with incomplete, lowly origins – orphans, really. They had to make it, together. Together, they were inviolable. They had respectability, were a family.

They had not discussed that condition, the stigma that came between them at night like a wall. No one had denied his accusation, told him that sometimes these things happen, or that he was only imagining, was guilty of that greatest sin: doubt. No, they had not come to her rescue; not her mother, nor her uncle, the mukhi; and her stepfather had actually confirmed the accusation, it was Rashid's voice that Pipa had heard outside accusing the ADC. And the girl said nothing.

But in the next few days his pain began to lose its edge. He told himself the adult world was not as pure as a child might imagine, the adult world was a soiled one. He recalled his mother. He realized he could have kept his shame a secret between these four walls; but instead he had announced it from the rooftop.

Her hair was dishevelled and she was in old clothes now; her bare feet gripped uncaringly at the rough floor. Some days ago she had been a bride. The jewellery, carefully accounted for, had been tied up in a kerchief and handed over, the clothes folded neatly, and put away. What remained was the ring, the nose stud, and one set of new clothes.

He had not left the house since that first night and was himself dirty and smelly, dressed only in singlet and a kikoi cloth round his waist. Only she had walked out a few times on errands, once bringing kitchen things from her mother. This evening, he now told her as she took the dishes away, they would go out to the mosque.

Let curious spiteful eyes follow them, for how long? He would show them who was cleverer, smarter.

On their way to the mosque, a chattering of boys and girls followed them, a youthful jeer sounded from across the road. As they entered, the singing chorus halted, letting the single lead voice continue the hymn. Curious, silent faces watched them. As Pipa walked up to the mukhi, joined hands in traditional deference to the office, the mukhi gave loud blessings, joyfully, kindly, as if prompting the rest of the congregation to show similar kindness and acceptance. The girl, now a married woman, was received with respect on the women's side and was given the chance to lead the second prayer. They ate at the mukhi's, where Mariamu's mother, Kulsa, was also present, and Rashid, her stepfather, conspicuously absent.

That night she looked desirable in bed, ripe and fragrant as a

Lamu mango. They lay side by side but he did not touch her, cursing the fate that was now his frozen heart, his inert loins. And yet she was his wife. He would take her to his home in Moshi, on the German side, where his mother was and he had a thriving shop, friends and benefactors.

The following morning he began preparations for the journey. There was a trunk to obtain for Mariamu, and his own had to be repaired. There was the account to settle with Jamali. Porters to arrange. The mukhi's wife, Khanoum, came and spent the afternoon with Mariamu. Kulsa, her mother, came in the evening and bade a tearful farewell. All being well, the couple could depart early the next morning.

But all was not well. By the end of that day the town was abuzz with rumours of war. The next day war with Germany and its colony to the south was confirmed by the ADC, the border could not be crossed, and Pipa was an enemy national.

10

For many people this Great War, the war of the Europeans, was a great riddle composed of many smaller riddles; it came unasked for, undeclared in their midst. For those not involved in combat, it also became a game – one of observation and commentary, of cunning and survival. In Kikono and other towns of the Tsavo, caught in the midst of the mischief of the mzungus, the telling of the war was often the telling of riddles.

The first riddle (how the war was announced):
    – A great cloud of dust moves quietly down the Taveta Road, leaves much destruction behind.
    – A swarm of locusts?
    – No!
    – Na-ni? What then?
    – It has many legs.
    – Why didn't you say so? Jongoo? Millipedes?
    – Not at all.
    – Na-ni? What then?

– Some tongues are mute.

– Ah! Your own tongue is not!

– Comes in peace, goes in peace.

And so on.

From the Mission on the hill one afternoon they saw the cloud of dust move slowly and painfully down the dirt tracks through thorn and bush. Mrs. Bailey watched it a while with her binoculars, then gave a sniff. "Mules. Ox wagons – two," she announced to her companion, Miss Elliott. They did not think much of it until a few hours later.

The caravan, belonging to two European families, struck camp on the other side of the red hillock where the road entered Kikono. They had with them thirty tired porters, who brought a good day's business to the town and were treated accordingly. The travellers were on their way west from Voi, the stop was going to be a short one. Baruti's tea shack reopened and dispensed its potent "gunpowder" tea, bottles of water and soda were fetched. The Indians sold khanga cloth and mirrors and perfumes that would fetch better prices across the border. The Europeans themselves stayed close to their wagons, where they awaited their African porters, but were happy to receive vendors. Then the last of the little caravan disappeared behind the bushes on the long road to Moshi, and when the dust had settled, the air in Kikono remained heavy with rumour and news of war. A war is on, kuna vita, they heard from the stores, from the vendors, from Baruti the teamaker. But where, this vita, and who is fighting it? In Ulaya, between the Germans and the British. You did not have to be told why that distant war was important here. The European visitors of a few hours ago were on their way from British to German East Africa.

It was not until the following day that the ADC, frantic for news, at last received it from Voi. The day-old *Herald* carried a one-inch-high headline in bold. It was August 6, 1914.

WAR IN EUROPE
Great Britain Declares War on Germany
Yesterday afternoon a cable was received at Government
House from the Colonial Office announcing that a state of
war is now in existence between Great Britain and all its
domains and Germany. The Governor Sir Henry Belfield
has declared a state of emergency in the colony . . .

A column analysed the recent problems in Europe, which had
hitherto not merited more than an occasional short paragraph.
The photograph under the headline showed a crowd of settlers
gathered outside Nairobi House – a ragamuffin mounted corps of
farmers waving their rifles. Leaving their wives and children to
mind the farms, off they had galloped to the capital on horse and
mule, ready to do their duty. A recruiting office was opened,
irregular units were in existence, and men were already on their
way "to the GEA, on the road to Taboray!" but actually to scout
the border. Other men heard their call in the distant home country and were boarding trains bound for the coast, where a Union
Castle boat was waiting. The DC's message from Voi to his assistant in Kikono was more to the point. "War declared in Europe.
Look out for raids from across the border. Await further instruc-
tions."

Corbin's little kingdom at the mbuyu became a theatre of war,
its fate now out of his control and in the hands of master pup-
peteers abroad. This outpost dominion, whose palace could not
even boast a proper ceiling under the roof, where quinine was
always an urgent priority, now had a role in the defence and
machinations of Empire.

He mustered his small force of police askaris and kept them on
alert. He posted scouts under the command of the albino, Fumfratti, several miles into the forest and hills, and alerted the towns-
people to the possibility of evacuation. He interrogated travellers
for news from Moshi and Tanga.

The second riddle:

A man clutching his wrap about him comes hurrying into town and sits on a box at Baruti's tea shack. Evidently a farmer – uncouth, dirty. The others sitting there avert their gaze or move away. A kindly old Swahili smiles and says, "Why do you shake, old man?"

"You piss under a tree and it pisses back."

"Ah, yes. That's the way of the world."

"From the branches."

"Naam?"

"It pisses from the branches."

"No doubt."

"A branch with many leaves leaps down and speeds away."

"Didn't I say so? It happens."

"Gives you the fright of your life."

"No doubt. Bila shaka. What did you smoke? – some bhang?"

"It has boots. And a gun, too."

Na-ni? What is it? They've all gathered around now, this sounds like no ordinary riddle. Call Fumfratti, says the old Swahili.

He does so and the colourfully dressed albino approaches.

"Lebeka!" Fumfratti replies.

"Listen to this riddle."

"You piss under a tree and it pisses back – from the branches," says the old farmer, fortified by Baruti's gunpowder tea and grinning.

Fumfratti listens, then speaks: "Idiots." He takes the farmer by the hand and walks him up the hill to the ADC's office.

This, then, was the first real contact the town had with the war. The farmer, having gone behind some bushes to take a piss, happened to be looking upwards at a tree close by when he saw drops of liquid trickling down. He gave a start; there was not a cloud in the sky. It could have been an animal. Then he saw the vision –

the branch leaping down, a figure with gun and boots making a dash for it.

Every able-bodied man went with the ADC's party to find this apparition – in uniform, as the witness now said – but the camouflaged soldier had of course disappeared. On the platform he had built using cross-planks laid over branches, they found a tin with remains of ugali and orange. In a bush nearby, the place where the farmer had relieved himself. It was probably trickling orange juice that he saw, although opinions varied.

The ADC dispatched a runner to Voi with a report.

This was a time to exercise the rhetorical flourish, allow the flight of imagination. And what better people to do it than the wazees – the elders – outside the Swahili mosque, or at Baruti's tea shack, or over cards in the evening in the light of a coalfire, while cassava or maize or cashew was roasted and black coffee was passed around in the little cups. Whenever a group of people gathered under a tree, the chances were it was not only a game of bao or three-card monte they were watching but war commentary they were giving ear to.

One favourite subject was (and remained for many years) the quality of the Germans' African askaris: hard, tough as nails, disciplined. They were taught well by their masters. And these European masters of the terrible feldkompanies . . . not for nothing was the German called hand of blood, will of iron, fierce as a devil. Those who remember will tell, of the Rebellion of Bushiri bin Salim long ago and how it was crushed. And then the Maji Maji uprising of ten years ago. That too was crushed. There were more men hanging from the mango trees, eti, than mangoes. Compare the stern, cold-eyed Germans (a word here, a word there, all is understood) to these British settlers who had come to fight them – here they referred to a mounted corps that had recently passed through (in safari suits and funny hats, sitting on donkeys with their pots and pans r? ᶾ, servants behind them, arrogant as if they owned the land.) Even the legendary Abu Nawas could not have assembled such a crew. What were they arrogant for – eh, jamani – and they with their guns and police? Abusing people, enticing African boys to go with them as scouts and carriers – more likely to test the first German bullets. Eti, who is at war with whom? Did we say we were fighting? Have we enemies, jamani? Since when is the Chagga tribe our enemy? And if a Taita lives across the border – eti, where is this border? – is he my enemy, bwana?

– You ask where is this border, eti, heeeh!

– Do you know?

– Nobody knows, my brother. See that mountain – the mountain knows. The British gave it to the Germans.

– How?

– They draw a line in the grass, then they rub it out and draw another one.

– So one day you are on one side, the next day on the other. Like chickens.

– Kuk-kuk-kuk-kuk-kuk, kuk-kuk-kuk-kuk –

– We are not chickens!

– That's exactly what we are. In Voi they started a little matata, a ruckus, to give the DC a little scare. The soldiers showed their rifles. Fired in the air and everyone ran. Like what? Like chickens into huts, into trees, under motorcars. Then they returned, scurried along to pick up spent bullets, even the old men – like what? Like chickens running after grain!

– One day all their lines will be rubbed out.

– Or their fingers cut. Some lines they draw are deep.

And then the first casualty, the blood-tie to the conflict.

Fumfratti's scouts, a few miles outside town, discovered what appeared to be bushes on the move, taking short hops. With a *whoopee* they gave these German askaris the chase. They did not have a single rifle among them, neither it seemed did the opponents. Just then a single shot rang out from behind them, bringing one of Fumfratti's men down. They gave up the chase.

But who had fired the shot? The albino, with golden flowing beard and hair, the yellow bandanna and cowboy hat, looked around. Cunningly he said, "First the bush moves, then an anthill smokes." This became the third riddle of the war.

With much ado the wounded man was carried to the town, while Fumfratti and another man stayed behind and crawled silently towards the large anthill. They came close to it, and then in a sudden move dashed against it, letting out shrieks that scared the man inside out of his wits. Then they pummelled him senseless.

The captured soldier turned out to be a Yao tribesman from Nyasaland, the British colony south of German East Africa. He had served the British army in the 2nd Battalion of the King's African Rifles, the KAR, near Voi, and then was discharged a few years before with the rest of the battalion in Zanzibar. The way back to Nyasaland was through the German colony. In one of the towns, a unit of the German Defence Force promptly recruited him and sent him on to Moshi. He and his men were the advance scouting party for a mounted patrol in the area. If Fumfratti and his gang had continued their game of tag a little longer – the prisoner had beat his forehead with his fist to punish his stupidity in firing too hastily – they would have run into the patrol, the real Germans on mules, who would have finished them off.

So the war was no joke. It was upon them. The ADC sent the captive to Voi that same evening. The town was quiet, the talk subdued.

As the first days of the war passed, rife with rumours and with isolated incidents to egg them on, the Indians in town began to panic with uncertainty: to go – abandoning all – or not. Every day the mukhi came to the ADC for advice, comfort, the latest news. To a man they had relatives in Moshi, Tanga, Dar es Salaam.

– The British have bombed Dar. Don't they know there are British subjects there? Our families, our brothers . . .

The mosque worked overtime, for prayers, for possible shelter and advice. And the young man Pipa and his bride were trapped in town, too afraid to leave.

One night, between four and five in the morning, the Shamsi mosque was enveloped by a deep silence – deeper than the surrounding night, its inhabitants would say. It was the hour of meditation, and not even the sound of breathing could be heard, for the breathing was controlled, relaxed, in order for the spiritual force Kundalini to move up the spine to the head. Only an occasional dry cough exploded, to be absorbed into the silence like a pebble into the infinite ocean. This night, to the distracted mind, the first explosion in the distance could have been a cough. But then the *ra-ta-tat* of the machine-guns, the crack of the rifles – and even those most immersed in the Universal were drawn out. The silence was no more, and the night filled with sighs, coughs, calls outside, each mind then acutely conscious of life, possessions, progeny, agonized about what was going on, what would happen. Because the hour was sacred, the sitting had to continue, and the mukhi waited till the clock chimed five before turning on the lamps. Then, after a hurried prayer, he despatched his people to their homes to await word from the government representative.

The distant shots became sporadic as the morning wore on. At midday a cyclist was already in town bearing news. The Germans – hundreds of them – had taken the border post at night, then attacked the border town Taveta early that morning. The ADC LeBlanc was on retreat towards Voi with his policemen, and the Germans were now at Salaita Hill, a strategic point outside Taveta. Then came news of people on the Voi road, carrying bundles, children, pushing carts; a few strayed into town, others moved on. The town sat tight. There was no sign, no news of the

KAR all day. Only at night came rumours that they had arrived at Voi, were on their way to Bura twenty miles away. The night air hung heavy with uncertainty, the Shamsi mosque was filled once again, everyone there listening eagerly to a refugee from Taveta. The Mission ladies, who had so far refused to come down to Kikono for safety, now withdrew to Voi.

The following night Alfred Corbin slept fitfully. Much was happening; too much threatened to happen. Rifle shots rang out in the distance; there came shouts, and the sounds of the crying of children, a woman pleading somewhere; and his mind echoed with the machine-gun *ra-ta-tat*. Scenes from the day's commotion replayed themselves again and again. As if this were not enough distraction, he could not help speculating about the fighting in Europe, and thinking about his family.

His father had by now retired and settled in Devon. It had been months since he'd last heard from his brothers – Kenneth in Nyasaland and Robert in India. He wondered how the war would affect their lives, and his. It seemed likely to end by Christmas, but that was only a guess. Anne had put off her visit to England and was a volunteer at a hospital in Nairobi . . .

Suddenly there was heavy pounding on the door. He thought the end had come, at least in this frontier town of Kikono. He gave himself a moment to dress. How would he surrender, what would he say? When he opened the door, a tall figure strode past him carrying a lamp. A shorter, African man followed. The lamp was put on the table and Corbin faced the intruders. The door was open, he could feel the cool air, hear the sounds of more men beyond it.

In front of him stood Maynard, in uniform, hands on hips, a smile on his face, eyes gleaming, perhaps from drink. He looked thin, emaciated. He had lost his moustache, but had a few days' growth of beard.

"Captain Maynard! Why –"

"A drink, old chum. And some information."

Corbin produced whisky and glasses.

"Surely you're not with the retreating party?"

"No. Came straight from Mombasa, via Voi. Intelligence. GSO, if you have to know."

The African who had come in with Maynard was in kanzu and cap, evidently a Swahili. The two men outside were invited in; one wore the dress of a Taita villager, the other, in khakis, was a Somali.

"Place is crawling with agents," Maynard said, with a sigh. "Voi to Mombasa. Surely you know of the sabotage on the railway line. Our train was fired at on the way from Mombasa. Lost one man, captured two."

The war was a godsend for him, a game designed somewhere and set before him to play. When had he arrived back in the country? The war was hardly two weeks old – the War Office must have rushed him back here, with his knowledge of the terrain.

"How long are you staying?"

"Not long. We need to talk to a man here. Coolie chap. Nurmohamed."

Corbin looked nonplussed.

"Pipa," the Swahili, named Shomari, said, a little impatiently.

"Why, he's from German East on his way –"

"Exactly. Could be a spy."

"Surely not!"

"Surely?" Maynard looked at him searchingly, and Corbin couldn't reply.

"Just point out the house, old chap."

"Over there – next to the mosque – your man probably knows it anyway," Corbin said, and sat down at the table.

He finished the bottle, waiting, he didn't know what for, staring in front of him as he heard first a shout or two, then a door banging. Then came more shouts, a scream from the girl. Mariamu.

Corbin got up to go, then stopped himself. He realized he could do nothing.

Pipa's howl bellowed through the town. It was probably exaggerated, but surely there was cause enough. The rest of the drama, it seemed, would proceed soundlessly, and Corbin waited for it to conclude, as did the rest of the town, which was unusually quiet.

Finally there were sounds: voices, the dog, footsteps approaching. Maynard's boots came thumping on the verandah, and he strode in triumphantly and headed for a chair. Corbin, on his feet again, watched him intently for signs of sweat, exertion. Which of them had applied the beating?

"A drink, I say —"

"Was the man a spy?"

"Don't think so. Now he is. For us."

"After the beating?"

"Don't be sentimental. The boy is tough. He knows it was necessary. There is a lot in it for him." He smiled his rabbit smile. "I hear it gets pretty lonely here. . . . Orders from Voi." He slapped a letter in Corbin's hand.

Voi Station

15.8.14

Dear Corbin,

The bearer is Captain Maynard GSO(I) — whom I believe you know. He will apprise you of the situation. You are to shut down your station and proceed to Voi. Please give him the men he needs and bring the remaining police with you. Take possession of mules and deposit them with Cmdr. F. Coy 4/KAR at Bura.

W. C. Hobson, D.C.

"A Government station here would inevitably draw an attack," said Maynard. "Propaganda victory – not good for us, we could have an uprising. LeBlanc is in Mbuyuni tonight. You could join him in the morning."

"Yes, I shall do that. I'll start preparations right now."

"By the way, I met some of your scouts. You trained them well."

"Yes . . . a fine bunch. They knew their job."

"The Yao you captured could be the first enemy soldier captured in the E.A. operations – he told us a lot. Well done."

Maynard slept in the spare bedroom for what remained of the night. The next morning he met Fumfratti and his scouts, recruited them, and had Pipa brought to him.

Corbin took with him only the most important papers. Others he burned or packed away in cases. Early in the morning he called a meeting of town elders, impressing upon them that they had nothing to fear, that the town was of no military value, and to be prepared to evacuate if fighting came close.

He left with a feeling that he was absconding.

11

The house that Pipa lived in with his bride, with its small shop-front at the side of the living and bed room, belonged to his wife's uncle, Jamali, the mukhi. That community stalwart had effectively shut up the stepfather, Rashid's, gossip about the wedding night upon threat of ostracism and had given respectability to the young couple. When news of the war came, Pipa had received the ADC's permission to stay in town and run his pili-pili bizari business, selling kerosene and copra oil, spices and tobacco. Like all the town's men, he gave up some of his nights to patrol the perimeter of the town.

It did not take long to reconcile himself physically to his wife. As the number of days of married life increased, her lack of innocence disconcerted him less. Men married widows, divorcees – the best example was God's own Prophet, as the mukhi reminded him. He had finally had a man-to-man chat with Jamali, who in a very worldly way had scorned his prejudice. The blood that they go around showing after the wedding night – do you think it is always the woman's, ay? Why not a chicken's, a goat's?

It was late in the night. Pipa and his wife had woken early that day, before dawn, to the distant sounds of guns, and like the rest of the town, had waited in anticipation of whatever else was to happen. At about ten in the morning, news arrived of Taveta's capture by the Germans. And shortly after that the refugees started coming, those who had fled Taveta and its environs. There had been moments of anxiety in Kikono, but it had quickly become apparent that the fighting was not going to approach them yet. Business had been good. In mosque that evening there had been much discussion about possible evacuation of the town's population, but it had amounted to nothing. Now having returned from that meeting, and after counting the day's takings, Mariamu and her husband lay down to sleep.

He was awakened by a loud banging on the front door, on the shop side of the establishment. He swore at whoever it was, then remembered the war and its uncertainties and became worried. Partly dressed, he opened a panel in the door, and held up a lamp. A man–giant strode in, in boots; then another man, and another. A European and two Africans. They entered without a word but with grim, purposeful faces, and stood around him, their legs firm and spread apart with authority, their accusing eyes upon him. He looked from one to the other, his heart beating in fright, vaguely guessing his crime. In the other room behind the rag curtain his wife stirred. He took a step in that direction, but the African in kanzu, who was evidently a Swahili, pushed him back. The other African, a Somali, took a step towards him and brought his face close to his, meeting his eyes. Pipa barely had time to respond, was recoiling, when the tall, bony Somali gave him a tremendous slap in the face. He fell back, reeling. The presence of the white man emptied him of all courage.

"Mama! What did you do that for?" He was hurting. He held his cheek.

They said nothing, but stood watching as before.

He choked back a sob and lunged half-heartedly at them,

more in an attempt to get it over with, whatever it was. He was from German East, that must be his crime. He had carried letters once. But these men could be from either side. Had the Germans already arrived?

As he came at them, the Swahili hit him with something hard in the stomach – a club – and he heard Mariamu scream. Doubled up, yet strengthened by her presence, he rushed towards the nearest pair of legs, but was felled by another blow. As he lay on his side on the floor, the European took a step closer to him, touching him with a boot, toying with his stomach. He breathed in deep, looked away, waited for the blow that would surely crush his insides and kill him. Mariamu screamed again, ran up to the grinning white man, pounding him with her fists. He shoved her away and she fell down. The two Africans escorted her to the backyard and returned.

The European was in uniform. He had a huge head, which looked so powerful it could break a wall. He was dusty, his face was flushed, his eyes were red as a drunk's. His hair was yellow, he grinned like a devil, exuding menace and terror. The Africans stood and watched.

"Tell me –" began the white man.

"What have I done? By God, hakia mungu, I have done nothing!"

"You work for the Germans, our enemies."

"Hata! No!"

"You are lying!" The boot pushed into his stomach, then pulled back, ready to kick in his insides – a thick black boot caked with dry red mud. Pipa's eyes remained fixed on this instrument of power, of terror, and he groaned, expecting the worst. Suddenly there was a pain so excruciating he thought his world had come to an end, and he screamed uncontrollably, passing out. When he came to, he thought he had been kicked in the groin, then realized the man had stepped on one of his hands, grinding the fingers into the floor.

"Do you deny having worked for the Germans?"

"No."

"What work did you do?"

"I brought some letters to post."

"Who gave you the letters?"

"Bwana Rudolfu."

"How many times?"

"Once! Only once!"

"You are lying!"

"No!"

"What did you do with the letters?"

"I brought them here to the post office . . . except the one for Bwana Lenz in Mbuyuni. . . . I was carrying it in my pocket – Bwana Corbin took it."

"Tell us about Bwana Rudolfu."

"A German. What do I know of him?"

Did he wear a uniform? . . . did he have a dog? . . . how many servants? . . . did he work at home? . . . what time did he get up? . . . was he married? . . . did he visit women? Which women?

"Tell us about this Hamisi the Arab."

Hamisi was an exiled Arab from Sudan who had escaped a warrant for his arrest for seditious, or anti-British, activities. He had left behind a wife and two children. He was now a teacher and head of a Sufi mystical order in Moshi, where he had another wife and three children and received protection from the Germans.

"A teacher of Quran. A wife and three children. A kind man."

"And?"

The men were seated now.

Yes, Hamisi knew Bwana Rudolfu. They were friendly, had long talks late in the night. Sometimes they argued, especially when the Germans tried to force people to eat pig. Bwana Rudolfu went to Hamisi's for coffee at night . . . they were friendly, weren't the Arabs closer to the Europeans?

How old were the children? they wanted to know. How old were his pupils? . . . did he write letters? . . . did Pipa deliver them? . . . did he teach him? . . . what else did he teach besides the Quran?

And Pipa told them what he knew of Hamisi, the Arab who had befriended him.

The white man leaned forward and looked Pipa in the eye.

"Listen carefully, you. My name is Maynard. Call me Fisi – what?"

"Fisi," said Pipa nervously. Like a fisi, a hyena, he told himself, this giant stalks his prey at night . . .

"All right. From now on, you run your shop here. And you be my post office. My own post office. You. In the dead of night, in the shop – anytime – you will get letters for me. Parcels. The man who brings these will say to you, 'Bones for the Fisi.' And from time to time a man will come to you and say . . ."

He stood up and looked at his companions: "What – what will he say to this our post office?"

The Somali scratched his head.

"The Fisi needs bones to chew," said the Swahili.

"Right. He will say to you," the white man eyed Pipa once more, " 'The Fisi needs bones to chew.' And you will give him all you have for me. Ume elewa? Do you understand?"

"Yes."

"You will be paid."

"Yes."

"If you tell anyone about the Fisi . . ." Maynard took out a pistol. "Risasi. In the head. Ask these two how many of your tribe I have hanged in Mombasa."

Pipa was silent.

"Ask!"

"Eti, how many did this one hang?"

"Two. And shot many in Tanga. And killed one with his own hands, one who refused to obey," the Swahili man said. "This game is dangerous. It is war. Life has no value. We serve now King George."

"You heard," said Fisi. "Not one word to anyone. Not even to yourself. Or . . ." He turned to the Swahili man once more.

"The owl will hear you and carry your words away."

"A mshairi," said Fisi with a sardonic grin. "Poet."

12

His given name was Nurmohamed – Pipa was the nickname given to the family by the neighbourhood, and it had stuck. It made him feel a lack: of respectability, of a place that was truly home.

He was simply an Indian, a Mhindi, from Moshi, a town in the vicinity of Kilimanjaro whose masters were the Germans.

He did not know where he himself had been born or when, in any calendar, German, Arabic, or Indian. Of his father he remembered only a tall thin man with a scraggly beard, a kindly grin on his face as he pulled the boy's cheeks, saying "Dhaboo." His father had not died – Nurmohamed could not recall grief, a graveyard. His father had gone away, and the boy carried this knowledge within him like a hidden deformity. He remembered him as Dhaboo, and for years lived in the expectation that his father would return, that one day when he came home from play Dhaboo would be there waiting.

Of his mother he remembered the long rains in the wet season falling through the cracks in the thatch roof, himself standing with her, shivering in a pool of water, his sister holding his hand. Another scene: squatting in the latrine with his mother, watching a fast and furious stream hit the ground under her and joining with his own wavering little spurt. He had looked in vain at her darkness for a member corresponding to his own, had had his arm smacked for pointing his finger at that mysterious shadow.

She was beautiful, his mother. An oval face with smooth cheeks and pointed chin, eyes as big as plums. She had a smile in those days. Big haunches and warm breasts and a smell that was all things to him. She had strong legs, and a little swell in the belly, and she was the most mysterious and lovely thing in his life.

There had been many uncles. There was Fateh, the short, fair shopkeeper with a nervous grin and a patch of white hair at the back of his head, who always brought sweets. Morani, the tall, stern, squeaky-voiced teacher, whose large and bobbing Adam's apple was believed by boys to be a trapped almond seed. And others. He would watch them intently when they visited and they would toss a heller coin at him to make him go away, and his mother would shut the door with that look which gave the secret away when he was old enough to understand it. One of the last uncles was a Greek doctor, who became more or less regular and the others stopped coming. His mother then walked out with a little style, becoming a woman of substance. The Greek was an older man, long-faced and quiet, always in a suit. He came in the afternoon during siesta time when the town was quiet. Sometimes he would bring a bottle of soda. When he emerged from the house later, word of his presence would have spread and there would be women with children waiting outside with ailments to show. He was a kind man and listened to as many mothers as he could.

They lived in a Swahili section of town that had a lot of women and children and few men. His mother made the fried sweet vitumbua and the vermicelli tambi and the candy called gubiti – whatever suited her moods and needs – to sell to the neighbours.

The boy was big and thickset, and the nickname Pipa, meaning "barrel," described him so well that it became exclusively his. Boys teased him by running past and jeering "pip-pip-pip Pipa!"

One day, when he was fifteen, he threw a stone at the departing Greek and drew blood. His mother called him in and scolded him. He told her exactly what he thought of her, and, wounded by his insult, she struck him with a broom. He wrenched the object from her and pushed her back, sending her to the floor in surprise and fear. He was a burly youth with an angry glower for a world that did not want him.

If guilt, in subsequent months and years, came at all, it came not from his having raised a hand against his mother – that blow became the single act of violence that absolved her in his eyes, a punishment for her sin. Instead, he felt a vague sense of guilt at his inadequacy, at not being able to do anything with himself that would raise his mother and sister from degradation to Indian respectability.

Like many of the boys in Moshi, he made a few hellers carrying at the railway station, and like them became more adept and aggressive as he grew older, jostling and shouting and crowding around the two weekly trains on the Tanga-Moshi line. And like many a young man, one day he allowed a Tanga-bound train to take him in its third-class carriage to wherever it would. It was grey dusk when the train left the station, and for a long time he watched the grassland and mountains he was speeding past on wheels of iron, captive to the roaring rhythm of the fire-driven engine. And at dawn he woke up from a snooze to gaze in wonder at the dense vegetation, sandy soil, palm trees, women veiled in black buibui, men in kanzus and kofias: a different world. The languid, casual world of the coast, made more so by the early-morning hour at which he met it.

There was no mountain in sight, the heat was like a weight on the head, his language sounded halting and uncouth in this town where talking could be a profession, where the nuances of words were many and could be used to wound or caress, to litigate or to tease, to rebuke or to make a joke. But the town of Tanga was beautiful. There was the ocean you could walk up to or sit watching, as many did, looking away into the distance or at the ships or at the island across the harbour where prisoners were sent to be hanged. There were houses with verandahs and balconies, the white ones of stone near the water belonging to the Germans. And there were the gardens with shrubs and flowers, and the promenade along the shore where men and women walked in the afternoon, and on Sundays a band played.

He found a job as a sweeper in the big hotel called Kaiserhof on the promenade. The German ladies came for confections in the morning, in the afternoon the men came to drink beer. Like most others, he feared these people. He found them amazing, dressed in the brightest white, stiff and composed. The women looked clean and pure as angels, pink and fresh-eyed; and they left behind delightful odours of flowers and creams. He would clean under the tables and chairs after they had gone, sweeping away cigarette stubs and crumbs, scraps of paper. On rare but not impossible occasions they left something behind. Once he returned a wallet – not before removing one note from it, a modest one – and was rewarded.

From this sweeper's job he moved on to pulling a rickshaw, rented from an Indian. It was around the Kaiserhof that he operated, especially at nights when the Germans went to drink and dance and there was greater chance of a fat tip or a wallet dropped (which as always he would return, minus a note). The only hazard was that a rough ride, an unexpected bump, could earn an awful oath or even a cuff.

The ships in the harbour were many; cranes like huge tame giraffes serviced them. Numerous visitors were brought to the shore, numerous others boarded. They came from all sorts of places – Mombasa, Bombay, Zanzibar, Dar es Salaam, Beira, Aden, Hamburg – some of which he had heard of before, others never; but all sounding wonderful and far. They did not fall into any recognizable arrangement in his head, and for many years they remained arbitrarily situated for him, until he had a son, who one day showed him the world, on a map.

Then, after eight months in Tanga, convinced by an old harbour hand that it was in Dar es Salaam that the real life of all the young men began, where his own fortunes surely lay, he bought passage on an outbound steamer and let it take him farther yet from home.

Dar es Salaam was all that he had been promised it would be. As he alighted from the ship onto one of the boats which rowed the passengers ashore, beautiful white buildings of stone lay ahead of him, and a motorcar drove along the paved promenade. He saw in the distance a lone dark figure of a man standing high above the ground, and realized with wonderment that it was a statue on a pedestal. Behind this calm government section, through which he passed nervously, was the bustling Indian bazaar, its streets filled with people, donkeys, horses, and even cows and goats. Here, surely, was opportunity; yet how was he to go about finding it? Who was he in this town, who knew him? As he was to find out, you had to be *somebody*. Of his savings, only a little remained, and certainly not enough to go back home the way he had come.

For a few months he did a number of odd jobs, beginning at the harbour, where porters were always in demand. He lived in Swahili quarters then, in the African sector. One day he was spotted, working for a butcher, by an Indian shopkeeper who gave him a job minding his store, which was near the Shamsi mosque in the Indian sector. On his employer's recommendation he was given a place to sleep in a rest house up the street that catered to travellers and the homeless. Outside this hostel at night, the local shopkeepers ate roasted meat and maize and played cards. Pipa slept for a few days in a large room set aside for hopelessly depressed and demented men from the community. But when he'd been to the mosque – largely to pass some time, there being nothing else to do in the evenings – he was surprised to be rewarded with a bed amongst the more normal guests. People talked to him, asked him where he came from, realized he knew their language. They sent him to Sheth Samji, a respected rich merchant, who employed him.

Sheth Samji had a produce shop on Bagamoyo Road. Every day gunny sacks of husked, dried copra, from the coastal towns outside Dar, arrived at Sheth Samji's. It was Pipa's job first to weigh the copra as it arrived in the morning, then to take sackfuls to the back of the shop and throw chunks of it into the oil mill, and later to collect and skim the oil. Often in the afternoon he would sit before the blindfolded camel that drove the mill as it walked perpetually in circles – patient, doggedly persistent in the illusion that it had a destination – and he would feel a surge of pity for it. Where could the beast think it was going – did it see rewards at the end of its journey, did it hope to meet a mate, did it hope for happiness, children, old age? The journey would end for the day when Pipa removed the blindfold and untied the camel (whom he had named Bahdur, "Brave"). He would then skim the crud off the oil and pour it into cans and bottles and go out with a servant to sell it.

The moral of the camel's story, a preacher at the mosque once said, for the benefit of all those young men who had taken shelter under the community's wing, was that of a man who had lost his home, did not know where he was going. Pipa thought of home; wondered when he would save enough to be able to go back, and, if he did return, what he would do there. On the other hand, he could stay and settle in this town among this community that had adopted him.

Dar es Salaam was an important place. It was the residence of the German Governor. There were many Europeans, many officials, whom it was best to avoid. Visitors poured in from the harbour. Within minutes a street could be cleared to make way for a dignitary – on horse, in a motorcar or rickshaw, or even on foot. There were people – from the interior, mostly – who would go down on their knees in fear when a dignitary passed and humbly touch the ground with their heads lest they offend. In a place like this there were many rules and regulations, and a police force to see that they were obeyed. It mattered who you were, where you belonged: you were your tribe, caste, religion, community. Sheth Samji was a former mukhi and now a community elder. From his vantage point at the till in his store, he watched carefully the goings-on at the rest house across the way and near the mosque. Many a guest had been threatened with eviction and loss of job if observance, attendance in mosque, did not improve. There was rivalry among Indian communities, jealousy and enmity from the old country. Many a lonely young man had been compelled to change allegiance, many a willing young man duly rewarded with a bride and a business.

Whether he was of the Shamsi community or not, Pipa could not say with certainty. But like many others before him, he accepted the Shamsis, and the rewards that followed: a job and a place to stay; eminent men to vouch for him; and, if he wanted, a bride. So he could become the camel who at last stopped his endless journey and found a home.

But one day a strange thing happened that he would think of many years later as a call of fate. As he sat watching Bahdur the camel make its endless journey to nowhere, he heard the sound of a drum outside, apparently coming up the street, and a commotion of people. He went to look, peeping out through a side entrance. A noisy procession was approaching, accompanied as usual by boys and the town's layabouts. A man in trousers and

133

shirt was playing the instrument with a regular slow beat. When he reached the middle of the block, he broke into a smart tattoo and stopped, as did his followers all around him, and signalled with a nod to his partner, a man near him in kanzu, who made the announcement.

"Tunawataka wapagazi! Tunawataka wapagazi! Dar-Moro-Kilimanjaro, Dar-Moro-Kilimanjaro – andisheni, andisheni – O!"

A European expedition of missionaries, on a tour to inspect the interior, needed porters on the foot route north from Moro-goro to Kilimanjaro. The Dar-Moro train fare would be paid. A handsome daily wage was promised.

And Pipa, as twice before, succumbed to the temptation to take off, and signed up with the caravan. But this time, he told himself, he was going home. With the money he had saved, and the porter's wages he would earn, he would start his own life in Moshi.

Leaving home had been easy, not so the return.

Three hundred men in single file snaked through the forest, singing, a seventy-pound load on each head and carrying in addition a spear, a machete, or a club. They would sing vigorously at first, then lapse into a low resonating chorus, responding to whomever happened to be leading. They were divided into companies of fifteen men, to eat and sleep together, under a leader. Four companies formed a larger company. The leader of all the porters was a man called Livingstone. They would wake up before dawn, wash, attend to nature, pack, and after breakfast, as a drumbeat sounded a signal, they would set off with the rallying song of "Funga safari, funga safari!" Let's pack up and go, O let's pack up and go! Who says so? Who says so? It is the mzungu who says so! The jungle would be still wet with dew, the air still cool, and the sun barely peeping through the trees.

This was work for only the most seasoned porters, as most of the men were. They spoke fondly of the days before the rails came, when they went on long safaris that took months, and the white man was completely dependent upon them. But to Pipa each day seemed endless. How far, how long? he asked each morning, even as others sang lustily away. He had to push himself to keep up, for to lag behind could be dangerous. By noon, however, even the strongest and most experienced of the men would be quiet, nearing the end of their strength. With hearts pounding, necks straining, backs running with sweat, and throats parched, the porters, in broken formation now, would approach the campsite, where the advance party of the six Europeans and a few chosen men had arrived. Cooking would begin among the companies, and it was not until two or three that they ate. Afterwards, the Europeans, sitting under a tree or beside a bush or a rock, would read from the Bible to a small gathering of the porters, as others attended to their own needs. Then gradually preparations for the evening meal would begin.

A dozen campfires would start, cooking meat, maize, cassava; around them men would be singing, shouting, playing bao or cards, smoking tobacco, telling stories and riddles, meeting to discuss the next day's route. After the meal the drum would sound, and gradually the campsite turned quiet and there would remain only the sound of the night forest – the chorus of insects, the hoot of an owl, the roar or grunt of an animal – and the occasional dry cough of a watchman, the moan of a worn-out porter.

The Europeans had separate tents. The chief among them, called Bwana Turner, was a big towering man with a fierce-looking curved moustache and fiery green eyes. He and the head porter, Livingstone, went back a long way, had travelled much together – from the coast up to Uganda several times before the railways were built. Livingstone was a short man with muscular limbs. The rumour among the men was that his hair was actually white – a sure sign that the days of the porter were numbered – but he blackened it using a concoction supplied by the chief bwana.

There were incidents on the way. Twice they were attacked by robbers; in each case the last man in the file had been speared, once fatally, and his load stolen. Once, caught between two steep cliffs, they were pelted with a rain of stones, which ceased only when Livingstone fired a few shots from his gun. Two snakebites were treated by one of the white men. A man was thrashed for insubordination. And a few porters deserted.

After twenty-nine days they entered Moshi.

"Hiyo mama, hiyo mama! . . ." Singing at the top of their voices like a triumphant army, Livingstone's porters arrived in the town. "Hiyo mama, tuna rudi!" Here we return, Mother. And the town treated them royally for the money they would spend. Shops brightened up, fruit sellers opened up on the streets, coffee sellers came by clinking their cups. In the evening the hosts roasted meat and cassava and maize for the travellers, the air filled with smells of woodsmoke and sizzling fat, perfume and local brew, curry and dried fish.

On an open ground the missionaries had set up a tent, outside of which was placed a table, and here they paid off their porters. The men queued up and one at a time said their names before the chief bwana, who sat at the table and ticked them off against a list as Livingstone, sitting next to him, paid the money. With a final, farewell salute they then turned and went away.

It was early yet, after the farewells. The men had been given tea, and Pipa was on his way, thinking of how he would start his new life in Moshi. He walked jauntily through the idle, chatting groups of discharged porters, feeling confident, resourceful, and impatient to begin.

"Weh, Pipa! Fatso, what will you do?"

"I'll open a shop, you mother's cunt!"

The questioner ran after him and Pipa dodged.

The tent at which he had been paid was open, now only a folding chair stood outside it. Pipa took a quick peep inside, saw no one, passed by the chair and noticed a valise on it. Swiftly he looked around him, then swooped up the valise. But two steps on his way, a voice, a very English voice, said loudly:

"Weh mwivi – you thief! Simama! Halt!"

He was pinned to the ground by Livingstone's lieutenants, and it seemed a mountain of men fell upon him. The valise was extracted from his hands by someone and passed on towards its owner, who stood stiffly away from the crowd.

– What is it – what is it – nini?

– The bwana's case.

– What's in it?

– Kitabu! A book!

– Only a book!

– The same book in which Bwana Turner writes carefully every night by the light of a lamp.

In the rush of hands, somehow the book – a diary – had come out of the valise, which itself quickly found its way to its owner's hands. The wondrous object, the book, lingered a while among the crowd until the last person had fingered it and taken a peep at the writing inside before delivering it respectfully with both hands to the missionary.

When Pipa got up he thought his back was broken. Why had those sons of dogs jumped on him? he wondered. What would these white bwanas give them? As if *they'd* never pinched a thing in their lives.

"Come here," the missionary said sternly, holding the book and the valise under one arm. "What is your name?"

"Pipa, bwana."

"Do you know the punishment for stealing?"

Khamsa-ishrin, the young man thought with dread, twenty-five strokes of the whip, pain and humiliation – the German punishment. Is this why I returned home?

"Mercy, bwana. I will not do it again . . ."

A German officer, having heard the ruckus, was approaching. Perhaps he had been fetched. All eyes turned towards him.

"Leave the boy to me, bwana," said Livingstone quickly to his boss. "He is my responsibility."

And Livingstone, pulling Pipa by the ear, took him aside and slapped him a few times on the face, saying, "You fool, you barbarian. Of which mother were you born . . . do you know the German could have your hands cut off!"

The German and the missionary walked away together. And the men who had watched the spectacle said, This old Livingstone may dye his hair, but what a man of the people. Weh, Pipa, go home now, open your shop, Indian. You are a lucky man.

When Pipa returned to Moshi it was January 1913, and, looking around, he knew this was no longer home. It had been twenty-two months since he left. But now he had the experience of a world inside him. What did this place amount to beside Tanga with its Kaiserhof, or Dar with its Government House, its monuments, its teeming streets, and visitors arriving daily from the ends of the earth? Where were the likes of Sheth Samji, who with a click of the fingers could command a community, to whom even the Germans paid respect? There was money in those places, opportunities to be grabbed, status to be bought. But he was here, in Moshi, and this was where he would start. The camel had opened his eyes, and he was home. And in the process of regaining his sight, he thought somewhat ruefully, he had almost lost his two hands.

His mother shared rooms, now, in a ramshackle house. She looked older and heavier. Her hair was greying, her hands, her feet, looked coarse. She had let herself go. The Greek doctor had left town and she now cooked for an Indian man and did some housework for him. His sister, Zaynab, had gone away with a merchant.

A sheet of torn tent canvas held up by poles was the first Pipa Store, selling cigarettes, matches, oil, tea, spices, and sugar.

There was an influential man in town called Hamisi the Arab. He had come from up north, Sudan. A tall and fair-skinned man of good looks, he always wore khaki trousers and tunic, over which he had a fine white cotton kanzu, and on his balding head would be a white Swahili kofia embroidered with light brown. He ran a noisy Quran-reading school every afternoon in his home, from where the alif-beh-teh chants of the boys rang out into the street. Three of the boys were his own. He was friendly with the commandant, Bwana Rudolfu, and it was rumoured that either he spoke German or the commandant spoke Arabic, or both. On Thursday nights the Karimiya Sufi order met in open secret – not just anybody could go – on the second floor of a prominent local building to discuss hadiths and whisper holy syllables. Hamisi would take the commandant to these meetings. There were many things whispered about the Sufis, including the wisdom of not engaging in whispers about them. The young men among them were particularly fierce – they took to the streets in their kanzus on Friday afternoons, when they wore green fezzes on their heads.

One day Hamisi stopped at Pipa's shop and asked if the young man could get him some English pipe tobacco. He spoke in a gentle, kindly voice; his manner was unassuming. Pipa, quite taken aback at his presence, said, Yes, bwana, I will get it for you. Hamisi's custom at Pipa's became regular after that. He would stop to chat after buying his tobacco or matches or sugar – a serious man yet friendly, with a distracted smile.

Pipa took pride in this friendship. It was a sign of his acceptance as a respectable even though young businessman of the town. With the benefit of this new patronage and its influence, his business increased. Every Friday Pipa sent a bag of dates to the Arab as a token of his appreciation. To demonstrate his newfound dignity he did not move into better accommodations – that would have been expensive and foolish – but instead enabled his mother to buy better clothes, to walk proudly in the streets; and he took her to the Shamsi mosque. As he had learned in Dar, you had to belong somewhere, have a people. Even Hamisi the Arab had inquired of him one day: "Who are your people?" And Pipa had had to hum and haw before saying, "The Shamsis." After all, it was the Shamsis who had adopted him in Dar, taught him the tale of the blind camel and what could be learned from it. Hamisi had been satisfied. And so Pipa accepted, once more, this fraternity, whose network extended into towns small and large among the shopkeeper communities, each praying to the same God in the same fashion as their forefathers, scratching out an existence and future in Africa. Their chants and prayers sounded less foreign to him than to his mother, who dismissed all questions about her past, her origins, any people she might have had. They went regularly, every day, to the mosque at the edge of the Indian quarter, one half of a building owned by the local mukhi. It was a small community and it embraced them warmly. His previous reputation as a ruffian became an asset, because the mukhi in the town, Jaffer Bhai, lived in slight but real fear of assassins after the recent murder of a mukhi in a small coastal town.

Naturally, the question of the young man's marriage arose, was quickly taken up by the community, for which he was grateful. Moshi had no eligible girls except for the two daughters of the mukhi, both young, and anyway reserved for the prestige of larger towns. But mukhis have connections, too, and this one put his to use almost immediately.

One Friday night Jaffer Bhai detained his congregation, as he was wont to do for special announcements. All those who could moved backwards or sideways to find a wall to rest their backs against. When it came time for the mukhi's announcements, the men would crack jokes and the women would get impatient. The mukhi was known for his impractical schemes and a tendency to lecture.

On this occasion, he stressed the great benefits for those living in the towns of Kilimanjaro to co-operate with each other. There were matters of trade, obviously, and employment of new or younger people and — he paused significantly — marriages and so on. As well, information could be exchanged regarding the methods of the governments on either side of the border. He announced a goodwill mission to Kikono, a new but growing town in the British area, whose own mukhi, Jamali, he knew to be a good man. He called for a delegation. Two men volunteered.

"How about you?" Jaffer turned to Pipa. "Would you like to explore opportunities there?"

The young man, not used to such niceties, blurted, "For how long? Is the town far?"

But, as the jolly Jaffer Bhai later explained to Pipa, "You naïve oaf! The mission's specially for you! There's a girl I want to show you in Kikono." Which was what the young man was waiting to hear.

One July morning Jaffer and his three community brothers joined a group travelling to the Church Missionary Society station in Taveta. They spent the night at the border town and early the next morning set off for Kikono, arriving late in the afternoon of the following day. They were greeted like high dignitaries, escorted into town, and fed at a communal feast that had been prepared for their arrival.

The next evening, after prayers had been said, and as the congregation sat around in the mosque, the local mukhi, Jamali, gave a long welcoming speech and stressed the need for co-operation among neighbouring towns in much the same way that Jaffer had done in Moshi. Pipa looked furtively towards the women's section. Jaffer had told him to watch out for the girl but had not described her. Pipa met one or two hostile looks and turned away, yet he thought he had caught sight of her, the girl who had been selected for him by his elders. She had a narrow face and longish nose, looked a little lost, just as he imagined he himself did. But she was pretty, he liked her, and his heart was full of excitement and hope. Then all kinds of apprehensions crossed his mind – would she approve? would her family approve? what would they demand from him? He did not even know what the custom was – and what if she did not approve of him: there were not that many girls around. . . . Mombasa had been hinted as a possible source; there was a Swahili girl in Moshi, daughter of one of his mother's friends.

He yearned for the stability of a home, the embrace and warmth of a marriage bed; he hoped he would make a good father. Marriage put a successful end to youth: the religion proclaimed that, the community acknowledged that. With marriage you were finally accepted: the women came and talked to you, called you "bhai" – brother – and men treated you as one of them.

Later that night, as the women danced a garba, the Kikono mukhi, Jamali, pointed out the girl and Jaffer Bhai's eyes lighted up in satisfaction as if he would marry her himself.

"Well? What do you say?" asked Jamali.

"Well?" Jaffer Bhai turned to Pipa.

"Well . . ." was all he could muster.

The older men laughed. "He's fallen. We'll take the proposal."

Pipa was told that the girl's name was Mariamu. She was

Jamali's niece, and the proposal, to the girl's parents, was a formality. An engagement was confirmed in Jamali's house, where sherbet was served to the small Moshi delegation.

Pipa had, of course, not yet met the girl. Now at this ceremony his eyes met hers, briefly. There was hope in hers, an acceptance, perhaps a plea. His eyes lingered on her as she turned away. Had she found them sympathetic?

Jaffer Bhai and Pipa with their two other townsmen went home after an excursion to Mombasa, where they bought goods to take with them to sell. Items of glass and perfumes were in great demand, and khangas of the newest fashions, inscribed with a current proverb or riddle, for which women fought and clamoured in the shops. And of course they took dried fruit and halva for presents. From Mombasa they took the ship to Tanga, thence a train to Moshi. Their profits would pay for their journey and more.

"Don't you think you should go to Kikono?" Jaffer Bhai said to Pipa.

Three months had passed since the engagement, when it had been agreed that a wedding date would be suggested by the bride's people, but there had been as yet no word from Kikono. Instead, they had heard once through the grapevine that the girl had been unwell.

It was Friday night, the young man and his mother were guests at the mukhi's. They sat with their host and his family outside the store, a lantern producing a dim glow around them and throwing flickering shadows on the ground. A girl sat at the open doorway.

"Have you heard from them, then?" said Pipa in response to Jaffer's question.

"No. But you should use this occasion to go."

The occasion was the October "happiness" to celebrate the community's founding in India.

"Go and find out what the matter is. If the girl is sick you should know. If not, what is holding up the wedding?"

"Will you come with me?" asked Pipa.

"No," Jaffer said. "I can't. But be a man and go by yourself. Tell them you bring greetings and presents for the festival, and you've heard that the girl has been unwell. They'll understand. And don't come back without fixing the wedding date – remember, insist on it."

Pipa said he would go. He exchanged a glance with his mother, who had finally looked up. Without any real status in the community, she had no say in this matter.

Hadn't he picked a date only to be told that they, his spiritual guardians and worldly fathers, would tell him when? But Jaffer Bhai had forgotten all that. "You'd better take charge, friend. There are all sorts of young men looking for pretty wives who might beat you to it."

"There's a group leaving tomorrow night for Taveta," Jaffer said. "Go with them. And Hamisi has been asking about you – he has an errand for you. I told him you are a good boy, with a bride waiting under a mbuyu tree."

The following afternoon Hamisi the Arab came round to Pipa's shop.

"Ah Biba, how are you?"

"Marhaba, marhaba, sheikh."

After placing his order, Hamisi said, "Your imam says you are travelling to the British side."

"Yes, bwana."

"Bwana Rudolfu has an errand for you. If you do it he'll reward you."

Hamisi's eyes met Pipa's briefly. The implication of his message was clear. Bwana Rudolfu was the German commandant of Moshi. Pipa had no choice but to go and see him.

The commandant was a short rotund man in khakis, with close-cropped hair and a light beard. He looked kindly and spoke softly, but you never judged a German by appearance.

"Ah, Mohmet," he said, standing up, putting his hands to his hips. "You are going to Kikono, I hear. An auspicious visit."

Pipa stood and muttered something.

"I want you to do something for me, Mohmet."

"Yes, bwana."

"Listen. They have a good postal service there. I want you to post these letters in Kikono. From there to Voi to Mombasa – and, fut! – to the world. To India, to your homeland. Also, give this to Bwana Lenz by hand – in Mbuyuni. You will be paid for your trouble."

Pipa took the bag of letters that was given him. Why should the Germans trust him with important letters? The thought of emptying the sack in a bush somewhere – a latrine perhaps – occurred to him. But they'd find out and have the hide off him.

On his way out he paused to look at the bundle of money Bwana Rudolfu had given him. They were used but crisp notes, like the ones he would pick up at the Kaiserhof in Tanga. These were not the smelly pieces of limp, moist paper that had seen tobacco boxes and armpits and bosoms and farmers' hands and whatnot. As he fingered and counted the money, he could not believe the amount and wondered if there was a mistake. Forty rupees! He should check. He could have received the wrong bundle of notes. Perhaps the German was testing him. Ruefully he walked back and told the commandant, "Bwana. You made a mistake." He showed the notes.

"No, no." The commandant raised a benevolent hand. "The government pays handsomely those whom it chooses. Go, now."

"Those letters," Pipa told his wife ten months later, "are what got me into this trouble, why Fisi now has me in his clutches."

She was quiet.

"One day you will tell me all about yourself," he said.

She looked away, deferential, shy, quiet. To him she would always be a mystery.

ᗡᗣ

The morning after Pipa was visited by the Englishman Maynard and his two henchmen, the Swahili, called Shomari, came over.

"Weh, Fatso, you are wanted."

"By whom?" Pipa asked sullenly.

"You have forgotten already? By the one who chews bones."

"You have been conscripted, my friend," said Shomari. "You are not free. Nobody is free in this war." As they approached the ADC's house, Fumfratti the albino was leaving it. He looked briefly at Pipa when they passed him, then strode off down the hill. Under the tree outside his house, Corbin was addressing the town businessmen. Pipa had already learned that the ADC was leaving town due to the war. Corbin was seated on a chair, using both hands to make a point, as his audience sat patiently on the ground listening.

Maynard was sitting at the table in the main room of the ADC's residence. In front of him were some papers, a pen, a box, and some keys. Close to the door stood an askari.

"Bwana," said Shomari.

Maynard looked up. He had been reading a pamphlet that had appeared recently in town. "Ah . . . yes. The Indian from town. My post office."

"Tell me," Maynard said to Pipa, "have you seen a paper – a gazeti – like this one before?"

"Like this one – yes – my wife brought it from the mukhi's house."

"Do you know what it says?"

"'The Imam of Istanbul says –'"

"So you can read!"

146

"No, bwana. My wife —"

"She can read!"

"No, bwana."

"No one can read, yet the whole town knows what this paper says."

The pamphlets had appeared that morning, bearing an anti-British message. But that was not Maynard's main concern with Pipa.

"Do you remember what you were told last night?" he said in a low, even voice.

"Yes, bwana."

"Do you have any questions?"

"No. But —"

"Baas, then. You do as you were told, and everything will be all right. We are all required to play our part. Sawa sawa?"

"Sawa sawa, bwana."

"And don't open your mouth, or —"

"The owl will hear you," said Shomari, finishing his sentence.

He was given ten rupees, made to sign for them, and dismissed.

On his way out, as he stepped onto the verandah, he saw the ADC was now on his feet outside, bidding farewell to the businessmen. The mzungu was all dressed up that day, in sparkling white tunic, trousers, and sun helmet. As Pipa watched, a boy gave a present to the ADC, who bowed and shook hands. Pipa looked away, proceeding to leave, when he saw a chair beside the doorway, pulled back against the wall. On it lay a book.

He could never tell how long he stood there looking at it, tempted by it. That whole moment could have been a dream, but he knew it wasn't. The book was lying closed. Beside it was a pen. The cover was yellow with red and black print on it. It was where the ADC had left it before going to meet the delegation of businessmen waiting for him outside under the tree. That it was Bwana Corbin's, Pipa had no doubt. It was the kind the old men, the wazees, called the book of secrets. He recalled the occasion before when, foolish and inexperienced, he had swiped a missionary's valise that had contained a similar book. He heard clearly in his head that voice . . . halt! No, he turned away, he would not take the book.

On his way home he met Mariamu and the mukhi's wife, Khanoum, walking towards the ADC's house.

"Where were you?" Mariamu asked.

"Oh," he said, giving her a quick but mild look of reproach for putting him on the spot, "that mzungu Maynard was asking about the pamphlet – it's come from the German side, Moshi. The sooner this war is over the better," he muttered. "And where are you two off to?" he asked her.

This time Mariamu was on the spot. She turned to Khanoum, who said, "Some of her things are still at Bwana Corbin's house, from when she worked there."

"Yes, go then," Pipa said, curbing the old anger erupting again at the thought of the mzungu with his wife. But, he thought approvingly, how like sisters the two women are, though one is an African and the other an Indian.

Back in his shop, at the till, he could not help thinking of the ADC's diary he had seen. If he had taken it he would have stolen something personal and mysterious – in an unreadable hand, a foreign tongue. But long before, he had been cured of stealing.

A little later that morning, he saw Maynard and Fumfratti come down the hill and head towards the Taveta road, where Fumfratti's men always prowled around looking for enemy patrols. Shortly afterwards the ADC took off, leaving Kikono with an entourage of askaris and porters, the dog Bwana Tim, and five mules.

So much for Corbin, Pipa thought. He need not enter our lives again.

≈

How do the little people fare in a war between big powers? In answer, the Swahili proverb says, "When two elephants fight, it is the grass that suffers."

To the religious, the wise have always said, "Pray wisely." Even in the best of times, prayer can be a mistake. In a war, the wrong prayer can be deadly. It is not only the Omniscient who listens — who might tune in only too well this time and grant the petition, so that you have only yourself to blame for the ultimate disaster — there are government agents and spies, too, who listen in. Jamali's followers in Kikono began simply enough in the first days of the war. "O, Lord," they beseeched in their best Hindu–Muslim fashion twice a day in their mosque, "O, husband of the earth and master of the fourteen directions, give success to the efforts of our wise and just government." But was this a wise prayer?

As if in answer, pamphlets appeared from across the border, sowing seeds of doubt and discord. "O, Muslims!" exhorted in them the Grand Imam of Istanbul. "O, brothers! The government of the Kaiser is our true ally! Pray for his victory and rise against your Ingleez oppressors! And verily, Allah will protect you from the unbelievers . . ." And though this was the first time the Shamsis of Kikono had heard of the Grand Imam of Istanbul, they wondered if they had not been too hasty. For the flyer to be distributed right under the noses of the British was itself an impressive achievement. The English agent Maynard questioned a dozen people. They all shrugged their shoulders: I found it with the sweepings; so-and-so showed it to me; a young man brought it and asked if I could read it to him; no, I don't know the young man. The young man could not be found, but he had entered several stores.

"Those who believe do battle for the cause of Allah; and those who disbelieve do battle for the cause of idols. Fight the minions of the devil," said a short message in Arabic from the Sufis of Moshi across the border, on little scraps of paper handed from person to person. A Quranic verse, explained the local skeikh, a message from God to the oppressed. Copies were scarce and in demand, were used to make charms. The Englishman Maynard was not around this time to ask questions.

At the Shamsi Indian mosque they began to wonder, too, what victory their brethren on the other side – Jaffer Bhai, the mukhi of Moshi, and his congregation – were praying for.

For the pragmatic there were tales of British defeats – surely one should pray for the winning side? Taveta had been taken within days of the outbreak of war, and their own ADC had retreated, unable to defend the town. There were rumours of Mombasa's imminent fall: Kisii, near Lake Victoria, had been taken. The German man-of-war *Königsberg* prowled the ocean from Lamu to Kilwa with its fearsome guns, appearing like a spectre in the mist and destroying British warships. The terrible German demoness Bibi Malkia went around with a troop of her own, appearing from behind hills and trees to wreak havoc on British forces, leaving hacked, mangled bodies behind, especially of the white settler troops. To top it all, there came pictures of the shameful British defeat at Tanga . . .

Three months after the outbreak of war, in November, a convoy of ships of the British army, called the Indian Expeditionary Force B, arrived full of confidence straight from India. Their objective was to begin the British takeover of the German colony at Tanga. It was early in the morning, and the Germans seemed to be in their beds when the British landed their troops. "Chalo! Maro! Tally-ho!" the British sirdars rallied their Indian men. But when the Punjabis, the Rajputs, and the Madrasis ran forward, bayonets fixed, they were set upon – not by African askaris, but by bees. In panic the Indians retreated; their British officers pushed them back, sometimes at gunpoint. Only after the Tanga killer bees had done their work did the German side, well prepared, start firing. It was a rout.

A few copies of German newspapers found their way into

Kikono – no one any longer cared how – with pictures of captured British officers, masking their faces with their hands; dead Indian soldiers piled on the Tanga beach; and German officers proudly posed with an oversized captured Union Jack.

Two Indians, it was heard, were hanged in Mombasa for signalling at night to the *Königsberg*.

With all this news, and more arriving every day, Jamali, the mukhi of Kikono, very prudently introduced in his mosque a neutral prayer for peace and guidance in the region.

His people had waited for word to leave – for Mombasa, for Voi. But stories of the near-siege of Mombasa, its evacuations, were discouraging; and Voi was more dangerous because it was the railway that the Germans were after. A German troop could come to your door in the middle of the night demanding shelter and information. And the next day soldiers from the King's African Rifles would come and beat you up for assisting the enemy. And so it was, right in the middle, between two warring sides, that the Shamsis of Kikono sat trapped and waiting with prayers in their mouths. Soon it became too late even to think of moving, as the area around them became a hunting ground for the marauding patrols of either side; it was only a matter of time before one of them set up camp in their town.

Jamali's neutral prayer was a wise one. One day, well into the first year of the war, a large German force raided and dispersed an advance camp of the British motorcycle unit at Mbuyuni, only ten miles away from Kikono, and set up a post there.

For Jamali and his people there was now no hope of evacuation from the town. They would have to wait out the war.

13

Mali kwa mali, mali kwa mali
nguo kwa mwili, risasi kwa bunduki
nipe suruali, mustini, khanga, mabuti
nikupe kisu, bunduki, mshale, na kuki
risasi kwa bunduki, mifupa kwa Fisi.

A pedlar in dirty kanzu and a cap that lies aslant, mouth running constantly with talk, brings his donkey-driven cart to a halt in front of the shops of Kikono. Doing his rounds from Voi to Taveta, he brings items ranging from the ordinary but necessary to the unusual and useless which the war is already beginning to disgorge. It is a wonder, they say wherever he goes, that his donkey has not been commandeered yet. The animal looks strong and is understandably dusty – as is its master, a veteran trader in the area. He sits on a tree stump, removes his sand-filled boots and empties them, orders a cup of tea and a pail of water brought from Baruti's tea shack, and begins to dispense the latest war commentary: "A station master in Ngozi killed . . . the Somali scouts of Bwana Cole mutinied . . . one man whipped, mutiny quelled . . . trouble in Giriyama . . . a railway line will be laid from Voi to Taveta . . . workers sign up . . . a new general arrived . . . a warning from the government: don't place food offerings for Bibi Malkia . . ." And then, suddenly, as if remembering, he begins his call:

> Goods for your goods, goods for your goods
> clothes for the body, bullets for the gun
> give me trousers, mess tin, khanga, and boots
> take away knife, gun, shield, and spear
> bullets for the gun . . .

Only when he reaches the last, discordant phrase *bones for the Fisi* does Pipa, watching anxiously from his shop, know for certain that the mali – the pedlar – calls for him today, comes from the dreaded Englishman Maynard.

Pipa Store of Kikono was a small provision store. It was here that the legend of the thrift and cunning of Nurmohamed Pipa first took hold. Sitting at his shopfront all day, patiently wrapping packets, dealing with customers one by one, taking in just a few hellers or paisa at a time. And one couldn't help noticing that the unfortunate young man seemed finally to have attracted baraka, blessings. Business at his store was brisk.

But some of the customers were fraudulent, as Pipa could have told them. Some came bearing cigarette tins and bundles tied with string, saying "Bwana Pipa, bones for the Fisi." Expertly, the burly shopkeeper in singlet would extend the long-handled tray to take their offerings and hand out something in return. "Thank you so much," the customer would say and walk away – the weary householder, the man about town, the idler, the traveller. Some of these messengers Pipa would see in town (but he avoided them); others simply passed through and disappeared, and he never saw them again.

At night when the town became quiet, with fires burning here and there and people gathered around them to talk in murmurs (Bwana Tim the dog, gone with the ADC, was always missed at this hour), while his wife worked in the kitchen which was a shed in the backyard, Pipa would bring in the day's takings for the Fisi – the tins, the bundles – and examine them. Much of what he received, he was sure, was rubbish, picked up on the road by those on Maynard's payroll. But then there were those other items that had the reek of authenticity about them, the look of having travelled far. He could tell even before they were in his hands by the manner and look of the messenger, the manner in which something was handed to him – and such messengers never stayed around. There were the photographs, newspaper cuttings, scraps of paper with writing, maps, sketches, all crumpled, stained, smelly from the numerous hands, the hiding places. And even among these, there were one or two special ones, scraps of paper with a peculiarity all their own: used, written on, encrusted with brown dirt, they had the revolting odour of human shit.

"Does the Fisi need shit to smell?" he asked of a messenger once, sardonically.

"Ehe," affirmed the old man who had brought the goods that time, "they bear the mark of German arses!"

Encrusted in foul dirt, and hiding the secrets of an enemy army, these bits of information would be sniffed at by Maynard, the Fisi – what an apt name, because the hyena is also an indiscriminate scavenger – who would piece together a truth, a story, the secrets of the enemy.

There was a strange intimacy about these scraps of paper. What manner of man had used this one he was looking at? A part of this German was being transported in baskets, pockets, and saddlebags, in bundles and kerosene cans, for the perusal of the Englishman.

He had formed a fair idea of his place in the information chain into which he had been coerced, leading from the German command to Maynard's eyes (and nose). The messengers who brought him "bones for the Fisi" were under the charge of the albino Fumfratti, and brought them straight from agents in Moshi or Taveta, or simply bought them at the busy Taveta market – or, as he suspected, sometimes picked them off the roads or the nearby rubbish dumps. Pipa collected these scraps and bits and, in a bag or large can, handed them over to the mali-kwa-mali pedlar who came to call. And from the mali-kwa-mali through unknown intermediaries they reached the Englishman.

Ten rupees a week was Pipa's token recompense for handling this dirt. At first he had felt burdened by this responsibility, awed to be participating in the waging of a war. But as the war progressed he became cynical about it, and he hoped whoever won would leave him alone. Or that they would knock each other senseless, and finally go away to their own countries, with their streets of glass and perfumed air.

The naval debacle in Tanga showed the British that the German side was no pushover. Their confidence checked, they bided their time – replacing generals, gathering forces, acting only to counter German forays into their colony and attacks upon its railway.

Finally, after months of waiting, the British army began to stir, like a lion after a snooze. With its forces amassed from colonies around the world, it began coming down from Voi on its way to Taveta to engage the enemy, and thence to advance south to German East.

The Taveta road from Voi was upgraded. Army brass from Mombasa and Nairobi appeared in open-roofed motorcars, surveying the desert terrain with binoculars. Lorries brought supplies, men; motorcycles carried messages. Close to the road, work began on constructing the railway that would take the forces west into the German colony. Hundreds of Kamba and

Taita men from the area worked alongside sappers from the Indian army, cutting bush, blowing up rock, laying tracks – a few hundred yards every day – until they reached Maktau and faced the German post twelve miles away at Mbuyuni. And one afternoon a wonderful sight in the sky: eyes trailed the droning dot for miles, pointing fingers converged on that speck in the sky, which approached and grew larger, creating a frightening racket, so that it seemed it would crash upon them with the man in it, but the airplane – the flying ship – simply dropped leaflets, turned around, and flew back. If there was anything to doubt the abilities, the akili, the might of the mzungus, this disproved it once and for all. There were of course those who had said this when they saw the first train approaching with steel and fire, or heard the murderous stutter of the machine-gun. The mzungu was truly mighty. But then there were also the old men sitting outside mosques, throwing curses at the object in the sky and at its makers: Eti, if He meant for man to fly, would He not have given him wings? Shetani, these white men – King Solomon's djinns – very clever, but. The leaflets raining on the earth announced the sinking of the dreaded German warship *Königsberg*, and contained exhortations for the British side from the Aga Khan and the Sultan of Zanzibar. It was now July 1915.

Three months earlier, Mariamu had given birth to a boy, and it seemed then that Pipa was being ridiculed again, for the child was fair and had grey eyes. Which didn't prove anything against his fatherhood, as the mukhi, who was the boy's great-uncle, said. But would he ever know if it was otherwise? Would he, Pipa, ever be certain? The child was called Akber Ali, Aku for short.

One evening a company of soldiers arrived in single file in Kikono. Such expeditions of dusty, exhausted, hoarse-voiced askaris were not unusual, but this time there was a difference: the

156

soldiers were from the German side. The townsfolk quietly shut their doors, fastened their windows, silenced their children. If you strained your ears you could hear the clank of steel not far away at the British army work-camps – yet the Germans seemed to move about at will. How could they be losing? There came sounds of the men singing where they had set up camp. Then two shots were fired, followed by shouts – someone caught sneaking off in search of British patrols. In the long unnatural silence that ensued came the faint smell of woodsmoke. But something had to happen, something dangerous was portended for the night. At last it happened. A tremendous explosion, then stillness, then the delayed rattle of utensils, vibrating doors and windows. Finally, distant sporadic gunshots.

Then silence once more, a silence pervaded by fear. It was two in the morning, and the people of the town tried to sleep as best as they could.

At four the mukhi stirred on his mat. He listened for sounds, but none came that concerned him. Not without fear he opened his door, looked out. There was no sign of life: but that could mean anything. "Rakh Molate," he murmured, Leave it to God. He brought out a lamp, turned the wick up, went out to wake up his congregation. He saw no sign of the night's visitors.

At a little past five, as they began to emerge from the mosque, there was already some commotion to greet them – there was news that the supply dump at the railway depot near Maktau had been blown up. An Indian watchman and some soldiers had been killed, and the British were searching for those who had betrayed them to the Germans.

"Mali kwa mali . . ."

One day the pedlar – the mali – Abdalla was his name, arrived in Mbuyuni from Kikono. It was ten in the morning. As soon as he stopped outside the town's refreshment store, ordering water for his donkey and ginger tea for himself, a German captain and a band of askaris walked up to him, surrounded him, watched him arrogantly. Abdalla looked at them, but he did not lose his humour. He was of that age at which an air of advanced self-respect — like that of a Muslim sheikh — attaches itself to certain men. He was also nervous. He cracked a joke and took a sip of his tea.

At once the German captain gave Abdalla a slap, sending the old man reeling, the contents of his cup flying out, his finger still wrapped round its handle. He was arrested.

In Kikono, Jamali hastened to Pipa's shop. "Aré, hide anything suspicious — your Abdalla's been arrested."

"Who . . . by whom?"

"The Germans in Mbuyuni. You and your secret games —"

"As if I had a choice. How did you know?"

"I am the mukhi, I know everything here," said Jamali. "Let's worry about you first."

Both agreed there was not much to do but keep their eyes and ears open. The new railway line was approaching Mbuyuni fast, bringing a large British force, and the Germans were bound to evacuate. Pray the Germans did not take it into their heads to retreat to Kikono first.

About two weeks later Jamali came over again to Pipa's shop.

"A letter from Moshi . . . we, too, have ways to send messages in this war," he said, answering the look on Pipa's face. "It has something of interest to you, listen."

He sat down, unfolded the letter, and read:

"'God grant Jamali Mukhi . . . etc., etc. . . .

"'Pipa's mother has left Moshi, with a man who has agreed to take care of her. Look after Pipa, who is a younger brother to us, and tell him not to worry about his mother. The man is good . . .

"'But this week we have been truly shocked. Hamisi, a kindly Arab sheikh and a very good friend of our community, was hanged by the Germans for spying for the British side. All went to see the hanging and grieved for him. Who knows what the truth is? Please give this news also to Pipa, who knew Hamisi well. Also congratulations and prayers for the birth of his son and heir. God grant . . .

"'As we agreed before, my brother, it is best for people like us to keep a low profile and out of the way . . .'"

Jamali looked up. "You should be careful. We all should be careful. These are treacherous times. There is no telling who works for whom." Jamali waited, looked pointedly at the young man, then said, "News of your mother doesn't surprise you?"

"No . . ." Pipa murmured. "She had to go wherever she found security – and with me here . . . what could she do?"

But Pipa was stunned by the news of Hamisi's execution. So the war could touch someone like himself, directly. Hamisi, his friend and patron, was dead; hanged by those same Germans whose secret papers he, Pipa, had received, handled, and then passed on to Maynard. Hamisi – working for Maynard? How could that be, when he had been so clearly the German commandant's friend? Would Hamisi have betrayed his friend? Pipa remembered that it was Hamisi who had sent him to see the commandant, whose letters he agreed to take with him to Kikono. It was these letters that had involved Pipa in all this trouble. Hamisi had been no innocent, then. Had he known all along he would be placing Pipa in danger?

What made these people act in such ways that they could not even trust each other? Their motives, like their war, were incomprehensible to him.

He stepped out of the shop for some air and walked over to Baruti's tea shack. There he found that the news of Hamisi's demise was known to everyone. An Arab sheikh, they were saying, a Sufi, had been hanged by the Germans.

"Eti," he said, "did Hamisi really work for the British?"

They laughed. You are naive, Pipa. Didn't your mukhi tell you? And so they told him.

Hamisi had *not* worked for the British. He had been defeated by them – or rather by Maynard, the wily Englishman.

Hamisi had been head of the Germans' African and Arab spies, whose agents were legion on the Voi-Taveta road and were even present among the railway workers. The explosion at the railway depot of a few weeks before must have depended on detailed information, even a guide. It had been costly for the British. This time Maynard had vowed vengeance, and he wasted no time. He wrote a letter to Hamisi, thanking him for his services, adding that his wife in Sudan was well looked after by the British. After the war he would be allowed to go back to his country with a suitable position and a decoration. To add to the cleverness, the letter had been written in Arabic. It was found on the person of Abdalla the mali when he was seized by the Germans in Mbuyuni. Hamisi was arrested and hanged.

"Everyone knows this here, and the Germans don't?" asked Pipa.

Everyone knows this now, period, he was told. What is victory good for if it is not broadcast?

"But Abdalla?" he asked. "What about the mali?"

"Abdalla?" the speaker paused. The British didn't commandeer his donkey, did they? They let him go about. Now we know why. The Germans also let him alone. Why? Think. A trader always carries things both ways – never one way, never empty-handed. So Abdalla carried messages for both the British and the Germans. This time the British betrayed him, the Germans hanged him.

No telling who works for whom – Pipa recalled the mukhi's words.

When relief came for Pipa, it did not come too early. One day the Fisi arrived in Kikono with his lieutenants and took over Corbin's former residence. Pipa's job with the British army was thenceforth terminated, and he felt as if an oppressive weight had been lifted from him and that he was free at last.

14

It was February 1916. The new railway line from Voi brought the massive British conquering army west to the midway point of Mbuyuni, and the small German force that had occupied the town dispersed. The next German line of defence was at the formidable Salaita Hill outside Taveta, at the border, which the British had now begun to assail.

Mbuyuni turned into a city of white tents against a background of desert brown and scrub. In the morning the flapping, cracking canvas could be heard for a great distance; as the day heated, the canvas would tighten, its surfaces smooth and blinding in the glare. At night lamps flitted about in the landscape, men sat and sang around fires, there were smells of food and gasoline. A makeshift hospital had been put up. Trains packed with soldiers arrived, later to depart for action at the border. Planes flew overhead. Troop patrols brought in prisoners and casualties.

Kikono, only ten miles away, saw its neighbour town thus overcome and was itself run over, but not so completely.

Prominence had been dreamed of, forecast for this little town between two railways, but not of this variety. The war was almost over for the area – and the town would never be the same again; already the townsfolk, not unappreciative of the added business brought by the war, had learned to regard the place cynically, without affection, as they would a whore. When they were done, they would go away and leave it, as the armies were doing.

At Pipa's one afternoon, a knock came at the backyard gate that led to the street. He and Mariamu were outside the kitchen shed eating their midday meal while the baby slept inside. Mariamu got up to look. A female figure draped in buibui stood outside the gate.

"Mama, I want to work."

"We have no work," Pipa called gruffly.

"Then give a poor woman some water, for kindness."

Mariamu walked to the drinking pot to fetch some water, and the woman stepped into the yard. Quickly she closed the gate and, undoing the buibui, revealed herself to be a man. A stocky man, moreover, with a moustache.

Mariamu gave a start. "To repay kindness you do this?"

"What do you want?" asked Pipa. "Take all you can, there's not much."

The man laughed. "Show me the hiding places, then. But I am not a thief. I come on business."

Pipa nodded. "The Englishman?" he asked casually. What could that devil the Fisi want now?

But the intruder said, "Bwana Juma sent me."

"Juma? Which Juma? Are you some kind of madman or what? I know of no Juma."

"After Thursday comes Friday," said the man implacably, playing on the names. "After Hamisi, Juma."

Pipa began to understand. The man was from the German side, one of Hamisi's followers. He sat down, looked at his wife, who was still looking startled, the cup of water in her hands.

"You go inside," he told her. "It's not her business," he said to the visitor. "She has to be with the child."

The man graciously agreed. "But stay indoors," he warned her as she gave him the water.

"Look here," Pipa said, pleading with the man. "This war is nothing to me. I just want to lead my own life."

"I understand, my friend," said the man. "I do too. But have we a choice? We have all become involved." He leaned forward and looked straight into Pipa's eyes. "Hamisi was betrayed. There are those among his followers – the Sufis – who think his death should be avenged."

"But it was the Germans who hanged him."

"He was betrayed from here – by a message given to the mali Abdalla. Some say it was you who gave it –"

The man sat back as Pipa erupted in his defence.

"The day the mali was caught he got no messages from me. This I swear, by God, the Prophet, and my mother."

The man shrugged: "What do details matter."

"Hamisi was my friend," Pipa said.

"Listen, Pipa." The man again leaned forward, as if to impart a confidence, and said slowly, "Prove to us that Hamisi was your friend, by working for us."

All Pipa had to do was pass messages on. They would come from the British camp in Mbuyuni. He would get little chits with his money from certain customers, and these he was to insert inside packets of spice, which he would hand over to any customer who said to him, "I thought it was Thursday, but Friday follows Thursday and demands a prayer."

"The war is almost over," Pipa pleaded. "Why now, why me? What for, all this treachery, this Thursday-Friday business that will surely cost me my life?"

"Everything counts," said the man, unmoved. "And as you yourself say, it will soon be over. One week, maybe two. But till then. . . . It is nothing, truly. Just a few messages – accept them, and hand them over. That is all, you know nothing else. Is that a crime? I will tell the Sufis you are innocent, a good man."

Pipa and his wife sat looking at each other for a long time after the man had left. The Fisi was not far, he was up the hill in the departed ADC's house. If they told him about Thursday-Friday would he protect them? And for how long? He would soon be gone, but there would remain Hamisi's followers and Abdalla's family. He and Mariamu went and talked with the mukhi. Do what the man said, Jamali advised. He could be desperate. It can't last long. A week at most. Then you are free.

The messages began the next day and came three days running, brought by an off-duty Sikh soldier from the British side.

Pipa eyed the man curiously, who ostensibly bought cigarettes, and once a packet of sugar. He was not very young, somewhat weary-looking. Each time he said something that Pipa couldn't understand. After the man had gone, Pipa would hide the messages in his packets, which then waited to be picked up.

On the fourth day following the arrival of the Thursday-Friday man at Pipa's, a British attack on Salaita Hill outside Taveta was rebuffed.

That night, as news of the setback spread, as the wounded and dead were being brought back, and as they talked once more in the town of the prowess of the German feldkompanies and their African askaris, a fist pounded on Pipa's door, threatening to bring it down. Pipa went and opened a panel. Two men strode in – Fisi and his Swahili aide. Pipa, still at the door, watched them with fright. If he had been alone, he would have made a dash for it. The game was up now, he thought, and probably his time, too. The baby, Aku, began crying, and Mariamu went and picked him up.

The Swahili brought a chair. "Sit," he said to Pipa. This was no kindness, but a preparatory step.

Aku was struggling in Mariamu's arms as she returned her

husband's look in terror. Inside the shop, now, the men were searching. Cigarette tins, cigarettes, shelves, kerosene tins, spice and grain boxes . . . all turned over and inside out; then finally the spice and sugar packets. Triumphantly they brought them out to examine them under a lamp.

"They forced me," Pipa said. "They forced me, what was I to do? They said —"

Maynard glared at the Indian and put a hand to his pistol: "For this he can be shot."

"No!" screamed Mariamu. "Please, no. He was forced —"

"Trial, bwana," said Shomari. "In Mbuyuni, with other traitors."

And so Pipa was marched off to the lockup, as the mukhi and one or two others hurried inside to comfort Mariamu and the child.

There was a hole in the roof which let in a dim glow that was the light of the night sky. This faint light cut through the dark hollow under the roof, illuminating the beams, exposing objects lower down as shadows and silhouettes. Through the opening Pipa saw the pinpoint flickers of the stars; the new-moon ceremony was a week past, now, but the moon was out of sight. He was nervous of sounds, afraid of snakes. At first he dared not move, but later, barraged by all manner of rustling, scraping, soughing, he made his own, propietary sounds in the dark. Later he became bolder still, egged on by a pack of hyenas who arrived outside, barking at him angrily through the wall where the mud had been washed or broken away, and in frustration rubbing their bodies against the gap, as if willing it to give way. And Pipa, on edge with fright but unwilling to show it, clapped his hands, stamped his feet, shouted at them to go away. But he was a prisoner and they knew it; they would not go away.

In this forsaken prison, with its small wooden bench, broken bed, and rotting mat, Pipa languished that night besieged by hyenas, until he started yelling to be let out.

Captain Maynard, commander of a military intelligence corps, sat at the table in the ADC's former home, surrounded by his chosen lieutenants, sifting through the messages they had found in Pipa's store earlier in the evening. Above them, hanging from a beam, was a powerful pressure lamp by whose bright light they went about their work. The strength of the army amassed to move into German East, and its momentum, were too great for these captured reports to make much difference – there was intelligence from the other side to indicate this. Nevertheless, the Germans had come up with surprises before, had repulsed several overconfident attacks, including the one the previous day at Salaita Hill.

German intelligence in the area had been in place and strong even before the war; German maps found on captured soldiers were accurate and were even used by the British to correct their own. Raids from across the border were persistent and effective, their successes depending frequently on collaborators. Although Hamisi the Arab had been killed, his network of spies continued to be active and was operating in Kikono right under Maynard's nose.

Maynard had four men with him, an Indian and three Africans; each was familiar with a different language, a different tribe. The search in Pipa's store had delivered six scraps of paper bearing messages. These messages were passed around, commented upon, put back in the heap on the table, picked up and passed around again, as the men tried to make sense of them.

Three of the messages were short cryptic notes: two in Punjabi and one in English. The remaining three were sketches of the local terrain, troop positions indicated with crude symbols and texts. Captain Maynard looked carefully at the sketches with a faint toothy smile. They contained up-to-date information: troop movements that had taken place over the past two days – even that very day. And the man – they all seemed to be the work of one hand – possessed a detailed knowledge of the terrain. They suggested, of course, that the man was now in the area; but more significantly, that he was a local; and not only that, one of the sketches hinted strongly that the spy was one of his own men.

Maynard looked at each of his companions in turn. Could it be one of them? The Indian: no, he was a stranger to these parts. Of the three Africans, one was also a stranger here, the other a local of whose abilities the Englishman didn't think much. That left the fourth man, Shomari the Swahili, crafty and capable; but he was much trusted, had been with Maynard since the start of the war. Maynard went back to the sketches, handed two of them around. He held on to the third, which aroused his strongest suspicion. It showed, with the symbol of a horsehead profile, the position of a mounted company in the countryside around Kikono. The town itself was marked with an open circle and named. Under the name of the town was scrawled the word "Fisi" (hyena), almost as an afterthought. The Englishman Maynard, who was also called Fisi, finally passed on this incriminating sketch with a glint in his eye.

A South African mounted company on its way to the Taveta front for regrouping – yes, he knew about that. But what was so remarkable about hyenas in the area? Why mention them in the intelligence? No, this was not a warning against the nocturnal scavengers they could hear outside the jail, rummaging among the refuse, barking at the prisoner. It was an indication of Maynard's position. Not many men knew of his code name; no one apart from his own men should know it.

Pipa could be heard calling out, "Let me out! There are snakes here!"

Maynard looked at Shomari and gave a nod. Two men went and brought Pipa in.

"What did the messenger say – the first time he came – about Thursday and Friday?"

"After Hamisi came Juma, after Thursday comes Friday."

"What was this messenger like – the man in buibui?"

"Black-black. Short. Good Swahili."

"Short as what?"

Pipa looked around. His eyes fell on Shomari: "Like him," he said. Five-foot-six. Shomari flinched a little.

There was silence, but for the sound of paper and pencil. Shomari noted down the particulars of the six identified messages in a ledger. Every intercepted message collected in his book had a number, a place. Gradually, some of the informers would give enough of themselves away to be identified. The Indian station-master at Simba Lala, twenty-five miles east of Voi, had been caught this way after three of his messages giving train times were intercepted. He had been hanged.

"You knew Hamisi," Fisi said, his eyes on a piece of paper he was holding. "Did you see anyone from Kikono with him there, in mosque or in his house, whom you recognized later?"

Pipa opened his mouth, then hesitated, and thus gave himself away. There was sudden silence, an anticipatory stillness; his interrogators were all looking at him.

He looked at each one of them in wonder. Who were these men? . . . Why did they play this game? What gave them the right to choose good and bad for him, right and wrong?

"Tumetega," said Shomari. We have caught it.

The others nodded and smiled.

Fisi opened his mouth a little, his face glowed with pleasure. "Yes," he said.

"Nani?" he asked Pipa. "Whom did you see with Hamisi?"

"Uso Shetani." Ghost-face, the albino. Fumfratti.

In the distance came the sound of railway cars rumbling, clanking, soldiers shouting or singing, lorries grinding their way west, some rifle shots. Below, little Kikono was awake, but keeping its silence as much as possible. Dawn had begun to break, more tea was brought in.

Pipa answered further questions, then was allowed to doze off. Intermittently, he opened his eyes; he was not comfortable, sitting on the chair he had been given. He thought of his wife who would have lain awake all night worrying about him. The four men at the table seemed calm now. The scraps of messages they had taken from his shop had been put away and they seemed to be simply sitting around, as at a game of cards, talking in murmurs. They would be deciding the day's course of action. Soon Pipa would learn his fate at their hands. But all anger at him seemed to have abated, a bigger prey had been scented. It was past noon when he was told to go.

He went down the hill from the ADC's residence, turned past the little mbuyu into the street of shops and houses. It looked like a normal day, except somewhat busier with all the military activity in the area. The number of layabouts was greater, which was a matter of concern. Baruti's tea shack on the other street was bustling; it was there that the latest news about the war would be available – what exactly had transpired at Salaita Hill, how strong the Germans were. He entered his home through the front door, whose main panel was open – but Mariamu would not have opened the store because everything had been turned over and inside out by the Fisi and his men in their search the previous night.

He saw her almost immediately. She looked dead. She was in a sitting posture on the floor against the wall, her head lolling sideways towards her right shoulder. Her eyes were open. Catching his breath, emitting a choking sound, he went over to her slowly and with tenderness picked up one of her hands. He felt her forehead, caressed strands of hair, and with the back of his hand touched her neck where the line of blood ran. He pulled the hem of her frock down so that she was decent, and dropped her hand gently to her lap. Then he ran to the mukhi.

Jamali walked hurriedly back with him. The baby, he said, had been brought earlier to their home by his wife, to relieve Mariamu. He was safe, playing, being fed – what was wrong with Mariamu? Pipa beside him, pulling him by the sleeve, was breathing fast, in large, audible gulps that might have seized and choked him.

"Oh, God!" gasped the mukhi when he saw the sight. "Oh, God and the Prophet . . ."

She had been violated, but there was no point in broadcasting that. All these foreigners about – brutal and shameless – Africans from all over, Punjabis and Baluchis and Rajputs, it could have been any one of those depraved men. Poor innocent, they all said when they buried her, who could have wished this for her, and why?

Could it be *them*, Pipa thought. The Sufis of Moshi. As revenge. Punishment. But why *her*? Why not me?

Later Pipa went through Mariamu's belongings, sifted through her trunk to look for things he could send as offerings to the mosque, whose value she could reap in the other life, but there was nothing suitable except her pachedi. As he extracted the green garment whose shimmer had once thrilled him so, he felt a hard flat object wrapped inside it. As he unfolded the slippery cloth, he found himself holding a book. *The* book. He was so startled he dropped it back into the trunk, then picked it up again. Bwana Corbin's book, he thought, which he himself would have so liked to steal that day, now hidden among his wife's things! He recalled the morning, coming from the ADC's house, seeing the book with a pen lying on the chair where Corbin had left them in a hurry . . . then meeting Mariamu and Khanoum walking in the direction from which he had come, to the ADC's house to collect her things. She must have taken it then, along with the pen, which was now here inside the book. But why?

He examined it briefly. There were some snapshots in it – in one of them the ADC Bwana Corbin on a horse.

Why? To steal back her secret – her shame – from the Englishman? To prove to her husband her innocence? Or to permit herself – and her husband – to take revenge on the mzungu? A revenge he himself had been unable to take. So was this her gift to him; one which she, one day, some evening in better times, would have shown him had she lived? . . .

He was convinced the book contained the answer to his torment. What was the relationship between the ADC and his Mariamu? Was the boy, Aku, really his own? He could not read it, yet he would take this gift with him wherever he went. It was from her and she must be in it, described in it. The book contained her spirit.

Miscellany (ii)

From the personal notebook of Pius Fernandes
April 1988, Moshi

It has been a little over a week since I came to Moshi and met
Young Jamali. Together we have visited some of the sites, and he
has told me stories and anecdotes he heard as a child in his home
. . . and much else besides that is not pertinent to my inquiries . . .

Yanga (Young Africans) have been beaten at soccer by their old
rivals Simba (formerly Sunderland), and for the last hour the
Moshi bus station has been in an uproar of celebration and
recrimination. The Taveta bus is, predictably, late, and when it
does arrive its passengers are celebrating and transistors blare.
   Young Jamali and I push through the throng with our tickets
and confront the conductor confidently. "We have seat numbers!" "Of course," he says. "Go right in." But the bus, coming
from Arusha, is smaller, does not conform to the seat plan flourished before us earlier at the ticket office. What we thought

173

would be the comfortable mid-section is, in this vehicle, the last row of seats.

It is a hellish, rattling ride. We cling to our seats as to our lives. We are on a trade route, and with us are seasoned, hardy passengers: Masai youths, Taita men and women. Now that market day is over, they bring fresh goods from Tanzania, pay not duties but bribes at the border, freely exchange and carry forbidden currency. The young man sitting next to us explains how it is all done: everyone makes a living – from the blustering policeman who first boards the bus to the bullying customs officer with darting eyes to the slow-witted immigration inspector who takes ten minutes to press a stamp on our papers. Who can survive on a government salary, our friend offers a truism, putting a candy into his mouth and once more taking a quick reassuring glance along the luggage rack where his goods lie, and an anxious look outside lest something of his be carried off the roof of the bus. We arrive in Taveta at about midnight.

It is a black moonless night folding in dim-glowing pockets of light. There is a slight chill in the air. To our right as we start off from the bus station is a large open area that has been used as a garbage dump. This presumably is where the market was held. The smells of the day have long ripened, though the crisp night air abates them and keeps them distant. We walk along what seems to be the only main street (the other direction, we have figured, goes out of town, Voi-way). Some doors are open, shadowy lights inside. Strains of music. Hardly a soul on the unpaved, cratered road. A sign on a wall, MODERN CINEMA NEW VIDEO, beside it posters advertising a double feature – Sylvester Stallone and Amitabh Bachan, Hollywood and Bollywood, facing opposite directions. The buildings are low, part mud, part cement, part brick – whatever fit – the roofs, corrugated iron. Suddenly we come upon an amazingly modern building. TAVETA INN is painted boldly in foot-long letters on the side wall. The doorway is lighted, orange. There is a tree outside, cars parked, an askari.

We enter and are greeted by a young man in blue Kaunda suit. "Welcome," he says. The rooms are, to our surprise, very good.

I have not felt so alone, so away, in years. The last time was when I first came to Africa, long ago. Outside, the music still plays. Downstairs in the lobby two men talk earnestly in the bar, their voices carry clearly and without inhibition. There comes the sound of water, from somewhere. Young Jamali sleeps in the adjoining room. So many times in the past few weeks I have seen this town, this area, in my mind as it must have been eighty, ninety years ago; imagined the thousands of troops and animals on the march across the dry land, digging in battle lines, relinquishing them; the guns firing, the bayonets thrusting; the disease and thirst and death. Now to be here . . . the feeling is eerie, unreal.

Morning, after a Swahili breakfast. The town is so exposed, so uniformly bright, the sun seems to have simply poured in, leaving not a spot untouched. This is the town at the edge of a desert that during the war had to be crossed to recapture it.

But there is no sign of the war here, no sign of the past. History drifts about in the sands, and only the fanatically dedicated see it and recreate it, however incomplete their visions and fragile their constructs. Yes, says the morning askari, at his post at the doorway, his grandfather would talk of the old days, of the war and the Germans. But he had died recently. If only we had come two or three months ago. The manager arrives, unhappy that it is the askari who receives the benefit of our conversation.

"The guests wish to know of old times, Germans and so on," says the askari.

The manager sends him off and eyes us. "Who are you?" he asks.

When we tell him he shakes our hands and says, "My friends, this place is full of history."

From then on he is unstoppable. His name is James. A slight

man of about thirty, with a thin moustache, a beige Kaunda suit today.

"Are you from here?" I ask hopefully.

He stops. "No, sir. I am from Rabai. On the coast." He is not going to say more about that. He continues: "Did you know that this town was the only British territory – anywhere on our globe, mind you – that was captured by the Germans in the Great War. They held it until . . ." and he goes on, telling us a history we already know.

"Are there people here – wazees – who remember the war, perhaps stories from their fathers? . . ." I ask.

"The last one died just six weeks ago. I doubt if you will find anyone else. . . . Come with me."

Dutifully we follow him back inside, take the stairs to the roof terrace two floors up. This is the highest point in the town, look-ing out upon the entire countryside for miles in all directions. Instinctively drawing our breath we gather to take in Kilimanjaro. There are huts on its slope, smoke rising at a few spots; the round peak is visible, capped with snow: so majestic and yet so benevo-lent. Almost emerging from its side is a range of hills. "In the hills there is Lake Chala, a crater lake," James says. "It is fed by an underground stream. The stream continues underground from there – look, you can see the line of vegetation that follows it above the ground – and erupts in a spring there." He shows us some dense growth in the distance. "Next it feeds Lake Jipe," he says, pointing now southwards, "and proceeds to the Pare Moun-tains in Tanzania. Taveta, you see, is practically surrounded by an underground river." He beams proudly.

We walk around, in different directions, pulled separately and privately by the awesome panorama that surrounds us.

Down below us, the mundane and gross world of the town is slowly but assuredly coming to life: the street with the sparse human traffic, the four-wheel-drive that's just arrived and parked downstairs, the video place with the double feature now with the radio on, blaring news interrupted by the jingle of an ad from Nairobi. Behind our hotel, rails of a defunct line that once carried an army; next to it a group of houses sharing a common backyard. A child emerges from an outhouse that is obviously doorless, a woman with a can of water goes in. I look away, into the distance.

Straight ahead, rising upon a bare round hill, an impressive church built of rough stone. Towards it, on a trail through bush and plantations, well-dressed but simple folk make their way to service. Could that be the CMS church, or its site, I wonder.

Towards the east, in the near distance, a quite distinguished feature of the local geography: a low circular hill, a gentle bump in a flatland. It would not take long to walk to it, just out of town where the thorny desert terrain is beginning to take over. "Salaita," James says, coming over to my side. "Here a famous battle was fought." He corrects himself: "*Three* battles. It was captured by the British after the last one."

Does anybody care about the history, I ask: does it matter?

"Ah, not to the local public, alas. But from time to time there are visitors like you. Last month there was a German expedition from Tanga – a man and a woman. They took photographs of Salaita Hill."

He has had a brochure prepared, he says, describing the local attractions for tourists. He would like them to visit this place for its history, as well as the wildlife and the mountain. "Why do you think I'm paying you so much attention? I like you, you are my brothers from across the border. But I also want you to tell people about us."

As part of his overwhelming hospitality James drives us to the church in the four-wheel-drive. A padre and a flock of his congregation come to greet us as we get out of the jeep.

"When was this church built?" I ask anxiously after an exchange of greetings.

"In the thirties," says the padre, a trifle disappointed we will not be joining him for the service. "After a fire," he adds.

"And before that? There was a CMS station here a long time ago."

"Ah," he says. "Long before my time. It wasn't on this site. I believe it was where the cemetery is."

He sends a girl with us, who does not seem too keen to miss the morning service. She looks committed, must be a favourite. In the middle of a mango grove, we find a graveyard. The graves have all been reused, very recently. Ancient carved gravestones, new graves, five, ten years old.

On our way back to the hotel, Young Jamali points to the old brickwork of what looks like a relic chimney. We stop. It is a surprising, somewhat startling sight on top of a bare mound identical to the one on which the church stands, directly across the road from it. The chimney rises next to a dull rectangular structure with grey concrete exterior. No one saw fit to mention it to us, yet it is a decidedly old structure; there is nothing else of that brick we've seen. The grey building is the parish office, partly rented out. A bent old woman interrupts her sweeping of the yard to show us the chimney, which is attached to an ancient kitchen now used as a storehouse; it doesn't have a roof. As far as she knows the chimney has always been here. The newer building has been put up on an older, larger site, whose outer brick walls are just visible flush with the ground, and from one of whose corners rises the chimney, scant reminder of the past.

Unlike Alfred Corbin we do not have Masai guides to take us up to Lake Chala. But on seeing this secluded jewel I concur with Corbin: this must be the sight of the Creation itself . . . so blue the lake surrounded by hills, so crystalline pure its water, so cool and gentle the breeze rippling its surface, so unspoiled the site. The vegetation all around the lake – thorn, bramble, small trees – not obtrusive. Nothing man-made here, except, on the lip of the crater, and only just noticed as we prepare to depart, is the remains of an old brick wall. This must be one of the emplacements for the machine-guns now long silenced. It takes a feat of imagination to people this terrain with the actors of war, to hear it echo with the boom of guns. What manner of men would let these slopes be covered with guns, blood, guts? Alien, I say; then remind myself of the carnage our own leaders have wrought on the land. As we go back we see a car from Nairobi driving away from a picnic site, leaving pizza boxes behind, Masai youths picking them up.

We drive part way on the unsurfaced Taveta-Voi road. It is a hazardous journey, the road is often not visible for the dust that rises, and the opposing traffic is frighteningly swift.

Mbuyuni, once a city of military tents, is now a gate to the Tsavo National Park. There is a sideroad that goes northwards, that takes us to a town on a site where Kikono perhaps stood. This one is called Glory: neat square church, tiny neat houses in immaculate rows. Under the only mbuyu tree (not remotely resembling a hand) a class is underway. I look around for a cliff and see a hill in the distance. Could this be the site of the MCA station? We have not seen a single wild animal on our journey.

"Please return," James tells us back at the hotel as we prepare to depart. "I have stories for you. I have talked to the wazees . . . including the old priest at the church – the one you met was his son. And the people of Lake Chala – believe me there is a tribe there – have a story about why and when the lake sank.

Young Jamali did not tell me his father was alive, was in Moshi, until my last day there.

He is a bent old man, in his eighties I guess, thin – grey hair, gummy eyes – wearing a wrap round his waist and an open shirt. I sit facing him, in the backyard of the house in which he has a room. His son, Young Jamali, stands uncomfortably beside us. The backyard is bare earth, stockaded, and there is a dark dilapidated shed at the end, which is a kitchen. The old man sits on a stool, chewing a piece of cassava, spitting out the hard bits and the fibres on the ground. Next to him is a pan of water. When he's finished with the cassava, he picks up the pieces from the ground and throws them to the far and littered end of the backyard. He picks up the pan of water, walks to the middle of the yard, and carefully pours the liquid out, spreading it about on the earth, which drinks it up. Then he comes and sits down on his stool.

"My father was a chief," he says. "In Kenya."

He has a confused memory of the war. He mentions it with the Maji-Maji uprising. But he was born after Maji-Maji, I quickly tell Young Jamali, who shrugs. Are you sure he is your father? I say exasperated. He is amused. Maybe not, he says.

The old man recalls a brother. He was stolen.

"Come," he says.

We follow him inside to a room so dark we stand still for a while to let our eyes get used to it. Young Jamali and I sit down uncomfortably on what looks like a bench. But the old man quickly tells us to get up. He removes the cloth which covers it, revealing an old wooden trunk, its sides carved in the coastal fashion. He opens it, motions for me to come and look. I kneel down beside him.

There are all kinds of knick-knacks: pieces of cloth; a mirror; a Swahili newspaper without a date but apparently from colonial times; coins, including a heller from the German period. There are photographs, including a framed one of himself and his wife. She is sitting on a chair, he is standing beside her. He wears a coat and kofia, she a dress. The photo was taken in a studio a good forty years ago or so. Then he pulls out a postcard-size one of an old African woman – his mother, Khanoum. I pick up the photograph, which I see was taken at the same time and studio as her son's. She's standing, staring directly at the camera; a short determined-looking woman. Her son picks out a scrap of aged yellow paper printed with an Indian script I cannot decipher. Then a remarkable thing happens: he starts singing in a low voice, watching me with amused eyes, moving his head a bit as I stare at him unable to tell the language. But very soon I know what it is: an Indian hymn. Young Jamali, obviously angry and embarrassed, says we must go.

"What was all that about?" I ask Jamali once we are outside. "Why did you get cross with him, your father."

"He's an old fool."

I ask him about the brother who was stolen.

"The story is that he had a fair-skinned brother once. He had been given to the family. Then he was taken away to Dar es Salaam. . . . That is why I don't like the old man speaking the Indian language, singing their song. For what the Indians did to my grandmother. They did not recognize her when her husband died, they took away her adopted son and let her die in poverty."

"And the boy – this fair-skinned boy," I ask.

"Yes, Pipa's . . ."

We go then to see the old graveyard. This part of town, shaded by large trees, is where the Europeans lived in colonial times. The old high-roofed red-tiled bungalows bear testimony to that period. The library search has been useful; Corbin's memoir has been found, and we've brought it along. The graveyard is fenced, surrounded by trees and park, and well-tended, probably due to foreign funds. We walk around.

To one side a monument to "Hindu, Sikh and Mohamedan soldiers," some small child graves. They don't tell us anything we don't know, but are worth a look as something tangible from the past.

We sit at the monument to the Indian soldiers. I think of the spy, the Sufi Hamisi, and ask Young Jamali if he knew what became of his family.

"Oh – they stayed in Moshi for a long time, until the sixties. . . .

A son, called Seif, ran a religious school, which closed at that time. Seif's sons went to the Old Moshi School. I knew them. Clever. Later, one went to Sweden, another to America."

In silence we share some food, brought for us by the graveyard caretaker, who joins us. In the ten days I have spent with Young Jamali I've come to know him well, I think, though I would be hard put to say exactly as what or in what way. I can describe this best by saying that there is an understanding, a mutual respect that transcends verbal communication. In his quiet fashion he has taken me around, told me things, and so shown his support for my endeavours. And finally he gave up his privacy, first by taking me to see his father, then by the verbal outburst that revealed to me his buried anger against the Indians. I don't quite know to what I owe this friendship – certainly to no gregariousness on my part, but perhaps to a need in him for communion with a like spirit.

"What about the albino, Fumfratti . . ." I say. "Did they execute him?"

Young Jamali is quiet, brooding. And then he blurts it out, a complete piece of information. "My grandmother used to talk about them – Hamisi and Fumfratti – the war, her husband. She was a bitter old woman but her memories were fond. Five years after the war, Fumfratti was seen in Mombo – on the Tanga route. He had a shop close to the railway station. He was seen by one of his own men, who had become a policeman in Moshi. He was hanged. Here, in Moshi."

The next day at the bus-stop, Young Jamali and I embrace. "We'll meet," I say.

"We'll meet," he says. And we part.

Appendices

(1) There are three chapters on the early years in East Africa in Alfred Corbin's memoir, *Heart and Soul*. In the first of these the

182

travails of a young Assistant District Commissioner are described in a somewhat dry fashion.

(2) Intelligence Supplement 117/16
Notes on the officers serving with the Enemy Forces in German East Africa (with specimen signatures)
Compiled by the Intelligence Section: General Staff
Dar es Salaam 17 October 1916
Introductory Note by F. Maynard, Captain.
(pg. 11)
Hamisi ibn Arab (no rank). Master of the Karimiya Sufi order in Moshi, which had maintained links with seditious elements in Egypt and the Sudan. Hamisi escaped from the Sudan in 1904. . . . The Karimiya order has engaged in intelligence operations against the British in East Africa since at least 1912, and after the outbreak of hostilities has been involved in hostile military operations. . . . Agents involved in bombing the Voi-Taveta Railway 4 miles East of Maktau on 29/7/15. Again derailed 4 trucks with a contact mine at Mile 36 on 22/8/15. Etc. Deceased.

From the personal notebook of Pius Fernandes
April 1988, Dar es Salaam

I return to Dar to find that Rita is already in town, somewhat earlier than we expected. Feroz is frantic, he wants me to return his diary. Clearly he wants to be the one to show it to her. I tell him I would like to keep it until my work is finished, and that I will not lose it. What can he expect to do with it – it has no monetary value . . . could it be that he simply wants it as a keepsake . . .

But Rita, who's left a message with him that I meet her at her hotel tomorrow . . . how do I respond to this phenomenon from *my own* past? Feroz tells me, again, that she's anxious to see me. I for my part would have preferred my tranquillity undisturbed; but it's already shattered and I, too, am anxious to see her.

She is Pipa's daughter-in-law – how much does she know of his story, how much will she tell? And of all the questions that the diary has churned up, does she have any answers? *Why* is she here? – not for me, certainly; but not as a tourist either.

PART TWO

I

The Father and the Son

He eats with you, but won't die with you
unless he's born of you.
— Swahili proverb

My relations are this prison around me . . .
— Gujarati hymn

15

The war, from what the boy had been told about it, would appear to him always in the same scene of utter chaos: dust churned up into a clinging choking mist; fires — a house burning, a garbage dump smouldering, smoky campsites dotting the grassland; people rushing about, bare feet thumping the ground; shouts of people and honking car horns and tinkling bicycle bells, whistling trains, bleating goats . . . and himself lost, abandoned, in knickers and singlet, running in and out between people's feet, crying. Kindly large hands picking him up and carrying him home. He had been a baby then, far too young to remember the war as it trampled and roared and clunked its way through Mwatate and Maungu, then Mbuyuni and Kikono, and beyond towards the mountain. But this picture of a lost child Aku carried within him always, having fashioned it as his own impression of those fateful days in the town of his birth.

In the years of his childhood that he would actually remember, the war was already the stuff of legend. He had been taken to Moshi by then. He recalled men sitting outside mosques or houses there, discussing positions, movements, and tactics, using twigs and stones on the ground, pondering outcomes as if over a game of chess. He played guns and armoured cars and planes in the streets. For many months there were the wounded without arms or legs or eyes, one Indian reputedly with a single testicle; another, a man with the top part of his head sliced off orange-fashion, as it was described. There were the boots and khakis and binoculars and mess tins and bullet casings and rifle parts and tires and belts and buckles and tiffin boxes and betel-nut crackers and shaving brushes and razors and tinned food that appeared on sale in all conditions. For many months in Moshi a favourite game of the street loafers would be to call out "Halt! Achtung!" in the market and watch the men who had worked as soldiers for the Germans stiffen reflexively, still showing that renowned discipline in spite of which they had lost the war.

He was a wonder child in Kikono, and later in Moshi. People pointed him out. Young girls in mosque, eyes dreamy with thoughts of marriage, would come to see him for themselves: the grey-eyed boy with fair skin, pointed chin, high cheekbones. The ideal-looking child they would wish for themselves. "Please don't let his eyes change colour, Mama Khanoum, please don't," the maidens would plead, as if his guardian, Khanoum, the mukhi's wife, had power over the boy's looks. Finally, before some evil could befall – before some djinn took it in his heart to possess him, or someone cast devil's eyes or put a jealous spell on him – she took Aku to a maalim for protection. The maalim tied a tawith around the boy's right arm, a little cylinder case containing papers inscribed with Quranic ayats for protection; the mukhi his great-uncle tied a thread with prayers round his neck. And his eyes received thick smudges of kohl from Khanoum just in case.

Of Khanoum, who swore she would hold him close to her bosom even if God's earth were to split apart under her feet, Aku would always remember a short black woman, who barely reached her husband's shoulders. She would stand at a distance to cast her eyes on him, and flash a smile. He would remember, too, the long arms and that engulfing hug that promised so much. Oddly, he also could never forget one story she told: how in her village two young men fought over a woman and one devoured the other's ear. He laughed and laughed. Even when he was much older and as far from that town with the mbuyu tree as one could ever be, he would smile at the memory.

Of his mother, as a boy in Moshi he only knew what Khanoum had told him: she was her little sister who had died. His father he knew to have gone away and left him. Khanoum and Jamali were his auntie-mother and uncle-father, who over the months became simply Mama na Baba, Mother and Father, as they were for the other three children in the house.

How does a small town like Kikono die?

Even as the armies of General Smuts were trampling past on their way to victory over German East, Chagpar the dispenser, one of the original settlers of the town – as if forecasting the future – had offered his services to a medical corps and departed. Pipa, having buried his young wife, left his son with Jamali and Khanoum and took off, in the same direction, to Moshi to begin afresh.

Suddenly, with the armies gone, it seemed that not only the rest of the war but everything of import was happening somewhere else. Within months, Dar es Salaam had been shelled from the sea and was taken, and soon the war was over. In the times that followed, small Kikono, situated with such great promise between two railway lines, was forgotten. No new ADC came to administer its affairs and those of the neighbouring area. Newspapers from Nairobi and Mombasa were slow to arrive, rumours came faster; speculation grew – concerning booming business in the large centres, cheap properties to hold on to in Tanga and Moshi and Dar as the Germans and their allies lost all.

The mukhi, Jamali, desperately held on to his people, for a

time. It will soon get better, he promised. Remember, in the past we almost got township status. With strength of numbers we can petition for an ADC, call for new immigrants. Nothing has changed, he said; but all had changed. Over the months, family after family came to bid farewell.

There was a bitter row over custody of the boy Aku when Jamali's sister, Kulsa, Aku's grandmother, came to say her good-byes. But the mukhi had status still as well as a letter from the boy's father, who had left Kikono after the war and had remarried and gone on to Dar. Jamali had prevailed. As long as that railway coolie Rashid hung around his sister, he would never give her the boy, he said to her, creating a schism between them that would never be repaired. Aku's grandmother and her husband, Rashid, slunk off Mombasa way.

The mukhi, who had been the first of the Indians to arrive in Kikono at the twisted mbuyu tree, who had seen his congregation grow from the twosome of himself and his wife, now saw it dwindle to himself and his family. Finally they too left for nearby Moshi, three years after the armies had gone that way.

They had taken to the Taveta road with two donkeys and a goat, a hand-pulled cart which could carry a few of them at a time, and a few porters. The twisted mbuyu raised a final protest-ing hand behind them, in the distance were the forest and the Mission hill, in front rose the mighty Kilimanjaro. The road, a dirt highway, was deserted. The war had left numerous scars on the land: rusting machine parts, piles of refuse reduced by the ele-ments and scavengers, charred campsites.

At one point some Masai emerged from the roadside and stood watching them – tall and erect at the side of the road, with spears and shields in their hands – giving them quite a scare. As they approached, the Masai started chattering and motioning. The head porter of the party went over to them. "They want us to see something – or meet somebody – don't know what, over there." They went, scrambling onto the grass, two servants remaining to guard their possessions. The Masai, bounding ahead of them, stopped at the bank of a dried water hole and pointed – a human skeleton. It was lying on its back, projecting outwards from the trunk of a young tree. It had the oddest look of having been dismantled, then put back together – the joints were not complete, the bones loose; and the head was placed upright against the base of the tree. This was a strange, eerie sight they never forgot. Who had taken the trouble of collecting the bones? How had the animals been kept away? What did it mean? And why had the Masai boys brought them here? The Masai were laughing now – perhaps the sight had become a joke for them which they had wanted to share. At another place they saw an abandoned vehicle in a dry riverbed, monkeys playing on it, having managed to bend a whole tree branch almost completely over it. They saw no bones about. They stood staring in silence at the wreckage for some time, then continued on their way. Of that journey, they would remember many things. The grunting of lions, the constant presence of hyenas spoiled on the remains of human warfare. The servants who accompanied them were armed with machetes and spears, Khanoum carried a club; the mukhi – lanky as a Masai, though a bit wobbly – walked with a spear and supplied comic relief. An impala gave them the run-around and they couldn't kill it; they wouldn't touch a dead giraffe. Finally one of the donkeys which was on its last legs was slaughtered. Their goat ran away, to its doom – if only it had known better.

Aku had been four years old then.

Aku remembered a holiday, a festival, when practically the whole town of Moshi went to the railway station to welcome the new District Commissioner. There were flags, banners pledging allegiance, and two bands; Europeans – the men in white suits and sun-hats, the women in dresses and wide frilly hats – stood in front with the police; Africans in all manner of attire, kanzus, tattered trousers, buibui, khanga cloth, stood behind on one side; Indians in turbans and fezzes, suits, dhoties, and frock-pachedis, stood on another. Aku stood with the mukhi amongst the Indians as the train arrived and a stool was produced and a white man descended from the train and then assisted a white woman, a rare delicate creature, to do the same. The bands played, there was applause, and the DC and his wife waved. Then the DC inspected a police guard of honour, after which he and his wife made their way to the awaiting motorcar. As the DC approached where Jamali and Aku stood, the mukhi tugged at the boy's hand and pulled him away.

The new District Commissioner was Alfred Corbin.

A year after that festival, the earth under Khanoum's feet split open and her world tumbled. The mukhi, with whom she had presided over a town, who had taken her down the slopes of the Mission hill to his world at the mbuyu and made her mother to his people, died, a king in exile. In Moshi he had not had quite the same prestige, but there were enough who knew him. Jaffer Bhai was one of them, though also reduced in stature, having retired as the mukhi of Moshi. With what he could bring with him, Jamali had opened a general store with dreams of regaining his past glory. He might have done just that, carried his family through a generation of respectability. Instead, with his death his family turned overnight into paupers. The store was not the kind of venture a woman, and an African one at that, would be allowed to enjoy credit on; it collapsed, its original promise coming to nothing. Without her husband, or material means, Khanoum was ignored by the community that she had embraced so wholeheartedly. The status she had held was forgotten. And so she turned away from them, bitter and sad, but not defeated. She had an Indian boy in her keep and three half-Indian children of her own; she was their Mama. The fact that Aku was so much fairer than the others did not seem to concern him, in the camaraderie of the streets where the sun tanned him and the dust covered everybody.

A poor widow sold what she could; Khanoum had her cooking, which she sold from her house. Her older son had left home, the other son brought in a meagre pay, and the third child, a daughter approaching marriageable age, helped her mother.

By the time he was six, a year after the mukhi's death, Aku was picking balls at the Sports Club for the mzungus when they played tennis, and receiving tips. And he was offered work as garden "toto" at the large house of a European. He would go at nine o'clock every morning to a house behind the closed cemetery where there were many large trees. The memsahib would be sitting on the front steps, resting after her morning's exertion in the garden – her face flushed, her pith helmet dropped beside her. The steps descended to a walkway that ran under a shady bower. There were many flowers and shrubs in the garden, of which the only ones he knew by name were the roses and sunflowers.

At first the boy did not understand the attention lavished upon a mere piece of ground covered with vegetation. Later he let his eyes roam discerningly over the garden and saw the clusters of golden yellow, the spears of white, red, and blue at the ends of long stalks, the pink and white ground cover, the thick large leaves like curtains and the numerous tiny leaves like lace, the difficult-to-maintain plants and the easy ones. He saw design in their timing and arrangement, and he felt a respect and affection for the garden's creator, this ruddy woman with golden curls, a smile on her lips, who was prone to chatting to herself.

He went around with a watering can, swept clean the path, arranged the flagstones, chalked them after rains. He always got a glass of lemonade after work. Once, he and the woman had killed a snake together.

One Sunday there was a party at the Club. He helped arrange chairs and tables on the lawn, and laid tablecloths and carried flowers. He ran in and out of the house conveying this and that, anything the panicky memsahibs demanded. The guests came in cars or on foot. Indians had been invited and came in two large groups, one of men, another of women, and they stood apart uncomfortably, huddled in their groups, watching the Europeans. The Europeans wore whites, looked pink and clean, their chatter crisp and starched. They sat down on the chairs. On the front tables silver trophies had been placed, polished that very afternoon, and so blinding in the evening light that some of the guests had to move their chairs. A man got up and made a speech, and the presentations began. The servants and the Indians at the back gawked. When the ceremony ended, sandwiches were served, and drinks. The Indians were concerned about ham and beef, and one of the mzungus came and talked with them. A little later a fresh tray was brought for them. "Cucumbers, bread, no harm here," the men said, and ate, but the women were shy and soon left. A little later the men followed, also shy, and apologetic, it seemed, but once the men were outside the gates Aku and the other totos saw them positively trotting away and laughed.

It was dusk, grey and breezy, and kerosene lamps were brought out. The trees rustled, emitting large expansive sounds, and the mzungus were ready to go inside.

As Aku was scurrying off with a liquor bottle a voice behind him said sharply, "Simama!" Stop!

The boy stopped, cringing, afraid of a scolding, even a cuff, and turned to look back. It was the European who had arrived on the train, the DC. He was the man who was the guest of honour, who had given out the trophies earlier. He had a thick moustache, kindly twinkling eyes. He was not very tall, carried his white helmet in his hand; his thin hair was combed flat. Beside him was the boy's memsahib and a tall young man. The woman spoke to the DC, who listened while staring at the boy. Then he came forward towards Aku.

"Kuja," come, the DC said in his English way, then stopped, and hesitantly the boy walked towards him.

"Jina lako nani?" What is your name? The man had bent down to speak, to look at the boy.

"Akber."

The man looked long and hard at him, into his eyes, until they hurt and he brushed them with the back of his hand.

"Baba yako nani?" Who is your father?

"Mukhi Jamali," the boy said.

"Yuko wapi?" Where is he?

"Amefariki." Dead.

And so Aku told him about the mukhi his uncle-father, and his auntie-mother, Khanoum.

The next morning Khanoum received a chit from the DC, brought by a messenger on a bicycle. At two o'clock, therefore, after lunch and rest, she went to see the DC at the government district office. Compared to what Bwana Corbin had been used to in Kikono, this was a palace: a large white building with an askari on guard outside. Another askari stood in the long corridor outside the DC's office. Inside, the DC sat behind a large desk, behind him a window with a grille. On a wall was the photograph of King and Queen.

As she entered he looked up from the papers on his desk, put down his pen, and stood up. She stopped in her tracks, bewildered, intimidated at the change – in circumstances, in him. He looked cleaner, heavier, and imposing.

"How are you, Mama Khanoum? Sit down . . . please."

She sat across from him, silent.

"It's been a long time . . ." he said.

"Ai. Much has passed."

"Yes. How is the family? . . . I heard Bwana Mukhi –"

"Passed away. It is as God wishes, isn't it?"

"I am sorry to hear that. Polé sana."

"And you, bwana?"

He told her he had been in Mombasa, then he had gone with the victorious army up to Wilhelmstahl, and stayed there for some work; then he was DC in Tanga. Later he had gone on leave and got married in England to a girl he had met in Nairobi (he nodded towards the framed photograph on his desk). He had returned to Tanga, then was posted to Moshi.

She accepted some water. How things had changed. He had been a shy guest in her home, once. He had been lonely. He had sometimes come to their home on a pretext and chatted with her husband. And the mosque had always fascinated him, he would peep longingly inside when on his evening rounds. Then there had been the incidents. First with the maalim, then the wedding. Mariamu had made him happy working in his house – that was her husband's idea, a stroke of genius he thought until it became a curse of the devil. All that, had been. Now they were in a big town. He was its ruler, with a beautiful young queen. And she, Khanoum, was a woman without a husband. She threw a glance at the photograph of his wife, a bright-looking girl with fair hair. The pose was stylish, the woman arching herself back and leaning sideways.

"I heard about you from the boy –" he said.

She nodded. "He told me. I didn't know it was your house he worked in."

"Mama Khanoum . . ." he began cautiously, searching for words. "I am deeply sorry to bring this up, but . . . I learned from government reports that Mariamu had been killed in Kikono. Please accept my sympathies . . ."

"Thank you."

"Who killed her – did the family have any suspicions . . ."

"No," she said. "There were many strangers about. But the matter is finished now."

"And the boy –"

196

"He is hers. Akber – we call him Aku."

He waited, then asked, "And Pipa – what o' 'm?"

"In Dar es Salaam. He married again and gave the child to us." She was staring at him and he became uncomfortable.

"If I can be of assistance, Mama . . . perhaps to help send the boy to school . . ." he said tentatively.

Proud woman that she was, she declined. "I have been remiss," she said. "Only, I have other children too. But I shall send the boy to school."

When she returned from the government headquarters, she told Aku not to take up odd jobs. And she herself found work in a European home, assisting its mistress with housework. She never met the DC again. Soon he went away, to Dar es Salaam, she heard, and another one took his place.

When she made inquiries at the Indian school, the elders of the Shamsis came to see her. Would she like to give up the boy? they asked. There were one or two Indian families who would oblige. The boy was good-looking and hard-working.

No, she told them, the earth under my feet has split open, but I shall not take charity and I'll not let the boy go. I am the wife of a mukhi, who left Aku in my care in the absence of the child's parents. I, too, have been leader of the community, looked after its welfare, helped run its mosque, buried its dead, welcomed new arrivals, nursed and fed the sick, cooked for its festivals, and danced and wept with the rest. So why do you come to harass me now that this husband is dead? Does this black self lessen in value now that its brown partner is gone? Has my soul lost anything, or my honour? Eti, have my abilities as woman and mother been diminished?

All arguments, she knew, were in vain. It was only a matter of time before her heart would be wrenched.

One day two Indian women came to see her. They were local women – Khanoum had seen them both before – middle aged and with the bearing that comes of status. They spoke clearly.

After the greetings, and refusing refreshments, one of them said, "We've come to see Pipa's son. The father pines for him and wants news of him." To explain this request, she added, "We have a letter from him . . . if you want to see it . . ."

Khanoum declined, and called the boy to meet the guests.

For two days they took him out on walks, talked to him. They bought him things, fed him. They told him about his father from whom he'd been separated and from whom he was now being kept away, no doubt due to the bad intentions of those who wanted to use his labour. "Look at you," they said, "just like a European. You have a great future, your father is rich."

One of these two "aunts" was on her way to Dar and would take him to meet his father.

Eight-year-old Aku was excited by the prospect of a rich father in Dar es Salaam. But he loved his Mama Khanoum too.

"Go," she told him. "Go and be with your father. You have a future with him. But don't think you'll be rid of me, you! Mama Khanoum will come to be with you . . ."

A few days later he climbed into the train with one of the women and went away. He would never see Mama Khanoum again.

16

For Pipa, the closing of the war brought a tragedy that marked the end of one life and the beginning of a new one in a world that had changed.

The day after he discovered his wife dead, Pipa and the community buried her in the little graveyard in Kikono. There was no civil government in town to investigate her murder; no witnesses were sought, no rewards offered, no evidence gathered. The Shamsis assumed that a marauding soldier had violated and killed the young wife, and – too conveniently in the eyes of the bereaved husband – had dropped the matter. They were a peace-loving people not in the habit of seeking vengeance. They could take comfort in the thought that Mariamu had moved on to a better life in the hereafter.

In a subtle, and to them compassionate, way they had so involved the bereaved husband in the rites and ceremonies of burial, that it was only afterwards that he could be alone with his grief. He had grown to love his wife. He felt cheated, felt her memory somehow violated by the quick resolution in the matter of her murder. But his elders had ruled; and there was no other authority — save the military, which he feared — to which he could turn. The town of Kikono now held for him the bitter reminder of a happy beginning cut short. Within days, as soon as the British armies had finally broken through into German East Africa, Pipa set off for his home town of Moshi. He left his young son, Aku, in the care of the mukhi and his wife, Khanoum, until such day when he could take care of him.

When Pipa arrived in Moshi on the heels of the victorious British forces, he was immediately offered a bride by his old patron Jaffer Bhai. The girl was none other than Jaffer Bhai's youngest, Remti, whom Pipa had watched growing up in her petticoats. Remti, contrary to the meaning of her name, "mercy," declared what most girls of her day would have agreed with, and something which she was most certainly coached to utter: I don't want the child of "that woman" in my home.

Children of a previous marriage polluted the new one. In most cases, however, some conscientious family member did the pious duty, for to adopt orphans is a great virtue. The mother or father would then take care to stay away, in another town. The price exacted by the new marriage, the abandonment of one's children for the sake of a new wife or husband and another brood, was seen as a necessary evil. Faced with this condition to his marriage, Pipa wrote a long letter to Jamali and Khanoum, asking them to keep the child.

Pipa was home now, yet lived in fear. He was a marked man, known both to the agents of Maynard and to the allies of the Germans; any of them could come to call on him as they had done in Kikono. He lived near the place where he had once run his shop, where Hamisi had come to buy English tobacco. In a way it was that tall, handsome Arab who had got him involved with Fisi; he thought of how the evil Englishman had betrayed Hamisi, who had been hanged by the Germans. Pipa was not the one who had passed on the betraying message, but in the eyes of Hamisi's followers his association with Fisi made him guilty. He saw Hamisi's children in the street sometimes, and once, through Jaffer Bhai, sent a gift of money to the widow. It was promptly returned. A young man in a white suit and with a stern face had asked for him at the door and peremptorily placed the envelope of money in his hands, without saying a word. He had worn the long green fez with the insignia of the Sufi order.

Pipa had come to town bearing another burden: a white man's intimate thoughts, memories, pains, committed to words in a diary, though he did not have the key to this illicit treasure, could not decipher it, did not have the language. He had hidden the book well, wrapped in canvas, inside an old trunk. The pen which had come with the book he kept with him.

He desperately wanted to get away, to Dar, to make a new beginning in that bustling city in which he had seen so much promise once. All kinds of opportunities would be opening up there. Even as preparations for his wedding were taking place, news came of the city's capture from the sea by the British.

Pipa was given a traditional wedding, regular in all respects. As Jaffer Bhai told him, "You have nothing to fear, she's my own daughter." It was as if his old patron was offering him his own daughter as replacement for damaged goods. But the memory of silent, beautiful Mariamu lingered, a cloud over the exciting event that was the wedding, casting a shadow that would only deepen.

Remti was a small figure of a girl, with thick wavy hair, full of mischief and vitality. She could cast seductive looks, as Pipa found, but she was practical and calculating. He had found a good match. In a larger town her prospects would have been brighter, but trapped in Moshi by the war, her choices were close to nil, until Pipa arrived. All this was no doubt reflected in the tears of her mother during the final ceremony of the wedding: the farewell after the feast on the day following the flawless wedding night.

Soon after the wedding Pipa took his new bride to the capital.

Dar es Salaam, 1916. A few decades before, the Sultan of Zanzibar, on an acquisitive whim, had paid a visit to the site. It was then a village beside a perfect, peaceful harbour. Highly impressed and feeling ambitious, he returned shortly with carpenters and planners to build up a town, and called it Haven of Peace. The Germans came and wrenched it from Arab hands; they built it up further, with beautiful white houses, roads, and monuments. It became now, for the British, the main military base for the remainder of the war. Gone were the rickshaws and handcarts, to be replaced by fleets of lorries, motorcars, motorcycles, roaring through the streets spewing black acrid fumes into the hot humid air. Villages of tents covered large, previously open spaces; restaurants and hotels overflowed with soldiers; fields and parks housed thousands of mules and horses. And everywhere the stench of dung, petrol, animal carcasses.

The Germans never surrendered their prize colony. Instead they kept getting pushed farther and farther south, and under their redoubtable leader von Lettow they kept fighting all the way into Portuguese East Africa. They had to be told that the war in Europe was over before they would emerge from the jungle.

And then finally one day came the end of military authority. The tents and uniforms, the animals and vehicles, the thousands of soldiers had gone; the town was cleaned up. And the residents of Dar took stock of what had happened.

There were those who had come from the interior wiped out, to unload their woes on family and community. And there were the others, whose fortunes had risen in the same war, who had bought out the Germans, foreclosed on loans, received outlandish collaterals, smuggled, hoarded, supplied the armies. Property was scarce in Dar. But the man who had been an unwilling agent of both the protagonists of the war had been paid well. He rented a house with shopfront; Pipa Store began anew.

His customers, as for the rest of his life, were the poorer Africans and Asians, those who could not stock their larders for more than a day – buying a little of this and a little of that. But bit by bit, as Pipa would say, the ocean gets filled. Haba haba hujaza kibaba. There are those who sit in their shops twitching their legs or picking their noses, saying their rosaries or singing hymns; I have my packets. A little bit of turmeric, chili, coriander, inside a flat cone of paper – fold, fold, fold, and a packet in the basket that would fetch an anna. It became a meditation for him, folding packets, an unconscious act during which he could think, come to himself, watch the world.

He had the industry of a spider. He hardly ever left the shop, until closing, when he would go to mosque. In a world in which he had neither family nor prestige, he found a niche, and that's where he built. Business came to him. Whole grain, from the farmers, which he would send to the mills for flour that he would then sell; copra, from which he would extract oil to sell; cashews roasted and raw; old newspapers; even screws and nuts, bolts and nails. For everything there was a buyer. And if sometimes a stolen bangle came his way, or a chain, or a forged hundred-rupee note, what matter? – he did not go searching for them. He even bought old German coins, now useless and despised, because he thought one day the price of metal would go up and they could be melted down.

In the evenings after supper his wife would help him count the day's takings – the coins would be rolled up and the notes gathered in bundles, and the money was put safely away. After a time they had a daughter. Yet there was nothing more compelling in the house than the Englishman's diary. It lay inside Pipa's black metal trunk by the bedside. It was memento, it was absolution. It harboured the spirit of Mariamu. By giving it to him – as he believed she had – by taking it for him when he did not have the courage to do so himself, she had chosen him over that other, had finally given herself to him. He should feel complete, and in a manner he did. But he felt possessed. If the book contained the spirit of Mariamu, she had not died. If through it she had chosen him, he could not cast it aside.

He knew, also, that it contained the answer to the one question that still haunted him, the answer he thought he almost knew for certain. What Mariamu had never discussed, never acknowledged, never denied. One day he would release the spirit in the book, and it would tell him. He wasn't sure how. In the single room behind the store, which was a bedroom at night, a living room during the day, the trunk with its sacred content was a charged presence that made him glow, tremble with excitement every time he allowed himself to think of it. That it had value to its previous owner he had no doubt – someone who had meticulously written in the book time and again, whose comfort he had sought like a woman, was bound to it by his memories, would come looking for it if he knew where it was.

But this did not happen and Pipa had put it out of his mind until one day, years later, while in the process of tearing up an old copy of the *Herald* for his packets, he found himself looking straight at the face of Alfred Corbin. Pipa couldn't believe his eyes, he stared and stared – but there he was, unmistakably Bwana Corbin, in the local newspaper.

He looked around desperately, then in great agitation ran outside with the paper to ask someone to read it for him. A civil servant visiting a neighbouring shop finally obliged him. By this time a bunch of curious shopkeepers had gathered.

– Aré that was the District Commissioner, Mr. Corbin – didn't Pipa ever see him? Eh bhai, didn't he come around this area ordering cleanups and the beggars to be picked up?

– That he was Corbin, two onlookers concurred.

– But I didn't see him, Pipa said, wondering at his good luck, letting out his breath at last. Has he gone, then?

— Yes, to Uganda. Look, he's saying goodbye. And that piece with him is the missis.

— What, Pipa Bhai, did you know Mr. Corbin from upcountry? What would he want from you?

— It's all right . . . I knew him up in British East Africa. He's gone now anyway — where and when will I see him again . . .

— No telling, said the civil servant. You know the sahibs, they come and go as they please. Don't they rule the world.

A discussion on the nefariousness of the Angrez followed, before the shopkeepers realized that business was meanwhile suffering and they dispersed.

Alfred Corbin had been District Commissioner in Dar es Salaam for eighteen months. He had then been briefly appointed Assistant Secretary for Native Affairs. He was a firm believer in, and made strong recommendations for, indirect rule of the former German colony, now a trust territory under the League of Nations. From Dar es Salaam, in 1923, Alfred Corbin was posted to Uganda, where he would spend a further twelve years.

Pipa found it difficult to get over the knowledge that Corbin had actually been in Dar, had walked the same streets he had, and possibly even stopped outside his shop. Had perhaps known of his presence in Dar. Suppose, he thought — just suppose — that Bwana Corbin had walked into his shop while supervising a cleanup of the street outside and had seen him, Pipa, sporting his fancy fountain pen. What then? A search of the house would have immediately revealed the diary in which the pen was found. Or suppose he had met Bwana Corbin in the street: how would he have greeted him? And he would have had this same fancy pen in his shirt pocket.

It was a miracle. He had been close to a calamity, but had been saved. This thought strengthened his feeling that the book was truly meant for him, and was under the protection of Mariamu's spirit.

And then news began arriving from Moshi, news about a boy, an angel of a boy, mistreated and used as a servant by an African woman. Was it the same boy? Pipa had no doubt. He had heard of Jamali's death the year before in Moshi, had sent a letter of condolence to Khanoum and had inquired in it about Aku. She had replied, thanking him and saying the boy was well.

Pipa then sent a letter to his father-in-law, Jaffer. The reply came: "The boy is yours, dear Pipa, living with the late Kikono mukhi's wife. She has left our community now that her husband is dead. The boy is dirty, wears no shoes, works as a servant and does not go to school. It is our urgent duty to take him back . . ."

Pipa guessed, correctly, that it was due to Khanoum's dire circumstance and outcast status that the boy's condition in her care was seen in this light. Yet something had to be done. It was as a result of his wife, Remti's, insistence that he had given the boy away. But seven years later Aku was no longer a threat to her; he could even be an asset. Besides, Pipa owed it to Mariamu's memory not to turn away from their son.

Find out, Pipa and Remti wrote back, if the boy would like to come to Dar to his father, if he will be happy away from Khanoum. The boy must be willing to come; Khanoum, who has been a mother to him and is his aunt, should not be coerced. If necessary, we will come to Moshi to discuss the situation with her.

The folks in Moshi acted upon this letter and took custody of the boy and sent him to Dar.

17

You shall not worship idols, say the scriptures.

"This is not right," said Remti. "It is sinful, this puja, this shrine. We are not Hindus –"

"I have to do this," he said. "Or there will be no peace."

Over the seven years since her death, she often came to haunt his imagination. At first, during his early days in Dar, she would appear as the helpless murdered figure he had discovered on the floor of their shop in Kikono: her head lolling to one side, a pained, surprised look on her face; strands of hair stuck together, a red stain on the throat, her dress soaked at the chest. The pachedi was somewhere on the floor. This bloody apparition would get up to claw at him in anger, and he would recoil with horror and surprise, saying, "This is not you, Mariamu, this anger," and she would become her normal gentle self and chide, "Surely we agreed to be together."

She is only jealous of Remti, Pipa would tell himself; she'll soon get used to my new life.

After a time, to his relief, the blood-stained figure disappeared altogether, and she came to him only as the gentle woman he knew so well. She would be sitting on a chair facing him, legs crossed in front of her, quite alluring in the green pachedi and the sparkling nose stud, her bare feet dyed with henna in bridal designs.

"Why this bhupko," he'd ask her, "this show, after all this?"

"Isn't this how you liked me?" she'd say with a smile.

Everyone he talked to, those who knew, told him with certitude that a jiv, a soul, whose body meets a sudden end must remain on earth for the specified period, until the time ordained for death. There were rituals to benefit the jiv: on the morning of Eid, when the choicest cooking is taken to mosque in the name of the dead (food for the body transformed into prayers for the soul); and on Layl-tul-qadr, when angels descend upon the earth to bestow blessings.

When Aku came to live with him, she said, "You've made me very happy. He's now with us, as before."

"I would so much like a corner to myself," she told him one day. "Nothing much. Just a humble corner of my own."

There was a small, square storeroom adjoining the shop, its warped wooden slab of a door facing the till. To its left was the doorway opening into the street; to its right was the entrance to the inner, living room.

He would make a home for her in this empty storeroom, he decided.

He had the room swept and cleaned. And then he went and brought the trunk, which had for so long sheltered the book, and placed it against the wall facing the door. There the book lay, inside the trunk, for some time. The room became hers.

One morning, on a Sunday, when the shop was closed, he went into the room, fetched the book from the trunk, sat on the floor. He flipped the pages, examined closely the sloping hand, the dates, the printed advertisements on the endpapers; he noted the change from ink to lead pencil and back, and the varying length of entries: all these signified, said something, he could not know what. Tenderly he closed the book.

He went and brought a white sheet, covered the trunk with it, and with reverence placed the book on it. This room, its door visible at the far end from the till, thenceforth he kept locked, for entry to no one but him.

Thus began his long period of private idolatry.

To Aku, his father appeared as a dour, silent, and strange character, though not an uncaring one. The boy went to the community school in the morning, and in the afternoons sat in the shop with his father, at his allocated place on the outside doorstep, looking out at the street but ready to help when called. In the evenings he went out to play. His stepmother he found attentive, though in a distant way; she had her own two daughters to look after, with whom he sometimes played. For many months he missed Khanoum's long arms with which she embraced him, and her carefree home that he had left.

Aku's introduction to his father's strangeness was the mysterious locked room into which no one but his father was allowed. It began with a peculiar incident, a Hindu ceremony to which his father took him one night.

They were in a large and bright room filled with thick incense fumes and the tinkle and jangle of bells and tambourines and the chanting of people. A thin, dark brown man sat at the edge of a stage, his legs dangling over the side, facing a throng of worshippers who sat on the floor. He wore a cloth round his waist, the rest of him was bare and hairless. A lightbulb hung not far above his head, creating an aura around him. The worshippers, men and women, chanted as they struggled to keep their eyes on the man, who went into a paroxysm of shaking and shivering, so that waves seemed to move up from his legs to his belly and neck. His eyes had become large and wide as if with fright, his mouth was a deep red, and there were white lines on his forehead. Suddenly there was a hush. "Look," people said: the man on the stage, his body taut, eyes wide, mouth puckered in a whistle, and hands on his knees, seemed to be changing colour, taking on hues from dark purple to grey to ashen white then yellow, orange, and red. And then with controlled undulations a wave went up from his vibrating stomach to the torso, and from the back of his throat there slowly appeared first a dim light, then a glowing object which so grotesquely filled his mouth it could not possibly be ejected, and the man, his lips stretched to the utmost, pulled it out, tearing his lip in the process so that it became bloody. The object seemed to be a sphere fused to one end of a cylinder. The man fainted into the arms of his attendants who had rushed to him.

Aku watched this spectacle terrified as he held on to his father's hand.

The next morning the man came to the shop, in dhoti and cap, grinning very broadly, with extremely white teeth. The boy was not frightened this time. His father served the Indian some tea, then showed him a piece of paper, and after that took him to the storeroom. A smell of incense began to come from inside, and the sound of chanting. The Indian came two more times, each time bringing unfamiliar pasty sweets for the children, who swallowed them painfully. On the last day he drew coloured chalk patterns outside the storeroom, on the floor at the threshold.

Thus was Pipa's shrine to Mariamu consecrated. If the room had been forbidden before, it became forbidding now. To Aku and his sisters it symbolized the mysterious, unspoken side of their brooding father. If they talked about it at all, it was to say that the room was their father's own private prayer room, and it had resident in it a holy presence.

To Pipa, the boy brought a comfort. He felt a tenderness welling up inside him, a need to reach out to the little fellow; but six years' separation had left gaps too large, they had not developed between them the codes and language of familiarity and affection. There was also that doubt, the question that stood between himself and Aku: Was he his son?

Mariamu spoke to him, but she did not say much. She had never been one for lengthy conversations; and now, as before, on certain matters she was completely silent.

So whenever he heard of the presence of maalims and joshis or others of whatever faith who had acquired local renown for their knowledge of the world of spirits, he went to consult them. To each he showed a half page from the book. Of each he asked the same questions. Where is she? What is she? Who killed her? What is in the book? Tell me about the jiv, the soul.

None of them could give him the exact answers. But they all concurred: the fact that she had returned to him, made her home with him again, so to speak, was proof that she had left something undone, had something yet to take from or give to the mortal world.

But what? – Pipa thought. Why doesn't she tell me what it is?

"Sometimes, my friend," one maalim, going further than most, told him, "all that these returned souls want from us is forgiveness in order to be released . . ."

Having heard this, Pipa went home trembling with the thought that he would release Mariamu. Why not? – she was dead, let her rest in peace. He would keep the book she had given him; and he had her son. He went to her shrine, sat in front of the book, and said, "I forgive you, Mariamu, if you sinned. Go now and rest in peace."

But that night Mariamu came to him, turning the maalim's

reasoning on its head: "I thought you forgave me already . . . back in Kikono . . . why then send me away now? And how do you expect me to leave my son?"

"Isn't he my son too?" Pipa said angrily.

He had been clever there, he thought. But Mariamu said nothing and made him angrier still.

And so Mariamu remained, as did Pipa's questions to which she would give no answer.

Pipa learned the English alphabet from his son, who was eleven years old now, tracing over the letters like a child as the two sat in the shop in the afternoons. At other times Aku read to him from his school readers. This is a dog. A farmer went trotting upon his grey mare: bumpety, bumpety, bump. Rule Britannia. It is the duty of all subjects to be loyal to their king. The boy was not sure when his father's limit was reached, at what point his mind simply refused to take in any more. But he read, and helped his father say words with him.

Several times Aku saw Pipa at the shrine, through the crack where the door was hinged, bent over something, poring over it — trying to read. He would come out quiet, at peace. Once, he emerged from the storeroom and said to the boy, "Can you write 'Mariamu'?" The boy wrote on his slate. Pipa looked around for a piece of blank paper. He couldn't find one. He became frantic. Finally, he took one of the last pages of a ledger and found a pencil stub. The boy scrawled *Mariamu*. Pipa took the piece of paper to the storeroom, studying it in his hand as he walked, and emerged a half hour later, rubbing his eyes and pleased with himself. He had read the book: one word in it.

The boy had felt his heart beating fast when he heard that word, Mariamu, his mother's name, on his father's lips. It brought them a little closer together. Until now he had been told nothing more than that his mother was dead. Now he knew: all his father's devotions at the shrine were to his mother. But he was afraid to ask his father about her yet.

Then a strange episode occurred that made him even more aware of her.

He was eleven years old. For a few days there had been much veiled discussion between Pipa and Remti, about some "they" who would be coming to visit. Pipa had fumed and raged. "After ten years they show their faces – for what? Now that he is almost grown, do they think they'll take him from me – or turn him against me? . . ."

The boy began wondering: Were "they" his other relations? Would they take him from Pipa and Remti as he'd been taken once from Khanoum?

The day they were to arrive there was much anticipation. The children were given new clothes to wear and instructed not to go outside. The rooms were swept more than once. At last, in the afternoon, the visitors came: a thin sickly woman, a robust big-bosomed lady who was older, two girls, and a man who was their local host. The adults all sat on the floor and the guests were given water. The children were presented and were admired before they, too, took their places on the floor. When Aku's turn came to be shown off, the happy scene broke down. The older lady began: "What a beautiful child! And the girls like angels! Such prosperity in the home!" And then, before anyone could respond: "Oh my poor darling if she had only lived to see all this . . ." With open palms she beat her white bosom, once, twice, and the women started wailing and the two men, at first taken by surprise, looked down and had tears in their eyes. The younger children giggled a bit before the older girls shushed them. Remti offered vague words of comfort.

As suddenly as it had started, the wailing stopped. The big

woman, wide-eyed, looked around. "But this is not good," she declared. The younger sickly woman, her daughter Kulsa, who was Mariamu's mother, blew her nose and said, "What's happened is done with."

This was the long-delayed sog ceremony after the death.

"She was a good soul," Mariamu's grandmother announced. She was the type called Zanzibari, one given to dramatic exhibitions of emotion.

The mood relaxed, tea was drunk, with biscuits, and they all talked matter-of-factly about "She," who apparently had been a great soul. When "She" died, there had been a peaceful smile on her face; a star had fallen from the sky during the funeral ceremonies.

Before the visitors left, Aku was brought before them once more. With tears and hugs he was given a present and told to visit his grandmother in Mombasa.

After they had gone, Mariamu, his mother, became real for the boy. She had had a mother and a grandmother of her own; what else? He began to feel that he belonged to more than just his father. But the world of adult machinations, appearances and disappearances, bewildered him still. Khanoum he remembered somewhat vaguely now. She had said she would come to him, but she never did.

Remti was a patient woman, bringing up a growing brood of girls, longing always for a boy. She did not resent the girls, the older ones helped with the younger, and about the house; they sang together while oiling hair, or cleaning rice and grain; and of course there were numerous squabbles. With the boy, Remti was less close – both remembered the circumstances of his arrival. But she was not unkind. With a pang of regret at not having her own son, she saw him grow older; soon he would be another man in the house. Her daughters would eventually be married away, and he would remain, its master when her husband was old or dead; unless she had a son of her own. Also, she knew that it was a son who preserved a woman in her old age.

She had her way around her husband, his moods, his obsession, which she treated as if it was a disease. She had known him a long time, longer than he had known his first wife. She could remember the day he first came to her home, with his mother, shy and gruff, and how her father had taken to teasing him as though he were a younger brother. He had set eyes on one of her sisters first but had been discouraged by the ambitions of her parents.

She was a good-looking woman of high spirits, astutely keeping out of her moody husband's way most of the time. But on festive Thursdays, cleverly and with determination she worked her charms on the man, coming to be beside him in the shop, solicitous, intimate, and good-humoured; he somehow expected that and responded. On those afternoons the rooms filled with the cloying sweetness of halud vapour, and she would bathe, and oil her hair and scent it with jasmine. She would have his clothes cleaned and pressed and together they would walk to the mosque with the children. They would return in high familial spirits and eat the evening meal in a festive atmosphere, her every move long and slow and voluptuous in the colourful frock and pachedi she generously filled. Still sweet-talking him, she would guide him to bed, in the corner away from the children, while the oldest girl turned down the lamps.

With the street sense he had picked up, the boy always knew the moment when his father mounted her – the rustling bedclothes, his growls, a short sharp cry from Remti, then an anxious pause followed by her tremendous sigh of abandon. And, after masturbating in his corner in the dark, the boy would lie awake for a long time, thinking about who he was, and about Mariamu, the mysterious creature with whom he was linked. For every time the name, or "She," was mentioned, a look, two looks, fell upon him.

If Thursday night was the boy's period of agony and sleeplessness, until he got up at four in the morning and trudged to morning prayer, the following night was his father's. All day Pipa would be in a foul mood; even the beggars were not spared on Fridays, their day. After prayers he'd go to play cards with other shopkeepers at the seashore, returning late after smoking bhang. On these nights Remti would find a pretext to sleep with one of the younger children.

One such Friday night the boy woke up to see a big shadow beside him; he opened his eyes wide and saw his stepmother, lying between him and the fourth girl, Zarina. The perfume on her from the previous evening was faint but sweet. For minutes he lay on his side, looking at her back curving towards him, his heart, his body aching, and then he edged himself closer to her, first to smell the halud, the jasmine, still lingering, then closer still until he was just touching her – and finally the wet release and his choking, confused torment. He was pressed against her, and she said angrily, "Move away." He began to cry then, and she turned and held him. "Did you have a bad dream?" she asked, and he said, "Yes." She must have guessed his torment – while her husband groaned in his. From then on, on the nights he found her close to him, he would move against her and find comfort, and admit to a bad dream afterwards. Her kindness then made him love her.

For Pipa those Friday nights belonged to Mariamu. He would dream or think about that wedding night, what a calamity it had been; how different from his other wedding night, with this healthy, spunky girl from Moshi – who had responded as he had expected, after which he had looked at the stain and knew, and handed over the bloody sheet to the women waiting for it.

Images would come to his mind of Mariamu and the English-man together in the ADC's house in Kikono, grotesquely sugges-tive; but they were kind, these spectres, shadowy and blurred . . . nevertheless sinful, deeply hurtful.

He would dream, too, about the days after, when they had risen above the hurt, lived up to their vows, become closer.

Yet she was not only a voice, an image in the past. She spoke to him in the present, as when she said, "Oh, but how easily men forget. You are happy now." The next day he had sent dried fruit, milk, a pachedi to mosque.

But she did not rest.

Another time: "Don't you think. . . . We hardly had time to start a home." She looked alluring, inviting, sitting on a chair fan-ning herself. Her nose stud sparkled, she had on the sparkling green pachedi (Was it really so fine as this? he wondered). And she gave a thin wistful smile before looking away. He had sent some furniture to the mosque as a result, but a little angrily because of the cost. He bought one chair back at the subsequent auction of goods and kept it in the storeroom which was her shrine.

"You don't have to give me anything," she said. "I come only to be with you sometimes, and to watch over you. And the boy. Do you mind that so much?"

Once he asked her, "Did you and the mzungu —"

She disappeared.

If the book were not there he would forget her. But it was there. How clever she had been – he admired her fondly – to leave the book for him, so that he could never forget her.

It was noon, on a school holiday, and Aku was sitting as usual on the step outside his father's shop. Pipa was seated among his wares, around him the gunny sacks and crates, behind him the scale for weighing produce.

"Eh, Aku," Pipa said to the boy. "Mind the store, will you, I'm going in for a minute to stretch my legs." A little later he called out from inside: "Aku, don't leave the store. I'm staying to eat."

The boy sat confidently in his father's chair, next to the till, and served the customers who came. Like his father he would extend the long-handled tray to receive the copper and silver coins from the customers, who stood outside, then extend it again with the change and the goods. A few of the customers paused to compliment him, quite a young man now, in his father's seat, and he felt proud. Between customers he watched the street outside. There was some excitement when a police Land Rover passed, making an announcement through a megaphone.

Suddenly a shadow fell over the street, a cloud had covered the sun. Everything became still for the boy – far away – he could hear a buzzing in his ears and distant, very distant sounds of the street, as if it had receded into a dream. He felt a call, an urge, a pull, from behind – from the storeroom, from Mariamu, his guardian angel. He got up, walked between crates and gunnies, past the doorway on the left that lead to the inner room where his father was, then paused at the threshold to the storeroom. It was a few days after the Diwali festival and his father had had the markings on the floor renewed, with blue, white, red, and yellow patterns in chalk for good luck. On the lintel above was a verse from the Quran. He waited to hear if his father was coming, then with beating heart and trembling hand he slid back the bolt, pushed open the creaking door, and there in front of him was the shrine he'd only glimpsed before through the crack in the door.

He hesitated once more, then walked to it, the chair which was an offering to her, sent to the mosque and bought back, on which now was the sacred book. There was an incense stand on a stool to the right; and some sweets on a stool to the left. The book itself was placed on a white doily of cotton needlework. Yellowish boards, red and black letters on the cover. He opened it gently, and looked through the pages inside, trying to read in a hurry, looking for the charmed word "Mariamu," without success. He turned around, then, to see his father approach.

He was beaten – until he ran fearing for his life – for the desecration, for having dared step on the auspicious patterns, for having slid back the bolt, touched the book and soiled it. Shaytaan, he heard, as the blows fell, you devil, *bastard*. He did not return that day, slept the night in the mosque, vowed never to return. He asked the caretaker of the mosque if he needed assistance, whether he could serve him. The next day the caretaker took him home, holding him firmly by the wrist, but grinning. "Many like you have come to me for refuge," he said. But he scolded the father: "Why breed if you can't look after them?" Pipa opened his mouth to reply but shut it.

The boy and the father looked at each other. The one searching, the other blank but without anger. Aku was forgiven.

One day he asked his father, "Shall I draw Mariamu for you?"

Pipa, somewhat startled, stared at the boy. "Yes, do," he said, struggling with a tenderness he did not quite know how to handle. And the son, sitting on the step next to the scales and the gunnies, drew a head, a chest on a piece of paper, and showed it to the father.

"The face should be a little narrower, you've made it round, like Remti's."

And the boy, with eraser and pencil, altered.

"Add the cheekbones. And the siri on the right side of the nose, not the left. It sparkles.

"Put a border on the pachedi. The shoulder doesn't droop so.

"The chest." (He meant the bosom. The boy made it fuller.)

Pipa held it, and stared long at it. "You draw well," he said.

"Can I have it back?" the boy asked.

"By all means, she is your mother. Every Thursday take a plate of sweets for her to the mosque and pray for her soul."

"She was a sati, wasn't she?" the boy said, chattily. Pure and pious.

Yes, she was a sati.

"And sinless, she did no wrong?"

Pipa looked at the boy. Here he himself was on shaky ground.

"Remember what they teach in mosque. Everyone, no matter how pure, commits at least seven sins a day. That is the nature of life. That is why every day in mosque we go to the mukhi and ask for forgiveness."

The boy took the drawing with him. He showed it to his step-mother and sisters. He kept it near his mat. And he also took to talking to her. She distracted him on Thursday nights, during the performance of his father's lust upon his stepmother; and other times interceded for him through his adolescence.

Akber Ali – Aku, as he'd been known – grew up into a dashing youth. Throughout childhood he had been considered especially well endowed with good looks: a local phenomenon, with beau-tiful eyes and fair skin. This glamorous reputation stayed with him in boyhood and beyond. It gave him a sense of specialness, which was reinforced by the less public, unhappy aspect of his upbring-ing as a stepson, a child of that other, mysterious woman from a war-torn country. And to this specialness he would attribute that certain longing he always carried for something he could not quite describe: a need to rise above others, to escape and move on, and the drive to prove himself, to conquer.

At twenty he was tall and somewhat burly. He preferred white suits, a style associated with an older generation of men, except that he also wore a striking black tie. His black hair was combed back above an ample forehead.

He was working in "town" – the business area – as a salesman for a wholesale firm. For the young Indian men in Dar, the first real job always was a watershed, the end of youth. Marriage

proposals would already be out in all directions, to families ranging from the upscale to the modest, girls from the beautiful and
smart to the demure and homely. Before he sank into domestic
oblivion, Akber Ali decided he would go to Mombasa to see his
mother's family and perhaps seek better prospects there. At first
his father would not have it.

– This is your place, with me, with your mother.

– But my mother wants me to go.

– No, she doesn't. I have known her longer. She left you in my
care.

– But I will return.

Without consent, without blessing, the boy could not go. The
stalemate lasted a year. And then: Go, his father said. But your
home is here.

In Mombasa, Akber Ali was apprised of some family history. His
mother's grandmother, he learned, had gone as a girl from Jam-
nagar, India, first to Zanzibar, then had married in the ancient
Swahili town of Lamu. It was from Lamu that her son – his great-
uncle Jamali – set off in the company of a British explorer and
founded the town of Kikono, where Mariamu, his mother, was
brought up, later married, and where he was born.

If Ali had had hopes of being reunited with Mariamu, of
finally getting to know her in her death, he was quickly disappointed. Here she was the "sati," the saint, and it was in these
terms that she was spoken of. Sometimes, at his grandmother
Kulsa's home, a relation called Rashid would show up, apparently
for handouts. With reluctance he was told that Rashid was his
grandmother's estranged husband and Mariamu's stepfather.

Ali quickly found work – and diversions – in Mombasa, a city
with long traditions, and multitudes of tribes, castes, races, which
offered greater allure and more freedom than the smaller, re-
pressed Dar. Life's lessons in the streets of Mombasa were learned

more easily; there were more corners and alleys, and ample curtains to hide behind. A city more experienced, sinful, earthy, was kinder to the yearnings of youth, less prone to condemn. Akber Ali travelled with friends, dressed well, and wherever he went he cut an impressive figure. He contemplated many ventures – apprenticeships in Lamu, Uganda, Nairobi, Mombasa. But two years after, he decided to return home to Dar.

Ali came back from Mombasa a dandy, and quickly found a job at the firm of G. R. Moolji, a successful wholesale distributor of khanga cloth. Soon Ali married one of G. R. Moolji's daughters. She was called Sherbanoo and was educated up to Standard Eight; she had been a teacher for a while and was on the prestigious Ladies' Committee, which ran classes in etiquette and "English" cooking (boiled or baked). But she lacked in looks – she was the darkest of the daughters when "beautiful" meant "fair," and by no means was she slim like the actresses in the films. But she had the name and was a good catch.

From the son of Pipa the shopkeeper to the dandified in-law of the "khanga king"; from salesman to part owner. He could have been exploited and mistreated by his in-laws, but he had a strong presence. His grey eyes were a source of wonder, family pride. He should protect his eyes and skin from the sun, he was advised. No point in acquiring a fair in-law only to have him baked brown afterwards. The family well remembered that their Miss Sherbanoo Moolji had been hard pressed for a suitor. The fact that she failed to conceive after marriage gave him a hold over his in-laws that was irksome to them, though they found consolation in his circular adopted name, Ali Akber Ali, which denounced his humble origins and protected their new mobility (and nobility). He still preferred white suits, but now wore a black astrakhan hat and carried a cane. In all this he had a model: none other than the glamorous Prince Aly Khan.

And so there was born the legend in Dar es Salaam of the

handsome boy who looked like Aly Khan but who had changed his name and denounced his father.

"I told you so," Pipa said to Mariamu, "when you said to let him go. They put all sorts of ideas into his head. Now he doesn't know me. They stole him from me."

I knew it, he muttered to his wife, Remti, and daughters.

"How long could you have held him prisoner?" Mariamu said. The other wife, Remti, concurred, adding, "He's showing his true colours, it was bound to happen. He's not yours. Now you know."

That, of course, was where the knife hurt most.

"Don't worry," Mariamu said. "No matter what, a boy always returns to his father; always the son becomes the father."

"You talk as if you know a lot about such matters, you who bore only one son and couldn't see him grow up."

"There's a lot of wisdom where I am," she answered.

But inwardly, he groaned. Always he becomes the father – but which father?

One afternoon, a European police inspector, accompanied by three askaris, called at the store. With them was another European, a red-faced stocky man in civilian clothes, who didn't say much but smoked a pipe and followed the inspector about. They were searching for smuggled items, the inspector told the shopkeeper. "Go ahead, then, look," said Pipa to the inspector wearily, and the men got to work.

Shopkeepers were used to these whims of the police – if it was not smuggled goods it was stolen property, or expired licences, or scales which had been tampered with. But something in the demeanour of the two Europeans, and that one of them was a civilian, made Pipa wary this time. Something else was afoot, but he could not be sure what. He had only one thing to hide, and it had ruled his life for almost twenty years. When the askaris reached the storeroom, Pipa would not let them through. "My prayer room," he told them. "Don't go in. Don't step –" he pointed to the chalk markings on the floor, pointed to the Quranic verse on the lintel. They insisted on peeping in. The bolt was shot back, the door pushed open. The two white men stared at the room for a while. It was quite dark and bare except for a shrine in front of them, consisting of a decorated chair with a garland hung on its back. There was the smell of incense. "Let's go," they said to the askaris and left.

The two men returned the next day to an even more agitated Pipa, and themselves very much impatient and bad tempered. They headed straight for the storeroom, and they entered, careful to step over the chalked markings. On the seat of the wooden chair, which was directly before them, they saw a book covered by a white doily and picked the book up. It was printed, in Gujarati, published in Bombay. No interest. There was a photograph. "Who is he?" asked one of the Englishmen. "Suleiman Pir," said the shopkeeper. "Our spiritual leader." The two men asked for lamps. Candles were brought, and they looked around. Their shadows loomed large against the walls, darkening large portions of the small room. The three men kept bumping against each other. The Englishmen yelled at Pipa to wait outside, but he wouldn't. In one corner of the room was a pile of newspapers, the floor was wet there. This was the corner opposite the shrine, towards the inside of the house.

Later no one could say exactly how it had happened. A candle fell, turned brighter on the floor, then the fire exploded in their midst, throwing them back and into confusion, and sped towards the walls, which burned in no time. The storeroom was destroyed, as was part of the shop and the kitchen.

It took Pipa some years to win his claim for damages from the colonial government. He moved his shop and residence to the African side of the Mnazi Moja no-man's-land, called Kariakoo, where land was cheaper. He also had a dark storeroom there, which acquired legendary status because even then subsequent police raids found nothing incriminating.

As the forties arrived, Dar es Salaam was a booming town and a capital surpassing Zanzibar. Here fortunes were made that would last a few decades, and more; family dynasties began that would replace the once glorious but now declined houses of Tharia Topan, Sewa Haji, Allidina Visram, who had gone penniless from Cutch to Zanzibar in the previous century and set up private empires while servicing foreign ones. The no-man's-land that was Mnazi Moja, a wasteland left undeveloped to act as firebreak and sanitary buffer between the African and the European sections, with the Asians living on either side of it, became a boundary between the town-wallahs and the Kariakoo-wallahs and a muggers' haunt in the dark. A mosque was erected in the Indian quarter, near the vegetable garden and the town well, a two-storey stone structure with a tile-roofed clock tower that dominated the shops at its base, tolling the hours and half-hours. Gradually mud and wattle and corrugated iron gave way to brick and concrete. There were motorcars, buses, and bicycles on the roads, several cinema houses in operation. India sent magazines, storybooks, missionaries, pandits, fortune-tellers, mullahs, new immigrants, and movies. England sent newspapers (which came second hand through civil servants and often as wrapping paper), textbooks, movies, teachers, administrators and governors, the BBC, and the law. America sent movies and Coca-Cola. English meant power, prestige, and wealth, while German was a quaint reminder of a bygone era. The pioneer days were over; the Indian communities took their ancient rivalries to the cricket pitch for "friendly" games that only occasionally turned bitter and became memorable. They had their schools now, and dispensaries; welfare organizations, community councils, sports clubs, youth organizations; proud Boy Scouts carried their banners at festivals, swore loyalty to God and King, learned survival in the jungle. Festivals lasted weeks, mournings forty days. Festivals opened with dramas – or "dyloks" – the most popular for several decades was *Hassan bin Sabbah*; but Indian musicals supplied endless plots and songs. The Empire Cinema entertained with Madhuri, "The Baghdadi Bul-bul," *Beau Geste*, *All Quiet on the Western Front*, *Her Private Life* (also called *The Fallen Goddess*), and much more. New products tantalized the new consumers. Cadbury's, cod-liver oil, Pagdiwala Coffee, Stephenson's pens, Aden-white salt, Odeon "talking boxes" with records in English, Swahili, Gujarati, Urdu, and Arabic. Star Printing Works was born, and with it a community newspa͡ ͡ vith national and international news: the Boy Scouts of Dodoma were arriving; Prince Aly Khan opened a school in Kathiawad, India; a religion teacher required in Nairobi; a widower in Masindi Port seeking a companion or he would marry his African maid, for the sake of the "comm" (the community) would a widow or older unmarried lady of experience please come forward. In these hard times, one Lalji Ramji exhorted the community, you could make a few extra shillings by selling him your old postage stamps, also those old German hellers and Maria Theresa dollars; a mosque gone up in Iringa; M. S. Meghji would have your lights fixed; Bharat Cinema pleaded for its customers to support it, its new seats were comfortable, a gallery was set aside for the ladies; we have spent a lot of money, announced the Empire Cinema, on equipment for talking movies, please support.

In short, a world that begins to look familiar emerges from the waters of the past, integrated.

Miscellany (iii)

From the personal notebook of Pius Fernandes
May 1988, Dar es Salaam

Rita and I see each other every day when she comes into town. There are not so many people she knows here now, and the relations that she does have become free from their shops only in the evenings. We discuss among other things the diary – the slim book that has enmeshed so many lives. She's curious about what I know, of course, but surprisingly she has been quite forthcoming with what she knows.

"You see," she says of Ali, "the son did return to the father. Just as Mariamu said he would. At least for a few days."

"And then?"

"They talked, had the talk they never had before, and then he went away – returned –"

"Went to his father in England?"

She gives an annoyed look.

Later, talking of her father-in-law, Pipa, as if arguing his moral right to the book, she says, "How much he put himself through just to preserve that book, to keep alive that memory, that name: Mariamu."

"A latter-day Orpheus –"

"A little different, surely – a humble shopkeeper."

She stops, looks at me impatiently, then smiles, surprised at herself.

"I'm sorry," I say, as she sips her coffee.

She has me now, as she's had me ever since I laid eyes on her again, after so many years, when I went to greet her at the hotel.

Still the Enchantress.

We sit in a café on Somora Avenue. It used to be Independence Avenue; before that, Acacia Avenue. It reminds us that much has changed (for one thing there are hardly any trees left), but life goes on; if anything there is more life now, in this teeming street, in this city whose population has more than quadrupled since she left.

Every day, for several days now, we have sat in the same place, the same cushioned corner seat, starting at ten in the morning: some idle chitchat, some reminiscences, and for me, in little bits, she gives the story of Pipa the father, Ali the son. And she, Rita, I think as I watch her, certainly no spirit across the table.

There is some grey in the hair, above the ear; the face is long, still smooth, with a dab of peach bloom on the cheek, a little tiredness around the eyes. She has a flower-patterned dress on, the brightest thing anywhere in this room (no one wears a khanga here), and sits straight but not stiffly; no longer a pupil but a rich woman of the world.

"And you have told me all this," I say. "All this openness about the family's past. Why? Is it the book you want?"

"Well, I have only told *you*, haven't I. . . . We go back a long way, don't we? I enjoy talking with you – perhaps all I've done is to repay you for your company. Haven't *you* felt the need to talk, after a long time?"

She stops, eyes me. For a moment, and only a moment, she looks vulnerable. "Your curiosity is irresistible, in any case. You already know so much. And — since you ask why I tell you all this — there's a price I'll want to exact from *you*." She smiles.

"I'll pay the price." So says the historian quickly disarmed.

"Any price?" Her smile widens.

"Any price that's mine to give."

"I wonder."

This new familiarity, I say to myself, watching her, is exciting. I never knew her like that. The mature, grown-up Rita, the full person.

I smile in return, as I must: "The story is all that matters. I can't stop now. I'll take it to its end."

Who owns the diary? Feroz and Rita stand poised, each with claims to it. Feroz with the finder's privilege. It is he who gave it to me, on trust; to him I should return it. Rita on the other hand represents the heir. That claim assumes that the diary was Pipa's. But it wasn't, it was stolen. A claim could be made for Corbin's heirs. But what guarantee do we have that it would have gone to them, or that they would have disposed of it in a manner he would approve of, or that he himself would not have ultimately destroyed it? The private diary of a public servant. Who are his heirs — his kin? The people he served among, whose lives he influenced? The government he served?

"How do you two know each other?" I ask Feroz light-heartedly.

In her absence, he's talked of her knowledgeably and famil-iarly, and now, watching them together, it seems to me that they go back quite some way. He is embarrassed by the question. She answers it: "I am his aunt, aren't I, Feroz?" She explains: "He is a son of one of my cousins. I remember him as a boy of ten when I left Dar. . . . He was a quiet boy and such a help around the shop." She turns to Zaynab, his wife, and asks almost impertinently: "Is he a good boy now?"

This is at lunch at Feroz's. We are on the second floor of a Msimbazi building constructed in the heyday of the sixties when such a building represented wealth, a move up. Since then, like others, it has been taken over, nationalized; and money has found other means, other havens. But in spite of the wealth amassed by Feroz (some in Canadian and British banks), in spite of the hot water and VCR and toaster, this house – everything from its oil-cloth on the table to the linoleum on the cement floor, the wooden pantry and scullery next to the dark kitchen, the sofas, the beds made up with mosquito nets rolled down and tucked in at the sides – belongs so much to the times Rita left behind.

"Hasn't changed a bit," she says. "Exactly like the house I grew up in. Don't tell me –" she tiptoes excitedly into the sitting room, with its television, sofa, and – she turns to looks at us triumphantly – the master bed. "Brilliant," she says, clapping her hands delightedly.

By this time the host and hostess are thoroughly deflated, shown up, reduced to the Kariakoo-wallahs that they are (foreign bank accounts notwithstanding, educated kids in the wings notwithstanding). There is a pained look on Zaynab's face. Her daughter brings Cokes on a tray. The room is air-conditioned, cold; curtains on iron-screened windows keep away all knowledge of the glaring melting heat (except for a stark bright triangle on the linoleum, broken by the diamond pattern of the screen). The guest shivers, the hair on her arms bristles. She has on a sleeveless dress, arrogantly white, with green borders; the shoes are green and white, the purse is green. She exudes freshness.

Lunch brings more awkwardness. The couple can only show off their children (of whom only the beautiful though unaffecting

Razia is with us) and the food they can buy here. Of the old school, Zaynab is taken to force-feeding, and guests cannot leave until they are practically bursting. Politeness will not do; at some point you have to look her in the eye and say, "No. I will not have any more." There is meat, of course. And rich biriyani, buttered lapsi. Kababs. Bhajias, potato fritters. "We do not believe in all this diet modern stuff," Zaynab informs us, excusing the abundance. Feroz concurs. "Eat, I say. There is plenty of food in this country. We have enough. . . . I understand there is much poverty in U.K." This last remark is for Rita, who doesn't seem to hear it.

After the meal, Rita brings out photos of her family. The first one is the daughter, a young woman of stunning beauty. Did Dar spawn this? I ask myself. But of course a lot of wealth and special schools have gone into that look – that face, that tall shapely body, that Princess Diana manner. Her name is Rehana.

"She is married to a European, isn't she?" Zaynab asks.

"Her father wanted her to marry the Kuwaiti ambassador's son – you know, to keep Eastern contact. But the girl was adamant. They are Scottish, her in-laws. They own resorts in Europe . . ." The second photo is of a boy and girl, eight and six years old. Rehana's children. "David and Leila . . . her in-laws were adamant about the boy's name . . ."

The third photo goes around – Hadi, her son. He's lost out to his sister in looks, is stocky with crew-cut hair and a smile that is thin and cruel. "He went off on his own – for some years," says his mother. "But he's now a director in his father's company."

And then the fourth photo, which Rita hands out with an anxious look. Ali.

It's a garden scene, in front of a house: a driveway, a portico. He stands alone, looking at the camera. He is not very tall, he has on a collared blue sweater and white trousers. He has a kindly face, well kept. There's no past in that photo, nothing that I recognize. For that there's Rita, the link.

"It's taken at Beech Grove," she says.

"That's your house, isn't it?" Feroz says. "In England they don't have house numbers, " he tells his wife, "just give the name, and the post office knows –"

"Well, not in all cases," Rita laughs.

"I remember," he says, "we used to hear Ali lived in a palace which had gold taps and –"

"Wouldn't it wear off?" murmurs Zaynab.

"Where does he live now?" Feroz asks.

There is a pause and she returns his look. "In Knightsbridge," she tells him. "Near Harrods."

"But he took good care of you?" Feroz says. Suddenly he is protective.

"He was generous," she says. "We could have fought. But it, the divorce – we are divorced now – was all amicable. We meet often. Rosita is my friend, actually. We often do our shopping together."

There is a photo of Rosita, the new wife, beside a horse. She is younger than Rita, but not by much. I look at Rita.

"He was always the playboy," she smiles, taking the photo from me, putting it away .

"It's as if he has two wives," she continues, wants to explain. "I am his Indian connection – that's why I am here. The community approaches him through me. For donations and so on, you know."

She looks around, then picks up the shopping bag she's had at her feet all along and brings out the presents. For Feroz, a smart pen. A dress for Zaynab, who says, "Hai hai, you shouldn't have troubled yourself." "No trouble at all," Rita says, and gives Razia hers: a suit. The girl beams, is almost in tears.

"And for you, Mr. Fernandes – sir –" Rita says.

I open the wrapping – from the weight, size, shape, I know what it is: a book. There's also a pen, like Feroz's. But the book . . .

Havin' a Piece: Collected Poems 1930-1967, by Richard Gregory.

"My, my." I am flustered. "Don't tell me – Dar, brought to the world through the poems of an expatriate teacher."

The name, the pun in the title, the photograph on the back, all bring back strong, vivid memories . . . of a long friendship that I could never quite explain. . . . The volume is posthumous, and recently published.

First Rita, then Gregory, they have entered my narrative, unasked, so to speak. I began a history, with an objective eye on the diary of Alfred Corbin, ADC, DC, one of the architects of Indirect Rule, later Governor – and so on. I saw myself as a mere observer, properly distanced by time and relationship, solving a puzzle. Now, strangely, I see myself drawn in, by a gravitational force, pulled into the story.

"Show me." Feroz takes the book from me.

"Haven of Peace, Dar es Salaam," Rita explains the pun to Feroz and Zaynab.

"You remember him?" I ask her.

She smiles. "We've turned thoughtful, haven't we," she says. And then: "Oh yes, I remember."

II

Ali and Rita

Now they all know what I am . . .
– *Gilda* (starring Rita Hayworth
and Glenn Ford)

18

No, you will not forget. You were our Rita, queen of the stars, queen of Dar, queen of the night. You shimmered and radiated, waved at the crowd, at us. Full of life, promise. Your sparkling star-strewn carriage driving you away to the music of drum and trumpet, still waving. In hindsight, a childish, girlish phase all this, replete with colonial innocence. Yet unforgettable. And hindsight is dead sight after all, jealous of memory that breathes.

How did I, a Christian Goan, Pius Fernandes, come to be in the midst of this Shamsi Muslim procession of floats, pining for its queen?

That was in 1950, November.

Three years before, in Goa, I had passed my BA in history and literature, upper second, University of London (external), and the world lay at my feet. So I was told by my principal. But that world lay stunned after another catastrophic war. The Empire was winding down. And those of us who had identified a little more with our colonial masters knew not where we belonged in the new order being fashioned out of the India that was breaking up all around us. Economically we were on no surer ground; hundreds applied for even the meanest clerical position – licking revenue stamps, as we called it then.

An advertisement from the colonial office had appeared in the *Goan Times*, inviting applications for teachers in Kenya Colony, Uganda Protectorate, and Tanganyika Territory. We Goans are a travelling people. There have been many Goans – Goanese as they were called – in Africa from earliest times. The prospect did not seem daunting. I remember how, during the subsequent interview in Bombay, we joked as we waited nervously. Aré, who wants to be Kenya colonized? And U-*gand*-a? It is T.T. for us – Tanga-nyika Terri-terri. We could not know of course that the differences among the three countries, their futures, were indeed as great as we pretended in our humour and would determine our futures in unique ways. I was selected for T.T., with two others, Steve Desouza and Kuldip Singh, and we walked out of the interview together and headed straight for the nearest teashop to speculate about our futures. Desouza was the scientist, Kuldip the mathematician, and I the humanist, which is how we called ourselves somewhat immodestly.

We had been told that all three of us had been posted to the government school in the historic town of Tabora, in the interior of the country. We did not know what to expect, none of us having taught school, let alone in a part of the world about which we had only the faintest notion – and a lot of fantasies culled from the likes of Rider Haggard, Tarzan, and Sanders of Africa. The brochures we were given with our appointments were less than useful – we already wore the kind of clothes we were broadly advised to take, we knew how to protect ourselves from malaria. Tigers, we were told, did not exist in Africa. The African servant, like the Indian, we learned, did not have a sense of "mine" and "yours." We were to wear shoes.

We dug up a teacher, a Scotsman, who had spent twenty years

in East Africa. "My boys," he said. "Take books – Voltaire, Wilde, de Sade! And," he paused to eye us over his glasses, "above all, the books in your particular specialties."

Three strapping young men facing into a head wind, on our second-class paid passage aboard the SS *Amra*. We had boarded ship at Bombay, and throughout the journey our spirits never dipped for a moment. The world seemed small and we were conscious that we were crossing it. We were sailing to freedom: freedom from an old country with ancient ways, from the tentacles of clinging families with numerous wants and myriad conventions; freedom even from ourselves grounded in those ancient ways. Desouza, big and dark in safari suit and hat, very much the magazine picture of an adventurer; Kuldip and I, ordinary Indians in light bush shirts and loose trousers.

We trampled through the market in Aden. We walked up and down the decks looking for interesting people to talk to. There were those returning to Africa – and these you could tell by their interest in the ship's amenities (mostly the bar) and nothing else – and others like us going for the first time, ready to romanticize any sight, eager for any piece of information. The third-class deck was a floating Indian slum, to which we were drawn by the attraction of the newly married brides, who in these crowded quarters had lost their colour and also much of their shyness. When we crossed the equator we joined the upper decks at the ball. None of us had qualms about taking drinks, and all of us took turns at dancing with an elderly returning headmistress of a girls' school. And finally Mombasa, when we knew we had come to Africa, where most of the Europeans disembarked on their way to Nairobi. Then Zanzibar, and, with beating hearts, Dar es Salaam. In Dar we slept the night in a hotel near the harbour and spent the following morning roaming the streets before departing on the afternoon train to Tabora.

It was in Tabora that I first recall that feeling of being alone in Africa. It was a feeling that would return, though less and less frequently; one learned gradually to guard against it. I remember vividly my first night, in my room on a ground-floor corridor. My friends were in other parts of the building. Frogs were croaking, crickets chirping, the khungu tree whispering outside in a breeze. The room was solid dark, and the night air was so depleted of substance it felt like a rarefied gas carrying just a trace of woodsmoke. No longer did I feel so sure of myself; it seemed to me as if I had come to another part of the universe, that the world I had left behind, my home town of Panjim, Goa, was as distant as the nearest star in the sky.

After two years at Tabora all of us opted to leave for Dar – Kuldip for the Government Indian Secondary School, whose cricket team and syllabus he would bring to be among the best in the country; Desouza and I for their arch-rivals, the Shamsi Boys' School or "Boyschool."

Boyschool was away from the downtown area, at the end of Selous Street, coming after the potters' village and the poor Indian area known for its prostitutes. Behind the school were the teachers' quarters where we lived. I was not allowed to teach English literature – that was in the able hands of Richard Gregory; he was many years my senior, so I did not mind. I taught English grammar, and my other specialty: history. It was a pathetic syllabus I was asked to teach: Mughal history with the deeds of Humayun the Kind, Babur the Brave, Akber the Great; and above all English history with the Tudors and the Stuarts. This was marginally better than the lower classes' staple of Hammurabi the Lawgiver, Cheops the Pyramid Builder, and Pheidippides the Runner. This, after two world wars, Hiroshima, Yalta, the independence of India. Yet what to blame – the backwardness of the community or the advice of government inspectors? And blame for what?

Years later, Boyschool moved to a better location, bequeathing its old grey building to the Shamsi Girls' School. But now the girls were kept secure, close to home, across from the mosque in the building that remains to this day a warren of rooms. There was always a shortage of teachers at the girls' school; the best went to Boyschool, the girls made do with the remainder. The result was that the boys dreamed of straight As in the Overseas Exams, and the girls were happy with a D pass.

Some of the Indian teachers were asked to teach at the Shamsi Girls' School in their free time. We did not ask why. It was understood that we were Indians and appreciated the need; and we had no choice, there were many more where we came from. And so off to the girls' school I went after recess on Saturday – down Selous, past Kisutu, on Ring, then Mosque Street. The girls were keen and lively, fifteen to eighteen years old, and would one day be homemakers in well-to-do progressive, respectable households. They were Girl Guides and junior members of the Ladies' Committee and the Former Girls' Association, where they took cookery classes to learn "English cooking" and did callisthenics to control their figures.

And they all wore "shortfrocks" – with hems that were a foot above the ground but already represented a revolution – and western styles and patterns and, significantly, without the head-covering or pachedi. In one fell swoop, the Shamsis decided – at least for their younger women – to do away with this remnant of purdah, with its various stylistic conventions for girls, married women, widows, women with unmarried daughters, women with married daughters. Meanwhile, in the streets, other women walked in buibuis, burkhas, saris, and pachedis; many still do.

I had then, even as a young teacher, a stern disposition with my students. Most of them had been boys. But these were girls – feminine, Oriental, and yet delightfully liberated from the traditions that would have put a physical curtain between the lot of them and me. Faced with their wiles I found myself often at a loss.

There were fifteen girls in my class. My first lesson gave a clear indication of things to come and filled me with much foreboding.

I arrived ready to teach the Mughal Empire to these Indian

girls abroad. What better introduction to the subject than the Taj Mahal?

"How many of you know about the Taj Mahal?" I began.

An eager show of hands. How genteel, I thought, how they raise their arms quietly only from the elbows, how unlike the loafers I taught at the boys' school.

"All right, girls, I am convinced. The Taj Mahal, as we know, represents the glory of the Mughal Empire – the emperors Akber, Humayun, Babur –"

"Tell us about Salim, sir." An innocent, almost idiotic request. And the beginning of an avalanche.

"What Salim?" I asked impatiently, turning towards the questioner.

"Prince Salim the son of shehen-shah Emperor Akber. And his lover Anarkali!" said a voice from another direction.

They were referring, of course, to the recent box-office record-breaker from Bombay about unrequited love in Mughal times.

"*Hm-hm, hm-hm . . .*" someone hummed a song from the film, and the ground seemed to slip from under me.

"Now what is this? Girls! Please!"

"*Yeh zindagi usiki hai –*" she sang, the girl called Gulnar, from the back of the middle row.

Then they all sang, "*The world belongs to the one who loves, who's lost to love and nothing but love –*"

"Now girls!" I shouted. "For God's sake!"

They stopped, somewhat ashamed at having offended. I caught my breath, wondering whether I'd ever had a sense of humour, and what I was doing in a girls' school.

Another time:

"Are you married, sir?" This, just as I entered the classroom, having cycled furiously all the way to get there in time, having run up the stairs. A two-minute delay could disrupt the entire school, not to say the neighbourhood.

"Sir has a girlfriend, perhaps."

Laughter, quite animated and open – this began to look like rebellion. Then Gulnar came forward between the desks and benches, smiling, bearing a cake with one candle, and they sang, "*Happy birthday to you . . .*"

Gulnar was the most attractive girl in class, if you count personality, which you must! Gulnar Rajani, nicknamed Rita.

Bette Davis was too thin for local tastes and too tart; there was Garbo, luscious and luxurious but a little too svelte for our small-town roughnesses; the pin-up Betty Grable pointed a mischievous tush at you. Dilip Kumar the lover and Raj Kapoor the charming fool with so much to teach were the male idols, along with Gary Cooper, Gene Kelly, and Cary Grant; there was Nargis the heart-throb, the West-in-the-East, the dreamgirl of the intellectuals. But for a brief period the imagination of Dar was caught by the brunette American beauty Rita Hayworth. The Love Goddess, the "Put the Blame on Mame" Girl, kneeling on a bed in black lace, looking coyly at you ("Am I doing anything wrong?") in the picture that hit Hiroshima before it blew up. And she was the gypsy girl Carmen looking so Indian. But let's not kid ourselves, Dar fell in love with her because she married an Eastern prince – Aly Khan – with a sheikh reciting the nikaa as the Vatican looked on uncomfortably. And she did come to visit us in Africa. If she was discomfited by requirements of modesty and women bowing worshipfully and touching her hem, that was understandable. If she left in a huff, from Nairobi back to Europe then America, such were the ways of the great and famous. To have been selected by the prince gave her qualities, a bigness of soul, that perhaps even she was not aware of.

Dar had embraced her wholeheartedly, nicknamed one of its beauties after her. Our own Rita was a scaled-down version, of course – this was Dar, not Hollywood – but a bigger heart-throb on Jamat and Mosque and Market streets. The yearnings went deeper: she was real – walked on earth, as they said – she would soon choose, marry. Who would be the lucky devil? Her friends in class reported the latest proposal of marriage that her family had received ("Sir, Rita is thinking about her future") and which the girl was bound to turn down.

She had black wavy hair down to her shoulders, a large mouth; she was fair-skinned and, except perhaps for a little at the hips – I blush – she was slim. She had a ready smile, which is hardly surprising – aren't those years the best of our lives? She had me in such a state that I would catch myself checking my appearance before class and seeking approval from them (her) instead of letting them (her) seek it from me, their teacher. I have never been lenient with myself and didn't fail to chide when the need arose.

I didn't stand a chance, of course; even the thought was a useless torment and I was determined to curb it. I was a complete outsider, without a common caste, religion, mother tongue, place of origin – I was a proper "over-comm" in every way. (Some weeks later, an incident involving a pair of unfortunates was to prove me right in my pessimism about anything developing between us.) The girls all knew of my condition. There were too many of those darting eyes and calculating brains, gauging my various fumblings, not to guess. And those asides – "Sir, she is dreaming, considering a maago (proposal)" – were surely meant to tease, and they hurt.

Rita's father had been a bank clerk in Zanzibar, now retired. What progressiveness that background (similar to mine) signified, perhaps was cause for her boldness, was why she stood out. I know that once she was mobbed on Market Street for wearing a sleeveless dress and high heels. But she was a community girl, only flirting with danger, and the next day she was again out in the street appropriately dressed.

One afternoon after class she and her friends walked downstairs with me. The mosque yard where we arrived linked two busy streets with its two entrances. It was always crowded with people: pedestrian traffic pausing to chat; lonely men and women without a relation in the world, a penny to their names, seeking refuge and companionship on its benches; the caretaker directing servants. Someone made a loud remark about the Govo – Goan – and I longed to pedal away.

"Sir, tell us what storybooks to read," she said, almost putting a hand on my arm. (I can still see it: my arm on the bike seat, her hand poised an inch, two inches, from it.) "*Little Women*," I said, though *Pride and Prejudice* might have been more appropriate. And then: "Sir, which book proves God exists – the boys know but won't tell us. Please, sir."

She was detaining me – or was I imagining?

"Why doesn't she – why don't they leave me alone?" I said to Desouza later. "I don't mind having regrets from a distance, but this flirtation across an impossible chasm –"

"Tell them you don't want to teach the girls," he said.

"They'll wonder why."

"Then ask for leave to go and get married."

We were sitting in the staff room, on a corner sofa, drinking tea and smoking. As Desouza spoke we both looked up to see Richard Gregory arrive and stand looming over us. "Mind if we make a baraza of this tête-à-tête?" he said.

Gregory was one of those idiosyncratic Englishmen who become an institution by virtue of the sheer consistency of their oddball – some would say perverse – nature. He had a family in England, we'd been told privately, perhaps to give the lie to his carefree existence among us. In those days it was the thing to do among the educated to make fun of Englishmen behind their backs. He seemed genuine enough to me. If he had pretended once, the role had since taken him over. He was a good deal older than Desouza and myself, a big, somewhat pudgy man with a dissolute look – dishevelled, scruffy, always in dirty khaki shorts and his shirt half hanging out, sometimes showing a part of his hairy midsection. The sun did no good to him, he would turn dreadfully red, yet he'd been in Africa for almost twenty years and had no intention of returning to England. He was a walking compilation of literary quotations, knew his Palgrave by heart, and carried the Shakespeare on the current syllabus in his head. Thus prepared in perpetuum, he would shuffle from class to class partly drunk, fumbling with a pipe that was rarely lit, trying to tuck in his shirttails, rubbing his dirty neck.

He sat down and gave a fart.

"One of the girls got your blood racing, dear boy? . . ." he said in his growly voice. "Sorry, couldn't help overhearing, you do sound distraught, you know . . ." He began purring into his pipe.

Desouza with a look of distaste was ready to get up, but I stayed him with a look.

"Mr. Gregory, what storybook – as they call it – would you recommend to a young Asian girl?"

"A young Asian girl? And upright too, I suppose? A virgin positively? *Lady Chatterley*, of course."

"Seriously, now. Not joking."

"Has to be a storybook? Have you read the poems of Sappho, now? How about –"

"My sisters read Jane Austen," Desouza said. "And Mazo de la Roche."

"They would." Gregory, in reply to Desouza's distaste for him, liked to needle him. My friend was bristling. Gregory was fumbling with his pipe.

"I wonder," he mused, "how my boys would respond to Donne. I'd have to spell it out, of course . . . quite the rage these days in Lon-don."

"How about this one: What book proves the existence of God? I don't think there is any, myself, but what would you say?"

"Saint Augustine. Bertrand Russell, of course, proves that God does not exist." That was Desouza.

"My dear chap. Spinoza, if you ask me." The pipe was firmly between his teeth, he was ready to go.

"How would you like to come and watch the Shamsi parade next week?" I asked him. "My girls are in a float and beg me to go."

"Love to," he said and shuffled off.

"Bastard," hissed Desouza at his back. "I don't know why you pay attention to him. You always were fascinated by Englishmen – even the one in Bombay, it was your idea to look him up."

"That was a Scotsman."

"All the same."

Desouza didn't come to watch the parade, so Gregory and I went on our own. He had a car and picked me up.

Twice every year, when the Shamsis celebrated, for days the whole town – from Acacia Avenue to Ring Street, Kichwele to Ingles – was in happy disarray.

The "happiness" began on the first day with a flag-raising ceremony at nine A.M. to the strains of the Shamsi anthem played by the scouts. Then came a semblance of a guard of honour formed by all of Baden-Powell's troops – the scouts, guides, cubs, and brownies – in the manner of the KAR but with a few loose feet; and then the march-past throughout the Shamsi area surrounding the mosque, the band blaring "Swanee River" and strains of Sousa, followed close on its heels by boys and the town's idlers and beggars.

Every night thereafter, after the religious ceremonies conducted with abandon over loudspeakers, there was sherbet and food. And then they danced the dandia, the garba, and the rasa to the beat of drums and the bleat of trumpets that were heard for miles around. The mosque was covered with lights, the enclosed yard outside jammed with people, overhung with flags.

On the final day, a Sunday, there was the parade of floats, led by the young troops. It took place at four in the afternoon, at a time, I supposed, when the sun was out of the competition and smiled benignly. There came – as Gregory and I watched, having placed ourselves on Ring Street where the crowds were less congested – a larger-than-life Churchill on the back of a lorry, puffing on a huge cigar (whose smoke we were assured was nothing but incense fumes), waving at the crowds; an Arab sheikh in a decadent posture in a very Oriental setting, lying back against bolsters, drinking, smoking, surrounded by screaming, giggling houris; a snake charmer with a real cobra; a mountain with Hassan bin Sabbah and disciples plotting some nefarious but no doubt worthwhile activity; and Hollywood, complete with sparkling stars (and moon), and on each star a human starlet, waving and flashing Hollywood smiles. The topmost star, the queen of all: our own Rita.

There were volunteers serving drinks, others spraying perfumes and flinging handfuls of rice from the floats.

Walking alongside the Hollywood float, striding, beaming, waving royally to all he knew, was a handsome man in white suit, wearing a black astrakhan hat aslant on his head, a cane in his hand. He was Ali Akber Ali, Dar's version of the prince Aly Khan.

How could names, nicknames, cast a spell over their bearers, moving them to immutable fates, combined destinies? It was all in the stars, shall we say.

19

All that week of the festival there would be a break in the religious ceremonies every evening between prayers: a procession would head off from the mosque, proceed at a stately pace around the neighbourhood . . . accompanied by the deep, lugubrious *dhoom-dhoom-dhoom* of a dhol and two trumpets bleating variations of the same ten notes in a wonderfully mellifluous refrain that echoed in the mind for days afterwards. Among dancing young men and women and elderly mothers of the community and shopkeepers turned noblemen in turbans and robes, went a lorry filled with Dar's "Hollywood girls" waving. They went past shops decorated with flags, bunting, and strings of lights, and stopped frequently for sherbet and sweets.

Outside the shop of the "khanga king," Ali Akber Ali, the son-in-law and prince, served the Hollywood girls, ladling the choicest sherbet into glasses with a flourish and a smart comment. At the variety show "dylok" (for dialogue, or drama), performed by the members of the Ladies' Committee later in the week, he helped to manage the sets and even acted a small part as a doctor performing a blood transfusion in a heartrending scene. By the time the shopkeepers went back to their businesses, satiated with celebration and sherbet and biriyani, Ali was on speaking – or bantering – terms with Rita.

To joke with a girl is to become intimate – to embrace and cuddle with words when bodies and even looks cannot but remain restrained, hidden. Joking, you can be a child, a brother, a lover. As a lover you embarrass, cause her to shift her eyes, to lose control in a peal of laughter and then stop, blushing as if kissed. Then you know you've got her; all that remains is to clinch it, take the first decisive step. If you're truly romantic you send a note with a quotation in it – from a ghazal, a popular song, even a line or two from an English poem – unsigned but with a hint of its sender. This is what Ali did.

> *The moth, madly in love with the flame,*
> *plunges in –*
> *And so do I, my love.*
>
> *"Your not-so-secret admirer"*

A somewhat juvenile tack for a man of his age, and married for twelve years, but he was stricken. And she, the seventeen-year-old, was impressed, but didn't quite know who the admirer was.

He heard, saw, nothing from her in response. He went into her parents' shop once and, in her presence, talked with her mother, joked, and recited a verse. Later he accosted her on the sidewalk, and, as she turned away shyly, he recited a sequel to the poem. He followed her to the seashore on Azania Front one Sunday, where she strolled with her friends, and in full view of them he walked along, on the other side of the road, keeping pace. In a few weeks a current of rumour, a little weak and perhaps outrageous-sounding, stirred in pockets of the community, especially among the youth.

His own marriage remained childless; there had never been much love in it. But he had acquired by it a status and a livelihood; he provided in exchange a stable marriage, and, though attractive, he had never strayed from the marriage bed. What he was risking now, in middle age, was much.

The whole of the Shamsi community was on a picnic at the ancient port town of Bagamoyo, having arrived in open lorries with cauldrons of pilau and channa and a gang of servants, the young people singing, "*ai-yai yuppie yuppie yai yai*," all the way there, as usual. On the beach: games of hutu-tutu and pita-piti, soccer and cricket with coconut branches for bats; boys teasing girls with film songs; tea and Coca-Cola, more tea and snacks. A batch of new teachers from England and India had arrived, and some of them were on hand.

Rita had walked away after lunch, away from the youthful games and elderly card-playing and tea-guzzling. Her dress fluttered in the breeze and she was barefoot. She picked her way among protruding tree roots and shrubs until she reached the sandy portion of the beach. The tide was in, and there were a few swimmers struggling with the waves, fishermen beside nets spread out on the ground, vendors of coconut. She sat modestly on a tree stump, legs tucked in, looking far away to the horizon. They say, when you first see a ship, she thought, you see only the funnel.

She could not say why she had walked away so. Only that she felt miserable, depressed, in the way of youth. To her right was an old cemetery. Souls lying exposed to the sea, she thought, and began to feel nervous, recalling stories of possessed women. At the head of the graveyard was an ancient mission house. Somewhere nearby, she knew, was a slave market, even more ancient.

Soon the picnic-goers, before the final long tea and after the games, would venture out for the mandatory stroll and a look at the sights. There was a remnant of the community here, one or two old homes left over from times of slavery and ivory and the explorer safaris. They would go to the old mosque and visit the church, point out the haunted sites for which the town was notorious.

A rustle behind her, from the shrubbery on the right, and she started, her heart racing. He emerged, large and splendid, pushing back branches from his face. He wore a knitted jersey, his grey cashmere trouser legs were rolled up part way, and he, too, was barefoot.

This was a scene reminiscent of many films of that period. Hollywood and Bollywood; this was Dollywood, Dar and derivative.

He entreated, begged, went down on his knees. He would divorce his wife, he said. He was going to London. "What for?" she asked. "What's here?" he answered. Indeed, she thought. What is here? The prospect of London, of going away, of escaping to the bigger, more sophisticated world . . . she had never thought of that before. She eyed him without a word. During the "happiness" they had exchanged friendly antagonistic barbs. Now words seemed difficult, awkward between them, demanded too much meaning and nuance. He was glamorous, so unlike anyone she knew – the family men of his age, shopkeepers mostly and government clerks at best, or the adolescent loud-talking and immature youths of her own age.

They walked back separately, without one more word. The friendly game of hutu-tutu between boys and girls was about to break up; now they would do a few skits. In one of them, a boy and girl would perform the nursery song "Where Are You Going to, My Pretty Maid?" It was the kind of thing they asked her to do, their Rita. And so she did, played the coy pretty milkmaid this time.

"Nobody asked you to marry me, sir, she said,
Sir, she said . . ."

❧❧

Ali's proposal was, of course, unthinkable. She was a girl in the prime of life; what family would give her away to a "once-married," to scandal and shame? Rita became quieter in my class, and would have been inconspicuous had she not already made her impact on me. She was prone to blushing, an indication that among the girls much was said that escaped me.

My own relations with my Saturday girls became formal; the girls lost their sparkle, their laughter, were more respectful. It was depressing to be the object of pity of those who looked up to me; more so as it was about something undeclared, out of reach. By their understanding, their respect, these beautiful pig-tailed, pony-tailed, and "boy-cutted" girls were telling me they understood my pain. *Stop it*, I wanted to shout. *Be your normal selves —* but that was impossible, they had grown up. Meanwhile, I went on with the Tudors, the Stuarts, and the Mughals.

❧❧

Ali and Rita used an "interpinter," an intermediary, someone who would pass messages between them. It was typical of his arrogance that he used the most public figure, the town crier, to carry his love notes to Rita.

Karim Langdo – Karim the Lame – went around the streets of Dar's Indian quarter proclaiming funerals and other special events. Block to block he would go, dragging his lame foot. He would stop at a crossroads, spit, and then with a flourish bring out a chit and read his message: Come to the funeral! So-and-so Bhai, formerly of Panipat, India, has passed awaaay! Funeral time Thursday at four, location Kichweleee! Which cry the street idlers would carry on in a long derisive echo. Karim Bhai, who passed away? a woman might emerge from a shop to inquire. So-and-so Bhai of Panipat, he would say sharply as he limped off. He did not like to repeat, but was frequently called upon to do so.

Karim Langdo and Ali had grown up in the same streets. And Ali, regardless of his status in the community, never failed to acknowledge the lame man, to exchange pleasantries and news when they met. Karim, therefore, worshipped the prince. He willingly, gratefully, agreed to be the interpinter, to carry a note whenever he had an announcement to make. And so one afternoon, after Karim had announced a funeral, he limped up to Rita's courtyard, asked for water, and told the mother: "A letter for Rita from a girlfriend." Rita, unsuspecting, breezed in and took the letter, opened it right there, and put a hand to her mouth in shock.

"What does she write, this friend – who is she?" her mother asked.

"Oh," she said, recovering just enough to appear normal, "It's Guli Sharif – the crazy girl!"

> *My lover's walk teases me,*
> *let our eyes meet,*
> *let our waters unite.*
>> *"Your Prince"*

Having answered her mother she walked away, beaming with happiness, heart beating wildly.

"Aré, no reply?" Karim called after her.

"No, not today."

Another time, straight from a film song:

> *The alley which doesn't have your home,*
> *I can't bear to tread upon.*
>> *"Prince"*

Even Gregory's Palgrave contributed to their brief epistolary exchange.

The messenger himself was unmarried, unmarriageable, and the sight of these modern girls as bright as sunshine must have tormented him. What better way to have one of them for himself than through his hero, Ali?

Rita would get impatient for the missives, not having replied to any. "Hasn't anyone died, today?" she found herself asking, to which her mother said sharply, "Be thankful, girl, don't tempt fate."

It took a couple of funerals and a few special services in mosque before Rita could pick up courage and say, "Karim Bhai, this – give it to –" And off went the happy messenger.

"Sir . . . I would like to borrow a book from you." She had come up to the table to make this request when, just after class, I was ready to leave. The other girls crowded behind her, sniggering. They were almost their old selves, the pack – but she, Rita, had only a shy smile on her face. She was close and I felt angry.

"Yes? What book? I might not have it."

"I mean, if you have it, sir."

"So? What book?"

"*Romeo and Juliet*," she said in a low voice.

"*Romeo and Juliet*?" I forgot discretion, my voice rose. Giggles rippled through the room in happy mockery and I looked up to show consternation.

"Laila and Majnun, sir!"

"Heer-Ranjha."

"Nala–Damayanti."

And so I got all of the many variations of Romeo and Juliet; the girls were unstoppable.

Thus Rita's next message to Ali:

If that thy bent of love be honourable
Thy purpose marriage, send me word tomorrow
And all my fortunes at thy foot I'll lay,
And follow thee, my lord, throughout the world.

Karim Langdo, after replying testily to the familiar query – Sunderbai Patel, Bagamoyo Road, funeral tomorrow at four, aré pay attention will you – cheerfully went hobbling along, when he heard a sound just behind him: "*pssst*," and some sniggers. He looked around and saw a gang of boys following him, imitating his limp. Then the leader of the pack went further, spoke an obscenity, then touched his bottom. This time Karim Langdo lost control and raced after them, dragging his bad foot. He stumbled on it, fell, and the boys ran away. Several men came running to pick up the lame messenger, who was wheezing, moaning, swearing, his foot a gory mess of red and black, the bloody flesh stinging, pricked with pebbles and sand. A crowd gathered to look.

Karim sat, leg up, on a store bench, pitifully examining his tattered foot. Ramzani the dresser came racing on his bicycle, saying, "Tch, tch, Karim Bhai, now what did you do?" And Karim replying, "Those bhenchod with bitches for mothers –"

In the street were two pieces of paper the messenger had dropped – one the announcement of Sunderbai Patel's death, the other a note from Romeo – which lay tenderly on the road like butterfly wings waiting for just the right breeze to lift them up. Two young men did so.

"Call me but love and I'll be new baptized," said the note from Romeo. What could it mean? Something illicit, no doubt. Sinful and secretive, so doubly sinful.

Youthful zealot minds got to work. The street where the note was found was not a clue to the sinners' whereabouts; Karim the Lame had a large territory. He said yes to the resulting inquiries without supplying names ("I have sworn on my mother's grave" was enough) and the scent grew stronger. Gregory was consulted, and he obliged by giving chapter and verse, more quotations, a literary evaluation, the story, and the meaning of the lines under scrutiny. ("Young love knows no barriers, no strictures.") All that remained was to keep a close watch on the girls. Already all this boy-cut hair and lipstick-lali and sleeveless dresses; now one of them had overstepped the bounds.

And Karim, passing by Rita's house, after saying "Today a special majlis – prayer time: six-thirty," followed with a muttered sing-song warning: "Do be careful, you two."

But the young zealots, a school failure, Habib Haji, and his cohorts, got their victims. The couple they caught in their net and demolished, however, was another one, and Ali and Rita took the warning.

There had come to town a young Hindu bookkeeper called Patani, who lived in a flat on Market Street in the vast G. R. Moolji Building, which had just risen up. He had a wife and a child in the suburbs of Ahmedabad, and was waiting for his immigration papers before he called them. His cause was in the able hands of the lawyers of the Hindu Association. In the eighteen months or so since his arrival in Dar, he had come to be well regarded and liked, as a clever and reliable bookkeeper and as a quiet and decent man, although somewhat lonely. Some of the older women in the building would tease him about his pining away in the absence of his pretty young wife. Patani, though, had in recent months found another source of comfort. He had fallen in love with a Shamsi girl who lived in the building, and was carrying on a secret liaison with her.

Her name was Parviz. She was a short girl, with two pigtails down to her waist, known for her piety, which she expressed with an earnestness and plaintiveness in the Mira Bai mode. Unfortunately for Patani and Parviz, their affair was going on at the same time as Haji and his agents were on the lookout for another pair of illicit lovers. Parviz aroused the suspicion of the zealots when she was seen once to leave the mosque in a hurry halfway through the service. She was soon exposed.

It was a night of festivities at the Shamsi mosque, another "happiness" – gaiety and food, sherbet and dancing. In the middle of the evening's festivities – after prayers, when there was dancing and milling around – Parviz took off, hurrying away along Mosque Street. The youths followed – four of them, two on either side of the street, as they had seen in American films. When the girl went into her building, they noticed from the street that the lights in her flat did not go on. They took the stairs but could not find her. They knocked on a lot of doors, without success. Finally they dispersed, posting themselves on different floors, and waited. At eleven o'clock a door opened and Parviz emerged. She gave a gasp at seeing a youth she knew. He instantly called out to his friends.

"What are you doing here?" they demanded.

"What is it to you . . ." her voice petered out as Patani, shirttails untucked, emerged wearing bookish spectacles.

"I came to pick up . . ." she started again, but there was nothing to say.

"Come with us – or don't you want to?"

She went.

One hears of larger terrors – yet how is one to compare? For this girl surely it was the end of the world. What must she have suffered on that walk along Mosque Street escorted by her captors? I still cannot make up my mind – the shame or the fury that awaited her, what weighed most on that beating heart? She was brought back with tears in her eyes, terrified, to be judged by a thousand people.

The "happiness" was at its zenith, the last rounds of the dandia stick-dance were being played in a crescendo towards their finale. At another end of the mandap – the tent – outside the mosque was the traditional procession of women. Older women supported brass pots of sweet milk on the heads of younger, unmarried women and girls. They walked in a long file through the crowds, to where the mukhi and other elders, in robes and turbans, would receive them and give each girl a shilling.

At the head of the procession, this remnant, surely, of an ancient goddess ritual, they brought her, the stained one, saying:

"Ask her where she was when we found her."

"And what she was doing."

"And with whom."

Her crime was compound. There was no way, no need, to disentangle the multiple strands of guilt; they reinforced each other.

"I only let her talk to him because she wanted to ask about the mystic Narsinh Mehta," her mother wailed. "How could I know he would make her into his gopi —"

The girl was shamed in public, from which she would never recover. But the matter did not end there. The next evening the zealots knocked on Patani's door. They went in, roughed him up so he fled, then they trashed his flat. Chairs, sofa, went over the balcony to crash on the sidewalk, three floors below. Radio, ice box, coal stove, primus.

The *Herald* carried a story about the event the next day. "Shamsi thugs vandalize," wrote the European reporter. "Storm troopers terrorize Hindu bookkeeper." At this criticism the youth of the community were in an uproar, even the moderate ones. How dare he say "Shamsi thugs." We had a lively debate in my boys' class, a liberal bunch with only one or two leaning towards the fanatic fringe. Wasn't the behaviour thuggish? I asked. Yes, but why "Shamsi thugs," why not say "thugs"? The behaviour was surely connected with the community, I said; they went as representatives of the community, they had the sanction of the elders — or didn't they? No! they said. They would have accosted the girl, some of them said, brought her back from that Hindu banya's flat — nothing wrong with that — but they would not have gone back and vandalized the man's flat. He surely deserved a beating, though. ("Sir, he was married! Surely he was only playing with her!") Write an essay, I said.

They did more. They wrote a letter to the editor demanding an apology. The editor refused, went into a long tirade about freedom of speech. The boys responded by going from store to store asking people not to buy the *Herald*. The editor relented, regretted the unfortunate choice of words.

If only it had ended there.

The girl Parviz, who had apparently fallen while on a search for mysticism, regained her fervour many times over. Every day she went to mosque, early in the morning before dawn and in the evening. But this did not wash away her sin; not in the eyes of the people. Women and girls habitually made comments behind her back. She said hardly a word in mosque, and not much more at home. Her silence was her guilt, wrapped tightly around her. One day a woman said behind her, but quite audibly, "If I were she I would jump into the ocean and die." The following morning Parviz went to mosque as usual. She drank the holy water. She stood before the takhat, the seat of God, and said a prayer. Then she went downstairs, put her shoes on, hugged her shawl around her, and left for the seashore. There she took her shoes off and threw down the shawl. Then she walked into the ocean and drowned herself.

That afternoon, Karim Langdo limped along the streets calling "Mai-yaht mé halloo" – come to the funeral – in a subdued, somewhat breaking tone, announcing the death whose unwilling agent he had become.

The incident shook up the whole city, most of all the girl's own people. What happened, why so fast? A quick judgement, a quick death. What have we done? What happened to "Forgive and forget," that motto of the forties that we so conveniently adopted? What happened to mercy? She will haunt us, this girl, we will never be sure of ourselves. She has judged us. She mocks us. In that, she lives.

It was a big funeral, the biggest I had seen. My girls wept without control, my boys gave shoulder to the coffin as they recited the kalima in that haunting call which at this occasion was a wail, a cry for help: There is no God but Him. . . . A cry for mercy?

When Ali told Rita, a few months before at the picnic, that he would go to London, he was suggesting to her an option that no Dar girl could have failed to understand. London was escape, a haven for illicit, unapproved-of relationships.

They had only engaged in a brief flirtation of letters; they had not met in private, they had not made love. They had engaged in an exploration, in joyful play. Parviz's exposure and suicide, linked to their affair as if by the hand of fate, suddenly brought to an end the play, the innocence of fresh love. The realization that theirs, too, was an illicit love was almost brutal. But they would not stick around for exposure and shame. They would escape.

It was not easy simply to go off to London without the whole town knowing about it well in advance, but Ali and Rita managed to slip away without event, for they departed at a time when thousands were flocking to Dar es Salaam for the Precious Jubilee of the Shamsis.

The spiritual leader of the community, Suleiman Pir, had been in office for sixty years, and it was thought fitting to celebrate this event in a jubilee – after all, Queen Victoria had had hers – that would culminate in matching the weight of the leader with a mixture of precious stones. The site chosen for the event was our beloved city, and a property was bought to hold it on.

They came to Dar in buses, trains, planes, and by boat. They came from Nairobi, Mombasa, Kisumu, Kampala, Tororo,

Mengo; from Stanleyville and Leopoldville; from Tananarive in Madagascar, Lorenco Marques in Mozambique; from Durban, Johannesburg, Cape Town, and Salisbury; from Karachi, Bombay, Poona, and Rajkot; from Rangoon and Dhaka. They slept in tents, ate in mandaps. Armies of cooks, servers, cleaners, doctors, nurses served them. Onions, potatoes by the sack were peeled and cut, cattle slaughtered by the herd. This was a far cry from the early days of the lonely traveller in the bush, fearing man and beast. They brought money now, they contributed millions. And the millions collected went into a fund for new schools and homes for every family so that East Dar is what it is today. The children born that year were special too, and they bore names to celebrate the event. In subsequent years I would teach many a Diamond, an Almas, a Jubilee Begum, a Jawahir, souvenirs of that happy time.

It was an event in the Empire which Movietone newsreels broadcast to cinema houses from Sarawak to Kamloops, Wawa to Wollongong, though London, itself pale under rations and drizzle, was understandably cynical.

In all the hubbub surrounding this jubilee, with so many strange, happy faces in town, with all the excitement of the ceremonies and keeping track of dignitaries, and the weddings and the births and deaths, Ali and Rita could quietly catch a plane to Nairobi. Before anyone knew exactly where they were, they had taken another plane, to London.

20

The news came to Pipa in his corner grocery store, as it did to most people in Dar, through the grapevine: Did you hear? Ali and Rita have run away together. To London.

The boy whom he had come to love in his own gruff way, who had sat quietly in the shop with him, who once with so much devotion sketched Mariamu for him, was now gone for good. Few people returned from London.

He was angry at Ali for not coming to take leave, ask permission, for such a momentous voyage. (He forgot that once he, too, had left home quite suddenly and without giving notice.) He was angrier at Mariamu. The son becomes the father, she had told him. Is this what she had meant, had known all along, that Ali would go away to the land of the ADC – become an Englishman? Was she telling him, now, after all these years, in such a treacherous manner, that Ali wasn't his son after all?

As if to assuage his grief, another son was born to him, late in life now, after seven daughters. And for the next ten years this son, Amin, born of Remti, was the joy of his life.

And for those ten years, Mariamu and her book were allowed to recede into the background; or perhaps she simply allowed Pipa and Remti to lavish attention on Amin unhampered. One day, when Amin was four, Pipa removed the book from its place and hid it elsewhere; the shrine room was put to the use for which it was originally intended – to store goods.

I did not get to teach Amin, but I remember him well as a primary-school child. A much-pampered boy, and handsome, which must have pleased Remti. He was driven to school and back by a chauffeur in a shiny new Ford Taunus. The fifties were a time of emerging affluence. Even away from the town centre, the Indian shop-houses were giving way to two-storey brick buildings, each bearing the name of a favourite child or vision. Pipa's Amin Mansion went up with Habib Mansion, Anand Nivas, Bismillah Building, and others on Kichwele Street, the Indian street that braved its way into the African section, Kariakoo. But Pipa's store in its new building looked as it had when he first came to Dar, and thence, after the fire, as it had in the mud house that preceded Amin Mansion. The only difference was that the family now lived in the second-storey flat above.

Times were moving fast for all of us. In Kenya, the Mau–Mau war was on, and there were fears it would spill over into Tanganyika. We had a labour union now, and political parties were in the making. It was a time of considerable confusion. To the shopkeeper, the British government, the Queen at its head, was absolute ruler. How could the mighty British give way to the African, the servant? Those of us who were a little more aware of the world knew that Tanganyika was only a trust territory under the United Nations and was approaching independence. We had seen the prize colony – our India – become independent, though not without pain. I, myself, had left it at an uncertain period, a time of considerable upheaval, and saved myself from difficult choices. Now those times, the choices, had caught up. Only recently, the fiery Indian foreign minister, Krishna Menon, had come with a UN committee and done us expatriates proud. The only question now was how independence would happen, and that depended partly on Kenya Colony (KC as we had happily called it once) and the federation of Rhodesia and Nyasaland, the two neighbouring domains of white settlerdom.

Then one day God died – for many of my pupils and their families – and for them the world changed in irrevocable ways.

I remember the day, but I don't recall how the sky looked, though there are many who remember it. They say it suddenly turned grey. In the distance you saw rain showers, thunder and lightning. For a few moments, seconds, everybody, everything, was still; not a whisper in the air. Even much later the trees remained motionless; animals would not utter a sound; flags drooped; the clock at the town mosque stopped, and stayed that way for forty days. Many said that a photo of their leader had fallen from a wall, and they picked it up, much concerned. The next day many incidents were reported: tomatoes, eggs, cucumbers discovered with the sign Ali – or Allah – written across them in Arabic script. The *Herald* carried a photo of one such miracle on its front page.

That fateful afternoon I had been teaching literature to a Standard XII class. After a long apprenticeship I was allowed this, though to everybody's embarrassment my students took extra lessons with Gregory. It wasn't that there were complaints about me, just that they wanted insurance against their anonymous external examiners in Cambridge, and who better to provide it than an Englishman, that old pro Gregory. Anyway, today it was *David Copperfield*. Halfway through the lesson, a messenger came from the headmaster with a note: "All classes let the boys go home at once." Moments later there followed another note: "Staff meeting in fifteen minutes." These sounded like war measures.

In the staff room we were given the news by Rahim Master, the religion teacher. Beside him was the headmaster, Mr. Shaw. The school had two governments, religious and secular, and they were independent. Rahim was a dictator, and none of us dared interfere with his administration of religious discipline. Of course he left us alone. But the students had to answer to two authorities. Rahim told us gravely that the leader of the Shamsis, Suleiman Pir, had passed from this world.

If a whole community were able to cry in unison, it could be said it did. For forty days the warren-like streets in the town — Kichwele to Ingles, Ring to Acacia — hummed with a chant, a prayer sung with one voice, occasionally reverberating with a wail for the person who had advised them on everything, from what was a good thing to eat for breakfast to the hazards of too much tea-drinking, from throwing away the burkha-veil to adopting English in schools, and then to more arcane matters such as the ascendancy after the Prophet.

Suleiman Pir had been around so long that to my pupils he was immortal. As Gregory said, "After this they'll graduate to Nietzsche." He was right, in his cynical way, and perhaps he even knew why he was, would be, right. Because Suleiman Pir was succeeded by Yahya Pir, a history graduate from Cambridge and Harvard, an academic. A Boston paper quipped: "Assistant Prof. tenured as God." But for the boys, the studious ones, for whom Standard XII and the Cambridge O level was only the beginning, a phase set in. They wanted to go to Harvard, become academics. That several of them did, coming full circle in studying their own phenomenon, is something to ponder over. (I have, of course, one particular student, my correspondent Sona, in mind.) I wonder if Gregory would have a ready response to that.

At long last the school that the Precious Jubilee had made possible was ready. A school so beautiful it took the breath away. There was nothing like it in the country. Only Nairobi's exclusive white schools came close. Community members came on excursions to see it, this monument they'd built, walking for miles, having their picnics, and walking all the way back to their shop-homes. It came with cricket and football grounds, running track. Its motto, appropriately Latin, was *Labor Omnia Vincit*, its symbol Promethean fire. The Shamsis had learned the colonial game well. They played by the rules but they played to win. The sacrifices they would count later – or their poets would, those who passed through our hands at the school.

∽∾

As for my own life in those days, I remember 1959 as the year when my homeland, which I'd left more than ten years earlier, now loosened its emotional grip on me, gave me away. I had not had much inclination towards marriage, much to the despair of my mother in Goa, keeping myself absorbed in preparing year after year fresh students for their final exams and the world. That year, however, I became engaged to a Goan girl who lived in Kichwele – in fact, diagonally opposite Pipa Store. I saw the engagement as a consolation for my mother, who, seeing me "happily" settled and taken care of by a woman, could put her maternal anxieties at rest. Though it did not last.

It was during this brief courtship that I would see Pipa counting out his minutes with his spice packets, as I imagined it. He looked old and sickly, walking slowly – on the rare occasions when I saw him on foot – supported by his son Amin or his chauffeur.

As the decade drew to a close, it seemed that an old innocence had slowly faded, or been sloughed off, and a new consciousness by inches emerged. World news was as action-packed as the movies – and somehow more relevant. The cold war was intense, and the atomic threat hung over our heads too. Sputnik had launched us into a new world of science fiction. Closer to home, negotiations for the country's independence were on, and we felt conscious of the eyes of the world upon us. The Christopher Cup in cricket was avidly competed for by the schools, the Sunlight and Gossage cups in football thrilled the entire country. And the youth drama competition took up a good portion of our year at school. One of the plays was even reviewed in a provincial newspaper in England.

I associated with Desouza and Gregory, but never the two together, because of Desouza's dislike of the Englishman. I found myself liking Gregory for precisely the reason he roused Desouza's special ire: Gregory was a challenge, an iconoclast, always the devil's advocate, with brutally honest observations – and yet with an underside as raw and delicate as the skin on his chest in the tropical sun. He was a rather lonely person, quite incapable of attracting any sympathy for himself, a modicum of humanity or understanding even from his compatriots. There was a certain secretiveness in him, a reserve; there remained sides unrevealed, a trait I attribute to national character. But why not? Gregory always had one or two favourite students – bright boys, of course, but what else in a boys' school? There was always some talk about that, whose truth I never tried to ascertain. I took him with a bit of humour but also with respect and understanding. He took quite readily to me. I found myself going to the Little Theatre with him, and, during the erratic existence of the Film Society, we saw a number of angst-ridden Swedish films together, wondering afterwards over a depressing drink why we had gone.

He had hired an excellent cook and was generous in his ways. He lived in a small bungalow on Seaview, an area then almost exclusively white. But he gave all his private tutorials in town and Kariakoo, where his pupils lived. He could be dragged to class picnics, to which he was quite unsuited, turning very red very soon; and he would participate in the annual staff-versus-students cricket match, bowling decent spinners until Solanki or Abuali or Bhamji or Visram began hitting them to the boundary.

Around this time, poor Desouza was hit by a disastrous string of events from which he never recovered. He became engaged to a nice Goan girl, a bank teller, who unfortunately jilted him for a bank officer. This wounded him so deeply he never talked of marrying after that, and even turned somewhat ascetic. A few months after he was jilted, he one day savagely caned a boy for a minor misdemeanour. This was the event that would complete his transformation. He came to the staff room weeping. He went to the boy's home and apologized, was slapped by the boy's father and chased back into the street. After that even Desouza's appearance changed. He wore dull greys or browns and grew a beard. He became softspoken, almost gentle, but was also distant and never seemed happy.

To add to Desouza's torments, for the past four or five years in succession a boy in his Standard XI class had died in an accident. There was already a belief in town that every year the ocean claimed one young soul for its own. In two of these successive years, the boy who died was Desouza's. One of these was a boy who, early one morning by the shore, had heard two women crying out for help some distance away in the water. He went in to rescue them, but was himself carried away by the current. The women were saved by a boat.

Then there was the time that a boy, while chasing or being chased during school recess, hit his head against a corner of an open window. The year after, on the first day of school, Desouza warned his students: "I don't want any of you doing silly things, getting into accidents – dying on me." They laughed. In November, four weeks before the end of classes, two of them were hit by a lorry while on a bicycle and died.

With all the changes taking place, and new syllabuses and new inspectors of education, and observers from overseas, I found myself for the first time in many years not quite qualified. By the book, that is. I had, of course, a BA (upper second), but I was told I should go for my diploma in education. This, by a shop-keeper turned educational administrator, so my persuasive powers naturally failed me. The real reason, I believe, was that with the country's independence almost upon us, Western coun-tries were indulging their consciences by donating teachers with whom I had to compete. The very fact that they came from the West made them – in the eyes of shopkeepers – more qualified than I. Upon recommendation from Gregory, I was admitted to the University of London in the autumn of 1960.

Much has been made of one's first sight of London, even by Englishmen. There are many Dick Whittington stories from the colonies with ironic twists to them. I had, of course, left Bombay for Africa, so a big city was not in itself going to overwhelm me. But a colonial city is different from the metropolis, that place to which all roads lead. To see history take substance before one's own eyes (and I was quite taken by monuments) is deeply impres-sive; to know things, recognize them upon first sight, as objects familiar and near, is miraculous; to see Englishmen in their own habitat, not all teachers, administrators, or governors, not all from Oxford or Cambridge, is curiously numbing. All this, yes – but just to have got out of the rut I had been in was refreshing, was to be living again. I met other students from different parts of the world, sometimes with very similar experiences to mine – how truly delightful to hear discussions about the merits or demerits of Messrs. Nelkon and Holderness by those from Hong Kong, Penang, and Accra. How wonderful to discuss Gregory and to realize that his other incarnations reside in Lagos and Khartoum.

But levity aside – and surely there are those who will blame our problems precisely on the presence of a Gregory in Dar, Lagos, and Khartoum – just to see the world from somewhere else, *out there*, was exciting. To be exposed to new ideas, to be made to read and understand so much, was a privilege. In my mind I thanked the shopkeeper-administrator many times over for having given me leave.

Many of my former students – and when not my own, those who had seen me in school and said "Good morning, sir" to me countless times – were in London, and I met them. I was invited, smuggled, to one of their functions once, in the second month of my stay. They held mosque in a residential street in Kensington. The scene was remarkable: from the tube station, and the bus-stop on Kensington High Street, young Asians converged upon a handsome town house with black door and brass knocker. Inside, the mosque was quite dingy, but that was London. There were two large rooms downstairs on either side of the hallway desig-nated for prayers. The prayer rooms were packed that Friday, mostly with young men and women all seated in rows on the floor. After the ceremonies, when all got up, there was a tremen-dous crush and one moved with extreme difficulty. Finally, there was a spillover into the street – which was the only place some of these young people who lived and worked miles apart could meet. At this point the neighbours complained to the police and the bobbies showed up. It was all very polite and, I was told, quite regular. About an hour later, with the mats removed, there was dancing, and, since not everybody stayed, there was room to breathe.

After prayers, and with a jolt, I saw Rita. But briefly and only at a distance. It had been nearly ten years since she'd left Dar. She looked older, which she was, and she had a young child with her, holding him in front to keep him from getting crushed. She hadn't seen me yet, and I quickly looked away, in a gesture that was immature and perhaps even cowardly. But I had made it a point not to be obtrusive during this visit to London, and not seek her out in her new life with her husband. I desired very much to preserve what I had come to think of as my growing equanimity.

I had heard, though, that she and her husband had run a café near the campus, frequented by foreign students, but that they had moved on. It was now run by a Greek couple, and I of course knew the place.

During the latter part of my nine-month stay, I had a brief affair, the chemistry of which I attribute to loneliness on my part and socialist patronage on hers. This utilitarian liaison ended upon my departure – with the passionless comfort it provided, how many desolately lonely nights had I avoided? Without it, I might have tried to seek out Rita.

Before I left, I met the dean who had read the recommendation Gregory had written for me and had admitted me to the program. During our friendly final chat he let drop a remark which was truly unsettling, which quite astounded me; how little we know those around us, how much less we knew then. He informed me that Gregory was a poet, reasonably well known in literary circles.

I left for Dar with some relief – for a place where I had no direct family yet so much else I called it home now.

21

I had returned to a country on the brink of independence, one that was preparing to transmute. The dat⁏ had been set for December that year, six months away, and the laid-back Dar I had known was bubbling with excitement. There was hope in the air, and a cheery confidence, symbolized in the promise of a torch of freedom to be mounted on the summit of Kilimanjaro for all to see, across the continent and beyond. If in later years bush-shirted demagogues waylaid those dreams with arid ideologies, and torpid bureaucrats drained our energies, at least we were spared the butchers. . . . But I am losing perspective.

They were exciting times, when I arrived back, and soon even I found myself sporting the bright collarless celebratory khanga shirt, which inspired Gregory to remark, "Have you become a man of the people now, Pius?"

Saturday was a half day at school, and on Sunday mornings the male expatriate teachers gathered in a driveway of the teachers' quarters for a shave from the barbers. Our barbers were a genial pair, father and son. It was a considerable coup for them to have a dozen prestigious customers in one place at the same time, submitting to their razors. We would be sitting ready for them in a straight line in the gravelled driveway when they arrived on their bicycles. We waited as one by one our turns came, making jokes, bickering and quarrelling about various academic topics, but converging always on the current rumour about the impending changes in the country.

We were intensely aware of our essential homelessness. Our world was diminishing with the Empire. We were all travellers who had on an impulse taken off, for all kinds of personal reasons, yes, but surely also to pursue a career we had all chosen – to teach. And we were all proud of our best efforts. We were now aware that we would have to choose: to return home . . . but what was home now? to take on a new nationality . . . but what did that mean? to move on to the vestiges of the Empire, to the last colonies and dominions, or perhaps to retreat to where it all began, London. I of course had chosen to throw in my lot with the new nation; being a solitary man without close attachments has been a help in living up to this resolve. But for the others, even after they had opted to stay, the question always remained to plague them – to stay or to go, and where to go?

The barbers would wipe their razors and then cycle away, leaving us in the sun, smooth-faced, uncomfortable, and exposed. And we would sit a few more minutes with our questions and anxieties before one last comment met a long, pregnant silence, and the first person got up to go.

After the Barbers' Club, as these shaving sessions came to be called, Gregory and I would go off for lunch, usually to Cosy Café or Hindu Lodge, and then repair to his flat on Seaview, where we would rest on lounge chairs, finishing off his single malt, dozing to the sounds of waves breaking on the shore and the BBC African Service testing English comprehension or telling a story. I would leave towards six.

There was between the two of us – Gregory and me – the

friendship of two men thrown together by fate who were reasonably tolerant . . . and, if I may flatter myself, who saw the humanness in each other. There were worlds yet that embarrassed us, histories that irked, that we would rather not discuss. In other surroundings, situations, we might not have spent the time together. When I had returned from London, I brought for him an envelope from his friend the dean. It contained, with a letter, a fairly long clipping; a review of his work, I believe. We were at the Cosy Café when I handed it to him. The look on his face when he opened it is something I'll never forget: at once sheepish, guilty, remorseful, crushingly sad; it takes slow motion in retrospect to tell the components apart. If he had had it in him he would have wept with frustration. The afternoon was humid, his pudgy red face streaming with sweat. Clearly, his art was a source of considerable pain. If I may venture further, it is to say this: the pain was that of the exile, not for the loss of home but for the loss of his inspiration. I did not quiz him about his poetry, and he was grateful, doubly so when I did not let anyone in on his secret. I must say that now I find myself surprised at my lack of curiosity about his poetry; I suppose I had presumed, with him, that it was of another world.

Soon after that incident at the Cosy, he came into the staff room one day and asked for a favour.

"I say, Fernandes – would you mind awfully if you took my tutorial tonight?"

"Where – I'm hardly prepared – *Julius Caesar*, is it?"

"Yes. Don't worry – they'll ask questions. Say anything – they'll learn something from it."

And so I began sharing with him those tutorials, which had been his privilege for many years, a mark of recognition by students and parents of his expertise in English literature. One of the places Gregory held his sessions was at the building across from Pipa's Amin Mansion. One Sunday, following a Saturday session, he brought a piece of disquieting news to the Barbers' Club, which was unusually silent and brooding because those of us there had already heard. There had been a death at the shop-keeper Pipa's home.

The tragedy is simple enough to describe: once more Pipa was cheated, robbed at the peak of promise and happiness. But I must give the man his due, tell his story. Pipa was thrown to his lowest point; he would never rise again.

Two years before, an educated black man – a teacher, in fact, because that's how people in the street greeted him – had come to the store with two companions, and had stood outside on the main street, facing Pipa, who was perched on his high seat. The teacher seemed cheerful enough, and knew the shopkeeper – but that was no surprise, few in the city didn't know Pipa.

"Pipa, let's have a cigarette!"

"Have you come to buy or to demand? Which ones do you want?"

"Sportsman. I've come to beg."

"Beggars come on Fridays. And they don't get more than a heller – except the big-headed one."

The beggar with the swollen head had a perpetual grin on his face; you avoided him in the street, and in the stores you gave him something large – a ten-cent copper – that would send him off so you didn't have to look at him. Children fled upon his arrival.

The teacher laughed. "Don't you know, I, too, have a big head!"

"Go away if you don't have money."

"Tell him, Mwalimu," one of the companions grumbled.

The teacher laughed: "It's his right. You know, Pipa, come independence and we'll send you back where you came from."

"I come from Moshi. My mother and father – I don't know where from. Many places perhaps. Where will you send me? Tell me so I can prepare. And you will give this store to someone who will give free cigarettes to lazy teachers — and perhaps God will supply your country with free presents."

Pipa was spluttering, red with indignation. A servant brought cold water.

"Ah, Pipa — I was only joking. You have put me to shame. Forgive me." The politeness was not politic, feigned, but customary, a gracious acceptance of defeat in argument.

"Bwana Pipa — you we won't send away, but the British government we will."

"I'll believe you when I see them go. You think if you tell them Go . . . eti, they'll pack their bags and leave?" He started coughing.

"Well then, to send them off is going to be hard work. To travel, to talk to people, to print announcements, to buy loudspeakers, Land Rovers!"

"So you've come to beg for money."

"Eh-e!"

The old man, who was not yet very old, the fat shopkeeper in his singlet, slipped a hand into the cashbox. He fumbled. Without looking to see, he brought out a note; without looking at what it was, he handed it to the teacher. It was a hundred shillings — and Pipa added as a bonus two Sportsman cigarettes. Onlookers gasped.

The teacher was moved, but as was his way — which he perfected in later years as father of the country — he hid behind his friendly laugh. "You see, Pipa, we cannot fail!" He walked away, followed by a crowd of admirers. He would yet draw them out in the thousands. They would sing for him and march across the country for him; young and old, men and women, educated and illiterate.

As independence approached, on Kichwele Street, on the pavement outside Pipa's shop, banners appeared in the green and black colours of the new nation. Broad multicoloured canopies were put up in the middle of the street at regular intervals, bringing a toy-town look to the busy down-to-earth drabness of the thoroughfare. One day a Land Rover arrived on the side street, parking quite close to the store, almost under the tarpaulin sunshade. A man got out and walked into the shop. He handed Pipa an envelope, saying, "Open it," and Pipa, bewildered, tore it open. There was a white card inside, but he couldn't read it, of course. The man explained: With the compliments of the teacher – our leader – you can come and see the independence celebrations, bid farewell to the mzungu. At the National Stadium, the man said – among thousands – but with a special invitation and seat. Bring your family – how many do you have, twenty, thirty?

I'll believe they are going when I see them going, he had said to the teacher. Now he was invited to see them go.

He went with Remti and Amin in the Ford Taunus stationwagon to see the event, along with two of his older daughters and their husbands and children. There was an air of festive expectation in the stadium, in the glow of a multitude of lights, everyone there waiting patiently and cheerfully for the hour of uhuru – freedom – to arrive. The family was given privileged seats on a side stand. Bands played and marched on the field not far from them, and from time to time they saw a dignitary arrive on the VIP stand. Finally, at midnight, a hush spread through the stadium. For some reason, all eyes converged on the Union Jack, calmly flying on the flagpole in front of them. The red-white-and-blue flag they'd known all their lives. Pipa had seen it first in Kikono outside the ADC's office. Suddenly, the lights went out in the stadium. When they came on again there was a tumultuous uproar, wave upon wave of ecstatic cheering that came from all around them. The old flag was gone, a new one was in its place. The Queen's husband, splendid in black ceremonials, made a farewell speech. The teacher – Mwalimu – was on his feet now, making promises to the people and the world. Then fireworks, and the sky lit up.

It was while returning home from the celebration, having turned into Kichwele, now Uhuru Street, that the incident occurred which began the tragedy. It was two o'clock in the morning, the children were awake and cranky. One of the grandchildren hit Amin on the back of the head, and Pipa turned and shouted, "Not on the head! Never on the head." Hitting on the head was dangerous, it could bring on a spirit, cause madness. After this, it seemed, Amin often complained of headaches.

Doctors were no help. Over the next few months the family tried several of them, beginning with the old Dr. Panwalker and ending with the expensive modern Dr. Singh. Between them they prescribed cod-liver oil, laxatives, vitamins of all sorts; they checked the boy's eyesight and gave him glasses; they blamed the sun and the heat and everything else, and only stopped short of blaming his parents for having him so late. Herbal, ayurvedic medicines were bought; an old woman began visiting the home to draw away the headaches with special prayers. Nothing seemed to help.

And then suddenly one day Pipa knew: It was *she*, who else? She had given the boy to him, she was worrying him now. In the last ten years, with the departure of Ali, she had receded from his life until she disappeared altogether, and he thought she had found rest at last. Now here she was again. He dreamt of her, once, lying dead as she had lain many years ago, as he had seen her in his dreams many times before. He started to bring food, furniture to the mosque. What more did she want? She had taken away one son, given him this one – couldn't she see him happy?

And then Amin's fevers started, and would not go away. The doctors came, prescribed malaria medicine, but to no avail. The fevers, which came intermittently, persisted.

Meanwhile Pipa prayed to her. I know you can do it, he is in your spell. He was certain of it when he dreamed that she was sitting, holding a boy in her lap. After a while, she said, "Take him –" The boy turned his head: it was Amin. "Go on," she said.

Pipa woke up in horror.

The next day the boy died. It was Saturday night, nine o'clock, and Gregory was climbing the dark flight of stairs to take a session in a second-floor flat across the street from Pipa's home, a boy leading the way with a candle. Gregory said he heard a scream, piercing through walls, through hearts.

Ali came back to Dar for the funeral. It was a citywide affair, as such events always were, and Gregory and I attended. A child of the community, of the school, had died. Viongozi Street was blocked off with cars, mostly belonging to teachers. People stood outside – the flat being too small – around the beige-and-green funeral van, open at the back, awaiting its passenger. And then it came, the little coffin bobbing on shoulders to the wail of the kalima – "There is none but Him" – and the sobs, of men, boys, in kanzus, coats, cloth caps. The coffin was pushed into the back of the van, then Ali in astrakhan got in behind with the others and began reciting the kalima. And I remember this, too: Gregory, wearing a suit, wiping sweat from his face, also mouthing the kalima along with the others.

There are certain events that make you a part of a place. This was one of them, for Gregory: the death of a child in a community he had served. What point in asking him, taunting him, at the Barbers' Club: Mr. Gregory, after independence, where next – South Africa? Where but Dar?

As the van pulled away, Pipa and his male neighbours followed in the Taunus; and Remti's screams echoed along the length of Viongozi, they said, from Gerezani all the way to the fire station, the United Nations Road, and the schools.

Ali stayed a week. He spent much of it with his father. "Tell

280

me," he asked Pipa. "What is this secret? Tell me about Mariamu – my mother – who was she?"

And Pipa told him.

Ali returned to London, shaken, in some ways a changed man; and a man without cares, a man who could not be stopped. Ali told Rita what he had heard from Pipa.

And Rita has told me, but at a price as yet unnamed.

22

This is Rita's story in London –

Goodness knows how, by the time Ali and I reached London there was already an air of scandal and excitement in the community. Every eye upon me in mosque; and the whispers. You can have no idea how difficult it was. So we were finally in London, now what to do? We had not married, he had not divorced. He had grounds, of course he had grounds: there had been no children by the marriage. He had written her a letter before we left, but her first response was to refuse divorce at any cost. I was staying at the Centre on Gloucester Road. There were a few girls there who had come "for higher education" – how simple we were! – but it was all shorthand-typing and hairdressing and nursing in those days. Ali stayed in a hotel near the university, and we were desperate for money. Finally she relented – *they* relented, the family – and in three months the divorce came through. He thought it was because of his threats of publicity – but it was more my family, going down on their knees to the G. R. Mooljis, the khanga kings; signing away the deeds to some piece of property. Ali and I were married in a small ceremony at the mosque, and we rented a flat. The community in London soon forgot the scandal of our arrival and we began to lead normal lives. I heard from all my friends in Dar, but I had no contact with my parents, even my brother and sisters. My parents never forgave me. I wrote every week, I pleaded, wept over my letters. Please, I said, please, please listen. What is done is done, I cannot undo it, forgive and give me your blessings. They did not reply. That hurt a lot. A wedding is supposed to be a joyous occasion – it is a family occasion, a community occasion . . . it's not only love, it can never be. There's always some bitterness in a marriage that is not blessed. And a girl needs her family to turn to even in the best of marriages. I never got over it, it came between us, Ali and me. And now – I don't think *I* have it in my heart to forgive *them* . . . not completely . . . for that rejection.

There were other girls like me, in London. One had run away to marry a Hindu from South Africa; she lives in Harrow now and they own a grocery store. Another girl, from Kariakoo, ran away with a boy from the Jafferi sect – a crime much worse than mine. She is divorced and lives with her daughters in Toronto. We used to meet and talk sometimes – go for coffee after Friday mosque. All of us bred on Schoolgirls' Picture Library comics and Enid Blyton and Indian films, with visions of Big Ben and the friendly bobby. Well, the bobbies were friendly, in the 1950s, and the postmen honest – you could post a letter with tuppence-ha'penny taped in place of a stamp, and the next day it would be delivered! There was a nice sort of innocence then. And we were still from the colonies, we were no threat. But we were coloured.

I took shorthand-typing and had work within weeks. They treated you like servants, then . . . but I don't think we minded, not at first, not that much, we were too thrilled to be in London, too honoured. We worked late, were asked to clean up, had our bottoms pinched; a girl was raped, another became pregnant. And then we learned to speak up.

But he – Ali – had it much worse . . . in the beginning. He worked as a waiter; the proud, handsome Ali, who had the bearing of a prince. He would leave at six in the morning – neatly dressed in suit and tie, full of high spirits, whistling – and return all dishevelled. . . . All the stories of London we used to hear – how many would have gone had they known the truth beforehand? And yet those who returned home kept coming back, couldn't stay away . . . from the cold winters, gas-heated bedsitters, in which a few even gassed themselves . . . in error or deliberately, who knows? Did I have regrets? Yes. Who wouldn't? From Dar's favourite girl, coddled and pampered, to this – a drudge. And he? He never looked back, not once even in the most difficult times.

So this was the once-glamorous Ali and Rita in London.

But you made it eventually, didn't you, Rita? You would always have made it, anywhere.

Ali finally had a decent offer: managing the Museum Café near Great Russell Street. It required both of us to run the place and it paid well. But it was hard work. We opened at five for the deliveries; there was the first rush at six-thirty, when the cleaners and lorry drivers arrived. Then, at eight-thirty, there were the secretaries and clerks and telephone operators; later the students. Then lunch, and tea. Oh yes, I saw everything, the grease pans, the scullery, the mop. Out in front, Ali. He was indomitable. However tired and defeated and broken down he was in the evening, the next morning, there he was, the prince – or deposed chief's son, as some believed, he never made it clear. Oh, he could have sold them the Taj Mahal. Especially when he wore his astrakhan; that wasn't often of course, he was into Homburgs. He learnt the English accent, the real thing; proper. And he was learning Spanish. That almost undid me.

I had had our daughter, Rehana, by then, and I was expecting Hadi. Ali took his lessons on Fridays when I went to mosque. He was out of the community by then – more or less . . . it's never complete, is one thing you learn; that was okay with me. It was over coffee after prayers when one of my friends said, "How do you know he's learning Spanish, Ri?" "He's learning quite a bit," I said. In all innocence. They all looked at me as if I was out of my mind. "On Friday nights? Do you know the teacher? *What* is he learning besides?"

How I wept, made scenes. Wrote home. Her name was Alice. She came from Spain but had an American mother. At LSE, and a little older than me. If I had heard from my family, I would have left. But I didn't. And he gave her up.

We ran the Museum Café for five long years. They were not all as bad as the first year. But still. My children were my inspiration then. And I went to mosque on Friday evenings – what a solace that was. Ali took courses and tried one or two business ventures on the side, which failed. We didn't know what else to try. There was talk of going to America, or Dubai.

And then our luck changed in the most fantastic way. A few families made their fortunes in property; you know, one day grocers on Stanley Street, the next, millionaires in London – unbelievable, isn't it? Those who came later, those younger than us, made it in hotels and nursing homes, and also in property. But our luck came knocking at our door – and it seemed that he was right, Ali was really chosen by fate. Well. There was this Jew who every Thursday was the last customer in the café, at five. Mr. Eisen. He looked old but actually he was only in his fifties; he was a big man. Sometimes he brought with him his wife and daughter. Always had a light supper – we served no dinners. He liked Ali . . . and me . . . very much . . . would stop him as he walked past. "Mr. Ali," he would say. "How is the missis – tell her the soup, it was good. Thank her for keeping it for me . . . I know she did . . ." He, of course, didn't believe for a minute that we owned the café.

"Why don't you work for me?" he said to Ali one day. "Your missis can then stay home with the children." Just like that.

This was shortly before *you* arrived in London. I saw you, of course – that day when you sneaked into the mosque – and I wished so much to meet you, discuss my problems with you. Ask you about home, how my parents were, give you letters to take back. Ask you to talk with them, intercede for me – did that occur to you? No, you stayed away, nursing a wound that had no right to be there in the first place.

The wound had healed, Rita. So well, only a nice memory remained, I simply didn't want to reopen anything. You say Ali was indomitable; to me, you were so. I was afraid of what you could do to me. Perhaps I *should* have come to you. A faint heart . . .

Mr. Eisen – I can't remember his first name, the relationship was so formal, though friendly – had his own finance company, the Athena. He was a refugee from Germany, leaving as a young man. He had a strong accent. We were fascinated with the history – from the films and magazines. The first time we invited them to our flat, we asked them a lot of questions about Germany; his parents and so on . . . and the war. As students we had read of the brave Maquis in berets and the girls in pigtails on bicycles who helped them escape through France. Anne Frank. And the films those days were all about the war, weren't they? . . . But of course we soon realized it was a subject not to be discussed. There would always be that distance between us, we were too naïve. They looked poor – which they were not – and outcast, but there was so much culture, things we could only get an inkling of. They were so European. They had a son, who was an artist, who was touring in the States. He had absolutely refused to join the business. The wife and daughter helped, but I don't believe they had a knack for it. Perhaps it was too much a man's world. Mrs. Eisen –

Ela – was undergoing therapy. Migraine, she said, but I think it was depression. A young typist was the only outside person employed in the office. When Ali joined it he came like a breath of fresh air. The prince – even they called him that. And he took to the new business, the new life, like a duck to water. It's what he was born for.

"What do you do – what is the business?" Ali asked Mr. Eisen when he made the offer that first day.

"Say the boss wants to sell this fine restaurant and invites you to make an offer. You don't have the money, of course, so you come to Athena Finance Company – to me."

"For a loan – but I could go to Lloyd's Bank."

"Would they give you it – give it to you . . . you know what I mean!"

"No."

"Exactly."

Should I be telling you this – a family secret? Behind many an immigrant success-story there is a guardian angel somewhere in the background. Mr. Eisen was ours. Where would we have been without his help. He was a good businessman, too, of course, and many immigrants and refugees ended up at his doorstep for loans to start again. Some of the new real-estate multimillionaires – including a few from East Africa – bought their first properties through him. He could take risks with them, he knew their mentalities. "They are not riff-raff where they come from," he would say. "They are workers, builders . . . sometimes crooked, but we won't say that aloud and we are not fools, are we?"

The night Ali's half-brother, Amin, died, Ali was phoned from Pipa's house. We could hear the wailing and screaming in the background – it was dreadful. And eerie, over such a long distance. And Remti blaming Ali for it – what had *he* done? We were *of course* shocked; we knew what the boy meant to his parents. Such a darling, everyone had so loved him. Having come after so long a time, when there was money and time to lavish on him. Ali was not, after all, Remti's son. And when she had her own son, it was a triumph, over Ali, over . . . Mariamu, *that* woman. He'll be a bigger prince, Remti had boasted, he's the real prince . . . and so on. Amin Mansion was built, then the signs of affluence, prestige – car, telephone, fridge (we can laugh at it all now; we *were* poor, weren't we?) – all because of Amin.

Ali caught a plane out of London that same night we heard the news. A strange thing happened when he arrived in Dar. He had automatically put on his astrakhan and he was wearing a white suit. He took a taxi from the airport. When it got into town, driving along Independence Avenue, he realized the car had a train of young men running behind it. He was amazed, thought he was being attacked; or that he'd arrived in the midst of a revolution. But these were Indians – Shamsis mostly – who were mobbing him. Finally, when the car turned in to Uhuru Street, the young men knew their mistake: he was not the real prince Aly Khan. It rather unsettled him. This was not the Dar he knew, he couldn't wear the astrakhan as nonchalantly as he used to.

He stayed a week, living in a hotel. In that week he became his father's chauffeur. They had long chats. They sat at the seashore . . . or outside the new Upanga mosque with its beautiful garden . . . or in the shop, where the two had spent so much time together. Ali was genuinely touched by this closeness. The old man, coughing and sickly now, opened his heart to him. When Ali returned to London, he was changed. Before, he had seen himself as somehow chosen. Now he was driven, and quite ruthless. His face had darkened with a seriousness.

Ali asked to buy into Athena, and Mr. Eisen offered him twenty-five per cent, this being his artist-son's share. And Ali began bringing in international business. That was his knack, he could make contacts fast, he dressed well, he spoke well, and he impressed. "Forget about real estate, and bed-and-breakfast

288

affairs in Victoria, and typing schools," he would say to Mr. Eisen, "international finance is where the real money is." Of course there was glamour in that, and travel, and the contracts were huge. The first large contract was from some Arab businessmen. A ship was chartered for East Africa . . . there was quite an uproar about it later – all kinds of claims, not true really, but it was turned back by the Royal Navy on its way from Aden . . .

The time was 1963-1964; there had been a violent revolution in Zanzibar in which the Arab monarchy was deposed, with the assistance of the Russians, the Cubans, and the East Germans. The chartered ship, the *Seyyid Said*, was suspected of carrying weapons and European mercenaries. There was a Russian submarine in the Indian Ocean, the three East African countries were nervous about coups d'etat, and the tense situation was very much the cause of the Royal Navy's turning back of the *Seyyid*.

Athena, of course, did not lose anything, everything was paid for in advance, but it was close. Mr. Eisen got very nervous and told Ali to go easy from then on. Ali, too, had got a bit scared; things had gone a little too fast. He's always been cautious since then.

Mr. Eisen died in 1966. His wife and daughter sold us their share and went to live in Israel.

Overnight, our fortunes had changed. The children, Rehana and Hadi, went to public schools; we moved to Eccleston Square and from there to Beech Grove in Hampstead. And yes, when Beech Grove was fixed up it was all over the community newspapers – yes, gold taps, antique-raj chandeliers, a Rolls-Royce used by Pandit Nehru at Harrow, and so on. As I said, there was no stopping Ali; such publicity didn't daunt him. *Nouveau riche*, so what, he still says; it is still *riche*; weren't the Normans *nouveau* once? And didn't the English live in caves once? But of course he was conscious, we were conscious, of who we were; in England, how you speak, how you dress, how you sit – it all matters, is what you are.

Athena Finance Company is rather unique, I think. It has its offices on Carlton Place, near Trafalgar Square. From the windows you can see the parade of the queen's Horse Guards in the morning. That never fails to impress clients, all dignitaries of foreign nations. The company undertakes international projects. It is a bank and contractor. It facilitates governments in buying services overseas. First, by offering financing, when required. And then by overseeing the project – secondary contracting, shipping, and so on. Of course risky loans are guaranteed – by a government, or an aid agency; another bank. . . . There have been projects in the Shah's Iran, in Manila, and in South America. Once the company became known, projects kept coming in – Ali knew princes and ministers. And he, of course, was our prince; many – all – of his clients believed that. Even the English media believe something of the sort. When the tabloids reported Rehana's engagement, they called Ali a son of an oriental chieftain.

Arms: he may have dealt in them if he thought it safe; he is a cautious man. There was a scientist from Qatar who wanted to build a Qatari bomb. It was to be called Algebra I; "algebra" is apparently derived from Arabic. Athena didn't bite. Then a Quebec man wanted to build a long gun. Ali wouldn't touch him. The man was later assassinated. Coffee from Uganda. There was a blend we drank in those days, which we laughingly called Ugando-Colombian. Idi Amin was in power then, and the coffee was smuggled . . .

It's difficult to say what, exactly, came between us . . . many things, I suppose. Marriage is a kind of death, isn't it – the end of youth and freedom, everything that made you attractive and beautiful – the beginning of responsibility. With me the bitterness and disappointment of my parents' rejection; the hardship and toil when we began in London. A dingy room, a crusty landlady, cold winters, used and ill-fitting winter clothes, and, to top it all, a baby. Nothing like hardship to kill a romance double quick, is there? And then when the breaks came, we thought we'd begin anew. You know when I was a schoolgirl my friends and I wrote in each other's autograph books: Friendship is like china. Well, love even more so. He drifted away . . . a simple home life was not exactly where he wanted to stop – he wanted more, and more, until I think even I was not enough.

Even after all the tuition in etiquette, I don't think I quite measured up. I was still the same old me . . . couldn't take to wearing hats . . . couldn't quite act the princess; and I was still religious. With the political problems back home, the confiscation of property, my family had finally made contact, needed my help, and I helped them, sometimes brought them home – those nieces and nephews visiting London – which didn't go down well, I tell you.

Ali was derisive of Indian ways by then. He began more openly to have flings with women, and he travelled a lot. It was in Peru that he met Rosita. I knew the moment he returned that this was something special. She's Argentinian, with some British ancestry; and she's somewhat younger than I am – of course – with two children by a previous marriage. A very nice woman. And, yes, glamorous – ideally suited to him. She was brought up in the European way, you see. She insisted the settlement with me be generous and amicable. So I am still one of the family. It's as if he has two wives.

Beech Grove is mine. It's a splendid house of white stucco exterior with dark oak inside, built in the 1930s. It has a long gravel driveway and a simply beautiful garden. The kind of house we saw in magazines when we were young. When you look out on a summer morning, especially after a rainfall, it's a sight to fill your heart with calmness and the joy of living. There are always offers to buy it, from embassies. Rehana and Hadi would like me to sell it, too, to be closer to the City. But I shan't sell it.

It is like a mother, Jackie says — she is my Filipino maid — because you always come back to it, it is there, and it is nice and warm. I have a small car that I do my shopping with, and go to mosque.

Jackie and I have long talks sometimes. She keeps me up to date on all the Filipino girls in the neighbourhood. Who's having an affair, who's been fired, who's going back, who's got a job offer in the Gulf, or Japan, or Canada. I don't want to lose her, but sooner or later she'll go. Saturdays, I have lunch with Rehana and accompany her shopping. Sunday afternoons, Hadi comes over and spends the night.

Last year Ali was on the New Year's Honours List — finally, quite a few years after the Falklands. Only then did I feel denied, and hurt at not being at his side. But that's not everything, is it? I am still Mrs. Ali.

Ever a traditional Indian wife, you like to call your husband "he," Rita. And what about the Falklands, Rita? Was this the Argentinian connection through Rosita, some service rendered in the war?

She declines to comment.

Miscellany (iv)

From the personal notebook of Pius Fernandes
May 1988, Dar es Salaam

She's bought khangas for Jackie, her Filipino maid, a large Makonde carving for Ali, and gold jewellery for herself. ("I just can't resist.") The coffee shop is crowded and sticky, but a welcome refuge from the blazing Somora Avenue outside. The street curio-seller from whom she's promised to buy something takes an occasional peep in at us through the window where we sit. He's so desperate, I've concluded, he'll wait a week if he has to. It's a pity, in terms of quality he just can't compete with the Indian wholesaler on Market Street.

She will go to the game parks in Arusha for a few days, then she'll return and leave almost immediately for London.

There are questions still unanswered . . . about this girl who has made such a place for herself among us – Mariamu – who stole the Englishman's diary and like that book refused to lie buried. Who murdered her in such a terrible fashion, exacting a man's toll from her? What was her relationship to Corbin? And, most important surely for Rita, who was Ali's father?

Rita looks at me over her raised cup.

"The coffee here has such a raw taste to it – you can buy Tanzanian coffee at Selfridges, you know, but it's not the same."

The buyers here get the last choice from the local crop, I want to tell her, but desist. The long eyebrows, they captivate me, and the sparkling eyes – were they really always so brown, those eyes?

This is perhaps the last time I'll see her like this, admire her openly, at this age, in a way I had not dared to before. Only days ago, months it seems, she extracted jokingly a pledge from me to pay a price for these tête-à-têtes, her information. That price I have long guessed: silence, an injunction on these proceedings. She's going to name it here today, but how?

"Do you think Pipa ever learned the answer to the one question that obsessed him all his life?" I ask her.

She draws a quick breath, then: "I don't know."

"I would like to believe that Mariamu finally told him, relieved him of his misery before he died . . . through some sign perhaps . . ."

"We'll never know, will we?" she says, a little too quickly, I think.

She becomes quiet, sips at her coffee. She has something – several things – on her mind, I can tell, and she'll let me fumble through to them.

"What else?" she says at length.

"It's all so maddeningly incomplete, so unsatisfactory, isn't it? Half-formed pictures, suspicions –"

"You can't know everything about the past, can you?"

"It's not that at all. But there are certain things. . . . For instance, the girl Mariamu, violated, murdered, have you wondered – ?"

"A stray soldier, perhaps . . . that's most likely, isn't it? The family didn't come up with anything else at the time."

"I wonder. Perhaps they should have."

"Yes? Why do you say that?"

"Maybe I carry Corbin's bias too far . . ." I pause to warn her: "You may not like me for saying this, Rita —"

"Go on, now," she attempts to scold, smiles, then adds: "Tell me first and let me decide." And she sits back attentively in a mock gesture, waiting for me to expound.

"All right. It's about the stepfather, Rashid. I never liked him. Even now he lurks in the shadows. Following the girl about so possessively, claiming to speak with the spirit who haunted her — making her do terrible things — and surely not out of fatherly love.

"Ali told me about his reputation in the family. He *was* strange — but would he have killed her? And why?"

"In a fit of jealousy?"

"I thought you'd say that. And that the family suspected but kept quiet about it. Yes, possibly. But how can you be *sure*?"

Outside the window, the curio-seller has now crossed the street to stand beside his wares. But he's watching, ready to come over and pounce on this lady tourist as soon as we emerge.

"Did Ali ever . . ."

"Yes?" she prompts.

"I've always wanted to ask this. Did Ali ever try to contact Corbin after Pipa's confession — in England, I mean, after he returned home in the fifties? Or was it too embarrassing?"

"We met Sir Alfred in London in the sixties, once, at an annual independence-day function. All la-di-da and formal. There were no other meetings — as far as I know. His wife was there — a rather batty old woman."

"And? The conversation? What was talked about?"

"Well, just the usual things — about the old country — nothing

295

personal. It was a short encounter, and he knew so many people from the colonies who were clamouring to say hello and to shake his hand . . ."

"Amazing. And Ali – what did *he* feel about this afterwards . . . at having seen Alfred Corbin?"

"You've got to understand Ali. He's not one to dwell on the past. It was never mentioned in our home. I was not interested, either. We had a family and our future to think of, we were out in the big world, we had made something of ourselves in it."

And if not for the re-emergence of the diary, I'm thinking, you would not have had to deal with that past, would you, Rita?

Her hands in front of her on the table between us, the fingers interlocked. Nails not overly long, painted.

She is the object of much attention, and not only mine. A few tables away, a man and woman sit, publishers, lamenting the death of their industry. They are both known to me, have eyed Rita rather suspiciously. A beggar woman in rags dives into the restaurant and heads straight for my well-dressed companion but is shooed off by a waitress and angry customers. The waitress brings two meat pies. I pick one up. Outside the window the curio-seller is back, holds up a gigantic, grotesque Makonde figure.

"Oh dear, I suppose I shall have to buy something from him after all, but not *that*."

And she is looking at me, smiling.

The same mischievous, enchanting smile of ages past. She switches it off. We're back to ourselves, wait in silence. Could we ever have come close? Is it possible to re-live that time and determine what could or could not have happened? She's speaking.

"You've never asked me . . . about us – you and me. I wonder why you've not asked."

"Afraid of the answer," I mutter. Then: "If it had been me would you have –"

"You'll never know," she says.

"Is it something only I will never know – or something even you don't know?"

She does not answer, says nothing for a while, and then: "Let me ask you this – would *you* have run away to London with a girl, risking all, as Ali did?"

There's nothing to say. I didn't, did I? Why this torment now – but I asked for it. . . . *Would* she have?

"And there was Gregory, of course." She smiles mischievously.

"What about Gregory?"

"Well, your friendship with him was rather peculiar to us girls. Gregory was a homosexual, as you know. Gay, he would be called today."

"Are you implying . . ." I am astounded, to be the subject of this inference . . . but then what made me think I was free of this kind of speculation. . . . "I've had my share of women, if you have to know –"

"What was between you and Gregory . . . only you know that. If you do."

Her eyes all aglow, passionate, like the girl she once was, Rita leans forward. But this time so confident, her experiences so much more deep, varied, felt. I have lived, she seems to say.

"And if you don't know these things about yourself . . ."

And so comes the injunction.

If you cannot know these things about yourself, she tells me, what arrogance, Fernandes, to presume to peep into other lives – to lay them out bare and join them like so many dots to form a picture. There are questions that have no answer; we can never know the innermost secrets of any heart. Each dot is infinity, Pius, your history is surface.

And how unfair, these speculations, to those who've lived a little more intensely than their neighbours, and so revealed a little more of themselves. What of respect for their secrets, their humanity? Of course the past matters, that's why we need to bury it sometimes. We have to forget to be able to start again.

Yes, why make public our pasts, belittle ourselves, when we've come so far. So what if he isn't a chief's son in exile, what if he was a Kariakoo boy covered with turmeric . . . a ball boy for Europeans . . . a garden toto . . . once you've arrived no one wants to know. Look at the Americans. And not only them. All the nobility, the dukes and barons, even the kings – who knows from where they came, who cares? So why should my Rehana lose face, why should Hadi's future be compromised . . .

"No, sir – Pius – this is the price I'm going to ask – which you've known all along, and I hold you to it. Let it lie, this past. The diary and the stories that surround it are now mine, to bury."

After lunch at his home, Feroz and I return to his shoestore, at the former Pipa Store, on Uhuru Street. He offers me tea from a thermos he's brought along. With Rita at the game parks now, Feroz and I seem to be where we were those days in March when he'd just placed the diary in my care.

I tell him that I must give the diary to Rita. He nods, giving me an indulgent look. He has known, ever since Rita came and began her long tête-à-têtes with me, that he has lost control of the diary.

"It has no value to me," he affirms. "And it's for family reasons she wants it, no, sir?"

"Yes," I say, not wishing to elaborate. It occurs to me that Rita has perhaps also had a chat with him, explaining and cajoling so he wouldn't make an issue out of the matter. And, he has a son in England, to whom she could be nice.

"That's that then, sir. It's as if it was never found in the first place –" He eyes me craftily, knowing that what he's just said can't be true. But I refuse to take the bait; I ask him about something that's bothered me from the first day he showed me the diary.

"You never told me, Feroz, how and where you found the book."

He looks at me for a moment and says, "I'll tell you. I'll show you – come to the storeroom . . ."

I follow him to the room at the back, Pipa's infamous dark room, now brilliantly lighted, its walls lined with shoeboxes.

"Anything unusual – you notice anything unusual in the room?" Feroz asks with a sweep of one hand, as if preparing to perform a trick.

"No," I say dutifully, "I see nothing unusual – what is it?"

"Saidi," he calls a servant.

With some effort Saidi and a helper drag an entire section of shelves, with shoeboxes, out and sideways. The bare yellow wall thus revealed looks at first ordinary – but no, I draw a sharp breath, one of the servants gasps more audibly and mutters a prayer. Down low, six inches up from the floor, is an old, torn plywood door, two-by-one feet – the size of four large bricks. It is held in place somehow, but a gap where it's broken in one corner hints at the dark recess behind, where the book presumably was found.

". . . buried and sealed behind the wall . . . all along . . . buried and sealed . . ." Feroz is going on in triumph beside me.

I turn to look at him. The two servants have moved back and out of the way, ready to leave the room but only if told. Feroz explains.

"One day – several years after this shop came my way – when we were installing these new shelves, I noticed a small hole in the wall – a piece of cement had fallen away. It looked like a nail hole. I put my little finger in it, and more cement fell. And more. And there, behind all the cement that could come off was this little cupboard. Finally, I thought, the old miser's fortune which no one could ever find – but there was only this book, wrapped in newspaper."

"Buried in the wall all these years . . ."

The wonder of it all. Someone else might have found it; it could have met an altogether different fate, perhaps never been found . . .

"Do you know the story of Anarkali, sir?"

I look at him: "Go on, you tell me."

"Well, sir. In Mughal times in India, the great Emperor Akber had a son called Salim, who fell passionately in love with a servant girl named Anarkali. Such a love, between the prince of a great dynasty and a servant, could not be allowed. It was forbidden by the emperor, and Salim was sent to war. But the lovers continued to meet in secret. Finally, sir, as punishment for disobeying the emperor's order, Anarkali was sentenced to be sealed up in a cave. But many years before, Akber had offered Anarkali's mother anything she wished in exchange for her services to him. Now, as the cave was being sealed up, Anarkali's mother came to claim mercy for her daughter. So Akber, who is famed for his justice, instructed that the cave be left open, at the back, and Anarkali was free – but she had to go away. She went singing, 'The world belongs to those who love . . .'"

I recall a pack of audacious schoolgirls singing this very song to me in class. Mocking. Rita and her friends, in the prime of youth and happiness almost forty years ago.

"'The world belongs to those who love.'" Forbidden love.

Perhaps all love is forbidden which is true, and it is true because the pain it causes makes us live.

Appendices

(1) In March 1964, von Lettow Vorbeck, commander of German East African forces during the Great War, died in West Germany. Upon his death, the Bundestag voted to pay off his askaris, and a Hamburg banker was dispatched to Dar es Salaam to make the payments. To identify the former askaris, he gave each claimant a broom and put him through the manual of arms. No askari, it was claimed, ever forgot the German commands.

(2) American actress Rita Hayworth (born Margarita Cansino) was diagnosed with Alzheimer's disease and placed in the custody of her daughter Yasmin (through Aly Khan) in 1981. The actress died in New York in May 1987. The prince had died in Europe in a car accident in 1958.

III

Gregory

Really, must you,
Over-familiar
Dense companion,
Be there always?
The bond between us
Is chimerical surely:
Yet I cannot break it.

— W. H. Auden

23

In the early 1960s, the first years of independence in the country, the breezy self-confidence of the new ruling class came mixed with a nervous insecurity. Loyalty – especially from those who had served the old order – had to be loud and unequivocal. Some countries allow dual citizenship, but not the new republics hungry for recognition and greatness, suspicious of new colonialisms, anxious for a clean break from past humiliations. You were asked to renounce your former citizenship, say goodbye to a prized British subjecthood for a brave new world. Not everybody acquiesced, and some gracefully left, including the country's first finance minister, who was an Englishman. We were not surprised. One was not used to seeing Englishmen renouncing England; though the world has changed since then. And so when Gregory gave up his British passport, I was rather astonished.

"I've lived here most of my life, now," he said. "This is home." Then he looked at me pointedly: "Besides, if something were to happen to me and I got kicked out, England, that bitch, would always accept me – but not you, Pius. Wrong colour."

Thus spoke the perfect ironist, who could not take the world at its word, or himself at his own, and continued to live in it as best he could, without committing himself to anything. There lay his tragedy, I thought even then: a man who was vulnerable on all sides, who had not saved himself a position to back into. And, indeed, it would not have been hard for someone such as Gregory to be kicked out – our leaders had no room for ironical ambiguities or other literary niceties, especially from those who had ruled over them. The *Herald*'s satirist, mocking a query in Parliament regarding mermaids, had been a recent persona non grata and had left for Australia.

For several years after we met at Boyschool, we called each other Mr. Gregory and Fernandes. He was much older than I, and perhaps even reminded me of my own teachers. There seemed a chasm between us, not wide, but deep. At some point, without much ado on Gregory's part, I became Pius for him, for me he was still a Mr., and only a little later was it Gregory, and finally Greg, but only to his face and with the British-hating Desouza not around.

The three of us continued, in these times, to teach at Shamsi Boys', or Boyschool, which was reaching even greater successes in the achievements of its students. We had, soon enough, among our new colleagues some of the students we had ourselves brought up. But Boyschool, in these its glory days, fell victim to the politics raging around us.

The early years of independence were years of political euphoria and self-confidence in the new nation. With both the eastern and western blocs wooing Tanzania, the country could play a game of radical and cocky nonalignment. But alignment proved inevitable; it fell eastwards, and there came towards the end of the decade an era dominated by an earnest socialism. Changes came at breakneck speed, dismantling old structures, racing us towards the egalitarian Utopia that most surely – we were told – awaited us.

One of these changes was the government's takeover of Boyschool. We had objected to this, of course: not to the control of
the syllabus – which was understandable in the highly sensitive
political climate – but to the takeover of the school which had
been put up with such devotion, was a monument to the labour
and ambition of a community. For a few years we had Mr. Green,
an Irishman, as headmaster, then Mr. Peters, an African writer
from Moshi. It was, however, with Mr. Joseph that we hit bottom; a Party cadre who came simply to occupy a post – which he
did armed with his government newspaper *Mwafrika* – and not to
administer a school renowned for its standards and facilities. What
surprise, then, that a storage shed was put up over the cricket
pitch, the tennis courts became overgrown, window panes went
unreplaced, the school bell disappeared, a plaque commemorat-
ing a heroic sacrifice of life by one of Desouza's boys was
removed, the boards containing the list of all the former graduates
of Boyschool were taken down – in the cause less of egalitarian-
ism than of erasing an irksome past. We lived in cynical times
then, when the Party youth wing, the Green Guards, in the manner of Mao's Red Guards, bullied people in the streets and sought
control over their lives.

I go into these details because they come back to haunt, were
so wantonly destructive. They are, to me, the markers of a period
– a short one – in which so much changed. Nothing was the same
again. Friends and colleagues began to leave, never to be heard
from again; and Gregory fell.

At that time every school was provided with a plot of land to
cultivate vegetables in the service of the school's coffers as well as
the students' characters. Every plot was divided into smaller plots,
one for each class. And twice a week came the dreaded shamba
period at Boyschool when these urban boys, who had never seen
a spade except perhaps in their fathers' shops, marched in the
sweltering heat for three quarters of an hour, up a hill past the new
bungalows and to the slopes behind the Jangwani Girls' School.

What I remember of that short-lived experiment is the diminutive Mr. Kabir the math teacher, bent over almost double under the weight of two spades; Gregory holding a machete as if in pursuit of a robber or beast; grey, bearded Desouza with a hoe for a staff, eyes on the hill ahead, a latter-day Moses; and boys digging, persistently digging, but with no maize, no yams, no okra, no crops to show for it.

It was during one of these shamba periods, as Gregory was overseeing a pack of boys digging the red earth ("I'm no farmer, Pius, but surely you don't have to dig this deep to plant maize . . ."), that he fell into one of these contentious three-foot-deep ditches, suffering sunstroke, narrowly missing the sharp end of a hoe.

He was half carried, half dragged out, what little water was at hand was poured on his head, and I dispatched two boys to the Jangwani school to fetch a teacher. The East German math teacher came, in his car, and Gregory was taken to the Aga Khan Hospital, which was near his house.

Gregory was released from hospital the following day, looking rather weak and somewhat sheepish. Thereafter he was readmitted several times with dizzy spells. He was not recovering properly. All at once he seemed frail and aged. He began to wheeze and had become thinner so that his immense shorts, which once were the joke of the town, were now drawn in by a belt, portending decay and worse. He was excused from his duties in school, and gradually it came to be understood that he would not return.

It was 1971. Around this time a new batch of teachers from England had arrived at Boyschool, one of whom, Fletcher, had taken over the dramatic society. I cannot say whether it was the calibre of the students or the talents of Fletcher, but drama took off as it had never done before under Gregory or me. For the first time in many years, the school won first prize in the Youth Drama Festival with a production of an adaptation of *Pygmalion* written by Fletcher using an idea of Gregory's.

On the night of the awards, a Sunday, I went to take the news to Gregory. His bungalow on Seaview, across the road from the beach, was a small two-bedroom affair, set back from a front yard and a driveway which had two concrete gateposts but no gates. A shadowy nightwatchman sat outside on the front steps; a light was on in the front room. As I entered, two boys – one of whom opened the door – were leaving, one of them saying to me, "Sir – he's very sick. You'll have to call a doctor," and the other nodding agreement with equal gravity.

I closed the door behind them, turned to face Gregory, who was sitting on the sofa, and opened the offering I had brought with me (now so inappropriate) – fish and chips from the new Wimpy's – and gave him the good news about the prize. He grinned. I thought, then, that only his face, with that smile beaming momentarily, had any life, any presence, so frail and insignificant was the rest of him in his soiled clothes.

He sat up, tried a chip, put it down: "Bring me the scotch, will you."

"No," I said with friendly determination. "You, my friend, need rest. I'll give you some warm water. Then some tea and biscuits. And then to bed with you."

His expression turned into a most hateful leer. "Always bloody correct, aren't you." His voice was hoarse. "Do the right thing by me – will you – you fucking – frigid – Jesuit – who never took a bloody risk – always proper – *Mister* Gregory – *Mister* Gregory – you colonial –"

The water spilled over his shirt, and I handed him a kitchen towel, somewhat taken aback, but not willing to take his outburst at face value.

The tea went down better, and we talked about the play. *His* play, he called it. He told me that the two boys who'd left as I came in had come to say goodbye; they were going to the United States on scholarships. They were the last of his favourites, all the others had left, none had ever returned. He sat there, hunched, with a pained look on his face as if the world had come crashing down around him and he was in the midst of the debris. I could catch a faint glimmer only of how he felt, but then I was younger and less drawn to alcohol.

"Tell me, Fernandes – Pius – if you had to do it all over again, would you? Dammit, spend a lifetime to teach, I mean . . . farther away than you ever imagined. Would you?"

I was dumbfounded, and for the first time the thought came to me: What exactly *had* we achieved? Some satisfaction, yes, in having brought up a generation – but what comfort that, in lonely old age?

"Why, yes – wouldn't you? You're being unnecessarily morbid."

He wasn't listening, was weeping. Then he wiped his eyes, stood up uncertain on his feet, shivered a bit. He was ready to go to bed. I helped him along, by the shoulders, and sat him on his bed, which was unmade. Hastily, I looked for his pyjamas, found them on the floor, and then, as he shivered and sweated, I helped him change. He lay down on his side and I put a blanket on him, which he kicked off, leaving only a sheet. I started to go.

"Wait here," he said. "Please. Sit."

I sat on the bed, watched over him. Sweat ran down his face. It was warm, I reminded myself, but not unusually so. He would shiver in spasms, then relax. I wasn't sure how long I would sit there. "I should have called the doctor," I said. "No," he said, "just stay." Without knowing why, I lay down beside him, also on my side, and held him. When at last he fell asleep, it was with a great sigh and shudder, as if he'd lost a battle.

Of that moment I remember a feeling of dislocation, a sense of empathy; a feeling of being utterly alone, with another human being in my arms. The sound of waves in the distance. An occasional car on the road outside.

It was the next morning when I left; he was still in bed, fast asleep.

I did not see much of Gregory thereafter, I don't quite know why. All I have are incomplete thoughts, half explanations – the hateful look and the bitter taunt I could not, cannot, forget; but we had also, that night, reconciled and touched. What more was there? I felt guilty at not seeing more of him, but took comfort in the knowledge that he was under the care of some ladies associated with the Anglican church. I am surprised, now, at this callousness on my part, and have often asked myself, was it because I was afraid of what more there was, or could have been? I honestly don't know. Gregory was a homosexual. Of his relationships with his favourite boys I never bothered to inquire; to innuendos about him I turned a deaf ear. Of all my acquaintances in Dar I found him the most easy to be with. I liked him. His quirks I treated with affection, sometimes tinged with exasperation. It was Rita who confused and tormented, who even now leaves me helpless by her charm and beauty, about whom the regrets are real and not unspoken.

Images of death come, now, and quite naturally so, with the recollection of an event that came to symbolize for so many the death . . . of a dream, a hope, a way of life. Nineteen seventy-two saw the ruling party's socialist policies reach their climax in the nationalization of rental properties. Those – mostly Asians – who had erected two-storey buildings as monuments to the labours of their families, who staked thus a claim in the country they had made their home, whose one investment was in two or three flats they would rent out, saw their hopes dashed in a betrayal of the faith they had in the country. Savings of a generation, two generations, were taken away. It was now the people's property, they were told.

Two deaths were immediately attributed to this news. One was that of Hassam Punja, probably the richest man in Dar, with numerous buildings to his name, and mills and factories (the monument to his achievements being for many years Dar's tallest building, the imposing yellow pyramid overlooking the Mnazi Moja grounds). The other death was that of Nurmohamed Pipa. Pipa, a cynical old man after the death of his son Amin, upon hearing that much of Amin Mansion was the people's property now, said, "Bas? Only this? Let Him take away me too, now." The next day he died.

The two Shamsi funerals were held together in a momentous event at town mosque. Both men had begun in poverty: Hassam Punja, as everyone knew, by selling peanuts in the streets; Pipa as a porter. They lay displayed to their people under white sheets, only their faces showing. Naked we come and naked we return, the Shamsis sang in their funereal hymn; but that teacher, Mwalimu, who became the president, didn't have to hurry them along, they muttered under their breaths. And many would say in wonder afterwards that Pipa didn't look so fat this time, and Hassam Punja wasn't so short after all – how we tend to exaggerate.

Over the years, the people of the neighbourhood of Pipa Corner, looking at the yellow building in their midst, had often wondered about the miser who had built it after decades of labour in his spice shop. How much? How much did Pipa have stashed away, how much was he worth? In death now, as he had in life, Pipa eluded his questioners. After his funeral, lights in the second-storey flat stayed on late into the night, downstairs the shop was busy with all manner of sounds suggesting furniture being moved or dismantled. But Remti and her daughters and their husbands were to find no hidden treasure – no stolen jewellery, no smuggled diamonds, no German gold coins. What Pipa left for his wife and daughters was worth more than any treasure there might have been: Amin Mansion – but it was now the people's property.

There was a third death that fateful week, but it went largely unnoticed. A few years before it would have been a local event of some magnitude and meaning; the teacher had been an institution, had taught their boys for two decades and more, they couldn't pass English Literature without him. But, occurring now, his death was essentially an expatriate event. Mr. Gregory of Boyschool: Oh yes, didn't he leave? No – he's just died.

Some hundred people – expatriates in the city and senior students from Boyschool – dutifully showed up at the Anglican church for Gregory's funeral. A eulogy was read by Fletcher, another by one of his students; two telegrams arrived from abroad. As little known to this gathering as was the dead man, I had no words to say to them, nor was I asked to contribute any.

It was a few weeks after the funeral, when I went to the grave to examine the headstone donated by a few former students and fellow teachers, that Mr. Anscombe, the minister, told me Gregory had left me a box. It contained papers and books, he said. I assumed they were the texts he had taught over the years, and the notes for students he had prepared, which we had once thought of publishing, before they had become outdated with the arrival on the syllabus of Achebe and Soyinka, and Miller and Ibsen. I didn't pick up the box, however, didn't examine the contents. Let them lie buried in some vault, I thought then, useless detritus from a life now, happily, for its owner, extinguished.

24

In the years that followed, through the seventies and part of the eighties, I continued to teach at Boyschool. In those years, under a socialist régime in the country, I saw the values that I had brought with me and inculcated with such ardour in the school become increasingly out of place. Mediocrity was the new order, and ideological correctness. The new generation of students who came were sent by a government seeking bureaucrats, not, as in the past, by a community eager to get ahead in the world. The Shamsis, who had built and run the school as the pinnacle of their ambition, now in large numbers began to pack up and leave for North America. I saw my best students come to say goodbye, never to return. And one by one, almost all of my fellow expatriate teachers left also. One of them, I heard through my former student Sona, taught math at a school in a ghetto in New York City. Another sold insurance in Canada. A few went to Zambia before retiring to India. And finally, in 1980, Desouza succumbed to the times in a typically drastic fashion.

He had moved to a private school in town and I saw less of him then. After Gregory's death in 1972, for a few months we did spend more time together, but we drifted apart again, though remaining friends. Too much, it seemed, had happened to us that took us into private worlds we were unable to share.

One day a student of his came and told me that Desouza had not come out of his flat for three days, and could I do something. I went with the boy to Desouza's flat, knocked loudly on the door and called to my friend, but to no avail. Finally, with everyone else gathered there – servants and hawkers – assuring me that the teacher was definitely inside, I agreed to let the door be forced open. We found Desouza in bed, shivering, starving, and almost dead. There was no food in the house, not even tea or sugar. He was evidently suffering from malaria; and although this was a time when medication had become scarce, he was soon rehabilitated with the help of a doctor who had been a student at Boyschool. Shortly thereafter, during December holidays, Desouza went to India to stay with his sister and recuperate; he never returned. He wrote me once that he was having trouble obtaining a visa to come back. Apparently, he had never taken the trouble to become a citizen. Now, according to the visa authorities, he was too old to come back to teach.

Three years ago the headmaster of my school called me into his office and asked me if I knew I was past my retirement age of fifty-five. Yes, I said, but I had many years of teaching left in me. He smiled, reminded me that rules were rules. So I bowed to his greater authority and accepted a pension.

I have felt alone for a good many years, now; alone and lonely. The admission doesn't come easily. I suppose I could have left after Gregory died. But where, and to what end? Only filial duty would have taken me to India, but by then both my parents were dead. And the loneliness of old age can come upon one anywhere. This city where I first landed forty years ago has so grown on me, it is like an extension of my self. I will never shed it.

One thought, though, has been a balm in my solitary days: that I continue to live in the hundreds of students who have passed through my hands. Such were the times I served in, such the nature of the trust placed upon us teachers. Gregory would have understood this idea of fulfilment in the eventual dispersal of oneself, but he was not the type to draw upon it for comfort. "Are we thinking of the next incarnation already, Pius? A shade of Mr. Chips, perhaps . . ." I hear the purr of the pipe, see the twinkle in the eyes.

Seventeen years ago he asked, Tell me, Pius, would you do it again, has it been worth it? I could understand the question then, though I couldn't feel the urgency, the anxiety behind it. Now, closer myself to his own circumstance, I hear his question only too clearly.

As my answer, three months ago, I would have proudly displayed to anyone letters from my former students, all doing well abroad – testimony enough to warm the heart of any retired teacher. I might have pointed out a visiting former student or two, if they were around, or a young bank official from among my more recent accomplishments. I would have confessed to dire financial straits, yes, but I would have shown all the satisfaction of having done a job well, having influenced a generation of students. Surely there is something to be said for that, even in this cynical age?

But there was more to my life than the satisfaction of teaching. There was Rita, the girl who so ensnared the earnest young teacher that I was; and there was the angry, later sad, Desouza, with whom I could not develop a complete friendship because of Gregory; and there was Gregory, whose companionship I valued but could never quite understand.

I am not one to dwell upon paths not taken, to speculate on what might have been. Here I am, where I have arrived; this is my credo. Gregory would say, To live is to risk, and so you did not live. To which my schoolgirls of 1950 would put a more filmic gloss: "The world belongs to the one who loves."

But at least late in life this kindness has been conferred upon me, an unexpected, perhaps undeserved, gift: I have sat with Rita as I could not have in the past and admired her openly, and we discussed the question I had been afraid to ask myself before, about my relationship with her and what it could have been. And I allowed myself to go back to that evening in Gregory's house, and I cannot turn away from it now.

I have with increasing interest and frequency been dipping into the pages of Gregory's posthumous collection *Havin' a Piece*, which Rita gave to me. It has brought back many memories of Dar as it used to be, some simply by the description of a familiar subject in a poem, others more obliquely. For example, the poem "Pili-Pili Bizarre" – punning on the words "bizari" (spice) and "bazaar" in typical Gregory fashion – describes a spice shop such as the one Pipa had, the likes of which still exist at the odd corner. There is an angry, irreverent though moving poem, "Kalima," which begins: "There is no Deity but He / Who plucks out the heart of a woman / and serenades the night with her screams." It refers, I believe, to Pipa's son Amin's funeral, which seemed to affect Gregory profoundly, and is a testament, moreover, to his denial of God and redemption. And I have no doubt who the brown man of this little poem is:

BROWN MAN

He will endure
in sweet tan innocence
inert untouched
hardy transplant
in the region's new sun . . .

> While I
> pale and larva soft
> wither
> in African heat.

All these Dar poems are haphazardly distributed throughout the volume and cry out for a context. At some future time I shall perhaps make a study of these poems of my friend and explain their references to this city in which he served for so many years.

That Gregory, through his poems, should remind me now of Pipa is not altogether remarkable, only indicative of the small place and the times we lived in. More intriguing for me has been the presence in his collection of some poems dedicated to "A. C." who clearly was a woman. One of these poems has an explicit reference to Kampala, Uganda. Gregory told me he'd been in Uganda in the early thirties, as, of course, had the Corbins, who were transferred there from Dar. Could Gregory have known the Corbins – was the A. C. of the poems in fact none other than Anne Corbin? The thought, a dim possibility at first, kept recurring with greater force and conviction. Yes, why not – after all, how many Britons had lived in Uganda in the early thirties? And if I was right, then all the years I had known him, Gregory had known Alfred Corbin, whom I was to resuscitate decades later. . . . How our paths have crossed and recrossed.

A few days after my last meeting with Rita in the coffee shop, I finally went to the Anglican church office to collect the box Gregory had left me. On my way I stopped briefly and somewhat guiltily at the grave I had not seen for over ten years. The site was well tended, like the others there, and that morning cut flowers had been placed upon it. The headstone looked more modest than I remembered, the engraving upon it quite bleakly to the point: "Richard Gregory, 1908–1972." Inside the office I identified myself to the young priest (his predecessor, Mr. Anscombe, whom I had known, had passed away, I was told), who took me to a storeroom. Without too much effort, and to my great relief, we managed to find my cardboard box against the far wall, somewhat misshapen but otherwise intact, at the bottom of a pile of similar boxes. It was marked "To Mr. Pius Fernandes (to be picked up)," and had been secured carefully with sisal twine. I couldn't help thinking, with gratitude, that old Mr. Anscombe, who had first brought me the news that Gregory had left me the box, had shown remarkable prescience in believing that I would come for it one day.

As I had already guessed long before, most of the contents of the box were textbooks and binders filled with notes for courses. But there were other things, more personal, which in an instant drew me away from Shakespeare and Dickens. There was a thick bundle of staff photographs, from Boyschool – looking through them in sequence one had the eerie sense of the school staff age-ing. In his early photographs, Gregory had not been as unkempt and overweight as he was in later years, though he had always been stocky. My own youth in some of them came as a rude shock. There were three issues of the *Manchester Guardian*, for which Gregory wrote a column called "Bwana Notes." Three hardback exercise books contained drafts of poems and, I believe, an abandoned novel. There were newspaper cuttings of reviews of two of his books. And, finally, there were bundles of letters, ordered roughly by chronology, and secured with twine. The four letters that I had written to him from London were among these, as were dozens from his students at Boyschool. Then, among letters from numerous people I didn't know, I found a number from Alfred and Anne Corbin, confirming my growing belief that the three had known each other in Uganda. Not an earth-shaking discovery at this stage, but a relief; a small victory; a gift, if you will, from Richard Gregory. There were just three letters from Alfred Corbin, all written within a few weeks of each other in 1935, and eighteen from Anne, written at various periods between 1937 and 1972.

I have been deeply touched by this bequest, which I had spurned once and forgotten for so long. The box contains, as I had thought, the debris of a life; but this debris is also a wealth. I don't know what I will make of all this – perhaps there is another project here for a retired schoolteacher. Perhaps I will be able to answer for Gregory his own question, more generously than he himself was able.

25

Gregory had been such a fixture at Boyschool, such a part of the local life and lore, that it always came as something of a surprise to be reminded that he had been elsewhere in Africa. He would admit to it – he'd been in Uganda before Dar – but he made it obvious he had no intention of dwelling on the subject; it was none of your business.

It had been a short stay, 1933-34, and, I always assumed, not a very happy one. It was not hard to imagine a younger, more brash Gregory, a poet straight from London, offending the small local community of officials and being left without friends. The Corbins, however, and especially Anne, took a liking to him.

Entebbe
15/3/35

Dear Richard,

You should by now have settled in your new position in Dar. I trust the town and its inhabitants are more to your liking.

Excerpts of your essay have circulated in the upper echelons (among "the gods") and H. E. himself asked me if you were indeed a socialist s—. What I said of you does not bear retelling, but you have been redeemed if only as a somewhat eccentric literary type with connections to the London papers.

I am afraid that Commissioner Barnes came to you before I could quite write to you myself. I met him here last month at the Police Conference, at which he brought out a fountain pen which I found rather disturbingly familiar-looking. It was a Waterman with a very distinct design, and I told Barnes – who caught me staring at it – that it reminded me very much of one I had lost years before. It could still be yours, for all I know, was his response. He said the police clerk in Dar had bought it from an Indian called Pipa a few years ago and presented it to him. I told him that a young man called Pipa had run a shop in the town of Kikono where I had been ADC at the start of the War, and that I had lost my diary with the pen. This set the commissioner's police brain ticking. Well, the long and short if it all is that he has set his mind upon raiding the Indian's store. Such raids, for stolen property, are quite common, and I myself have been party to a few in Moshi and Dar. I told Barnes that in the – extremely unlikely – event of his finding my diary, he was to place it in your hands immediately . . .

Anne remembers you fondly. The Ladies' Reading Group has folded, much to her annoyance, and regrouped as the Child Welfare Clinic. Washing and weighing native babies is not quite in her line of interest and she looks forward to the Little Theatre's production of Shaw's *Pygmalion*. The garden thrives.

Yours truly,
Alfred

Dear Richard,

    I am sorry about the fiasco. I had no idea the police would take you along on the raid, and I apologize, again, for involving you in this silly affair. You are probably right that the fire was no accident. Your conjecture that Pipa is just the kind of shopkeeper who would hoard a diary is somewhat disturbing. I had hoped that it was dead and buried. The idea of it lying hidden in an Indian duka is revolting.

    The diary, a gift from my mother, contains entries I began upon departure for East Africa, and is a record mostly of my first posting as ADC in the town of Kikono next to the German border. I met the shopkeeper Pipa in the most odious circumstances there, engaged in a scuffle with two askaris and my cook, who had objected to his transferring a large quantity of German mail into our postal system. He had come from nearby Moshi to take part in a local festival. Later he married a local Shamsi girl who was in my employ at the time. I gave the couple permission to stay in my district when the War broke out, and later Military Intelligence found use for the man's connections in German East. Soon afterwards when the Germans occupied Taveta on the border, I evacuated my station upon instructions from my DC and proceeded to Voi. It was in Voi that I first missed my diary, and I recalled writing in it in Kikono immediately before meeting a delegation of the town's elders. I had placed the diary and pen on a chair before going out to the meeting. I have given up hope of ever getting it back.

    Anne sends her kindest. Your suggestion of using a native girl in the role of Eliza Doolittle raised some laughs. The police captain's wife can do the Cockney accent quite well.

As ever,
Alfred

Dear Richard,

The woman you met in the shop was Pipa's second wife. The first wife, as I think I wrote earlier, was a most striking-looking woman called Mariamu. She was also in the most pathetic of circumstances you can imagine, suffering ill treatment at the hands of her family, and in particular her stepfather. Before she entered my employ I rescued her from a ghastly exorcism rite.

After my departure from the town, Mariamu met a tragic fate – she was brutally murdered. I conducted a brief investigation into the affair after the War, when I was DC in Moshi, but came up with nothing conclusive. What I found appalling was the lack of interest shown by the family in pursuing the matter further – the crime was not reported to military or civilian authority. All this is ancient history now.

We are preparing for home leave, after which I take up my new posting, whatever the gods ordain. Rumour has it that this time it may not be in East Africa.

Anne sends her warmest.

Yours truly,

Alfred

How remarkably close Corbin came to his lost diary – first as DC in Dar, when on any day he himself could have walked into Pipa Store but, purely by chance, didn't; and twelve years after he left Dar, when Commissioner Barnes's policemen raided the store and were outwitted, leaving behind them a fire for which Pipa was able to win damages. I can only smile at the thought of Gregory in the store, among the spice crates and gunnies, following behind the inspector in charge, sniffing around, observing much but picking up nothing to dirty his hands. Did he feel like a dupe, then – or did he enjoy the experience? I remember him at the funeral of Pipa's young son Amin; he could have let out that he knew something of the boy's father, but he didn't. He did mouth the Kalima with the others, to send off the coffin, and wrote an emotional poem about the wastefulness of a child's death.

In his letters to Gregory, Corbin shows the reserve we have come to expect of him; yet I wonder if behind the neutral language in a letter, almost exclusively about Mariamu, he hides any feeling for her. About the loss of the diary he appears almost indifferent; that he felt more strongly about it, at least later in his life, we learn from two of the many letters Anne Corbin wrote to Gregory.

Anne Corbin's letters to Gregory are more spirited, and suggest a relationship of friendly intimacy that is somewhat reserved in the early years, becoming more open, admiring, and dependent towards the end. It was a relationship, one must conclude, whose nature is open to speculation by those interested in the intimate life of the poet.

October 23, 1946
Government House
Entebbe, Uganda

Dearest Richard –

How absolutely thrilling to meet again! Unfortunately our stay in Dar was brief – and sudden. Both factors beyond our control, I assure you. But to see you again!

Thank you so much for coming, as I assume it was for our sake – and yet I do recall that you rather enjoy such occasions once in a while, don't you, if only to needle the officials and their wives.

What *did* you say to the two junior memsahibs that scandalized them so? Freddie came to your rescue, saying something about the temperament of the artist – but, may I say this, Richard, you were watched like an explosive device on the move with its fuse burning ever shorter!

It was nice to see you again and in your element. You seem happy in Dar, one day you must tell me about it. Please do write.

It is so strange returning to Uganda. There is a feeling of dêjà vu at seeing it all again, yet everything is decidedly different. Rumour has it soon it will be packing-up time for the Empire, which is why we are here. Freddie still has the trust of the old chiefs, who may be needed when the time comes. After that it's retirement for us in good old England, though I wonder how we'll adapt to the little island after a lifetime of exile in the tropics.

Freddie loves being back in E.A. He became quite nostalgic in Dar and asked for a tour of the Indian and African districts. I think he was looking for the store where his pen turned up. He must have found the store, but I didn't ask him about it. He still has the pen – it has a special value for him.

Thank you again for the book. I am enthralled.

But now I must rush – the Girl Guides are expecting their badges and we mustn't keep them waiting.

Love,
Anne

April 6, 1965
Sevenseas Manor
Burntoak
Surrey

Dearest Richard –

The seasons are still difficult to adjust to but spring is always welcome. The daffodils are out, masses of them, and other bulbs – hyacinths and anemones. It only remains for the sun to come out to brighten the colours. Life is calm here, and not bustling and constraining like the Service. But Sevenseas is not exactly Government House, nor the residence of the British Representative on some lovely tropical beach.

Peerages were handed out to some former governors, though we were passed over. It came as a bitter blow, though he did not say much but sent a letter congratulating Sir Edward of Tanganyika. This was just the jolt he needed to get back to his memoirs and he is working hard at them. There are many photos and scrapbooks to sift through, some of them still in crates. They brought back a lot of memories. He missed that lost diary again. I wish I had it, he said, looking up sadly from the piles of snapshots and papers.

Fate works in mysterious ways, and the *strangest* coincidence happened to us recently. At a colonial "do" in London, a charming couple from Tanganyika was introduced to us. When Freddie mentioned that he had served in Moshi in 1920, the man said, why, he had lived in Moshi as a child at the same time. His name is Ali Akber Ali and he is rather pompous in a stiff sort of way. Freddie took to him. Where were you born? he asked, and Mr. Akber Ali said, "In a place that's not on any map. I wonder if it existed at all." Queer, wouldn't you say? Try me, said Freddie in that way he has, and guess what our Indian replied: "Kikono!" Freddie met Mr. Akber Ali one or two times in the City after that, for old times' sake, but I declined to go.

Do write, dear Richard, and write often. Poems and published books are welcome as always, but to this pedestrian soul a simple letter brings more joy.

With kindest thoughts and the warmest wishes from

Yours,
Anne

And so, Ali met privately with Alfred Corbin and did not tell Rita about it. Did Corbin tell Anne what they talked about? I see two men at a table in a spare yet exclusive club that would have befitted a former governor in the colonies, a knighted public servant. As he looked at the elderly Englishman, the mzungu, Ali must have thought: In the colonies he was king of kings, here simply a respected member of the establishment. Ali would remember him dimly from his childhood memories of Moshi; Pipa had told him much more about Corbin. Ali also remembered his wife, having helped her in her garden as a boy; she had not come, perhaps had not remembered him. But Sir Alfred had, and had suggested this meeting. What did he see in the younger man before him? – shades of Mariamu? And the urbanity, the polish, the acquired Englishness of the Indian – how much did they mock him, the real Englishman, bring to the fore the events of fifty years ago? When he had told the girl, Wherever you are, if you need me, don't hesitate to call upon me. . . . It would be easy to find him, a colonial officer, in any part of the world. Now, in London, her son sipping an expensive wine, discussing the Labour government and its prospects, the Common Market, the Commonwealth. . . . With questions on the mind of one, answers on the other's. What more was said; how many more times did they meet? Was the relationship between the two, whatever its precise nature, acknowledged . . .

Miscellany (v)

Appendices

(1) "Many are the conditions of life we met that would sound unbelievable today, many customs we saw that have disappeared from the face of the earth. Today the word Empire is taboo and colonialism is discredited. We do not have subject races but underdeveloped nations. A chapter of world history has therewith been closed. We went with the best of intentions, to give of our best . . ."

From the conclusion of *Heart and Soul* (1966),
the memoirs of Sir Alfred Corbin, KCMG, OBE.

Correspondence

Cambridge, Mass
May 2, 1988

Mr. Fernandes:
. . . Sir Alfred Corbin died in his home in Surrey in July 1971.

He was at that time consulting with the BBC on a drama titled "The Barons of Uasin Gishu," based on the lives of the white aristocratic settlers of Kenya. It appeared much later here on public television in 1982, on a show called "Sunday Night Theatre," which every week brings (somewhat wistfully) Old England and the Empire to the American republic. Anne Corbin died in 1980. There are two sons and a daughter.

Good luck with your reconstruction – can I call it that? – I still have to see it – will I see it? I myself have come from a major battle regarding authenticity and authorship, at a conference in Toronto, where the big question was: Have our texts come to us interpolated by succeeding generations – a question of reconstruction of another sort, but with certain similarities to your efforts, don't you think? Guess which side I was on. . . . An inconclusive battle, with much at stake. Watch out for future developments . . .

Regards,
Sona

Epilogue

Three months have passed since I last saw Rita, almost three months since I handed over to her Alfred Corbin's diary as I had more or less promised. It was a brief meeting, at the airport lounge, prior to her departure. She took the diary gratefully from me, then pointedly asked, "And everything else?" "I will not disclose," I said. And so we parted; she to return to London.

What I can never disclose, give to the world, is mine only in trust. The constant reminding presence of a world which I created, a history without the relief of an outlet, can only serve to oppress. And so I have decided to relinquish it. Only then can I begin to look towards the rest of my life and do the best with the new opportunity that has come my way.

In a short while, a man will call to pick up this package of material – notes and scribblings and research I have put together for Rita. It is, as she put it, "everything else," everything I have written and compiled in relation to the diary – what I have come to think of as a new book of secrets. A book as incomplete as the old one was, incomplete as any book must be. A book of half lives, partial truths, conjecture, interpretation, and perhaps even some mistakes. What better homage to the past than to acknowledge it thus, rescue it and recreate it, without presumption of judgement, and as honestly, though perhaps as incompletely as we know ourselves, as part of the life of which we all are a part? For Rita, then, all this. To do with as she will, to bury it if she must (and if it will allow her).

After I have surrendered this material, which overtook my life for these past months, I will go out and take a walk along Uhuru Street, and perhaps even stroll into the mnada, the bustling discount market where it all began, where Feroz, my former student, recognized me and stopped to give me a lift, and later put an Englishman's diary into my hands. Some shopping may be in order, now. At the end of a recent letter, Sona invited me to visit Canada and the U.S.A., where he says many of my former students will be eager to see me. A fare has been offered, and I have gratefully accepted the invitation. A holiday abroad at this time will not go amiss.

When I return to Dar it will be to this same apartment, thanks to Feroz, and — more important — to a new position which, after much effort, he has finally found for me. It is that of a part-time teacher at a new private school that has emerged to meet the recent growing demands to reinstate the rigorous standards we had once in education. The headmaster of this school is from Kenya, and he has already given me a tour of the place. I must confess, rather unfairly I started comparing: the grounds of this school are not even a fifth of those of the old Boyschool. But it is a new generation of pupils I will teach, boys and girls of mixed race, bright, with fresh hopes and promise, whose up-to-date experiences and outlooks are bound to challenge and rejuvenate even this old teacher. I don't know the full story behind the job, what strings were pulled, and I will not speculate at this point. I have told the headmaster I will take a month off, to go abroad, before returning to take up my duties. The new job, I expect, will allow me to undertake some projects that I have recently promised myself to pursue.

But I must stop now, the man has arrived for the package.

Pius Fernandes
12 August, 1988
Dar es Salaam

SELECTED GLOSSARY

The symbols ★ and † following definitions indicate Swahili and Indian words respectively. These words, especially the Swahili, may have origins in Arabic.

askari – a policeman, guard, or watchman ★

avatar – an incarnation †

ayurvedic – herbal; using ancient Indian medicinal traditions
    and methods †

baazi – a bean curry ★

bagala – a boat ★

bao – a board game ★

baraza – a public meeting ★

bhajan – a devotional hymn †

bhang – a drug †

biriyani – a rich, spicy Indian rice dish †

buibui – a thin black veil for women ★

bunduki – gun ★

bwana – used as title, equivalent of "Mr."; used to address
    someone, as in "sir" ★

carom – an Indian game for two or four, played on a square
    board, using black and white discs †

channa – chickpea curry †

dandia – a traditional stick-dance †

dhol – a kind of drum †

dhoti – loincloth †

dhow – a lateen-rigged boat or small ship

djinn – a kind of spirit; a jinnee †,*

dudu – insect *

duka – a shop *

Eid – a Muslim festival

eti – a word used to draw attention, as in "I say" *

feldkompanie – German army unit

fisi – hyena *

garba – a traditional Indian dance †

gharry – hand-drawn tram

gopi – cow-girl lover(s) of the god Krishna, with the union
    being sexual-mystical †

gyan – hymn †

hadith – Muslim text relating Prophet Mohamed's life and
    deeds

halud – a kind of scent †,*

Hamisi – Thursday *

heller – a unit of money introduced by the Germans

houri – a beautiful woman promised in the Muslim Paradise

hutu-tutu – a territorial game involving two teams, often played
    on picnics †

Jambo – a greeting *

jiv – a soul †

jumba – a house; corruption of "nyumba" *

Juma – Friday †,*

kalima – the Muslim creed that begins "There is no God but
    Allah"

Kamba – an African people

kanzu – a cotton smock, frequently white *

Kaunda suit – a kind of suit popularized by President Kaunda of
    Zambia

khanga – colourful printed cloth with a catchy line of text
    on it *

kiboko – a whip *

kikapu – a basket *
kikoi – a kind of cloth, with a border *
kofia – cloth cap, hand-embroidered *
Kundalini – a spiritual force †
Layl-tul-qadr – a Muslim festival
maago – a proposal of marriage †
maalim – an exorcist; a learned man †,*
maandazi – a sweet fried bread *
maghrab – dusk †
Maji-Maji uprising – a revolt by Africans against the Germans
    in 1905; from maji *, meaning "water"
mandap – a large ceremonial tent †
Marhaba – a greeting *
matata – a bother, fuss, or hubbub *
mbuyu – baobab tree *
Mfalme – King
mganga – healer; doctor *
Mira Bai – a famous Indian female mystic of medieval times †
mnada – market *
mshairi – poet *
mukhi – a spiritual and temporal leader of a Shamsi community,
    whose duties are performed voluntarily †
Mwafrica – (meaning "The African"); a Tanzanian pro-
    government newspaper of the 1960s and 1970s
mwalimu – a teacher; a respectful title for President Nyerere, a
    teacher by profession *
mzee – old man; used as form of respectful address *
mzungu – a white man *
namasté – a greeting involving joining one's hands in front †
ngalawa – a dugout boat *
nikaa – religious text read at a Muslim wedding
nyanyi – baboon *
pachedi – a woman's head-cover †
paisa – an Indian unit of money, smaller than a rupee †

pandit – a Hindu learned man †

pilau – an Indian fried rice dish †

pili-pili bizari – chillies and spice *

pita-piti – a picnic game †

pombé – an alcoholic drink *

Ramadhan – a sacred month in the Muslim calendar; observed
    with fasting in daylight hours

rasa – an Indian folk dance similar to a garba †

shaaytan – spirit †

shamba period – a school period allocated for cultivation

shetani – spirits *

Shikamoo – a greeting *

simba – lion †

sirdar – a person of high political or military rank †

Sufi – Muslim mystical order or sect, or a person belonging to
    one

tabalchi – a tabla player †

tabla – a drum †

tambi – vermicelli *

tawith – a charm containing Quran inscriptions †

toto – servant boy; a corruption of mtoto *, meaning "child"

ugali – a preparation of maize flour, to eat with stew *

vitumbua (pl.) – sweet fried bread *

wazee (pl.) – elders *

ACKNOWLEDGEMENTS

This book is a work of fiction. The town of Kikono, its ADC, and the other characters are all fictitious. Only the historical back-drop and geographical settings are real, though even here the purist may find some liberties taken.

I would like to thank the Rhodes House Library, Oxford, and the Imperial War Museum Library, London, for their open and generous facilities; and in particular I wish to acknowledge a debt here to the Librarian and the Assistant Librarian of Rhodes House for clarifying certain matters in relation to the bwanas of this book. This is also a good place to thank Begum and Pyarali for a dusty ride to Taveta; and the various folks in Tanga who welcomed a weary, curious, and unknown traveller one dawn, with a taxi driver who had been forced to foot it; and Zahir Dhalla for introductions. As well, Caroline Avens and others at Heinemann in Oxford have been generous with their hospitality.

I must thank various friends for their support – Arun Mukherjee, Issa Shivji, Walter Bugoya, Fatma Aloo, and Francis Imbuga.

The Canada Council has been generous.

And so have Nurjehan and Anil, in their own way, with their encouragement and their patience even when it was difficult.

Finally I must thank Alex Schultz for sensitively and thoroughly reading the manuscript. And of course Ellen Seligman, who probed every secret in the book – patient, thorough, and persistent; the debt is enormous.

Excerpts titled "Governor's Memoranda for PCs and DCs" in Chapter 2 have been taken from "Confidential Memoranda for Provincial Commissioners and District Commissioners," dated 1910, signed by Governor E. P. C. Girouard; excerpts from the Quran are from the translation of Mohammed Marmaduke Pickthall (Mentor Book); and those from *Romeo and Juliet* in Chapter 19 are from the Alexander Text (Collins, 1951).

The epigraph on page vii is from the translation of the *Ruba'iyat* by Peter Avery and John Heath Stubbs (Penguin, 1981); the one on page 9 by Sir Thomas Browne is taken from the *Oxford Dictionary of Quotations* (1979); the riddle on page 101 is from the book *Swahili Tales* by Edward Steere (Society for Promotion of Christian Knowledge, 1933) and modified by me; the epigraphs on page 185 are my own renderings of a well-known Swahili proverb and an Ismaili ginan; the quote on page 235 is from a movie poster for *Gilda*; and the one from Auden on page 303 is from "You" in *Selected Poetry of W. H. Auden* (Vintage, 1971). And finally, the line from the Anarkali song in Chapter 18 and Miscellany (IV) is my own rendering.